TRULY LIKE LIGHTNING

TRULY LIKE LIGHTNING

LIGHTNING

DAVID DUCHOVNY

FARRAR, STRAUS AND GIROUX

NEW YORK

Farrar, Straus and Giroux
120 Broadway, New York 10271

Frontispiece art by Glot Furman / Shutterstock.com.

Library of Congress Cataloging-in-Publication Data
Names: Duchovny, David, author.
Title: Truly like lightning / David Duchovny.
Description: First edition. | New York : Farrar, Straus and Giroux, 2021.
Identifiers: LCCN 2020040448 | ISBN 9780374277741 (hardcover)
Classification: LCC PS3604.U343 T78 2021 | DDC 813/.6—dc23
LC record available at https://lccn.loc.gov/2020040448

Designed by Gretchen Achilles

Our books may be purchased in bulk for promotional, educational, or business
use. Please contact your local bookseller or the Macmillan Corporate and
Premium Sales Department at 1-800-221-7945, extension 5442, or by email
at MacmillanSpecialMarkets@macmillan.com.

www.fsgbooks.com
www.twitter.com/fsgbooks • www.facebook.com/fsgbooks

1 3 5 7 9 10 8 6 4 2

To West and Miller, may they know they are
the miracles they are waiting for.

And to Margaret, my first teacher,
who esteems the written word above all.

Not only was his robe exceedingly white, but his whole person was glorious beyond description, and his countenance truly like lightning.

CONTENTS

PART I

JOSHUA TREE

Standing there, gaping at this monstrous and inhuman spectacle of rock and cloud and sky and space, I feel a ridiculous greed and possessiveness come over me. I want to know it all, possess it all, embrace the entire scene intimately, deeply, totally . . .

—EDWARD ABBEY, *DESERT SOLITAIRE*

1.

BRONSON WAS UNEASY this morning. He'd been awakened by a silent flash of lightning and found himself slipping out of the house almost without thought long before dawn, leaving Mary and Yaya in bed, and stepping into the cold desert alone. It felt like rain to him, and rain in this part of Joshua Tree was an event, a divine missive from a god stingy with his communiqués. Bronson's God was the one announced by the angel Moroni, the deity from the Book of Mormon, all of it a joke to the big cities, the coastal elites of his country. Mormons were generally known for their freaky polygamous ways, but also, paradoxically, for their whiter-shade-of-pale, clean-cut lifestyle, which included abstinence from coffee, alcohol, tobacco, and premarital sex; as if lack of twenty-first-century hipness was any reason not to believe.

No clouds, but damn did it feel like rain. Bronson kept venturing, blind in the night, his cowboy boots cracking the sand and dirt, moving every bit as much away from as toward something. In his pocket, he played with his "peep stones"—two worthless, jade-colored gems that he used to cover his eyes when he wanted to pray deeply and look within and see the writing on the wall of the sky. The desert seemed on schedule to receive about only two thirds of the 28 inches of average annual rainfall. It could be climate change. It could be a sinful, wayward flock. Bronson was known to his family as a rainmaker, like the old hucksters who used to travel the drought-ridden Midwest claiming that magic. He could feel the barometric pressure announce itself in the bones that he'd broken. Maybe it was just a trick of timing. He didn't know. He just knew he seemed to be able to make it rain.

Like the Mormon prophet Joseph Smith, Bronson did not have a surplus of formal education, but he had read on his own through much of Western civilization, Eastern too, in translation. You would be forgiven if you assumed that this Mormon cowboy jumping on a horse in the middle of the Mojave Desert adjacent to Joshua Tree National Park was not as well acquainted with Shakespeare, Nietzsche, Lao-Tze, and Marcus Aurelius as any tenured professor at Pepperdine, the school he had dropped out of before the end of sophomore year (after a balky knee and chronically sore shoulder cut short his baseball career) in order to pursue his taste for speed, controlled chaos, and beautiful machines as a Hollywood stuntman.

It was a good thing to be moving. Bronson owned so much land, so much unforgiving dust, miles of nothing, immune to the human hand of the Anthropocene age. His father's mother, Delilah Bronson Powers, had bequeathed this Eden of cactus and rattle-snakes to him. Throughout his childhood, Bronson's father, Fred, would tell him stories of the legendary Powers family, real estate visionaries who had made Los Angeles the quintessential American city, rising, he would say, like a man-made mirage from the desert by the Pacific. Fred Powers bemoaned his lot as a thrice-married car salesman, amateur poker player, golf shark, and minor league Ponzi schemer. Barred from practicing his most lucrative trade at many a golf course, the man kept numerous disguises and wigs in the trunk of his Cadillac to sneak onto the greens and cadge a few bucks off the fa-mous actors and rich doctors before the sweat compromised the gum arabic and his phony mustache drooped. He could've been an actor. He was that handsome. He was charming and good with accents. But he had no need for love or admiration, only for the powers the world had denied him, his very name itself; he only ever wanted to be feared by a world that paid him no mind.

Kicked out of the family for unspecified (or so he told his son) sins and forced to live in the squalor of West LA ("East of Bundy, south of Sunset!" he would shout, like a curse), his looks and his health faded quickly with two packs of Kent and one bottle of Smirnoff a day. When he sporadically visited his son—that is, when he remembered that every second Saturday was his—he read to him Twain's *The Prince and the Pauper* over and over again, filling the impressionable boy with infinite entitlement but no clue as to how to claim it, as if certainty and ambition itself were the only life skills necessary. He would tell him, "You're the pauper prince. You're Hollywood royalty, related to the great swashbuckler, Tyrone Power." Fabrications and fantasies. But to the young boy, his father was a charming, all-powerful, capricious apparition who appeared now and then to remind him of his true destiny, as in any Saturday matinee, a kind of anti–Jiminy Cricket—"and never let your conscience be your guide." He was Hamlet's father's ghost still living. In reality, Bronson's father taught him nothing but a restless, free-roaming resentment and a love for baseball and the hometown Dodgers.

Bronson could clearly remember that, in 1974, his ailing father took him down to Grauman's Chinese on opening day to watch the movie *Chinatown*, the epic Polanski / Towne thriller of water, greed, and incest in 1930s Los Angeles. Fred filled Bronson's head with the bullshit yarn that the Mulwray family in the film was an opaque nom de cinema for Powers (this was a lie, of course—Mulwray was a front-rhyming stand-in for Mulholland—true California royalty). Sitting through a matinee in that dark theater on Hollywood Boulevard, Bronson marveled at how his father must have modeled his brand of practiced insouciance on Jack Nicholson in his very own fabricated origin story. Or somehow Nicholson was imitating his father. Fred did claim to know the movie star because he'd won thousands off him on the links. He leaned over to his boy, arched a cocky eyebrow, and crowed, "Sonuvabitch, that's my eyebrow! Jack's doing me, ripping me off."

At the climax of the film, when the unspeakable incest is finally revealed, Fred took his son's hand in his and squeezed. It was the first time Bronson could ever remember his father holding his hand. Something heavy and unworded passed between them, like a dark blessing. Bronson glanced over to see Fred crying as the credits rolled, another first. When Fred passed away the next year, he bequeathed to his son no money or skills to speak of, but rather an awe and disgust at his ancestry, having planted the seeds in the next generation of anger over lost birthrights, unacknowledged genetic superiority, unimaginable wealth, and influence denied. Like psychic DNA, Fred replicated, forged, and minted a copy of the resentments a long life of scamming failures had made of his own soul upon the impressionable soul of his boy. Bronson grew up unconsciously carrying that paternal chip, with an unrequited sense of entitlement and unrecognized nobility.

Though Fredrickson Powers, an only son, had been kicked out of the clan, predeceasing his mother, Delilah, Bronson, in his early thirties, with no savings to speak of, and with the aching body, broken bones, and the manageable but growing opioid reliance of a working, often banged-up stuntman, was flabbergasted to find himself inheriting an unimaginably sizable chunk of undeveloped desert in the Inland Empire. Why him? He didn't know. He'd never even met his grandmother. He figured it was a fuck-you to his father. And every fuck-you, he knew, contained a bless-you on its flip side. He was his wayward father's son, and this was his birthright and blessing. The Pauper had been recognized as Prince. And when he rode fast through his land today, he could feel the blessing press on his face and body like an embrace.

Delilah Powers had converted in midlife to the Church of Jesus

Christ of Latter-day Saints. Bronson's dad mocked that conversion to his son, claiming, "It's only 'cause she wants to fuck Donny Osmond. And, it gives her scriptural license to be the repressive asshole she's always been. Let me tell you, that stingy bitch has a rage for order." The conversion had stuck its landing. Delilah, like Brigham Young himself, had chewed tobacco her entire life—a cowboy weakness she shared with her grandson. But now she gave up her chew, her six cups of coffee, and her Johnnie Walker Black, and moved from Los Angeles to San Bernardino County, which she knew had the highest concentration of Mormons of any county in California, more than 2 percent of its almost 2 million residents.

Mormons had, in fact, founded San Bernardino in 1851, setting up the city's grid and initial government structure. But in the mid-1850s, even as tensions between Mormons and the U.S. government intensified, the local LDS leaders chafed at the tight rein of Brigham Young; and the westernmost outpost of this American religion was abandoned. Brigham Young called all the San Bernardino Mormon founders back to Salt Lake City in 1857. Most Saints, close to three thousand, were obedient, and left San Bernardino. But the city and surroundings continued to grow into the fifth-largest county in the continental United States. Long gone is the dominant Mormon presence, replaced by Walmart, Amazon, and those who are paid barely a subsistence wage to keep the warehouses stocked and full. Present-day San Bernardino also boasts some of the worst pollution in an infamously smoggy state. But the Mormon footprint, the ghosts and the names, remains.

The one behavioral stipulation Delilah Powers had put in her will for her grandson, Bronson, was that the executors (all upper-echelon LDS elders) must make sure he "prove a good-faith show of conversion to Mormonism" in order to receive his inheritance. Mormonism? Bronson knew nothing about it. He thought it might be something like Scientology, which he'd tried for about a year at the behest of some globally successful, goofy little actor that he'd doubled on a few action films. He was initially drawn into the Scientology orbit because he shared that church's disdain for psychology, both in template and treatment. Bronson instinctually hated the navel-gazing reductionism of the "talking cure," tracing all ills back to early family trauma like some stuck parrotlike infant nattering obsessively about Ma and Pa. At Pepperdine, after quitting the baseball team because of injuries, Bronson suffered infrequent hallucinations, searing flashes of light, like lightning, that would drop him to his knees, followed by intense, debilitating three-day migraines. He underwent some tests, which found nothing; talked to a therapist, which did nothing. He was summarily diagnosed with depression and prescribed both prayer (Pepperdine was a Christian, dry campus) and an early SSRI, Prozac, which helped for a time. He didn't feel happier, but at least the Prozac seemed to stop the lightning flashes and the migraines.

As a budding man of action, Bronson became a seeker of his own cure. In L. Ron Hubbard, he encountered a flamboyant con artist who sought to replace Freud's neurotic cosmology; and though the call to power and its promises of getting "clear" from the past were enticing, Bronson didn't jibe with the upbeat Stepford vibe or the Randian masters-of-the-universe arrogance. Plus, the guy, like Freud, had pseudoscientific jargon that pinged Bronson's bullshit radar. And the loopy, B-movie, sci-fi top level secret sauce? Bronson couldn't hang with an alpha and omega named Xenu. He would not pay the pyramid scheme cover charge to join the Sea Org and party on with John Travolta, Tom Cruise, and the rest of the clear folk till that volcano erupted and all the imprisoned Thetans were freed.

In comparison, Mormonism, the dark-horse nineteenth-century American adjunct to Christianity, was a fairly uncomplicated breeze to embrace. And for thousands of acres of pristine desert?! He'd fart "One Bad Apple" through a keyhole for that price. He figured he'd have to hide his tats and sit a test with some old fuddy-duddy named Brigham or Jedediah or Uriah, so the badass stuntman

Bronson, popping more pills and fucking more women than was perhaps wise, got himself a Mormon "gold bible" and a biography of Joseph Smith and, never a good student, set out to ace his charade.

But a funny thing happened as he crammed for his spiritual audition. He started to get it. To *feel* it. Sure, most of it was semitransparent hokum in the great American tradition of positive-thinking, world-beating hucksterism from P. T. Barnum to L. Ron Hubbard, from Werner Erhard to Deepak Chopra to Tony Robbins, from Jemima Wilkinson to Marianne Williamson to Elizabeth Holmes; but there was something more. Hidden beneath its reputation as the most staid and repressive of American religious cults, Smith's original Mormon vision was a rejection of the white gospel of success, a repudiation of Calvinist divine economic selection. The end-times here were reclaimed by the Native Americans ("Lamanites") and the darker races, and the industrious, capitalist whites ("Nephites") were doomed precisely because they worshipped money and success more than God and righteousness. To the backlot cowboy, this was a true revolutionary pearl obscured by the huckster's smoke and mirrors.

Though he might not have been able to put it into words at the time, Bronson's fall for Mormonism had been prepared by his own father's disgust for his social betters. Fred had been a rebel without an adversary, and Smith chose the same enemies, but he fought them more poetically and powerfully—the establishment, the counters of money and arbiters of sexual morality, the so-called successful, the owners of this land—he called them all phonies, as Fred had. Bronson had been raised in the shadow of his father's own Joseph Smith–like alienation from the status quo and was thus vulnerable to this attack, this call to overthrow the man.

The boy in Bronson, raised on Westerns, but always playing Indians rather than cowboys, was thrilled that the land would be returned to the Lamanites in the end-times, and that Europeans were called "gentiles"—foreigners on this new American soil. Bronson was painfully aware that he was only a drugstore cowboy because, coming so late in history, he had no choice but to play, rather than be, the part. Stuntmen were where cowboys went to die. All the actual skills of the cowboy, no longer demanded by the twentieth-century economy, were part and parcel of the stuntman's playbook as the existence of the real West and real cowboys were nostalgically relegated to Westerns. Stuntmen tended to chew tobacco, drawl like stereotypical cowboys, walk and talk slowly and slightly bowlegged like John Wayne. Famously, John Ford ascribed the mysterious, enduring appeal of John Wayne, née Marion Morrison, to his ease in the saddle—he "looked good on a horse."

Bronson, six feet one and a vascular 185 pounds, with a passing resemblance to a more macho Montgomery Clift, also looked good on a horse. And on a motorcycle, or in a helicopter. If it was fast, and lack of coordination, preparation, or attention could kill you, Bro', as the fraternity of stuntmen called him, looked damn good on it, in it, or hanging off it. In fact, one of the reasons he quit the movies was because they started doing all those computer-generated special effects in postproduction and made everything on set safer. Why expose a man to actual fire and explosives if that fire can be painted on just as convincingly by some geek with a computer? Well, because daring men like Bronson had trained for real fire, that's why.

When he was rehabbing his knee for baseball at Pepperdine, a girl he was dating from the diving team had introduced him to the trampoline by the pool that the divers practiced on. She thought it could be a way to keep his balance fresh for baseball. He was skeptical, figuring it was for children, like a bouncy castle. He hadn't executed the old "seat-knee-seat" since grade school, but he was immediately struck by how demanding and athletic the moves were. He loved learning to fly upside down, spinning, the sky and the ground exchanging places. He had an acute gyroscopic talent, his body acclimating naturally, unconsciously in the air, always knowing how and when to right itself. Impressed, his girlfriend said, "You got proprioceptors for days, dude." The divers wanted him to try out for the team, but all he wanted to do was the tramp. At the apex of his highest bounces, he could see the ocean just a few hundred yards across the Pacific Coast Highway. He spent hours suspended like this, weightless as a bird, careless as a child.

He'd thought of being an actor for a time, an ambition he shared with no one, out of embarrassment, and eventually decided that it was too coddled and phony a life, but as he somersaulted and fell and dove, and reveled in his own natural gifts and ease, he began to wonder how he might stay in this feeling longer and about what daredevils and stuntmen did. And maybe a stuntman, invisibly replacing the more "valuable" actor in dangerous circumstances, was actually the more real one. And yet, years later, even as he succeeded in this field, he knew he was a ghost, an echo of the real men and real cowboys; he was a double, a shadow, and when he doubled the lead in a film, he was further removed from authenticity—the shadow of a shadow casting yet another shadow on the silver screen. This latter-day impotence gnawed invisibly at his soul till he read about Joseph Smith and heard the first stirrings of a call, what Descartes called the "holy music of the self."

Authenticity, the substance and very marrow of life, according to Joseph Smith, was still in the late air; you can write your own story, your own bible—"wherefore, because that ye have a Bible ye need not suppose that it contains all my words; neither need ye suppose that I have not caused more to be written. For I command all men, both in the east and in the west, and in the north, and in the south, and in the *islands of the sea*,' that they shall write the words which I speak unto them." The bible is still being written. Everybody has a bible in them. Everyone *is* a bible.

Twenty-four-year-old Joseph Smith, whose very name could be a synonym for "everyman," had somehow authored a true declaration of Emersonian spiritual independence and a religious companion to its 1776 political precursor. Bronson read somewhere that Thomas Jefferson had crossed out all the miracles in his copy of the New Testament, leaving only the teachings and parables of Jesus. But where was the fun in that? Essentially Jefferson had cut all the movie-worthy moments in the old book, leaving no place for a stuntman to turn water into wine, cast out demons, touch lepers, or return from the dead. What was a movie stunt but the performance, through painstaking preparation, of a miracle? These macho magic tricks had been the heart of Bronson's calling, and now it thrilled him that Smith had rightly turned the overly rational Jeffersonian trend on its head. Smith seemed hell-bent on effacing everything but the stunts and miracles; his soundtrack, Jesus Christ's greatest hits. Joseph Smith was the magic, Bronson's spiritual father and new lifestyle guru. It was Smith's improvised, vital worldview, more than the dubious events described in his bible, that whispered truth to Bronson: one of presence, not absence, of here and now, not there and then.

Bronson's conversion was not as out of the blue as it might have seemed at first. A few years earlier, he'd already been softened up for God by attending 12 Steps of Narcotics Anonymous meetings. A girlfriend, upon finding him one last time passed out in his car on a neighbor's lawn, left Bronson with a note on the cracked windshield: "You need a shrink, or a meeting, or a mother." Bronson had no patience for the slow psychobabble of therapy. No, talk was not for him, action was, and that's what the 12 Steps promised, decisiveness, not chatty hand-holding and procrastination—taking bold steps into a future, not reclining languidly on a couch staring at the ceiling. The presence in the "rooms" of a higher power had back-doored a notion of God into his brain, and the parabolic slogans functioned like touchstone precepts from Christ's lost sermons as dictated to one Bill W. The theologian Reinhold Niebuhr's 1944 prayer on all the anonymously abstinent lips—"God, grant me the serenity . . ."—was the wide gateway to Christ. A stubborn, animal-loving Bronson had first quietly muttered and transposed the serenity prayer to "Dog, grant me the serenity . . . ," but the steps baptized him, gradually priming this agnostic for belief. Forsaking chemical transcendence, he knelt down to God the drug.

Though Bronson, in Step 2, "came to believe that a Power greater than ourselves could restore us to sanity," that higher power had no face, and consequently lacked immediacy, intimacy. So, first, Bronson configured this higher power as Yoda for a while, then Mr. Clean (in that Bronson himself was a toilet to be scoured), then a kind of pulsating, glowing, orgasmic, androgynous blue-eyed orb, but nothing stuck—no imago pierced him through, and this was a serious problem of scale and reverence, getting in the way of his recovery. Ultimately, he began to feel like a fraud in those rooms because he was still taking his Prozac, and that was a drug, wasn't it? His commitment felt half-assed and hollow. By the time he was on the sixth step, he was using again and on the verge of quitting the program, or quitting quitting.

But as Bronson read more deeply into Joseph Smith, his nascent shape-shifting, inoffensive 12 Steps God started to come into focus. Bronson began to see Smith's semiliterate biblical retread as America's true origin story, and accepted that its core thesis could be his birthright of original vitality and an antidote to the entropy of belatedness—that miracles are not over, but still happening. Freud looked backward to Mom and Dad, Hubbard looked even further back to past lives, the 12 Steps wallowed so long in past wrongs and amends, only Smith looked forward: cowboys could still be cowboys on wild horses in Anywhere, America: "a voice of the Lord in the wilderness of Fayette, Senneca County . . . The voice of Michael on the banks of the Susquehanna."*

This proximity to the divine, both geographical and temporal,

* Joseph Smith to the Church, September 7, 1842, in PJS, 2:473–74.

engendered in Bronson an organic rebirth. Why couldn't Bronson
Powers, sure-handed shortstop, college dropout, righteous pain pill
abuser, in his late prime as a stuntman, hear the voice of an angel
on Hollywood and Vine or Fairfax and Highland? As his spirituality
blossomed, it sparked a ranging curiosity he had never known. His
new faith made him thirsty for knowledge.

Back when his fascination with physical bravery and defying
death had announced itself, he had sought out the best in that world
and managed to apprentice himself to the legendary stuntman Dar
Robinson. Dar had instantly seen potential in Bronson and had
drilled into the impulsive younger man the importance of nurturing a passion for methodical preparation to undergird the preter-
natural kinesthetic sense that he'd discovered on the Pepperdine
trampoline—the catlike genius for always knowing where your body
is in space. But Bronson needed another mentor now of a more ethe-
real falling art to teach him a kinesthetic-spiritual sense, as his soul
tumbled head over heels through its own eternal quintessence.
Yet Bronson was ever impatient and could identify no immediate,
living guru to provide that mystic guidance. Always in a hurry, like
a man convinced he would die young, Bronson did not wait for the
teacher to appear; he taught himself. This is when his true education, a rabid autodidacticism, commenced. He took to his literal
heart the audacity of Smith's oration at the funeral for Elder King
Follett, "God himself was once as we are now, and is an exalted
man, and sits enthroned in yonder heavens. That is the great secret."
He looked for kindred spirits through the Holy Books of humanity and the lightning-bolt conversion stories from Saul of Tarsus,
Aquinas, Bunyan, Milton, Merton, Niebuhr, Malcolm X. He ingested
the Western canon like a third-year graduate student cramming for
orals. He embraced as living contemporaries in no chronological
order—Plato, Foucault, Rousseau, Donne, Shakespeare, Melville,
Whitman, Blake, Rabelais, Kierkegaard, Stevens, and Girard. He
whimsically created batting orders out of his intellectual heroes:

Emerson, a speedy, aphoristic singles hitter, led off, Nietzsche pitched (mostly curveballs and change-ups), and Dickinson was always trying to draw a walk or get hit by a pitch and leave no mark on the box score. The greats were speaking a language he understood now, whispering bons mots, a chorus singing in his ear. This omnivorous hunger to know the best that had been thought or said acted like a natural amphetamine, his brain on the mind trampoline literally bursting through its bone-bound, finite skull to touch the infinite. This was no half-assed quest or passing fad. Bronson rarely slept and was never tired.

He had no use for Freud, he had Marx. He was suddenly in love with the world as an organism, really, America as a being, not the self as a thing; enthralled with the macrocosm without, not the microcosm within. He devoured American history textbooks, cottoning initially to Richard Hofstadter before being further radicalized by Howard Zinn's *A People's History of the United States* as a continuation and companion to the Mormon bible, the Pearl of Great Price.

He visited Delilah's legacy and surreptitiously built a shed the exact size of Thoreau's cabin. No one ever saw him on the land, no one cared to. He'd spend undistracted solitary weeks there when he didn't have a gig, filling his trunk with five-gallon gas cans of LA tap water and subsisting on Skippy's peanut butter and apples, just reading, reading, writing notes in the margins. For the first time, he recognized the inchoate restlessness in himself for what it was—a rage for order that his father had identified in his own mother, seemingly having skipped a generation, alive in him through Delilah. Like his father, Bronson had been born a man of prodigious gifts and energy, but outside a system or timely mentor that could harness those energies. Fred Powers had died, broken over the years by the wayward lightning strikes of his own untethered demon, but his son had found the sticking place where his grandmother had led him from beyond the grave. Bronson felt the holy authenticity, a calm descend like the holy spirit, but it was an energetic calm, a wild, ambitious calm.

By the time it came for Bronson to sit for his "show of good faith" test with a church elder and chief executor of Delilah's will (actually named Elder) to prove his Mormon bonafides, he was more than ready for this "worthiness interview." Hoping to throw Bronson off, Elder began by asking if he'd ever met his grandmother Delilah. "Not that I can remember," Bronson answered, "maybe when I was very little."

"Well, you must've made an impression on her. She loved you quite fiercely."

"Yeah, I was a supercharming three-year-old," Bronson joked.

"She was your secret benefactor. She paid for Pepperdine, you know?"

"I didn't know that," Bronson replied, and immediately felt off balance. Why hadn't he ever wondered how he afforded Pepperdine? He had accepted his father's explanation that he was paying tuition. Transparent bullshit, of course, from the deadbeat dad, but Bronson had never looked deeper.

"I don't know that she loved me so much as hated my father. Her son," Bronson said, and that felt like an apt epitaph both for this mysterious and suddenly powerful old woman he would never know and for his long-dead dad.

Elder Elder squinted and tried to intimidate Bronson, asking him to identify scripture from the Mormon bible by rote. Before answering, as if to undercut memorization and blind adherence as faith, Bronson quoted Smith word for word, "I am not learned, but I have as good feelings as any man." And then he nailed, chapter and verse, each citation Elder floated, from the most obvious to the most obscure.

By the end of the first hour, he had the elder Elder backpedaling, made dizzy by the antiestablishment heresies Bronson revealed hiding in plain sight beside the orthodoxies. This Elder, like so many modern-day Latter-day Saints, preferred to dismiss polygamy as the religion's equivalent to the appendix—a useless relic, a toothless anachronism and fringe belief, but Bronson attacked that shifting line, claiming it was Smith's core tenet and a restoration of the polygamy practiced in the Old Testament. All exalted beings must be sealed to an eternal spouse, Bronson proclaimed, so a man had a duty to seal, to make a marriage; for a single woman would not, could not be exalted. It was a spin on the apostle Paul's "it is better to marry than to burn" that equated sexual singlehood with damnation, or in Mormon cosmology, at least another round of reincarnation and terrestrial prison, heaven still waiting. The celestial nature of marriage far outweighed the nineteenth- and twentieth-century squeamishness with the concept of multiple partners. This was a matter of your eternal soul, Bronson asserted, not of sex and schoolboy snickering and political gerrymandering.

"I'd rather be a polygamist than a hypocrite and adulterer," he said.

Bronson had the facts at his once nicotine-stained fingertips: "1852—Brigham Young tells the world about the until now secret practice of polygamy. Brigham displays the depth of his belief by having fifty wives. This catches people's attention. 1856—the Republican National Convention denounces polygamy and slavery as 'twin relics of barbarism.' 1862—the government passes the first Federal legislation, the Morrill Anti-Bigamy Act, signed by none other than Abraham Lincoln. More antipolygamy federal laws passed in 1882—like the Edmunds Act, and in 1889, we welcome the Penrose manifesto, approved by LDS brass, that denies the Church has any right to overrule any civil court, also denies the doctrine of blood atonement. 1890—the fourth LDS president, Wilford Woodruff, reveals a manifesto that informs the Saints plural marriage is no longer commanded by God. Huh. Time cut six years, to 1896—presto chango, Utah becomes the forty-fifth state with a ban on polygamy written into its constitution. Funny coincidences."

Bronson gradually became aware, during the interview, that he was also preaching to himself, as he had never preached to anyone else before; this was his first time articulating his new beliefs and his passion to a stranger. He was cognizant of a certain sadistic satisfaction in making Elder squirm; it was undeniably enjoyable to watch this complacent, establishment fat ass shift about in his temple garments, but more than that, Bronson the seeker had split off into Bronson the preacher. In a kind of unplanned performance art, Bronson was consecrating his own personal conversion, boldly anointing himself before the elder man had the chance. He was performing for Elder, in real time, the daring act of a man converting himself.

Elder tried to move on, he was more than ready to sign off on the deal fifteen minutes into Bronson's exhaustively footnoted harangue, but Bronson, growing in confidence by the minute, began to push the old man on the Church's treatment of people of color and the indigenous of this continent. After listing some atrocities perpetrated upon Native Americans as the Mormons pushed westward in the nineteenth century, which Elder framed as merely a competition over resources, Bronson quoted from memory a letter from Joseph Smith to Noah Saxton, January 4, 1833, where Smith describes "Indians" as covenant Israel, and America as their promised land, which gentiles can join if they accept the Mormon gospel.

"It's their land," Bronson said, "and where the Puritans from Plymouth Rock used the bible to steal that land, Smith gave us the Mormon bible as our only way to share in this land, our only way to be as holy as the natives of the Americas, the Lamanites. Smith is an antidote and divine correction, not a continuation of manifest destiny." Elder began to sweat. Bronson began pushing harder, sweeping out the weirder, less canonical corners of Smith's vision and the possibility of secret teachings that were not only polygamous but achingly polytheistic. There was an abundance to Smith—a plurality of wives and gods and men becoming gods—that inspired Bronson and scared the Mormon leaders who publicly kept a lower profile on the fringe teachings in the hopes of quietly folding into and alongside the American Christian establishment. He goaded Elder by alluding to rumors that Smith had tried to negotiate with Mexico and France as a Mormon nation apart from the United States.

"That would be treason," Elder said.

"Only if you believe in countries," Bronson replied. "Do you think God organized the world with the United States and its laws in mind?"

Elder didn't know that this was going to be his test, his worthiness interview. His mind kept wandering for some reason to the placement of his season seats at BYU's Marriott Center for the upcoming basketball campaign. He kept flashing on the silly mascot, Cosmo the Cougar. He was panicked. He had to pee. He tuned out. Bronson held forth uninterrupted for another excruciating eighty-five minutes.

By the end of the interview, Elder nearly begged Bronson to exile himself to his plot of land and please stay there where he would not make any waves in the faith he was now welcome to join. He didn't want to kick this loose cannon any further up the Church's chain. Elder certainly recognized that though Bronson knew more about Mormonism than most any Mormon, it was a very personal and idiosyncratic version of the faith, almost his own religion. The Church of Latter-day Saints had fought a long, strategic battle to be accepted in the mainstream of the American separation of church and state, from downplaying polygamy in order for Utah to attain statehood (as Bronson had pointed out), to the previous generation's validation of trusted national figures like George Romney, Mitt's dad. At each inflection point where the Mormon Church had soft-pedaled the antiestablishment aspects of Smith's vision in order to gain American acceptance (polygamy, baptism of the dead, blood atonement), Bronson would not back down. There was no compromise in the man, no tact. Elder didn't want to tussle with this fiery iconoclast any more than Dostoyevsky's Grand Inquisitor welcomed the appearance of Christ Himself. Bronson was no more of a traditional Mormon than Christ was a traditional Christian. He was that most dangerous man, an originalist and a true believer.

Elder gave Bronson the LDS stamp of approval that Delilah had demanded from the great beyond and wished him well far off in the desert. Bronson accepted his inheritance, and this friendly banishment, and moved, sometime after the millennium, after a period of homesteading and building, to his birthright. He would raise a family free of the wounds an unjust society of men had inflicted upon his father and that his father had inflicted upon him. He would finally meet himself unadorned out there in Joshua Tree, an honest-to-goodness, real, working cowboy/Indian. He would order a desert in which to raise free souls that would return to heal the world. He would turn inward first so his legacy could turn outward.

Could it be fifteen years ago now? More? Must be. There was no way of telling time like that anymore. He owned no watch or clocks or calendar. The day began when the sun rose and ended when it sank. The desert had seasons, but they were subtle and resistant to the calendar mind. It felt like he'd been here forever. Born in the saddle, incubated among the hot rocks, suckled on rattlesnake venom. Years of living off the grid with his books, solar and wind power, his own well, chickens, cows, sheep, snake meat, making his own cheese and tending his own garden, had killed time itself; he'd been wandering this desert forever and he'd got here just yesterday.

Bronson rarely went into "civilization"—tiny Pioneertown (population: 574), or the "city" of Joshua Tree (population: 7,414), or the "big city" of San Bernardino (population: 209,924)—but when he did, when he needed seeds, or canned goods, livestock, gas or parts for "Ol' Unreliable," his '68 Ford F100 truck, or one of his seven "Frankenbike" motorcycles that he had cobbled together himself over the years, or a solar panel repaired or replaced, he tried as best he could to stop up his ears and hear nothing of how the world was spinning. He knew the Twin Towers had come down, but his was a cloistered, timeless world where the "internet" was not a word and the cell phone did not exist, America had never had a Black president, and Donald Trump was nothing but a laughable comb-over and failed Realtor. And yet somehow, without this seemingly vital knowledge, he continued to draw breath. His land was the world to him, a physical and mental landscape; he lacked for no other. He christened it "Agadda da Vida" after the muscular and mysterious Iron Butterfly song.

In the beginning, to build out beyond his little reading shed, he'd needed the muscle of his fraternity of Hollywood below-the-line tradesmen to dig the well and help him with soil. He was lucky that the water table under his land was around three hundred feet; in some places in the desert, it was as deep as six hundred. He was able to get a drill rig as a favor—so the well had cost him less than five thousand dollars, which nonetheless nearly bankrupted him. His stunt brothers were so goddamn helpful and charitable—they worked for days for free, and without them, he could not have conjured Agadda da Vida from the dust alone. And at first, for a few months anyway, some old drinking buddies would come and hang out a bit with their strictly sober, formerly hell-raising, newly Mormon friend. But Bronson was no longer the gas he used to be. The men now found they had little in common without the work and the booze; and after about six months, with lives and families of their own, no one ever visited again.

Since then, only the occasional park ranger had made contact, but most of them were dissuaded from venturing farther by the "No Trespassing" signs and eerie, apocalyptic scarecrows, as well as rumors Bronson himself had started about booby traps, land mines, and punji stick hellholes. In this way, Bronson created a wide, scary, barren buffer around the compound that he liked to think of as the "Forbidden Zone" in the *Planet of the Apes* movies.

Bronson could ride a horse for an entire morning and not reach the end of his land. He was like some biblical figure that way. Lightning illuminated the landscape briefly. He let loose with a war whoop, a rebel yell, even a Maori haka chant, and other vocalizations of warriors he had impersonated during his years on-screen as bad guys had gone from Indians to Englishmen to Russians to Middle Easterners and around again. More lightning as if in response. There it is, thought Bronson. The sign. Followed by balls-rattling thunder. Thunder was God clearing his throat, about to speak. But no rain yet, no precipitation.

Bronson brooded on the word. *Precipitation. Precipitate. Precipice.* Yes—the rain god was calling him to the edge of a cliff, and the rain would be the sign, and the lightning would show him where, show him the way, and the thunder he would translate. He had forced himself to give up the Prozac cold turkey upon entering the desert, and he now came to see the recurrence of the lightning flashes for what he believed they always had been—visions. Not hallucinations, visions. For the desert had cured him of the migraines that used to follow these episodes. Bronson was not sure if the lightning flashes were originating in his brain or the heavens tonight. This was either a sign of recurrent illness or heavenly wellness, but that discrimination no longer interested him. Perhaps they were one and the same. It was his duty to watch and listen for the gems. But Lord, he was troubled by new thoughts.

He looked way ahead to where the cities lay, past the San Jacinto Mountains—he couldn't make out any lights along the ground, but he knew where the modern world began because its light pollution made the stars fade and lose their brilliance up ahead. The stars could not compete with man-made interference. Bronson did not want to draw closer to that shit. He dismounted and walked toward three simple stone markers, one larger and two smaller. They were not part of the natural landscape. They had been shaped and placed there by human hands with great care. He ran his hands along each stone like a blind man reading Braille. Then he looked straight up at his stars. The lightning was a feint. Nothing, the night was clear as day.

He reached into his pocket, pulled out his peep stones, his absurd technology, held them to his eyes, and again peered up at the heavens, trying to read God's pointillist writing.

"I beseech Thee for guidance, for forgiveness, but Thou givest me nothing but empty noises. Why has Thou dried up and turned Thy back?"

Bronson waited for a reply. The god of the desert gave him nothing but a cold shoulder. He knew his impatience, his neediness, his lust, his pride, his lack of gratitude were all sins, compounded now by anger. As the deadly sins came cascading down upon him instead of the life-giving rain, he shouted, "I am angered by Thy absence, Father, for keeping such distance."

His horse snorted. At least someone is listening, Bronson thought. He recalled a touchstone from one of his dark angels, Captain Ahab—"I now know thee, thou clear spirit, and I now know that thy right worship is defiance." And he knew this was not blasphemy. Timid piety was a lukewarm embrace, and Bronson was hot to trot for his God—he was the last true cowboy and he was gonna lasso the fucking truth. His defiant faith was alive with curses and recriminations, spitting, raised fists and middle fingers, alive. Outweighed and outclassed though he'd always be, Bronson wrestled with his God. He knew what the ancients knew, that prayer and violence were brother vectors throughout all time. He knew that where he stood, God once stood, and as God had been man, man would be God. God and man were one in the same, at different stages. He was really listening in the intense dark and quiet for himself, for his future, improved, perfected self.

Bronson was at home here with an Old Testament God in

Joshua Tree, and at home with the legend that the treelike plant had been given its name by Mormon settlers for a resemblance they saw to Moses reaching his hands skyward in supportive prayer as Joshua fought Amalek in Exodus 17. Unlike Moses, whose tired arms were held aloft by Aaron and Hur, Bronson didn't need help to keep his hands up all day—his prayerful stance was similar to a boxer's. His fight was his prayer.

He'd been born the wrong color in the wrong century to the wrong father and the wrong mother in the right country. He was meant to be a Lamanite, a Native American, an Israelite. His spirit was meant to take a body in the time of miracles and authenticity when men could be men and cowboys and prophets. But no matter, Smith had shown him, the way a lightning bolt reveals what the darkness conceals, what he was truly meant to be. He had been illuminated by Joseph Smith, and he would live the ancient way in the latter day.

More lightning, more thunder, and still no rain.

Unsatisfied and jangly, his simmering rage for order unslaked, Bronson jammed the peep stones back in his pocket. Dawn was coming and even the stars above the empty desert were diminishing naturally with the still unseen rising sun. He kissed the three headstones, jumped back on his horse, and turned him for home. For sure, God was trying to tell him something, but God, playing hard to get, would have to wait on Bronson now. He knew you shouldn't quit five minutes before the miracle happened, but he had two wives and ten children back at the house to breakfast with and instruct this morning.

2.

"FUCKING SOUTHERN CALIFORNIA RAIN," Maya Abbadessa cursed, as she stepped out of her rented bungalow on Princeton Street toward the matte black Tesla she couldn't really afford, parked down the block. She'd cut an incongruous figure anywhere but in Santa Monica, in her tight black millennial businesswoman's dress, black heels, and stuffed backpack over one shoulder, a purple yoga mat sticking up out of it like a Technicolor exclamation point. Bare shouldered, she shivered and recalled what a good friend back east had said about living and dressing for the day in the conundrum of atmospheric sameness punctured by occasional biblical catastrophe that is Southern California—"It's hot *and* it's cold. At the same time."

It was a Friday morning, and Maya had to pack to leave for her weekend from work, hence the weighed-down, chic Sherpa/Zen escort look. Her commute to Praetorian Capital, where she found employment after graduating from the Wharton School of Business three years ago, was only about a mile; walkable, but not in these heels. She'd wanted to grab one of those Bird scooters and roll to work like a ten-year-old as she sometimes did, but she needed to stay dry enough to keep her outfit from getting obscene. Her long-range weekend plans rendered her pricey car impractical today. Elon Musk's electric unicorn felt more like an Edsel when you contemplated finding convenient charging stations on the 300-mile round-trip to the desert, which was where she was headed directly after work today. Running out of battery in the Mojave was an option, and therefore not an option. The young guns, the Young Turks, at Praetorian were having a semi-sanctioned Molly / Ecstasy / peyote / cocaine / Casamigos / Cuban cigar / Corona vision quest / weekend getaway / spitball session (a phenomenon not covered by the Wharton curriculum) in Joshua Tree this weekend.

This would be Maya's first desert sojourn. But these weekends were near mythical ("what happens in Joshua Tree, stays in Joshua Tree") for the ill-advised hookups, bad acid trips, and off-the-wall business ideas that erupted from them like lava from a dormant volcano that wreaks Pompeii-like devastation or the happy miracle of more Hawaiian real estate. And real estate was mostly what Praetorian did. Legend had it that the idea to buy Michael Jackson's Neverland estate a decade earlier had come from one of the now fired, tripping Turks after seeing an image of the ceramic Bubbles the Chimp, from the Jeff Koons piece, spring to a kind of Claymation life and float before him, whispering the enigmatic phrase "never . . . land" in the young man's ear, along with a quarter-billion-dollar bid. That the monkey's name was Bubbles was tragically overlooked by the would-be real estate titan, as these men and women were lifelong literalists who played with numbers, not words.

The mile commute to the Praetorian offices could take anywhere from three to thirty-five minutes in the clogged arteries of West LA traffic. The offices were nestled into a full block-long complex on Colorado Avenue that also housed the HBO, AMC, and Hulu television networks, along with myriad law firms and other businesses. Once entering off Colorado, Maya parked two floors beneath the earth. You could tell a person's Praetorian status by how close to Hades your parking spot was—Maya had moved one floor closer to the sunlight in her three years there but was definitely still a Satan-adjacent Persephone. Her commute within the building was nearly as long as to the building.

However, as a bonus, she would sometimes run into celebrities coming and going to and from meetings with the gatekeepers, searching for their cars. Nicole Kidman had asked if she had any gum once. Or a mint. She didn't. That was a bummer. She fucked up once by mistaking Seth Rogen for Jonah Hill and purring "Super-baaaaad" at him, not realizing the faux pas till a week later. Whoops. Keanu Reeves had once held the elevator door for her. He was cool. That was cool. She had said to him, "You're the best."

Keanu'd said, "Thank you." It was a story she often told.

The founder of Praetorian was the American Dreamer success story and self-made billionaire Robert Malouf. The son of a Palestinian immigrant set carpenter in Culver City, Malouf had Gatsbyed himself, despite a baldness so complete he bore a passing resemblance to Stanley Tucci on good days, and Klaus Kinski's Nosferatu on market-turndown bad ones, into a jet-owning, polo-playing playboy with billions in assets, debts, and connections to seats of power in the States, Europe, Russia, and the Middle East. The Neverland debacle notwithstanding, Malouf was the sole center of Praetorian's $40 billion in assets; an early rising, maddeningly nonlinear thinker, and a whiz at bending financial guardrails and identifying distressed assets and undervalued real estate. While the market had contracted in fear after 2008, Malouf expanded his portfolio in a mammoth buying spree and scored the biggest wins of his storied career.

His business mission, "alt-cap"—he branded it for "altruist capitalism"—enabled middle-class families, like the one in which he'd been raised, to stay in their overleveraged family homes even after those properties had tanked in value after the crash. And he had done that. A savior of the American Dream. That these families had gone from owning to renting from him, and that those rents kept rising, was not his fault, but rather a consequence of their overreaching minor greed and subsequent bad debt. He had almost single-handedly (along with assists from his compadres at the lending banks and money houses—Steve Mnuchin over at One-West, Jamie Dimon at JPMorgan, et al.), using the housing crash of 2008 as his pivot and the Obama too-big-to-fail bailout as his back-stop to protect him from loss, transformed American small-home ownership, mostly in the west, into a type of feudal serfdom. See-ing the future, actually making the future, he had gambled with the American taxpayer's house money and reaped billions by borrow-ing millions to gobble up thousands of modest foreclosures for-feited by the suckers who lost their life savings to the mirage of the subprime and the reverse mortgage. "But they're not homeless now," he liked to say. "We are the good guys."

But that legendary play was almost ten years ago now; he him-self had largely cashed out of that market, and there were whispers that Malouf's best days and ideas were behind him, that he had surrounded himself with yes-men who shielded him from the word on the street. Two deals in the last few years had netted more than $4 billion in losses and cost one president of the company his job, and there was no doubt that the Praetorian board now had their omnivorous eyes on its founder. That's where Maya saw herself coming in. She would tell him the truth, the hard truth, and thereby save his ass. He was gonna have to hear it from a woman, a young woman with her finger on the pulse; she would be the only one with balls enough to hold up the mirror and deliver the news. That was her ticket. The readiness, the timing was all.

Though he could be generous with himself and often took his private plane (earning the admiring sobriquet "King Learjet" from his worshipful minions) for five-minute air commutes from Holly-wood Burbank Airport in the Valley to Santa Monica Airport, Malouf could be cringingly cheap with his employees. Legend had it that a former assistant once handed him a receipt from the car wash for his McLaren, and Malouf, spotting an additional charge on the slip of $1.50 for something called a "Cokie," stopped the young man at the office doorway, handing him the receipt to check, and then curiously inquired as to what a "Cokie" was, and why was he paying a buck fifty for it. The assistant laughed at the misprint. "Oh, that's a cookie, while I was waiting for the car I got a cookie, they left out an 'o.'" Malouf smiled, nodded, wagged his finger, and said, "No Cokie." And then he fired a grown man for putting his hand in the Cokie jar, taking the dollar fifty out of his last paycheck.

He was a constantly smiling presence of practiced avuncularity, with the studied air of a man who didn't have a care in the world while he gambled daily with millions of dollars. His habitual greeting, "How can I help?" was quite disarming, even though one came to quickly realize that he meant it more as a rhetorical question than an actual offer of assistance. The young guns, of which Maya was one, knew that the correct response to "How can I help?" was "I got this, Boss." Whatever "this" was. Just get 'er done.

And, oh, how Maya wanted to get it done, get something done, a big score that would bring her closer to under the big man's wing, make her his anointed one. A Neverland-type outside-the-box vision, only profitable. She was already pulling down low six figures, but with a good commission and a nice ride upon the two sweetest words in the big realty business—carried interest—she could really start to feather a serious nest. Her own father had died when she was three; she had no memory of him. Maybe that's why it felt good to want to please an older man like Malouf. She knew maybe that was a little fucked up, not pervy, definitely complicated, but she figured the end justified the means—what's the problem with wanting to be great at her job? Some people carried their wounds into adulthood to hurt others; some used them to rule the world. Pleasing a Daddy Warbucks figure like Malouf would only mean great things for her. Win/win. She knew the score.

The Praetorian workplace was a frat-like nest of vipers, mostly men in their early thirties, and Maya, the only woman. Insecure about his own intelligence, Malouf didn't like to surround himself with the smartest guys in the room, not the Harvard/Wharton nexus. He preferred the community college scrappers; he liked to hire the late bloomers with chips on their shoulders, the C students with something to prove to all those who had underestimated them in high school and college—in his sage words, "Fat girls are grateful for the fuck." The most prized asset here was not book learnin', it was loyalty, complete and, many had found or would one day find, unrequited loyalty to the big boss man.

In his own starfuckery way, Malouf had named his newest group of nascent killers the "Young Turks," emulating that tired moniker from the overhyped agents in Michael Ovitz's late '80s/early '90s CAA talent agency. Malouf had been obsessed with moviemaking since he was a child. His father would bring him to work constructing sets for movies on the Paramount, Fox, and Warner Bros. lots.

It was on the Paramount lot in 1963, building sets for *Robinson Crusoe on Mars*, that an inattentive nine-year-old Bobby Malouf had lost his left index finger to his father's electric saw. He remembered in hyperreal detail his father's expression turning from anger to horror. He could still see his father retrieving the sawdust-covered, lifeless finger like a dropped, bread-crumbed hors d'oeuvre, jamming it into his coverall pocket in the vain hope that it could be reattached and his boy made whole. Malouf could recall the shocked silence of the trip to the lot hospital in a golf cart, a bloody dishrag, with the stitching "Watch and Pray" needlepointed on it, over his throbbing hand. Almost since that day, he had harbored dreams of revenge, of owning the business that emasculated his father and took his own finger; to own a studio like Murdoch owned Fox—that was his white whale lurking beneath the surface.

Maya was the only female Turk. She could be loyal, but she was also street- and book smart, and that's how she was gonna rise, an undeniable combo. She wanted, needed, to distinguish herself from the backslapping loyal boys, while simultaneously showing the boss that, as a woman, a brilliant woman, she brought an XX factor to this macho game, that her wo-machismo was different and useful, that she was a banger and street brawler in three-inch heels. She could be it all, and she wanted it all.

The last two years of #MeToo had brought a strange sense of empowered powerlessness to a young woman in Maya's line of work. She could feel the eyes of the men shifting to her nervously during conversations to make sure she wasn't miffed, while at the same time wanting to be acknowledged, desiring credit for checking in. Even when talk turned to something as neutral as the Lakers or the Dodgers, she could feel the men longing for her to join in and give her blessing to the suspiciously and traditionally masculine workplace topics. Because of what her mother had suffered at the hands of motherfuckers, and her mother's mother, and all the mothers dating back to Lilith, Maya now had the power to destroy men's lives with a wave of her hand and a couple of words. She had the nuclear codes. Would she be a righteous or a capricious Shiva? The boys did not know, so they were always on their toes. And though they liked her, they hated her for it. She was an impossible thing, both slave and master.

And it wasn't only about matters sexist or misogynist that she was the token voice of authority—by some transitive law of oppression, though she was white, cisgendered, and straight (okay, she'd tongue kissed a girl sophomore year at a frat party, but that didn't really count), she was now the one turned to if a discussion suddenly veered in tone to possible racism or homophobia. That was not a job, arbiter of all social injustice, she had signed up for. Hell, she wasn't even an expert on women. She was twenty-seven. It was exhausting. And boring. And deeply dishonest. She knew all she needed was an even playing field to win. All she wanted was a fair shake.

She thought the workplace sea change was generally superposi-
tive and a long time in coming, but she also sensed in its long-repressed
vehemence a psychosocial overcorrection, as in the stock or real
estate market, and that things would, in time, swing back slightly to
a way better place than before, and even a better place than now, a
new normal, eventually. She sensed that mighty pendulum would
be swinging back soon, and it would crush some heads as it did.
In her bones, she feared the reactionary momentum of potential
male vengeance as it tracked back from this moment. Those were
the claws out for *Roe v. Wade*, as well as for the innocent woman
on the street.

In the meantime, she didn't want to overinvest in her newfound
and what she felt to be inflated, illusory, and largely negative power.
So now she was the one who brought up tit size/authenticity, dick
size, cock sucking, pussy hair, asses, and orgasms; she was the one
who fired the first innuendo—clearing the way, opening the gate, and
waving the boys forward into the breach; the cool, fun gal giving the
okay for the men to indulge nostalgically in some good old-fashioned
misogyny lite and twentieth-century sexual banter and shenanigans.
Yet another role she didn't really want, but there it was.

Her office door was always left open when a colleague visited
her. An insurance policy, a literal transparency against litigation.
Through that open door now, Malouf popped his turtle-ish, leathery
bald head, while gently tapping like a shy schoolboy wishing an
audience with a superior. "How can I help?" he asked, stooping in
the entryway as tall men will even when they have no reason to.

"I got it, Boss."

Malouf smiled. "I hear—actually, I have heard nothing about you
going to Joshua Tree this weekend with the Young Turks."

"Yeah, I want in on all that nonsense. I mean I don't."

"Well, if I'd heard anything about it, which I haven't, I'd advise
you not to, that mostly bad things happen in the desert, which I
won't 'cause I'm not even aware that it's happening."

"Copy that."

"And if you were to ignore my suggestion, and go to the desert, I would in no way be impressed when I heard later that you outpartied, outingested, outgunned, and outfucked all those callow pups and pretenders."

"Of course not."

Maya had the sense of all these lines of communication crossing between them—flirting, exhibition, inhibition, resentment, age, sadism, dominance, submission—a twisted mess, like when you live under humming power wires and hope the wind doesn't blow too hard, and even if those Gordian braids never blow down and destroy your house, just living under that dark vibration over time could give you cancer.

Even with your newfound power, Malouf seemed to be saying, you are but a plaything to me. She could hear him hissing underneath his purr—it's not about sex; it's about money. Money will always beat pussy. Money outspends outrage. She didn't disagree and wondered if he knew she was on his team. She'd only been playing this game a few years, but she was a natural. They smiled harmlessly at each other, and Maya remembered something she'd read about the social origins of the smile—the baring of the sharp teeth in friendship, not anger, the display of weaponry in a cold war show of peace.

"Come back from the desert with the biggest fish," he said, smiling or grimacing benevolently; it was hard to tell the difference with him. His face was unique, yet hard to pin down, hard to remember when you were away from him. Maya had often thought there was an uncanny aspect of pareidolia to Malouf—she'd had to google stuff like "seeing faces in things" before finding that term, for the psychological phenomenon that causes one to "see patterns in random stimuli," sometimes leading to "assigning human characteristics to objects." She'd once tried to relate what she meant to a friend as "looking at my boss is like seeing a face on a piece of toast

or Jesus Christ in a potato chip—it's like, I know he's not an inanimate object, but his face looks like the face of an inanimate object if
an inanimate object could have a face." It was hard to explain.

That's what she was getting lost in when he added his other
favorite rallying cry, "Bring me a unicorn."

"A whole herd. That's the plan. Or a black swan." She winked.

"Attagirl, any of those endangered species. I'm glad we never
talked."

"Me too."

"What?" Malouf asked in mock horror, and put his right index
and left middle fingers forward like a crucifix, which made him seem,
paradoxically, like a nine-fingered Dracula himself invoking the power
of the Cross while simultaneously flipping the bird. They both forced
a laugh. He left the office with the door wide open behind him.

3.

BY THE TIME BRONSON had returned from his unsuccessful pre-dawn petitioning to his God, prayers had been spoken and the Powers family breakfast was in full swing. A couple dozen eggs had been gathered from the coops by the youngest children—Joseph aka Little Joe (~5) and Lovina aka Lovina Love or Lovey (~6)—and the three loaves of bread had been baked by Yalulah aka Yaya, his second partner. Hyrum (~11), Ephraim aka Effy (~10), the twins, Deuce and Pearl (~17), Alvin aka Little Big Al (~7), Palmyra (~11), Solomona (~12), and Beautiful (~13) had slopped the pigs, milked the cows, hayed the horses, tended to the ostriches, and were just now washed and sitting down with the appetite of those who have already done a full day's work. Later, after breakfast, the middle kids, Palmyra, Solomona, and Beautiful, would tend to the gardens and the irrigated fruit trees. Bronson and Yalulah, because she'd graduated with a literature degree, would then conduct the classroom for five to six hours, with a deep assist in visual and musical artists from his other partner, Mary. As such, without outside influence or events, or even news of outside events, each day had an insulated but flexible sameness to it.

There had been a third sister-wife and mother, Jackie, who died of cancer years ago. She hadn't sought treatment, would not leave the grounds of the compound, forbade Bronson from bringing any painkillers or even aspirin back from civilization, and her death was protracted, painful, and macabre. Jackie would accept pain relief and medicine only from the immediate surroundings—learning and teaching about native remedies for fatigue and swollen limbs—the ocotillo and the globe mallow for her weeping sores, and California poppy for the anxiety. She would be healed by the desert or not healed at all.

Bronson had been in awe of Jackie's stubbornness, faith, and genius for pain. She had said, "Suffering is the Guru. Let my suffering teach the children." What it taught them was hard to say; that fruit was yet to ripen. Her own children, Deuce and Pearl, had found it hard, by the end, to look at her or to keep from retching in her presence, her tumors so hideous, her smell so rank. Half dead, covered and colonized by spreading tumors, she lingered in bed for almost two years, seemingly unable to die, like in some obscure Greek myth. Bronson dwelled nightly upon ending her misery by suffocating her with a pillow, but dared not contravene God's mysterious plan for his wife. Her will, her holy masochism, was infinite, saintly. Bronson had loved her deeply as a man loves a woman, but now she became a martyr in his eyes, and his love for her became a thing of transcendence. When the end finally, mercifully came, Bronson built and carved an exquisite coffin with his own hands, and the entire family dug a hole for her far out there in the anonymous dirt of the endless desert, an area Bronson had visited that morning and which served as the family's natural, sacred temple.

Pearl and Deuce, who came so young to Bronson when Jackie followed his promises into the desert, had vague memories of the world outside. Their sleep was haunted by tall buildings, highways, and asphalt jungles densely populated, magical, glowing, multicolored boxes full of friendly faces, and roaring, blue-green horizontal walls of water—images that were indeed dreamlike to them, and surreal. They really were not sure from where these nostalgic/futuristic thought-pictures came. The youngest seven kids, sired by Bronson, were desert tabula rasa—all they knew of the modern world, except for the thundering metal birds/sharks flying overhead, was this patch of dry earth and what they read and saw in the books their parents taught them. They "knew" about planes in the way the rest of the world "knows" about Martians. You might call them deprived, but you would not call them unhappy. They were too busy to entertain the blues.

The lack of outside stimulation caused an equal and opposite lack of discontentment in the younger ones. But a teenager is a teenager, whether on the surface streets of Hollywood or the surface of the moon, and those hormones know no master. Bronson knew this. It troubled him, kept him up at night like any father—how do I prepare my children for a world I have forsaken? The initial project, as Bronson, Jackie, Mary, and Yalulah had formulated it, was to create a generation of spiritual revolutionaries who could see through the status quo bullshit of the world at large. A brood of Joseph Smiths. When the time came, and that time was coming soon for Deuce and Pearl, the children, nurtured in the hothouse of the desert brain factory, would be unleashed upon the world to make it a better place.

That was their version of a Mormon Mission—their children. The four parents, the teachers, concluded when they came to the desert that they themselves were hopelessly blinkered and injured by the way they, and all children in present-day America, had been raised, and that, try as they might to remove the blinders from their own eyes, they were always drawn back to illusory and imprisoning thought systems and chimerical hierarchies by the unconscious patterning of their early, even preverbal years. The adults were helpless against the invisible bars. This would not be the case for their children. Their children would be free, and would, when the time came, then teach their contemporaries how to be free.

But, as the day to set loose his eldest kids approached, many nights Bronson lay awake, his mind tumbling with these questions that might send him riding out in the darkness looking for answers. Especially one question he could not even name that appeared to him only as a dark cloud, more like an interrogating omen than a question. He could not even put words on it. He would peer into that cloud, looking for shapes or words, and then turn away in fear to repeat the more traditional lines of parental anxiety—when are the children ready to leave home? Will they venture out into the world as soft innocents and get corrupted? Were they going to go to college? But then he would argue with himself that society itself is the sickness. Can they learn of and cure that sickness without being infected by it? Is there an inoculation for the incurable mental disease that infects every participant in the civilization? Can they be in the world one day but not of it?

As the children grew, these questions grew more pressing with each day. He still had no answers, but the day was fast approaching when the answers would be demanded by time and fate. These were the running conversations he had with his wives. These were the arguments. And though Bronson was the only man of the house and there were two sister-wives, theirs was a working democracy, a small village. The wives had strong, singular voices, and if they voted in a bloc against Bronson on an issue and he lost, as he had with the planting of avocado trees, which he deemed decadent water whores, he would go sulking off to camp in the desert for a few days, burying the debated issue in the middle of nowhere in the sacred spot he had buried and baptized his two dead infants, asking their spirits for guidance and perspective, and then return reborn himself, cleansed of resentment. And a year or two later, he would be the one planting more avocado trees for his beloved wives. If he and Jackie were the original visionaries, the ones with eyes to see, all the adults were equals, prime movers, and he was, he knew, not whole without them.

After breakfast had been consumed and the kitchen cleared and cleaned, the family moved into the "schoolroom." It was the largest room in this house that had been designed by Bronson, and built and furnished with the help of union set designers, scenic painters, welders, and carpenters that he'd befriended over his years spent employed and bullshitting on sets and partying after work. The men who helped him build his very real house had been construct-ing sturdy sets for decades—fake rooms and false worlds—from the back patio of *The Brady Bunch* to the hallways of Versailles.

The house had gone up in a matter of months, and though built by men who constructed fakes for a living, was made to with-stand whatever the desert heat and cold and wind could hurl at it daily. Much of the furniture came from huge warehouses on the back lots of Warner Bros., Universal, Fox, Paramount, and Sony. Pieces, even an old trampoline, that had been used in films and then stored away for possible future use, were pilfered and then recycled in this hidden desert home. It was quite possible that this or that chair, bed, or table had been seen in a famous movie or TV show. While cleaning up a couple years ago, Bronson had pulled a tag off the underside of a couch that identified it as "Bev Hills 90210/Walsh House." Bronson threw away the tag, and kept the couch.

So these Powers kids, most of whom had never seen a movie or even a TV set, were living on and among pieces of showbiz para-phernalia that might drive fans and niche collectors insane with envy. Bronson would have enjoyed the irony, if he were a man who habitually enjoyed irony. Instead, he thought the pervasive irony of the culture he left was evidence of its decay, impotence, and lack of original energy, that it could find sense and pleasure only in flot-sam and jetsam, and indirect, passive-aggressive, "funny" attacks against an entrenched status quo.

He was a man who took almost sensual pleasure in efficiency, lack of waste, and poetic justice—nobody was using this real/fake furniture, it had already been bought and its makers compensated. Perfectly good, well-made things just gathering dust—it would approach sin not to take them so they could be used, not to give them life again. And it jibed with the tenor of a worldview, formed by the Mormon Baptism of the Dead as Bronson understood it, and its vision of souls in the prelife and the afterlife—like a huge warehouse for souls, waiting to be reused. There was no need for God to make more of anything; it was for man to figure out how best to use what God, and the IATSE Local 33 stagehands, had already made.

If his interior decoration was out of style, or indeed, had no style at all, Bronson didn't care. To him, "style" was only skin deep, merely capitalism's way of getting you to buy new stuff. God was a recycler. Souls and plastics and armchairs must be reused. This was the type of associative thought-flow he tried to model for and engender in his children during school hours. He wanted to teach them what to think, sure, but more important, how to think, and how to think about thinking. He had not been taught how to think, for which he blamed a broken father and a broken American pedagogy, and he was determined that his kids not suffer the same retardation. In this educational endeavor, he was blessed that his wives had areas of expertise to impart that far exceeded his own. The schoolroom was conceived with no set schedule, with "learning centers" where the kids could gravitate depending on their whim and curiosity. Something like a Montessori classroom is how Yalulah envisioned it. There was a science corner, a math center, painting, engineering, chemistry, music, literature, and history nooks—with a "teacher" standing by or nearby in each. Bronson taught history and religion. Mother Mary taught visual arts and music, and Yaya took the rest.

Mother Mary was raised in Elizabeth, New Jersey; adopted at eleven months old into the Castigliones, a sprawling Italian family with eight other siblings. Free-spirited, misfit Mary quit high school her junior year to hitchhike west till she ran out of road and ended up sleeping on Venice Beach for a couple months, where she had to use her capable fists more than once. She ate very little, did and sold drugs, and turned a couple tricks when necessary, but in a few years, by the mid-'90s, she had transformed herself from an under-age vagrant with no skills and no money into a transgressive street performer (combining sword swallowing, fire eating, and contortion on the Venice Boardwalk), graffiti artist, skateboarder, and out loud, proud bisexual. Small, boyish, and muscular with thick, wavy dark hair she dyed sometimes purple, sometimes green, smooth olive skin, and yellow-brown eyes that seemed to glow in the dark, she had a seemingly unbreakable constitution and would put any drug or any person in her mouth.

Mary could never sit still, neither her body nor her mind, and was ever in search of a big system, the Answer, to explain the madness of her existence. She had read Marianne Williamson's gooey *A Return to Love: A Reflection on the Principles of A Course in Miracles* (almost thirty years before her unlikely and quirky presidential bid) and dug it for a spell (i.e., thought Williamson was sexy), but drifted away from the gauzy, soft-focus, witchy love babble. She was a functioning drug addict and drinker; had been through all of the 12 Steps four times. Forty-eight steps for Mary, and counting.

In fact, she met Bronson at a 12 Step meeting on Fairfax and Highland—during someone else's share, he had brazenly reached under the table to hold and still her ever-fidgeting hands. Mary was stunned to find that she did not pull back and slap away this super-forward dude, but rather watched, as if from a sweet remove, her hand stop shaking, calmed in his large, warm palm. She kept it there for the rest of the share. They put a couple rumpled singles in the plate, skipped the after-meeting coffee klatch, and thirteenth-stepped it straight to bed.

In the first iteration of their relationship, they had bonded over the similarity of their addiction's origin, to deal with the pain from his stunts and her street-performing, sword-swallowing life. He saw her as a female mirror to himself. Marveling at her flexibility and strength, he taught her the fundamentals—how to shoot, how to ride a motorcycle, how to fall, how to take a hit—and got her into stunt work. She already knew how to fight. She was a natural. Mary loved the thrill of the job, the danger, and the money. And even after they drifted apart, Mary had a legit, taxable career if she wanted it. Bronson always dug her out-of-the-box mentality and kindred, boundaryless spirit, and suspected that their story together was somehow not done.

More than a decade later, when Bronson was making the move to the desert, he tracked Mary down out of the blue and asked if she'd come homestead with his wife, Jackie, and him and make it a kind of commune/Mormon kibbutz. Mary had become a single mom just months earlier. Her first response to his proposal was to say, "I'm pretty much gay these days."

To which he replied, "A sword-swallowing dyke . . . what a waste."

At the time Bronson reconnected with her, she was no longer doing much stunt work because the irregularity of the gigs and long hours were going to prove impossible without a partner or child care. Fed up with busking, bartending, and temp work, a soul-sucking combo that was barely break-even with babysitting, she thought—Why the fuck not? She was Bronson's second believer.

"Okay, Bro'," she'd said, "but before I marry you, I have to meet your wife. She cute? And if I find out you're going for the Manson family starter kit, I will fuck you up." She met Jackie and they hit it off surprisingly well. Bronson could see the forms of his new existence taking shape, recombining his past with his present time. As Jackie's twins, Pearl and Deuce, took turns holding Mary's infant girl, Beautiful, Mary married Bronson. Both bride and groom wore black tuxedos.

Raised Catholic in Elizabeth by the Castiligiones, but having rebelled mightily and lived without rules and regimen for her adult life, Mary was relieved by the return to structure and coherence that the familiarity of the Christian/Mormon faith gave her. If Bronson's entry to salvation was this angry rage for order, Mary warmed to a simpler, less volatile thing, more like a schedule, a to-do list that gave shape to her formless days. If pressed, she probably thought most of the specifics of the origin stories that she had acquainted herself with and the Joseph Smith legend itself were bullshit, but the vector, the aspiration, she felt was true—and the charity, other-centeredness, and responsibility sat well with her. She had only ever lived for herself and the moment, and those were shifting sands. That changed when she became a mother and Bronson came back for her, changed more deeply still within the desert, within the family. Religion and family duty had the same calming effect on her soul, circumscribing its urge to fidget and wander, that Bronson's hand had upon hers years ago. She still had her moments of untethered panic here and there, but she didn't miss the boardwalk.

The third of the sister wives, Yalulah Ballou, was born back east to Yankee money and had gone to ersatz pastoral Putney for high school in Vermont and preppy Bennington for college, where she studied English and was an editor on the *Bennington Review*. After graduation, she headed west, like Fitzgerald and Faulkner before her, hoping to write for movies or television. She envisioned for herself a wilder, more improvised existence than the blue-blood blueprint her parents had boozily outlined for her. Unable to sell anything quickly, she ended up taking a job as an on-set script supervisor for a television show to learn how the sausage was made and to feel closer to the action than she would sitting in front of a blinking cursor all day, checking and rechecking her paltry word count in the house her parents had bought for her in Los Feliz.

The bone-dry, clerical nature of the job chafed against Yalulah's self-conception of herself as an artist. She was miserable all day making sure hungover actors and actresses had regurgitated the exact ifs, ands, or buts of the hungover hack writers. If this was the road not taken, she'd rather not take this road. That's when she met Bronson, who was working on the Paramount lot at the same time. With her family stretching back to the *Mayflower* and her identity forged in books and narrative structure, she saw the ever-tan stuntman as a real-life cowboy and rule breaker, a second-act complication, a Springsteen B side incarnate. Neither plain nor pretty, Yalulah Ballou was dubbed "jolie laide" by one of her Francophile aunts, and "as angular and unmarriable as a Picasso" by another. She was quick to flush red in impatience and had a tendency to scare handsome men away with her biting wit, but not Bronson. He cherished that anger, and her sharp tongue, and he found her off-kilter looks exotic amid all the symmetrical, plastic Hollywood beauties. He christened her "Yaya," after the Stones' *Get Yer Ya-Ya's Out*.

Yaya and Bronson would meet in the corners of the cavernous soundstages and steal thirty lunchtime minutes making out in the semidarkness, secluded by scrims and green screens as the hammers hammered on nearby sets and the radios of the construction crews both covered and inspired the sounds of their congress. They sought out sets that weren't being used or were tucked away from the action for the moment, made quick, quiet love in roofless living rooms that had fake sinks with no pipes, and walls that could separate and fly away on thick metal cables—almost playing house where movie stars played house.

The Scripty and the Stuntman—she began to think it was a good screenplay idea, calling it *Stages of Love*—how the two humble, below-the-line main characters would appear to make romance around the world and in dozens of exotic homes, hotels, and vistas overlooking (courtesy of giant high-definition backdrop photographs) oceans, mountains, the New York City skyline—without ever leaving the one soundstage off Melrose Avenue—a metaphor of change without change, or the emptiness of wealth, or the thinness of identity, or something or other. And then she realized that she'd never write it and maybe that was for the best, and maybe she was just falling in love.

But they had no commitment. They weren't boyfriend and

girlfriend. They were just fuck buddies, so Yalulah found herself way sadder than she'd ever expected when Bronson said he was quitting the life and moving to the desert with two other women. Yalulah shocked herself by asking Bronson if she could follow him. He smiled and said, "Yes, if you become my third wife." Her extended family back east, stretching from Providence to Boston, threw up their Brahmin hands. Her mother's scarlet heart was broken and her father humiliated. But then again, she came from one of those old, unfathomably wealthy Wasp families with seven kids that seemed almost engineered numerically to withstand and even revel in one or two of their offspring veering colorfully and tragically from the law offices and charity boards onto a wacky, decadent path. Like a Doris Duke or an Edie Sedgwick. Though it may still be whispered about her parents, the Ballous of Providence, salaciously, that they had a "daughter in a Hollywood sex cult, and worse, a Mahhhmin . . ." Yaya hadn't heard from them in more than ten years. She drifted in a low-level state of alert that they might try to find her and "deprogram" her.

But, as the years slid by, that humming dread and paranoia receded to a duller and ever more distant drone. She didn't miss them. Or LA. Or trying to write. Now, instead of supervising a script for a half-hour sitcom, she had four children of her own with Bronson and six more of an extended family to ride herd on. Regret was a luxury she had no time for, and was not spiraled in her Yankee DNA anyhoo. If she were not the writer she thought she would be, she would be a mother to writers, artists, and revolutionaries. Honestly, the hardest thing had been giving up Starbucks.

As her physical passion with Bronson mellowed over the years and the pregnancies, she had been drawn to Mary, and the two had become lovers. For a heady time, the three of them shared not only a bed, but a vertiginous, triangulated passion. After Jackie's death, Mary and Bronson even rekindled a physical connection through Yalulah for a while, but soon that, too, receded.

Yalulah found herself, with Bronson's sidelong blessing, falling in love with Mary. He had been a jealous man once upon a time, had knocked out the stray eager suitor of former girlfriends when he used to drink, but since he no longer felt incomplete, he no longer felt threatened. This mellowing didn't happen overnight. When he first realized that Mary and Yalulah had fallen in love separately from him, he spent many a night sulking horizontally between the two women, a mopey, forbidding, cock-blocking presence. Or he might brattily, sighingly make a show of leaving the marriage bed to sleep alone away from them, taking his pillow with him. He thought about forbidding them with scripture. He thought about leaving them or kicking them back out into the world. What did it say about him, as a man, that this type of love would flourish apart from him? He asked himself and his God questions like that over and over, until the answer came back in silence: nothing at all, not a damn thing. It was love, and all love was good.

Bronson's natural and potent, sexually fueled anger lived on, but was better suited to other midlife combatants, like his mano a mano with God. And Bronson was no fool. He knew Mary's transgressive, sensual power and her playful shine. He loved both Mary and Yaya, and loved that they loved each other. They were bodies and souls. They would have their ebbs and flows. They would have their seasons. They would wax and wane all three together, naturally, in elliptical orbits, an eternal, inviolate marriage of true minds. They had met through him; they had found their love for each other through loving him. Through Mary to Jesus, as the cult of the Virgin goes, and through Bronson to Mary and Yaya in Agadda da Vida. He was an invisible presence in their love. It was a human trinity as mystical, disparate, and intertwined as the Holy Trinity.

Yaya taught all her children to read by the age of three. She shared the literature and history duties of the school with Bronson, in addition to yoga and meditation. Today, Yalulah was teaching the younger kids *My Father's Dragon* by Ruth Gannett, and Randall Jar-rell's *The Bat-Poet*—with possible excursions into Fenimore Coo-per's *The Last of the Mohicans*, Whitman's *Leaves of Grass*, and Allen Ginsberg's *Howl*. The history lesson supervised by Bronson in an hour or so would be a hagiography of Eugene V. Debs. Philosophy today would be Lao-Tze, René Girard, and Nietzsche. The school day always culminated in a reading from the Pearl of Great Price (Smith, Abraham, and Moses) or the Old Testament.

Yalulah moved to teaching the teenagers from William Blake's *The Marriage of Heaven and Hell*, a late eighteenth-century revo-lutionary text she had turned Bronson on to when they first got together, when she was still entertaining Pygmalion / Sam Shepard fantasies of educating her as yet unlettered cowboy—another screen-play scenario that had never been, and, God willing, never would be written. Blake, an uncanny genius, both simple and mysterious, worked equally as well for older and younger kids.

She asked Deuce, Jackie's boy, to read aloud the more than two-hundred-year-old words. The young man, tall and handsome though still lanky and gangly as a daddy longlegs, read: "Man has no Body distinct from his Soul; for that call'd Body is a portion of Soul; discern'd by the five Senses, the chief inlets of Soul in this age. Energy is the only life, and is from the Body; and Reason is the bound or outward circumference of Energy. Energy is Eternal Delight . . ."

"Amen," called out Bronson. Addressing the younger kids clus-tered around a finger-painting area, "'Energy is eternal delight,' says the bard. What are the five senses?"

The children stirred happily and looked up at the ceiling, thinking. Little Big Al said, "Sight, smell, taste, touch, sound . . ."

"Well done."

"And farts," giggled Joseph, the five-year-old boy.

"Farts isn't a sense," said Lovina Love, the six-year-old girl.

"Farts *aren't* a sense. That would come under the rubric of smell and sound," Beautiful offered helpfully.

"And taste! Sometimes!" Little Joe challenged.

"Ooof, he's got a point, Beautiful. The boy's poots transcend even Blake's genius to classify." Bronson laughed. "That's six, the sixth sense has been discovered by Little Joe Powers."

"What does Blake mean?" Yalulah asked, steering them back to the text.

"He means that God is energy," Deuce answered. "And the Soul of man is like a little piece of God cut off from God and surrounded by a wall called Reason."

"So how, then, if we are cut off by our reasoning minds, to come to know God?" asked Bronson.

"Through Faith," Deuce replied.

"Like Joseph Smith said," Beautiful spoke from memory, "'There is no such thing as immaterial matter. All spirit is matter, but it is more fine or pure, and can only be discerned by purer eyes. We cannot see it, but when our bodies are purified, we shall see that it is all matter.'"

"Yes," affirmed Bronson. "All spirit is matter. Well done, Beaut'."

"Maybe," said Yalulah.

Bronson furrowed his brow and looked at her quizzically. Because Bronson's grasp of the greats was akin to that of a precocious high schooler or a college freshman, he would more often than not defer to Yaya in literary matters. Autodidact that he was, he had come to the great books of the world so late that he was nearly blinded by his own youthful enthusiasm and struggled not to swallow them whole and be swallowed by them. Even though he himself was middle-aged, his academic mind was still, and perhaps forever would be, in the honeymoon phase of his relationship with books. Yaya, on the other hand, had grown up a reader, attended the finest schools, was to the manor born. Her enthusiasm was still alive, for sure, and she let it come through for the kids, but it was tempered by years of mental sedimentation and familiarity.

Pearl, Deuce's twin sister, who was supervising a music session with Mother Mary for the younger ones, interrupted the "Hey Jude" sing-along to call out from across the classroom.

"The body," she said. Without missing a beat, she jumped seamlessly back into the Na Na Na Na's of the "Jude" chorus. Pearl, along with Deuce, the only child here who remembered the outside world, had taken piano lessons when very young. Bronson's worldview that America had gone hopelessly wrong after the '60s was mirrored in his musical and history curriculum. So, like Plato, who insisted poets be banned from his perfect Republic, Bronson, the architect of a perfected Mormon society and under the sway of his first wife, Jackie, who was naturally a hard-liner, had wanted to ban all music from his Republic of Agadda da Vida. "The Amish have no music," he said, "and they're fine."

Once Bronson had overheard Yalulah singing "Wild Horses" as a bedtime lullaby to one of the kids, and later that evening, in the marriage bed, had admonished her. He liked the song too, it wasn't that, it's the principle, he argued, a song could be a Trojan horse of mental infection, and the Rolling Stones did not exist. "I am the immune system," he said. Yalulah was unconvinced of Jagger's danger, but felt that maybe this was not the battlefield to die on. She did not persist.

But Mother Mary, a music lover, had patiently negotiated with him. And it was clear to her from an early age that Jackie's Pearl had a gift. She would often hear the young girl humming beautiful melodies of her own making. Bronson called them "wordless hymns." After Jackie's death, Mary got Bronson to allow Mozart, Brahms, and Bach into Agadda da Vida. And after months of running arguments and Yalulah's backing, the Fab Four were admitted to the kingdom. Bronson even got with the program and

returned from one trip to civilization with an old mono phono-
graph from the prop room of some period film. Bronson also managed to lift an old upright piano from a Fox prop warehouse, found
a few pawnshop guitars, some yellowing Mel Bay guitar books, and
drumsticks for plastic buckets. The kids taught themselves how to
play and then taught one another. One morning, Mary walked into
the living room to hear Pearl playing the guitar line to "Blackbird"
perfectly. Making music became their entertainment. They weren't
the Jacksons, they wouldn't scare the Osmonds, or the Partridge
Family; hell, they weren't even the Cowsills, but they had fun.

"The body," Pearl repeated, a little louder. Bronson turned in
Pearl's direction like he'd been startled by a loud noise, but then
covered that start with a slightly embarrassed smile. "The body,
huh?" he mused.

Mary watched their eyes meet, could see the connection between
them, tense like the ropes that join climbers to one another on a
steep mountain. "What do you mean by 'the body'?" Mary's tweenage
daughter, Beautiful, asked.

Beautiful's father had been a male model that Mary had impressed with her muscular stuntwoman legs and sword-swallowing
skills on the Venice Boardwalk one afternoon so many moons ago.
"Mr. Beautiful," as Mary dubbed him, had hung around her like a
stray puppy on the boardwalk for a couple days conspicuously dropping twenty-dollar bills in her sword case as she juggled live chain
saws. Then he continued to linger for a couple months doing print
work, repainting Mary's run-down surf-ghetto beach pad, and making love to her before moving to Vancouver, B.C., to pursue acting.

He was long gone before Mary began to show and swell. Mary
had once known Mr. Beautiful's real name, but had long forgotten
it. He might've made it big in the movies, he was charismatic and
ambitious, she wouldn't know. Mr. Beautiful knew nothing of his
kid's existence, and the child knew nothing of his save the name
Mary had bestowed upon her. For all practical purposes, the young

girl was a miracle born of a Venice Virgin Mary, and as far as Mary was concerned, that's exactly what Beautiful was.

Jackie's Pearl looked older than seventeen, with her mother's long black hair, large green eyes, and defiant set to her strong jaw. Unprompted, Pearl elaborated, "We don't need purification, we are already pure. The body is all of the soul that the senses can access in our fallen world. The only way to God is not through faith, but through our bodies. The body isn't a wall, it's a portal. The body is the only God we can touch, God trapped by time." She set her chin high and smiled.

The children stopped singing and the room fell quiet, their little heads pivoting to Bronson to see his response. You could almost hear dust motes landing. Yaya seemed for a moment to want to silence Pearl, but that was something she would never do to her students. Bronson nodded for a few moments longer than was customary; it almost seemed as if Pearl had entranced him, short-circuited him. Mary saw in Bronson a look that he used to give Jackie sometimes when she teased him, a discomfited delight. Bronson inhaled deeply. Young Joseph picked his nose nervously. Bronson exhaled audibly, then stood up and left the room.

Moments later, they heard a man yell a command and a horse speed off. Yalulah handed Deuce the well-worn copy of *A People's History of the United States*, its broken spine duct-taped many times over, and told him to read the next chapter aloud. He thumbed through to find where he'd last been.

"Chapter fourteen," he began, "'War is the health of the state' . . ."

4.

THE DRIVE FROM the Praetorian offices in Santa Monica to Joshua Tree National Park takes about three hours. For Maya, this meant three hours of riding in the back of a black Mercedes G-wagen inhaling an unholy combination of exhaled weed and Cuban cigar smoke that framed the words out of the mouths of the Praetorian Young Turks. They played the music du jour at ass-tickling volume. Rapping along with the misogynist, money-centric, status-obsessed lyrics was one of the last refuges where Caucasian men could freely and enthusiastically refer to women as bitches and hoes. It was truly a modern blackface. The Turks were able to voice things, even JJ, who was African American on his birth certificate—it was a veritable minstrel show for him, too—that they could never get away with coming out of their privileged white faces. The Turks were indulging in a philosophical nostalgia of sorts as they threw up incoherent and incomplete gang signs and chanted along en masse: "I ain't sayin' she a gold digger / But she ain't messin' with no broke niggas."

At least she didn't have to golf with them tomorrow. The Young Turk weekend plan was twofold—a Friday night of epic drinking and drugging with trust building, tall tale telling, and desert spitball sessions while slumming in one of the Joshua Tree campsites, followed by a late Saturday check-in to recover at the Mojave Hotel, while the boys hit the links and Maya hit the spa. Sunday they'd all meet up and drag their ruined body chemistry, dry mouths, and dried-out spinal fluid back to the real world. Sure, it was conforming to sexist role-playing to skip golf, and even though Maya knew a lot of business got done on the course and the lame nineteenth hole, she fucking hated that game, everything about it—the clothes, the visors, the pace, the lingo and time-suck; plus, her toes were a mess. She'd be more than fine hydrating on cucumber-infused water all day and getting a mani-pedi after a wild night.

The G-wagen pulled up to the Black Rock campsite, four thousand feet above sea level, around 7 p.m., as the sun was beginning to sink and turn the desert postcard pinkish. They unloaded the tents from the car and set to work. At twenty bucks a night, at least Black Rock had water, flush toilets, and fire grates. To the Turks, its low-tech accommodations passed for slumming irony for one night. Once the tents had been secured, out came the peyote, the Molly, and the ayahuasca—the Father, Son, and Holy Ghost du jour of the modern desert vision quest. Each picked their poison.

Maya had done Molly in college at Penn, and liked it, but associated it with dancing all night and love feelings, and she didn't want any love feelings in her tent tonight. She'd heard a lot recently about ayahuasca, but was pretty sure it was a good idea to have a mediator there or some kind of shaman to see the trip through. She'd taken an intro to anthropology course (known as "Easy-A 101") at Penn where they read Carlos Castaneda and learned about the peyote culture. She chose the dried little *Lophophora williamsii* cactus button and awaited the thirty-minute ETA of mescaline in her blood.

In Easy-A Anthro, she learned how mescaline works chemically, and she liked the idea of a serotonin agonist. Her Econ. major's understanding of the drug's mechanism was shaped like the chemical that was supposed to lock up and inhibit serotonin. Serotonin she understood to be a kind of a happy, up-mood chemical, but that too much of it was not great for focus. So if you had too much serotonin you wouldn't be able to prioritize or hierarchize reality or your senses—the sounds and colors and taste and feel would all be present at maximum intensity; all life and sensation would attack at once. So her takeaway (given to her by a friend who was fulfilling his science requirement by taking the soft "Physics for Poets" class) was that this was not a trip that added anything to what was there, it simply made you unable to edit the world. Whereas you lived the rest of your life in a diminished sensual prison of your own making improvised through generations of chemical survival mechanisms, what you got when you tripped was the truth, the whole truth, and nothing but the truth, the chaos of the world all at once.

She wasn't feeling all that much, so she grabbed another button, washing the bitter pill down with some lukewarm rosé. By the time the drug came on for real, the Turks were blasting a confusing mélange of Jay-Z and Florida Georgia Line. They had moved, though she didn't remember moving, out to the fire grates, and the games had begun under a clear cold night sky that looked too big to be true.

There was a hodgepodge, *Lord of the Flies* element to the night's proceedings, in that the Turks seemed only half educated as to what they were supposed to be doing, like they had recovered the ritual on ancient stone tablets in a language they didn't understand. They knew this was supposed to be sacred or sacredish, but they had no idea how to proceed. At its best, this was gonna be like a really good TED talk, but Ted himself, or any kind of visionary leader, was nowhere in sight.

They began with a trust-building exercise that was most probably lifted from acting classes, in which one person would close their eyes and blindly fall backward, trusting that the person behind them would catch them. They called it the "Catcher in the Rye game," 'cause each time someone caught a falling comrade, the falling one had to take a shot of rye. Get it? They did this for about three days, it seemed, and Maya realized that her sense of time had fled.

When it was Maya's turn to be the catcher, she let this

annoying, know-it-all dude, JJ, drop and smack his head on the ground. She hadn't made the decision beforehand, but, as JJ was falling, she stepped back and made a flourish like a matador side-stepping the bull. The rest of the Turks gasped and laughed.

"The fuck, Maya, what the fuck?" JJ said, as he cradled his head.

Maya didn't apologize. "You see that? 'Cause that's the way it is out there, homie."

"In the desert?" JJ whined as he checked his fingers for blood from his scalp.

"No, not the desert, JJ," Maya preached. "The trust part here is me letting you know how it really is in the big out there, the macro out there—it's dog eat dog, but you can trust me to always tell it like it is, I'll always have your back."

"Bullshit, you literally just didn't have my back."

"But in a larger, macro sense, I did. I do."

JJ wasn't convinced. He said, "I think I'm bleeding."

"I think you're a pussy."

Well, maybe that wasn't very Ted of her, but, game, set, match—Maya.

This wasn't really in Maya's character; in fact, if one of the men had done it, she would have shunned him. But she knew this was the type-A behavior she had to exhibit if she was going to be accepted as one of the guys, as a shark. She knew that it was JJ who had coined the office nickname for Maya—HH, for Hope Hicks. And she knew why. Hope Hicks, Trump's trusted press aide before he became president, had model good looks and a high-class-escort fashion and outer-borough makeup sense that no doubt made Donny Drumpf feel sexy. Without any apparent qualifications aside from her pretty face and loyalty, Hicks ended up working at the White House, in a position of influence with global power and ramifications. Hope, like her boss, was hopelessly underqualified for her job once Trump upgraded from being a reality TV actor and real estate money launderer to the president of the United States.

That's what JJ was saying when he called Maya "Malouf's HH."
And even though Maya secretly felt that Hicks was more of a tragic
figure than the one so easily derided, trapped by over- and underes-
timation by both men and women, she still had to distance herself
from any whiff of being an ornament. So tonight, Maya knew, if
she wanted to shed the HH moniker forever, she'd have to humili-
ate JJ, she'd have to skew her nature to outman the men, to err on
the side of asshole by being the non-catcher in the rye.

"Jesus, JJ, stop being such a whiny little bitch." One of the other
Turks, perhaps the alpha, Darrin, chimed in, the rest of the men
guffawing like a morally stunted and inarticulate Greek chorus.

Maya extended her hand down to a still stunned JJ on the
ground. He looked at the hand as if he wasn't sure she was going to
pull it away and Lucy/Charlie Brown him again. She winked and
smiled. He grasped it and she helped him up to standing, patting
him condescendingly on the top of his head for good measure, like
a primate grooming another primate to welcome him back into the
fold after an altercation. Mission accomplished.

Darrin stood up. "I got it. Check it out. Here at Praetorian, we are
doing God's work. What's the best real estate scam of all time?"

Turks started answering—Manhattan, the Valley, the Hamptons,
or maybe that halcyon day in the aughts in Georgia when the Turks
had descended, like Bluetoothed, bespoke locusts, on county courthouses and snapped up over one hundred foreclosed homes in one
morning. Darrin had been in one of those courthouses that bright
day, all of twenty-three years old, his briefcase bulging with cashier's
checks, and he smiled at the memory of youthful conquest. But still,
he waved off all their answers. "Heaven," he said, his pupils so expanded that his eyes appeared entirely black. "The Catholic Church
says, 'Yo, there's this place called Heaven where everything is perfect
and you can go live there after you die if you join this club called the
Church and pay your dues year after year'—you'll get a little piece of
land in heaven, and there's no end to the real estate up there 'cause it's

fuckin' made up—they can keep selling it till hell freezes over, the bubble never bursts. Best Ponzi scheme ever. The Vatican are straight-up pimps with inexhaustible inventory, yo!"

"Heaven! Heaven! Heaven!"

The Turks shouted like Heaven was a football team.

Maya watched the men bark in approval of Darrin's perception. And she agreed, it wasn't a half-bad insight, but she found herself struggling for air. She knew the mescaline could cause respiratory tightness, so she was trying not to panic about it. She worried that her breathing was no longer part of her autonomic system, but rather was dependent on conscious effort; that is, she felt like she had to think to breathe, and by consciously controlling her breath, she was, in fact, starting to hyperventilate. She wretched. She vomited. The Turks applauded. "Good out!" one called, which is what you say when someone hits a nice golf shot out of the rough. Ha ha ha. They began chanting "Semper Re-Fi! Semper Re-Fi! Semper Re-Fi!"

They looked ghoulish laughing in the firelight. Her trip took a turn.

She felt some panic sweat cold on the back of her neck, but she didn't want to be perceived as weak, didn't want to ask for help. Her breath got tighter, labored, and even though she was outside, she felt claustrophobic. The sky looked too low to her, like she might bump her head on it. She had an image that if she could just take off in a car, the wind would force air down into her lungs if she drove with her head out the window, much like a shark must continue to swim to run oxygenating water over its unmoving gills. That's the last coherent thought she could recall until she found herself behind the wheel of a car speeding along a desert road, her foot plastered down on the pedal with her mouth open out the window like a happy dog. The speedometer hit 85.

She didn't know this car. This wasn't the G-wagen. It struck her as universally humorous that she was driving a vehicle unknown to her. But it had serious pep. Had she stolen it? she wondered. She'd certainly never stolen a car before. No, she or the mescaline reasoned, she had not stolen it, because there was no such thing as personal property, everything belonged to everyone, all is all for all, therefore theft is a chimerical, capitalist, bourgeois designation. She didn't need to know how she came to be behind the wheel or where she got the keys. All she knew was that the difference between what was outside and what was inside, the native and the foreign, the desert air and the air inside her lungs, was being erased by the holy serotonin lingering overlong. She felt the tightness leave her chest like a bird taking flight, and she could breathe again, she was breathing again. A bug flew in her wide-open mouth— "Protein," she thought, "we are all one, thank you for your sacrifice, sir"—and swallowed. The speedometer hit 100.

She had no idea how long she'd been driving, but at some point, she had to slow down because of the road. If there was a road any longer, it had gotten more grabby, soft, and treacherous. In her expanding mind, she had switched to "automatic pilot"; that is, she had stopped driving consciously and relegated the act more to a more basic bodily function akin to breathing or blinking or her heart beating. And the move had worked; she was alive and at one with this gleaming machine, and she was driving in complete darkness somewhere off-road deep in the Mojave. The wheels spun out and lost traction as the car fishtailed sideways, spraying sand and small rocks, and stopped. Maya inhaled.

It felt like the end of a movie, but she was still climbing higher; the second peyote button, like a booster rocket piggybacking upon the first, ignited and kicked in with a silent roar. Maya pictured herself wrapping her arms and legs around a rocket as it blasted into space, waving a ten-gallon hat like Slim Pickens in *Dr. Strangelove*.

Maya got out of the car and took in the sky. She had driven so far from road lights or ambient civilized light that the stars were bright hieroglyphs, blinking like cursors waiting to be lettered. She saw a curving cluster of stars that looked to her like a chevron or an arrow or a greater-than sign or the logo on the *Star Trek* uniforms pointing in a certain direction. Her feet began to move where the chevron pointed her. She walked fast, even faster when she closed her eyes, following the sign in the sky in her mind. Gradually, she heard music. Must be the music of the universe, the theremin music the planets made as they danced around each other, the music of the spheres. She took her eyes off the stars and followed where her ears led. She could only handle one sense at a time, it seemed.

As she crested a rise, her dime-size pupils tried to contract against a dancing light on the ground a couple hundred yards ahead. Her first thought was—downed UFO. But, as her eyes focused and she calmed down, she saw that it was a bonfire, and she could make out human shapes clustered around it. Something told her to hide, so she hunkered down. She heard the music of the spheres morph into the Beatles—the Na na na / Na na na na refrain of "Hey Jude." She vomited again till she was empty. When she finished, the music had stopped and she could hear human voices carrying on the cold air.

A thought dawned that she had stumbled upon a lost tribe of humans, perhaps even prehumans or desert Neanderthals. How they came to know the Beatles music catalogue, she left for some other time. Now and then she peeped her eyes up above the rise to get a better look at the primitive humanoids. She surmised that it was probably an extended family of early primates, like *Homo habilis* or *Homo erectus*—goddamn "Easy-A Anthro" coming in clutch with the terminology again! Looked to be about fifteen of them, though every time she tried to count past ten, she failed and had to start over. The group consisted of three or four adult males and females and a cluster of mostly younger ones closely resembling modern human children and adolescents. She saw the male one she took to be the leader rise and speak. "We are the bad animal created in the image of the baddest cosmic *ur*-animal. We are the naked apes," it said. Maya nodded her assent. Wow, she thought, either these strange beings speak English or I can understand their primitive tongue.

Behind the alpha male, she noticed some rocks stacked as if to make a headstone, and then a couple smaller stacks nearby, like graves for pets, a couple of mini-graves; this struck her as both sad and cute. "Aw," she said to herself.

Then the male continued, "When I was learning stunts, Dar told me to hang around with the animal trainers, study the animals, how they move. I always got along better with people who got along better with animals. This one trainer had a crescent-shaped scar on his cheek where an adolescent male chimp had attacked him while he was driving. He had a male and a female in the back seat. The male was grooming him, you know, going through his hair looking for bugs, which is a submissive act, but it was a ruse in this case, 'cause all of a sudden, the chimp got him in a headlock—they're five times as strong as a man, so he's got him in an iron grip and he full-on bites his cheek, right here. Removes flesh, a real bite, blood everywhere. The female is screaming, upset, but not helping. He didn't blame the chimp, that's what a chimp does—challenges the dominant male. He was able to stop the car and run out, the chimp followed him, ready for the finish, and my friend ran back in the passenger side and slammed the door before the chimp could kill him or rip his balls off. That's a move they like, very effective. We are about ninety-eight percent identical to chimps. The other two percent is God. Without God, we're all chimps. So, I got my eye on you, Deuce." They all laughed, some, it seemed the younger males, uneasily.

Holy shit, thought Maya, what the fuck is going on here? Early monkey-man talking about monkeys—weird shit. A small, muscular adult female with long dark hair stood, dramatically backlit by the flames. She spoke the same language that Maya could understand. "When I did stunts, I apprenticed to this legendary dude who was about sixty-five at the time, been an animal trainer for forty-five years. We're on location somewhere and we've got to handle a bunch of baboons for this movie, there's a knock on my door at five a.m., and it's the old man, he says, 'Come with me to the barn, I gotta get down with the 'boon and I need you there in case he kicks my ass.' And I'm like, what? What do you mean 'get down with the 'boon'? But he turns and leaves and I get dressed and follow him out to the barn where he's got this big male caged. Baboons are nasty, mean. The old man shuts the barn door and takes his shirt off. He opens the cage and him and this big baboon start going at it, I mean, punching and biting, throwing as hard as they can, and they're both getting good shots in."

As Maya was listening to this parable, it seemed like a subtitled movie to her—she saw the words embodied and screened across the black canvas of night as if it were a film. She wondered that these primitive souls could speak in images that were projected outward. She saw green lights shoot up from the ground and into the sky, turning the stars into dollar signs. This was the omen she had come here for—the barren desert would transform itself into money. But how? Were those precious minerals shooting into the sky turning into dollars? Silver, gold, oil even? Was that the play she would bring to Malouf? Or maybe a resort? She would bring a resort unicorn to Malouf? Another Twentynine Palms, only so much bigger—Twentyninethousand Palms? Another Vegas? She was in the right place now, she knew why she'd gotten this high, stolen a car possibly, and off-roaded this far. But she didn't have the answer yet that she'd come for.

The female primate continued her story, and as she spoke, the group around her seemed to turn into monkeys as well, and strobed back and forth in the pulsing firelight between human and monkey like a bunch of black-light Jesus paintings. "A couple times, the baboon landed some shots and I thought about stepping in, calling it, and pulling Hank out of the barn. But I knew that if the baboon won, that would be the end of Hank as alpha, and I sensed he'd rather die than be a beta. And wouldn't you know it, even at sixty-five, ol' Hank had enough for this big baboon, and the tide soon turned, and Hank's straddling this monkey and landing haymaker hooks to his head and body till the 'boon turtles and starts to whimper and cry. So Hank lets up. He stands up, sweating and bleeding and scratched red, and he pounds his chest like a silver-back, and points to his head. The baboon jumps up, jumps on Hank's back, and starts grooming him. You see, after the battle, Hank was welcoming the 'boon back into his proper place in the pecking order."

A younger female stood and said, "That's all macho bullshit. What about bonobos?"

"Pearl . . ." warned the older dark-haired female who had been telling the baboon story, motioning for her to stand down. But this Pearl did not stand down. The one called Pearl continued, "Bonobos are almost identical to chimps and also ninety-eight percent like us, but they are matriarchal and they resolve conflict through sex and physical affection rather than violence. That's just as much human nature. We are both chimp and bonobo, and we can choose the better way."

Maya felt herself rise up and walk toward them. "Greetings," she said, "I am called Maya. I am a *Homo sapiens* from the kingdom of Santa Monica."

The hominids turned in her direction. They seemed shocked at her presence. She saw a young male spring up and assume an athletic stance, seeming to point at her, and then she heard a whirring sound and felt a sting on her upper left arm. She looked and saw an arrow sticking out at an almost right angle from her triceps. It hadn't landed squarely or deeply, but she was bleeding and looked up to see that the small hominid was reloading his bow. Before Maya could say another word, the alpha male pounced on the arrow-wielding little one and confiscated his weaponry. She looked at her bleeding arm again, grasped the arrow, barely inside her, and pulled. It dropped to the ground like the punch line to a bad joke, and she lost consciousness.

Maya came to on the back of a galloping horse, her arms around the waist of a man she had never met, his one huge, rough hand grasping both her wrists in a fist so she would not fall. He smelled strongly of sweat and fire. She heard nothing but the sound of the horse's labored breaths and the wind in her ears. She felt lost, but safe. She tried to get a look at the man's face, but saw only long dark hair and a short beard in the moonlight. He turned to look at her. His eyes were like two burning stars, his pupils looked like lightning bolts. She was still very high, but she was coming down; lights were losing their trails, sounds their echoes.

Her arm throbbed. She looked at it. It was bandaged cleanly, a spot of blood seeping through. "Thank you, Bronson," she heard herself say. She didn't know how she knew to say his name. Magically, the horse transformed into an iron horse, and Maya, arms still clasped around the cowboy savior's waist, was hurtling through the desert night on a motorcycle. She held tight, looked up at the stars, and passed out again.

When she woke up next, it was late Saturday afternoon and her back felt like someone had drained it of all fluid and suppleness. There was a clean bandage on her arm and she wore a thick cotton robe, her skin oily all over from what must have been a massage she could not recall, a Bulgarian woman at her feet asking her what color she would like her toenails, black or red? "Paint them black," she said, "please."

Sunday morning came without warning to Joshua Tree, and Maya, sacrum locked tight and achy, slumped gingerly into the car with the boys. She was cagey about what she told the Turks on their way back to Los Angeles in the G-wagen. She let ride the narrative that had begun in her absence Friday night, that she was a total boss who had stolen ("borrowed," she amended) a Maserati and taken it on a screaming joyride into the night only to return hours later on a motorcycle with a silent cowboy and a fucking arrow wound in her arm! Epic! That was pretty close to the truth, and she was fine leaving it at that.

Feigning to be unimpressed with herself and uninterested in her adventure (no biggie), she asked what the boys had gotten up to. Not much of note. JJ, no doubt still smarting from being bested by Maya, had tried to walk through the fire grate, something he had heard Tony Robbins does in some mind-over-matter malarkey. Didn't go so well. He was now elevating his burned and bandaged feet in the car, his stigmata a beige Band-Aid of shame compared with Maya's red badge of courage. She was well on her way to becoming a legend even as the Turks eventually tired of being stonewalled on specifics about the mystery cowboy who had, speaking not word one, dropped her off safely and then vanished with a roar back into the desert. She honestly didn't know who the silent horseback/motorcycle hero was, but she was damn sure going to find out, all by herself, in secret. Sphinxlike, she declined to elaborate on Friday night's events.

So the Turks moved on to an excruciating verbal replay of each and every one of the thirty-six holes of golf they had played on Saturday. The heated dissertations on the proper dispensations and accurate length of "hangover gimmes," the upper limit of "tequila mulligans," and the merits of 3-irons versus 5-woods was a perfect soporific, and once again, Maya passed out, in triumphant lack of interest, until home.

5.

ONCE BACK ON PRINCETON STREET, Maya took a long, hot shower and went straight to bed, hair still wet. She could feel her body coming to, annoyed with her for the chemical trauma of Friday night. Her arm was fine, it didn't hurt much, didn't look to be infected. She privately hoped it would leave a decent scar to accompany the story. At about 3 a.m., she awoke from unrecalled dreams that were the dying embers of her nightlong mushroom hallucinations, and fixed herself a triple espresso. She sat down at her computer to research the part of the desert she had, both psychically and literally, stumbled into.

Her initial Google searches turned up some cool facts, but no gems. The park itself was massive—790,636 acres, 1,235.4 square miles. The nearest major city was San Bernardino. A nonstolen, not speeding Maserati drive through the park might take a couple hours. As she read through these easily discoverable facts, she felt like a detective taking the first broad steps to tracking down a mysterious man and woman; the woman happened to be herself in the lost hours of peyote-induced happy madness, and the man was this Bronson fellow. She intuited that this cowboy and his extended family were not squatters—she entertained vague images of getting bandaged by one of the women in a well-managed home with many children around, including the little shit who had Rambo'd her. She knew these things had happened, but it was also bleeding

into things she'd read and movies she'd seen about the Manson
Family on Spahn Ranch (her ear tricking her into a false equiva-
lence of Manson/Bronson). She wanted to try to nail down some
hard facts before real memories twisted forever, like wild vines,
with false memory and word association.

But this was not a murder mystery, and this wasn't true crime;
well, yeah, that kid had shot an arrow into her, and that could
be filed away as an assault chip to be cashed at a later date, but if
the Bronson family weren't squatters, drifters, or killers on the run,
they were landowners in a pristine and likely infinitely valuable part
of California-America. And if they were landowners, they could be
land sellers. The park had been established only in 1994. It wasn't
that long ago that all this edenic "wasteland" was privately owned.
Praetorian was in the business of buying land. A pristine sizable
parcel abutting a national treasure, Joshua Tree National Park, would
be worth untold millions in possible mineral rights—gold, silver,
oil? In possible housing development rights? A resort? What if the
private land was, like the famous Twentynine Palms, on the waters
of the Oasis of Mara? Or something bigger, flashier, and more
starfuckery than Twentynine Palms, as per Malouf's Hollywood
leanings.

Was the land Indian-designated and therefore possibly zoned
for gambling establishments? Fuck the Mohegan Sun; build a second
mini-Vegas out there. Now we're talking billions. That would appeal to Malouf's thirst for a final score to shore up his legacy as he
approached his mid-sixties. He could be the second coming of
Bugsy Siegel. A sexy, biopic-worthy figure whom the next generation's Warren Beatty would play. Malouf would come in his pants
over that idea.

The Bronsons didn't seem too worldly or too wealthy—in
fact, they looked dirt-poor, perhaps they'd want to cash out? Could
it be that she had indeed, as her stoned self thought, discovered a
lost primitive tribe in America or, better yet, a wormhole in time to

prehistory, and that she would be their educating savior, buying their arid, "worthless" land and educating them in modern ways before relocating them into the easy pleasures and accumulated wisdoms of late capitalist, twenty-first-century civilization. She could be a good person in this feel-good story *and* make a ton of money. Win-win. These were the absurd fantasies spinning through Maya's whiplashed consciousness as the caffeine kicked in and she clicked randomly at her laptop hoping for a clue to open windows to new worlds, or knock some valuable perception free.

Who was this Bronson person? She googled "Survivalist Bronson" and "Cowboy Bronson," stumbling onto a quintessential 1969 TV series, *Then Came Bronson*—"a disillusioned reporter quits his job and starts wandering the road on his motorcycle." Ah, those must have been simpler days, she thought. She tacked back, typing "Horseback Bronson," only to be euphonically led down a "best of *BoJack Horseman*" cul de sac for about ten minutes, which felicitously, algorithmically, curved her to the oeuvre of a thespian named Charles Bronson. She'd never heard of this macho, mustachioed actor from the '70s, but she meandered through the thread of his apparently very big box office life. *Death Wish* sounded like an awesome flick. She would look for it on Netflix sometime, or Hulu or Amazon. She was on IMDb scrolling through Charles Bronson titles when her frazzled cerebral cortex flashed on the stories that the alpha male had told around the campfire, about a monkey fight or something. He said he'd done "stunts"—he must've been in the movies too, like his namesake. Maybe they were related?

She IMDb'd "Stuntman Bronson" to see if this generic person might have a Hollywood profile. And indeed he did. When she saw the credits listed for a "Bronson Powers, Stuntman," her breath caught. The list of movies he'd worked on was three pages long, impressive. There was no bio on the page, no personal details, as stuntmen were generally unsung heroes, but Powers's last credit was 1996's *Independence Day*, the Will Smith sci-fi blockbuster. And then he had disappeared. But he hadn't been killed or abducted by aliens after all. It seemed he had vanished into the desert for decades, and had been fruitful and multiplied. Maya did not know she'd been searching for this particular man, but she'd found him.

By the time proper morning rolled around, Maya knew most everything the internet had to offer on a middle-aged former stunt-man named Bronson Powers, and had the incipient makings of a plan to pitch to Bob Malouf.

6.

CONTACT WITH THE OUTSIDE WORLD necessitated a thorough cleanup. The "temple," the sacred site where Jackie and two babies were buried, where they held weekly fire meetings, was razed and relocated. Above and beyond all else, Bronson knew that the buried children should never be found. There would be too many questions. The tiny handmade coffins were dug up, the half-burned firewood reclaimed, and the sand raked by Bronson and his kids. Signs of man were erased from this holy spot. They would make another shrine. What made the spot holy was the presence of the baptized loved ones now removed, and the holy value given the barren land by meaning-making humans. Once Bronson removed his children and beloved wife from the land's embrace, it became palimpsest, unremarkable. Nobody would ever find this place where the woman had surprised his family. It was mute desert again. Only the homemade, weather-distressed spooky scarecrows and "No Trespassing" signs remained.

That was the easy part, the physical work. Processing how this intrusion had upset the bubble—that was a more slippery psychic cleanup job. It had been ten years, at least, since the older kids, or the wives for that matter, had had real contact with an outsider, when some old work buddies had come out to help Bronson dig a second well and work on some trails. Ten years since they had gotten so much as a whiff of a world outside their small tribe, and the first time the younger ones had ever been exposed to such contamination.

Bronson knew the desires and fears such contact made arise in him, so he could only imagine the inchoate intensity of that within his kids now, and his women.

There was the problem of spiritual contamination, but there was also now the nagging, more pressing and practical suspicion that other intruders might follow. The woman had been wounded, and even though it wasn't serious and she seemed grateful for the care, she had been assaulted and could make trouble. Bronson prayed on the matter, but he couldn't see his way through. He had dropped her off in the dead of night. He had spoken to no one. He had driven the Maserati back himself that same night (fun, he had to admit), then had Mary come pick him up and take him back home on horseback. He had vanished without a trace. They had been ghosts in the night. He had done the best he could, but now, for the first time in a decade, matters were out of his control. He knew that. It aroused his rage for order. He recognized the familiar feeling from so long ago; he hated it anew.

First to minister to was the eleven-year-old boy, Hyrum, who had pierced the interloper with an arrow. Bronson found Hyrum this morning with their milk cow. Mary's boy, whom he'd named after Joseph Smith's loyal brother and disciple, seemed more at home with the animals than his siblings. Hyrum was a wild child whose nature was perfectly suited to the farmwork and the hard subsistence of desert life. He loved his chores—haying the horses, slopping the pigs, gathering the eggs from the ostriches, and milking the cow. He was also keen when it came time to slaughter. While the other children seemed to understand the necessity of killing for food, Hyrum looked at it almost mechanically, watching his father in those moments of life-taking with a removed fascination, like some other child might linger with a large puzzle split again into its senseless pieces—not malicious necessarily, just fully engrossed, at home. Still towheaded, untamed, undomesticated, he had never shown much of an interest in book learning like Deuce and the others. But like his father, Hyrum was a natural on the trampoline. Many nights, Bronson might wake from sleep and step out of the house for a cigaretteless cigarette break, only to be startled by the silhouette of his son flying through the air, casting night shadows—jumping, tumbling, falling, rising off the crosshatched canvas high enough to blot out the moon. When he beheld his boy in such unguarded, ecstatic private moments, Bronson thought of what Joseph Smith had said about himself: "I am a rough stone. The sound of the hammer and chisel was never heard on me nor never will be. I desire the learning and wisdom of heaven alone."

For sure, Hyrum reminded Bronson eerily of his own father as well, especially in the eyes and the defiant set of his downturned mouth. The kid could be a stuntboy, the way he rode a horse and shot. Try as she might, Mary could never see herself in their son. "I carried him in my belly, but he's one hundred percent yours," she would say. "That's your clone."

"I think he's more like my dad's clone. He's like my wild ram of the desert. He came out of the womb pissed off," Bronson responded, unable to hide his admiration.

"Like I said—you to a T." Mary laughed, Bronson didn't.

Hyrum was quiet. He usually did not speak unless spoken to. As always, he wore a shark's-tooth necklace that he'd made himself. This desert had once been a huge inland sea, and the boy found loads of the fossil fish teeth, ranging in size from a dime to a finger, as he roamed freely what used to be a prehistoric ocean floor. He was patting the old cow, Fernanda (named after a beloved baseball hero of Bronson's—the portly Dodger great Fernando Valenzuela), on the top of her head. Bronson began to pat Hyrum's head exactly the same way; the boy brushed his father's hand away.

"How are you feeling, son?"

"Feeling?" the boy replied, as if he'd never heard the word. "You mean what am I doing?" For in his boy's world there was only doing.

"You know that was a woman you fired your arrow at, Hy."

"I thought it was a coyote."

"Coyote, huh? Mighty big coyote. On two legs."

"I seen coyotes that big walking like that."

"Uh-huh."

"Maybe. It came to kill us."

"Were you scared?"

"Scared?" Again, like he didn't know the meaning of the word, like he'd never heard or considered the concept before.

When the boy was seven, he had developed a large pustule under his armpit. Yalulah, who crash-course trained as an EMT in preparation for joining Bronson in the desert, lanced the boil and drained more than a quarter cup of bloody pus out of it, squeezing and kneading until it deflated. Bronson had held his son as his wife cut and probed. The pain must have been searing, not that you could tell by looking at the impassive Hy. The boy didn't even need to be held. He just stared curiously up at his father's eyes while one of his mothers cut him open, as if looking for clues as to what a vulnerable human should feel. Much as he was looking at his father now.

"If I tried to really hit it, I woulda really hit it. I jez wanted to clip it."

"Well, boy, you clipped a her, not a it."

"Her."

"You gotta know that more people might be coming down now, and you can't be clipping any more of *them*, okay?"

"Why more gotta come? I like it the way it is."

"I like it the way it is, too. I'm not saying more are gonna come; I'm saying it's possible, and if I'm not around, you can't just shoot at them."

"It's them or us."

"It's not them or us. It's them *and* us. Them over there"—he pointed southwest—"and us over here. Okay? Put it there, Pilgrim." Bronson extended his hand.

"Okay."

Bronson shook the boy's little hand. It was remarkably callused and strong for his age. "Have I ever told you how much you remind me of my father?"

"No."

"Well, you do. You look like him, a redheaded him."

"What was he like?"

"I'm not sure how to answer that, Pilgrim."

"You brought it up."

"Yes, I did. He was very funny."

"I'm not very funny."

"No, I guess you're not. Though that was kind of funny."

"I don't get it."

"His name was Fred."

"Fred?" Hyrum laughed at the name, as kids do.

"Yeah, and he was not a good man, Hyrum. Not at all."

"Thanks a lot."

"See, you are funny like him." Hyrum didn't laugh.

Bronson didn't know why he'd brought his father up and wished now that he hadn't. He just knew that his son was a mystery to him, as his father had been, unreachable in some primal way, and dark. "Anything else?" he asked. "You seem like maybe you got something else on your mind."

The boy took a few breaths, almost starting to say something a couple times, then . . . "If I'da wanted to hit its . . . her . . . heart, I woulda. I don't miss. I hit where I aimed. Exactly."

"I believe you, Hy. You're the best shot of all of us."

The boy brightened. "Better than Deuce?"

"Way better than Deuce. Bow and gun. And slingshot."

"Better than you?"

Bronson took a fake dramatic pause like he used to see the hammy actors do in the action films that were his bread and butter once upon a time; the directors would say, "Take a comic beat." The muscle action guys always thought they could be funny, which usually meant arching an eyebrow muscle. He held his index and thumb a small distance apart and nodded, raising the Nicholson eyebrow his father said had been stolen from him. The boy, his boy, this rough stone, smiled wide. He still had a couple baby teeth left.

That night in the shared bed, Bronson lay with Mary and Yalulah. The three of them made love all together for the first time in years, as if they needed all their bodies to reaffirm some broken circle and to form a blockade against intruders by their sheer joined moving mass. Bronson felt like they wanted to keep him in their bed. He hadn't felt that in a while. Keeping him close like this seemed both a desire for and a fear of him—he would be there, yes, but he would also not be somewhere else. There was something between them they were trying to squeeze out, to kill the distance, and it hadn't quite worked.

In the dark, spent, he still felt alone on one side of the bed, the two women together on the other side. They all stared up into their own shared darkness.

Mary spoke first: "I think we're in trouble." Yalulah, often the voice of mediation, was quick to defuse: "Well, we've had park rangers come by a few times over the years and nothing's come of that."

"Did Hyrum shoot an arrow at any park rangers?" Mary challenged.

Bronson stirred. "No, he did not. He wasn't old enough." They laughed, they could still laugh at that, at the boundless nature of their wild son.

When Mary stopped laughing, she said, "You can't blame it all on Hyrum."

"No one's blaming it on Hy, seems almost a miracle it hasn't happened before." Yalulah was trying to help Mary inoculate her son against blame.

Mary turned to look Bronson's way in the dark. "You brought her here, an outsider, into our home, Bro'."

Accused, Bronson held where he felt Mary's eyes to be in the darkness. "What was I supposed to do? Leave her out there to die of exposure? No way she would find her way home. She was high as a kite."

"Maybe."

"Maybe?"

"Maybe nothing will come of it," Yalulah interjected. "It's been almost a week."

"Things are already coming from it," Mary continued. "Questions in the kids' minds. In mine."

"What do you mean?" Yalulah asked.

"Don't be blind. The kids are getting older. Even before this, I've felt maybe they want more, Pearl and Deuce, especially."

"Not Pearl," said Bronson.

The two women fell silent for almost a minute. The conversation was poised at a fork; both threads led into a different kind of darkness. Mary forged on—"Even without this, the time is coming when we have to make some big decisions about the older kids. College."

"Yes, we always said they'd go to college," Yalulah agreed. "But that's not for two years."

"Two years is nothing. Two years will be here tomorrow," Mary said.

"Go to college and then what?" Bronson asked.

"We can't know that." Yalulah sighed.

"I need to know," Bronson stated firmly.

"How? How can we know? There's no test. Bro', just because your father taught you nothing doesn't mean you have to teach your kids everything," Yalulah said, as sympathetically as she could, knowing Bronson hated to be put on the couch like that.

"So all our talk"—Mary kept at him more directly—"about releasing them back into the world was bullshit?"

"No one is saying that," Bronson said. "The kids got us out here, but maybe we have to keep our eyes open for more miracles. Maybe God has other plans. The kids are happy here."

"Are they?" Mary asked.

"What do you mean?" Yalulah asked Mary.

"I mean," Mary replied, "we have nothing to compare it to and neither do they."

"We can ask them," Yalulah offered.

"Ask them what?"

"When they're eighteen, ask them if they want to stay or go."

"They may be eighteen now. We haven't been keeping track like that. They may be nineteen. And why eighteen, anyway?" Bronson argued. "Eighteen is an arbitrary designation. 'Cause the government says that's when you're an adult? Why not thirteen? Why not twenty-one? Thirty? As arbitrary as a fucking speed limit. Bullshit."

All three of them fell silent again, imagining the possibilities, and the impossibilities. "Deuce is fine," Bronson finally added to the fraught silence, choosing the more obvious path. "Do you want for more, Mary?" he asked.

"No," Yalulah answered for the woman she loved.

"No," Mary agreed softly. "But nothing lasts forever. We never came out here saying 'forever.'"

"We take eternity day by day," Bronson said, and it felt like an empty platitude immediately.

Mary ignored it, moaning, "Are we the worst parents in the world?"

"We're the best," countered Yalulah. "Have you seen what's going on out there? It's a disaster."

"How do you know?" asked Bronson. A very good question. How would she know?

Yalulah raised herself up on the headboard. "'Cause I've snuck into town once or twice a year the past few years and I sit and have a coffee at Starbucks in San Bernardino and look at the world and go on a computer in the library with my library card and it scared the living daylights out of me."

"Yalulah Putnam Ballou!" Mary gasped with mock outrage. "You sneaky bitch! Busted."

"I had no idea," Bronson said. "You had coffee?"

"You have a library card? That's so . . . you." Mary smiled, having fun.

"Yes, I had a Venti Mocha Frappuccino. Or three. And I fucking loved it. That's what you want to focus on right now, Bro'?"

"Did you drink alcohol?"

"Maybe."

"You're a badass, sister," Mary said, with a laugh.

"Please, I had a beer. A cold Corona with lime! It was heavenly. And I'm not joking. It's so much worse than you can imagine. They all have their own phones now. No one looks anyone in the eye. There's something hideous called 'social media.' It's the worst of the worst. Like when Sartre said, 'hell is other people' . . . he must've been prophesying this. Hell is other people with phones. You must've seen the changes, Bro', when you have to go into San Bernardino."

"It's true, I've seen the changes, and it is bad, accelerating, but"—Bronson wagged his finger—"I didn't have any coffee. No freedom without obedience, baby."

He kissed Yalulah on the top of the head, and she looked up into his eyes, challenging. "Amid all that noise, you're still gonna get hung up on the Starbucks of it all?"

"I'm a lawman, Yaya." He smiled, using the old TV Western terminology for himself. "God's law, Mosaic law, Christ's law, Mormon law. It's the ground beneath my feet. It's how I stand upright. I can't pick and choose what I believe like from a menu. I believe all or I believe nothing. And if I believe nothing, I am nothing. I swallow it whole."

Yalulah snarked, "Are you done, Lawman?"

"Jesus, Bro', it's just a cup of coffee," Mary interjected.

"The outrageousness of God's demands is a precise validation of their holiness." This was one of Bronson's self-coined aphorisms. It drew a smirk from Mary, who promptly high-fived Yalulah. Bronson clenched his jaw. "And the beer, if I'm being rigorous." Yalulah shrugged. "Yum. But I want to be *here*. My kids are here. I never want to go back there. You two are here. My love is here."

Mary seized the opportunity to steer the conversation back to the children. "Are they going to go out into the world? The kids?

Eventually? If that's the case, well . . . fuck. What the fuck are we doing? How are we preparing them for that?"

"This is the world, right here," Bronson asserted.

"No, Bro', it's a world, not the world." Mary rose up in bed.

"It's Eden," Bronson said, trying to settle his wives. "And there's a snake come in the garden. But God created the snake, too. The snake has always been part of the garden. Where the path is bad, the obstacle is good. We will see our way through this. Together. In time, we will be shown the way as we always have been."

The three stayed in the silence, as if waiting for a blow they wouldn't see coming but knew had to come. The first hint of daylight was creeping through the windows. Bronson felt he had made himself known, that was all he could do. He would leave them alone for a couple nights now, let them come to their own understanding; then they would speak some more. That's how they'd always done it. He would have them feel slightly lost with his absence. There was another room for him, another bed.

The sun was coming up now. There was work to be done. "Time to make the doughnuts," Bronson joked as he got out of bed. Decisions would have to wait. Bronson dressed, temple garment first, as he said, quoting his old NA sponsor, "Don't future-trip. Expectations are future resentments."

"Ugh. Fine," Mary replied. "Just show me how not to expect, and I'll be good."

Yalulah kissed Mary and stood up and, while pulling on her own temple garment, smiled hopefully. "The kids could be park rangers and stop by for lunch all the time."

Mary shook her head and turned to face the wall, eyes open. "But what's the plan? Like, what do we do?" she asked. "I mean, like right now? Like today—what do I *do*?"

"We wait on the snake," Bronson said, and left to begin another day in paradise.

7.

AT HER PRAETORIAN DESK, a couple months after the now legendary Joshua Tree debacle/revelation, Maya shuffled some PowerPoint printouts together preparing to ambush Malouf with a presentation that would blow his greedy mind. In the intervening weeks, as she had researched the enigmatic cowboy, Bronson Powers, and the valuable real estate he had inherited from his unimaginably wealthy, land baron ancestors, she had acquired her very first tattoo. Among her classmates and peers, she had been the only remaining tattoo virgin. Hers was a reflexively self-scarifying generation. Right above the arrow wound on her upper arm, now healed, she had added the simple black, fine-point image of a snake swallowing its tail, the Ouroboros. No color, tasteful as shit.

This was an ironic and/or very brave move, as Maya suffered from a rather stubborn case of ophidiophobia. She was terrified of snakes; a sad fact she discovered at a very young age when meeting the Sterling Holloway–voiced Kaa in *The Jungle Book* animated movie. The meeting did not go well. The mere mention of a snake caused her to freeze, and when she watched *Planet Earth*, her finger was poised nervously on the fast-forward button in case the awe-filled, priest-like Richard Attenborough encountered a serpent of some kind. And, conceiving of making a deal for desert space, she knew she had to somehow come to terms with the reptile whose natural domain it was. She told herself that the snake on her arm was a type of inoculation against her mortal fear, and besides, the Ouroboros was a kind of snake suicide, or making itself disappear. Win-win.

She wanted all her ducks in a row, and didn't want to alert Malouf to her scheme until all he need do was add muscle and cash and appear to be the savior riding in on the white horse. That's the type of deal the boss loved. But Maya's proposal was tricky, too. She would have to convince Malouf that she was like one of those speed-chess players in Washington Square Park in New York City who helm five games at once. Her scheme involved seeing ahead a few moves on multiple boards with different sets of adversaries, and she hoped to circumvent Malouf's overriding instinct for instant gratification with a more sober eye to the long game.

Maya was led into the boss's expansive corner office by the first male assistant of Malouf's life, courtesy of the rampant #MeToo-phobia ever so legitimately sweeping social media in general and the Praetorian business culture in particular. Backlit by the room-length window with an LA-skyscraperless view all the way to the blue Pacific, Malouf appeared lost in his *GQ* magazine, no doubt a source of torture for him as he beheld people who appeared even richer, ever younger, and more beautiful and copiously fingered than he. With his slick, bald head, skinny shoulders, and long sinewy body, Malouf in silhouette looked, Maya thought for the first time, like a human snake himself. She shivered.

She watched as Malouf became aware of her presence and, hiding that awareness, quickly switched out the lightweight mag for a weighty tome, pretending to be engulfed. The book was *The Accidental Species: Misunderstandings of Human Evolution* by Henry Gee. Maya cleared her throat. Malouf acted surprised, as if he'd been shaken from deep contemplation, and stood up in gentlemanly fashion. He was wearing beige jodhpurs and a $200 black T-shirt. Maya dully surmised he had come from or was about to go play polo. On a horse. All she had ever played was Marco Polo. In a pool.

"There she is," he said, gesturing with his four-fingered hand to a seat facing his long desk, "Maya Abbadessa. My favorite name and favorite gal. I heard you got a tattoo. Sassy. May I see it? Leave the door open, please, Trevor. Have a seat, Miss Wharton. How can I help?" He waited for her to sit first.

His desk was always empty of clutter, no computer, or paper, save for that omnipresent *GQ* and a changing stack of nonfiction hardcovers, like the one he had just closed, that seemed to be in the Stephen Hawking *Brief History of Time* genre (or the more recent iteration of the book that absolutely everyone is not reading, Thomas Piketty's *Capital in the Twenty-First Century*)—books that promised to make science, or economics, easy for the layman and to deliver the key to the universe without the pesky math, granular Marxism, or physics in fewer than 400 pages. Books that signaled to the world that Robert Malouf was more than a moneymaking machine—he had interests, he had curiosity, he had a soul. Maya had seen Malouf ostentatiously toting these types of books before. She'd watched him lug around and appear to read Yuval Harari's *Sapiens* like an overeager undergraduate for almost a year. In a small vertical pile today she spied *The Selfish Gene* by Richard Dawkins, *The Soul of an Octopus* by Sy Montgomery, *Y: The Descent of Men* by Steve Jones, and *12 Rules for Life* by Jordan Peterson. The spines of the books were all cracked, too cracked even, more pages dog-eared than not, as if someone in a movie props department wanted to make them look well-read and digested.

Maya handed him the thick sheath of her presentation. He accepted it graciously, and then slid it into his trash without hesitation. "I don't like to read business and I don't like paper trails," he said, sounding much like his good friend, the current occupant of the White House. "I prefer-bal the verbal."

Maya swallowed hard and launched into what she knew from memory about Bronson Powers and his land. She told him to think of the Powers clan like the Mulhollands. "Like *Chinatown*," he muttered reverently under his breath. She knew she had him then. A Hollywood story.

She told him that the land was purchased for thousands and was now worth possibly billions—ripe to be stripped of its precious minerals—obviously gold, silver, and copper, but also, intriguingly, tungsten, which was suddenly rather valuable as a component of electric car batteries. Malouf's Muppet eyebrows danced up when he imagined himself rubbing elbows with all the Tesla-proud celebs.

Maya brought Malouf's attention to the Opportunity Zone initiative tucked into the 2017 Republican tax cut bill. "Look at what Michael Milken is doing in Reno. You could do that in San Bernardino, with your connections—I bet you could get the area designated as an opportunity zone and qualify for a massive tax break."

"That's the Mnooch." Malouf smiled, referring to Steven Mnuchin, the former "Foreclosure King," *Lego Batman* movie producer, and present secretary of the treasury of the United States. "He's the best, a good friend."

Encouraged, Maya then spun scenarios of exclusive resort building. She saw Malouf recoil a bit at that because Praetorian had recently lost a billion dollars buying a resort management company that had been humming along very well, replacing experienced management and promptly running it into the ground. But, Maya said, we would be in on ground zero here. She brought up his archnemesis and feral competitor, Barry Sternlicht, and inspired visions of vanquishing him, and outstripping Vornado, Starwood, and Mack-Cali, even outflanking Blackstone. She kept reminding herself that Malouf had had a few bad years running, that the board was moving against him, that he needed her perhaps more than she needed him. Always vulnerable to the Hail Mary idea, Malouf, whose sequential thinking was not his strong suit, in times of stress would look that much harder for the lightning strike, the one in a million.

When she was finished, Malouf licked his lips, visions of a thousand Mohegan Suns dancing like sugar plum fairies in his head. He tried to tamp down his excitement. He had made billions from buying cheap one-family homes, but when he had taken a big swing, like on Neverland, he had whiffed mightily.

"Been there, done that, cashed out. San Bernardino is a shithole. Believe you me, I know."

"So was Vegas. So was Reno."

"So *is* Reno."

"Yeah, maybe Reno is a shithole today," Maya persisted, "but again, let's look at what Milken is doing there with the Trump/Mnuchin opportunity zones." Malouf allowed himself a smile; he could be a world maker; in his mind, he already was.

"Milken is a fucking genius. He's OG. Thank goodness he stopped wearing the perruque, though, huh? I'm intrigued. I used to describe my present level of excitement as 'half hard,' but I don't do that anymore, do I?"

"No." She smiled.

He bit harder. "What's the catch, then? What's the plan? How can I help?"

"Well, here's the greatest obstacle and the greatest opportunity— this dude Powers seems to be a rabid Mormon, as I said, which I think is initially an impediment to selling, but, as in all epics, the impediment will become the opening."

"That's a very philosophical position. Usually, when I am persuaded by philosophy, I lose money."

She settled in to tell the story. She knew that dealmaking was all about storytelling, the ones with the happy endings.

"He's got his own private world up in there. I took a ride to the outskirts of his property, it's impressive in size and scope. He might have access to the Oasis of Mara—which would be worth untold millions—even the mineral rights alone. But there's no record of the kids in nearby schools, so he's homeschooling his kids, that's the key here, which, if he were a Utah Mormon like most of these guys, would not be a problem, 'cause Utah has very lax homeschooling laws, but, aha, not so California."

"God bless California."

"Yes, because the Golden State has some of the strictest home-schooling laws in the country. Can you imagine the creationist, Book of Mormon, anti-science curriculum that's being forced on these in-nocent kids? That is, if they're getting any kind of instruction at all. I mean, on the happy side, we might have an Angulo family situation, and on the dark side, we might have another Turpin family deal here."

"Who?"

"There are pictures in the presentation I worked so hard on that you threw in the trash," she teased.

"Oooooh, pictures . . . why didn't you say so." Malouf could enjoy taking the piss out of himself if he could be the one controlling the intensity and duration of the piss. It made him feel known, and liked.

Maya got up and retrieved her presentation from the garbage and found the pages with the photos. She hovered over Malouf, pointing as she spoke, aware that their bodies were touching and that her left breast was making "unintentional" contact with the back of Malouf's shoulder. She was momentarily insecure that her breast implants did not have enough give and did not feel real, but she soldiered on. "The Angulos are seven children that were raised in an apartment in New York for years, never allowed out by their parents. All they did was watch movies, thousands of movies. There was a doc made about them in 2015."

"A movie, huh? Cool. They look Indian. Who played them?"

"No one. It was a doc."

"Right."

She turned the page for him. "And the Turpins here in California, kept thirteen kids locked up in a house for years. The Turpins will be in prison for the rest of their lives."

"Hmmmm, white trash. They need a housekeeper. I think I know where you're going with this."

He didn't really, it was her story, and an original, surprising one, and she knew he didn't know it, but she stroked him anyway.

"I'm sure you do," she said as she went back to her seat across from him, "but let me lay it all out, 'cause I rehearsed it soup to nuts in the mirror at home. And this is where I need my eight-hundred-pound gorilla."

"Me?"

"Of course."

He smiled and shimmied in his seat when his ass was kissed. "That eight hundred pounds is mostly muscle." He winked.

"I need access, through you, to a heavy-hitting board of education member, someone like that, who will do our bidding."

Malouf tapped all nine of his fingertips together in a kind of praying posture while Maya told herself not to stare at the deformed hand. Malouf liked his hands front and center. He knew it made people uncomfortable; he knew it gained him sympathy, revulsion, and engendered self-consciousness and a false sense of superiority in an adversary. And everyone was an adversary. "My adult kids went to Crossroads," he said, peering over the fingers, "my kids go to Crossroads today, my unborn kids by the wife I haven't met yet will go to Crossroads. I've donated hundreds of thousands. I'm on the board there. I know everyone in that world. What are you thinking?"

"I'm thinking we go in with the board of education, quietly, don't make a big deal, find someone that can handle social services, and we go out to the desert and say, Look, Mormon dude, I don't know if you're like the Angulos or the Turpins, but at a bare minimum, your homeschooling isn't up to par, in the twenty-first century you can't teach that the ancient Israelites settled the New World, you can't teach that dark skin is a sign of God's curse and white skin a blessing."

"No, I suppose you can't *teach* that," Malouf said strangely.

"Aside from the fact that you've got multiple wives, you gross, kinky motherfucker—"

"Hold on. You lost me there." He held a beat, then smiled, and added, "Just kidding. Go on. Entangle me further in your web."

Maya chuckled and continued, "We come with the child abuse angle, and we will be saviors in the media if it gets out and gets to that, but we also come like we are on his side, the Mormon side. We say the board of ed is bent out of shape here and they want to take your kids away from you, and we want to think of a compromise."

"We do?"

"Yeah. 'Cause we're the good guys."

"We are."

"And we want to buy that land. We don't want the government confiscating it."

"What's the compromise?"

"That's where we get creative. We could say—sell us half of your stake in this land and we will make this headache go away and we promise not to develop or sell mining rights in the next twenty years, a promise we will break as soon as we want. You could make in one move what it used to take you a couple hundred deals to make; you wouldn't be fucking with the little green houses on Baltic Avenue, you'd be building big red hotels on Broadway."

"That a Monopoly reference?"

"I guess it was, yeah."

"Wow."

Malouf looked out the window to the sea, then looked back at Maya. "Maybe. You think the Mormon will take it?"

"I don't know. I don't know him yet."

"He doesn't know you."

"He doesn't know me."

"Anybody else sniffing around?"

"Not a soul."

"No Vornado? No Sternlicht?" The two competitors Malouf always felt over his shoulder like twin grim reapers. "No Tom Barrack? Colony? No Steve Dwarfzman?" he asked, referring to the diminutive Steve Schwarzman of the behemoth Blackstone.

"I don't see how. There's barely any record of this guy or his land. He's like a lost tribe unto himself maybe as far back as the turn of the century. I stumbled onto it and then I had to dig."

"How are his real estate taxes?"

"No record of him paying them."

"But he's not like that Ammon Bundy guy, is he? The cattle rancher guy who decided one day that federal lands belong to the people? I think he was Mormon, too."

"No, Powers owns the land outright."

"Astonishing."

They sat nodding at each other and blinking. "You know," Malouf said, "I seem to recall rumors of Sternlicht trying to make a big play out there about ten years ago that didn't pan out. Maybe this was that. Maybe this guy won't sell."

"Maybe he won't," Maya guessed, "probably won't."

"And if it turns out his kids are happy and it's not like the, the . . . the white trash people."

"The Turpins."

"Turpins, yeah. If the kids are alright?"

"Probably won't have to sell either."

"So it could be a nothing burger." Malouf sighed. "And where does that leave yours truly?"

Maya went all in: "We take a gamble. You wouldn't be sitting where you're sitting if you didn't gamble. You're a gambler." She saw him inhale the smoke up his ass, as he shifted happily in his seat; he held it in and felt its warmth, and she could see it felt good to him.

"I am? I am." He smiled. "Broad numbers?"

"Upside is huge. Hundreds of millions. A billion. More. I almost don't want to put a cap on it."

"Then don't. Downside? Exposure?"

"Not bad at all. Couple million for land that has to be sold for pennies on the dollar and no one else knows to bid on. A steal."

"So we keep it very quiet. Go on. What's the play?"

Darrin popped his head in the door. "Hey, boss man, you got five minutes?"

Malouf turned on his number one, glaring with a mixture of boredom and contempt that froze the young man in the doorway. "Get the fuck out of here, Darrin, can't you see I'm doing actual business with the lovely Maya Abbadessa?"

"Sorry, Boss. Sorry, Maya." Darrin skulked away like a dog.

Malouf turned his dark eyes back to Maya. "You were saying before we were rudely interrupted by my former favorite courtier?"

Maya could barely suppress a smile, and Malouf noted her glee. He winked at her to continue, and she did. "We say something like—'Mr. Mormon, we don't want you to lose any of your land, but we are having trouble seeing our way out of this dilemma. We are here to help.'"

"How can we help?"

Maya nodded at the inside joke. Malouf was responding like a trained seal to her well-timed prompts. "Exactly. And I came up with a gambit."

"A gambit beyond the half deal worth hundreds of millions?"

"A gambit for billions that also aligns us with the educational policies of the great state of California."

"I miss the way Arnold used to say it, don't you—'Galeefvawnya.'"

Malouf was the kind of golfer who liked to talk while other people were putting, to see if they could concentrate on the kill. It wasn't mere gamesmanship, it was part of the game to him.

Maya held firm. "We say, let's make a wager."

"Who? You and the Mitt Romney?"

"Yes, I'm betting a guy like this Powers—off the grid, mountain macho man with a harem, has got a pretty nice-size ego—"

"Safe to say."

"Yeah, and pride goeth before a fall, so we say—'You think you're doing things so right here in your little world, but it's not clear to the government at all' . . ."

Malouf raised his hand. "I'm gonna stop you right there."

Maya felt whiplash; she had been ascending so fast, the glass ceiling hurt her neck. "What? Really?"

"Oh, look at that face. The pout. You're adorable when you're disappointed, sexy."

"I don't get it. You don't like it?" She sounded to herself like a six-year-old whose parent has disliked her finger painting, and immediately hated herself for it.

"I like that we are helping kids. I like that a lot. And I am a gambler, but I don't gamble so much on things as on people. And I'm gonna gamble on you. I love you, so I love the play, and I don't know it, which makes me love it more. Also, I'm thinking that a man with multiple wives does a fair amount of thinking with his dick, and your pretty face, not my mug, will encourage that bad habit to continue. At the very least, an old-fashioned dude like that underestimates women. Let him underestimate you. Capisce?" Oh, the bad Italian from the Palestinian man, the faux mobster talk, the *Godfather* references—seemed the only movies these Praetorian capitalists had ever seen besides porn were *Godfather* One and Two, *Glengarry Glen Ross*, *Pulp Fiction*, and *Happy Gilmore*. Odd because Malouf struck her as a man that would dig *Citizen Kane*.

Malouf continued, "Is this gambit legal? I feel I should ask."

"Probably mostly. I wouldn't call it illegal."

"Extralegal? Legal adjacent?"

"I think it's more like something the law hasn't seen yet, and as such, it will be up to us to bend the legal criteria to our own demands. When the time comes."

"As a rule, I feel my good friend Mr. Koch's dictum of ten thousand percent compliance to the law might be a little exaggerated, a little . . . fundamentalist."

"I'm aiming for somewhere around one hundred percent compliance."

"I have found the sweet spot to be around eighty percent. Nobody's perfect." He shrugged comically, like Jack Benny.

"I can work with that."

"And don't repeat that."

"Repeat what?" They laughed at how clever they were being.

Malouf nodded and put his finger over his surprisingly full and sensuous lips for her to be quiet. "Seems to me," he said, "that you're a chess player. But you like to move people around the board rather than wooden pieces. Right? But you can gin up the old empathy when you need to, right?"

Maya liked that description of herself; it flattered her. Though she also liked to think of herself as a lover and a nascent spiritual person. From somewhere deep in her mind she recalled the camp-fire story of the chimps and the bonobos, and that we humans were descended from both, so Maya felt both, the warrior-like chimp and the lovemaking bonobo; she was a chess player of human pieces with heart and sympathy for her vanquished and bloodied victims. The whole package. She snapped herself out of that self-aggrandizing revery. Malouf was floating compliments her way in order to distract her precisely like this. Obsequiousness from a man like Malouf caused her alarm to sound. She knew weaponized flattery was one of his sneakiest business go-tos.

"How much time do you need? And how much capital?" he asked.

"I might need a year," she replied, "maybe a little more, maybe less, and the capital is nothing. Maybe a hundred K or so, maybe . . . You can keep the whole thing in-house, no loans . . ."

He chuckled at the pittance she would need, a genuine laugh, like a little boy. "In-house is right, I have a hundred K in my couch cushions."

The *GQ* had remained open on Malouf's desk to an ad where a young man with cut, wet abs whose beauty seemed generically familiar, wearing only a bathing suit and a glistening watch, stared out at them, seemingly issuing some sort of absurd and empty challenge. She didn't know if he was selling a fragrance or a movie or a timepiece, or simply wanted a slap fight. Malouf snapped closed the magazine, like it had suddenly said something impudent, and swept it off to the side.

"I thought you were my Wharton gal, my numbers guy, my face man, my play-by-the-book gal. This is biting and fighting—street-fighter shit."

"I'm both. All of it."

"This makes me happy and sad."

Malouf swiveled his chair to face the window. Maya imagined he was looking all the way to the water, and beyond that to Hawaii, where he owned a beautiful property on Kauai that he often spoke of like a spiritual retreat but never visited, his tropical Lake Isle of Innisfree. And staring past that unused haven to God knows what.

"You know why I love the water?" he mused, as if they were old friends.

"Don't you surf?" she asked, bringing up one of the many rumors about Malouf that lingered about him like a halo. The worshipful Young Turks would sometimes compete in who could ascribe the most outlandish talents and feats to their mysterious boss, like those "most interesting man in the world" commercials. Malouf taught Kelly Slater how to surf. Malouf raised mink in Russia with Putin. Malouf was the actual inventor of the margarita. Malouf was the Zodiac Killer. Malouf was the sailor about whom the '70s hit "Brandy" was written. Malouf taught Chuck Norris how to fight.

"Oh no, I can't swim." He said, "I grew up poor. Poor people don't learn how to swim—that's extra. I have two yachts now, though, you'll come out with me sometime, on the *Santa Maria*—that's the nicer one—on the water, so I like to go on it, but not in it." He had invited her on the yacht. That was like the bar mitzvah for Praetorian Young Turks. It marked that she had come of age, was worthy. She swelled with feeling.

"But," he continued, "you know why I love to work where I can always *see* the water?"

She was growing a little antsy about this sudden detour, and hoping Malouf was momentarily waxing philosophical before flashing his capitalist claws again, simply creating a backstory or moral narrative to make the kill palatable. He continued in what was for him a deep and poetic vein, "I love it 'cause it's always changing, yet always the same—you know what I mean? See for yourself."

Maya got up and went to stand behind Malouf. She looked past his shaved shiny head out to the Eternal Mother—and there she was, the end of America, waiting, rolling in and rolling back, changing every moment, always the same.

"Like people," he said. "You gotta look past the movement, the smoke and mirrors, the waves—to see their unchanging essence." He seemed to have mesmerized himself. "The ocean always tells me the same thing."

"What's that?"

"You're a dead man, Malouf. I got your fucking finger, and I'll have the rest soon enough. Soon you'll be gone and I'll keep rolling along." Each statement was emphasized by a graceful hand gesture like a wave gently breaking. "Nothing matters. What are you staring at, you bald, nine-fingered piece of shit? Fuck you."

She tried to lighten him up. "Wow, the ocean's kind of a dick."

"Yeah, but it makes me happy, puts me in the right decision-making frame of mind."

She was a little confused about his weird mood change and what this oblique gabfest demanded of her. Was she supposed to massage his shoulders now? Tell him she'd heard Sternlicht wore a hairpiece and had ED? Or that Schwarzman wears lifts? Tell him that he's immortal too, especially if he does this deal? That his wasteful lifestyle, polluting businesses, and heedless energy consumption may very well kill this nemesis, the ocean, in which he cannot swim, in his lifetime? Would that be a happy thought for such a man so afraid of death? That his name and his monuments will outlast the rapidly warming, fished-out, soul-sick sea?

Theoretically, Maya cared more about the health of the planet and its animals: she drank her margarita rocks through a metal straw. But she also didn't understand why she had to curtail her use of God's green earth just because the generations before had been so profligate. She would look for ways to be more conscious, greener, eventually, but first she had to score. Like a boyfriend or a husband or children, the Green New Deal could wait until she was sitting pretty on her nest egg. She realized her own sliding hypocrisy on the matter, and that made her feel bad, but not bad enough to spur action or change. Once she had power and some security and eyes on her, then she would lean in, make a turn to the good, to charity and conservation. Like Bill Gates. Like a reverse Koch bro. More like the self-made version of Bezos's ex.

Malouf turned away from the Pacific to face Maya once again. "I know the perfect board of ed guy; he's been wanting to get on the Praetorian board forever, too. If I dangle that, he will do what I tell him. I'll get you guys together. Maybe you can figure it out, Killer." The water had whispered to him. He was in.

"You're amazing. Perfect," she said.

"I am? I am."

Maya bent down and spontaneously kissed the top of his small oblong head, like you might a beloved dog or a small child. Immediately, she felt wrong and awkward. She was in his space now, too close. Malouf took another long pause—he seemed almost on the verge of tears—then he continued, "After I get you guys together, though, I'm gonna stand back and trust you, Killer. I won't know the details of what you're doing, and I don't wanna know. You'll be on the hook, morally, the face, the face of this company, till we make a deal. If asked, you'll deny that I'm involved in any details, you were a rogue agent, I knew nothing. Only speak to me of this deal in person and in private. Do not text or email me about it. And absolutely no fucking paper. Don't even call me to talk about it, only face-to-face, *mano a womano*. If it works out, I'll take care of you, believe you me."

"Believe you me" was another of Malouf's verbal tics. It was a bit of an archaic phrase, but Maya liked it; it felt almost like a homey mantra to her; it made sense beyond its grammatical brevity, like a circular haiku. You believe me, I believe you, believe you me—both a promise and a threat. She knew that any man who habitually used such a phrase about his own trustworthiness was not a man to be trusted, yet it comforted her to be asked about her belief, her trust. Even though she really didn't have much of a choice, her belief had already been sold to this strange, bottomlessly needy man when she joined Praetorian and accepted his money.

"Yes, sir, I do," she said.

"If it goes south, you'll take the brunt. I'll be a fucking vapor. You can trust that, too. Believe you me."

"Of course."

They stayed quite still, both nodding, but breathing quickly and deeply now, like they'd run a relay race together and pushed through the tape ahead of the pack. He extended his large, leathery, manicured hand. She took it and shook it. It was surprisingly tough and callused, probably from wielding a polo mallet.

"Show me." He tilted his chin at her.

"Show you what?"

"You know, Killer. Show me."

He was teasing, raising his Muppet eyebrows. She clocked that he was now calling her "Killer," which was a damn sight better than HH. She also noted that it made her nipples hard. She hoped her bra was thick enough to hide those stigmata. Wait, show him what? Her tits?

"The tat," he said.

Oh. She rolled up her sleeve to reveal the newborn snake. The needle scabs had recently shed for good, the skin molted and healed. The snake was smooth and permanent. She was fearless.

8.

THIS WAS THE THIRD early morning in a row that a Scott's oriole had perched outside Mother Mary's bedroom window, singing. It was rare to see these tiny yellow-and-black beauties anywhere but in the arms of a Joshua tree, so Mary had been delighted the first dawn when the distinctive, gentle song stirred her and she had opened her own eyes to find the jet-black eyes upon her, the shy little shadow of a head swiveling and questioning on her window-sill, just inches away. But three days in a row? And uncharacteristically, unnaturally even, before any true morning light. She wasn't one for omens. She left the interpretation of signs and wonders to Bro' and his peep stones, but this seemed like God was slapping her upside the head. What could it mean?

She looked over at Yaya sleeping beside her. Who was this old woman? This woman she had come to love deeply and completely—the source of such physical pleasure and companionship—was old. She remembered the Talking Heads song—"this is not my beauti-ful wife." Sometimes her mind was like an oldies radio station (for the music that she grew up loving would surely be oldies by now). It had been years since she'd actually, physically heard any of the songs on her daily mental playlist, only Beatles Beatles Beatles, and yet still her mind played deep tracks in familiar rotation, the groove of her memory imagined like the spiral groove of a vinyl record.

One little bird. She recalled Bob Marley sang of three. She

missed reggae. She missed Tom Petty and the Heartbreakers, wondered if he was still alive. She'd seen him in concert, so frail, color-
less thin blond hair framing the big teeth, sneering but gentle; he
was ugly and pretty up there, fully in command, barking, "You
don't have to live like a refugee." Maybe Bro' was right, maybe
songs were Trojan horses, shiny shells overpacked with marauding
significance. Was she living like a refugee? She had learned over the
years to be vigilant about smuggling evils unaware into their spiritual
paradise, but contaminants crouched in her memory, waiting.

"The waiting is the hardest part." Oh, shut up, Tom. The oriole
flew away, her job done, her indecipherable message delivered.
Mary got out of bed quietly so as not to disturb her sister-wife.

'Twas fuckin' chilly. She'd never gotten used to how cold and
sharp the mornings were in the desert. She'd never admit it, but it
hurt her bones more and more. She felt her face as she brushed her
teeth; the lines by her eyes and in the grooves around her mouth
felt deeper today than yesterday even. She knew this could not be
so, change did not happen so quickly, and that such a thought must
be an indication of some sick state of mind or weakness. There
were no mirrors here or anywhere in the home. Sure, there were
windows from which she could coax a reflection, but that was a
swimmy, unclear, forgiving image for the most part, or easily dismissed as a funhouse mirror obviously warped. Even so, Mary
could tell she had gotten old too, like Yaya. The drying out and
destruction of her youth by the relentless Mojave sun and time
were almost welcome to Mother Mary. Almost. She drove a finger-
nail questioningly into the lines around her eyes, trying to put a
human measurement on time, to plumb the depths of change.

So Mary knew that without mirrors, or boys her own age for
that matter, her child Pearl had no idea how beautiful she had
become. There were times when Bro' was out in the desert com-
muning with his uncommunicative God, and Mary would brush
Pearl's hair by the big window in the kitchen, angling the girl so she

might see herself, tempting her to behold the power of the post-adolescent beauty announcing itself, sculpted as if by a great artist out of stone as the baby fat left her face. Mary waited to punish the girl for her vanity, but Pearl would only stare blankly, mind elsewhere, unreadable, and then her reflected eyes would shift to meet Mary's in the clear glass, the big empty desert still visible in the frame beyond. Asking. Asking what? Am I beautiful? Why am I beautiful? Where did your beauty go? What does beauty mean? What is all this beauty for?

The magnitude of Pearl's beauty felt dangerous to Mary, like a temptation of God himself. Mary was both proud and terrified of it. She wanted Bronson to bring back sunscreen from one of his trips into the city, to protect against damage, but she refrained from asking for fear he would interpret it as this pride for herself, or for the children. She was so grateful to Bro' for this life, for his vision; she wanted him to know this, and her devotion to him, to Mormonism, was her daily, living evidence. Now she was a Christian again as she had been as a child; that's what she was, what she had become to save herself and her child, Beautiful. And unlike Yalulah, she had never once ventured beyond their property in the intervening years. She knew herself better than to do that. She had never had any boundaries, as a child or adult, such concepts were all or nothing to her; if she left, if she colored outside the lines she had been given, there was nothing but chaos on the other side, and drugs. And if she sometimes looked at a cactus and thought, How the fuck can I make tequila out of that? she could be forgiven. She was forgiven.

But it was a health issue too, the sun, wasn't it? Skin cancer. If it be Thy will, she supposed. A hard pill for a parent to swallow. As often as she could, though, she made Pearl and Beautiful and the other kids wear wide-brimmed hats. All the kids, but especially Pearl. Pearl didn't like to wear one. Pearl didn't like to be hidden, in shadow.

Mary slipped into her ancient, tan, fleece-lined Ugg boots, her one extravagance. She demanded that Bronson bring her new ones from civilization whenever a pair shredded after several years of active mornings. Silently, she padded through to the part of the house she called the 'kids' wing.' There they all were sleeping, the whole brood, except for Hyrum, of course. That wild child might've slept outside for all she knew, looking in the rain-shadow desert for rattlesnake eggs that he would fry for a breakfast none of the other kids would eat. Lovey, Beautiful, Little Joe, Little Big Al, Effy, Palmyra, Solomona. All ten accounted for and breathing the new day, except for Hyrum. And Pearl. Deuce, yes, but no Pearl. Maybe Pearl was a-milking. She was "an American girl." Okay, okay, Tom, I hear you, now fuck off.

Mary glided as silently as a ghost on her soft Uggs, thinking of Pearl and the uncanny collages she used to make from the colorful paper coverings of the canned goods Bronson would bring back from his trips to town. Those familiar, even nostalgic, labels were mere background noise to Mary but magical to the girl, her only contact with the world, and you could see her puzzling through the images that had no referents for her—gluing them, recombining them, painting over them, looking for clues and expressing her desires like in those hostage notes made from magazine snippets in the movies. The impressive kid had kind of reproduced a Warhol Pop Art sensibility without ever having seen a Warhol. Mary didn't know what the girl was trying to say about the world, but she knew she was *interested in it*. Maybe that's what she was saying.

Mary found herself approaching the back bedroom where Bronson spent his nights alone more and more the past few years, and, as quietly as she could, opened the creaky door. She was surprised to see Pearl first, on her side facing the door, sleeping. That was curious, and as her eyes adjusted to the dark and took in the rest of the room, she had the sense of a dread prophecy being fulfilled. The meaning of the oriole's song. For beside Pearl in bed, incongruously, was an old man. That was her first thought. There's something wrong with this picture. The old man she knew was Bronson Powers.

Pearl opened her eyes and looked at Mary, sleepy, guiltless, and free. The girl's face was radiant, flush, the skin on her chin chafed a bit and red, not from sun, but from kissing maybe. Pearl held her mother with clear, challenging eyes, unblinking, seeming to communicate—*There is nothing wrong with this. What did you expect? What else is there for me? He saved us both. There is no other. I am a woman now, a beautiful woman. This is not my father. This is as natural as the sun rising right now, and the animals eating each other and fucking each other. As natural and real as blood, as the blood that flows from me monthly. I love and I am loved. This is no lie. This is the covenant. This is the truth. This. This. This!*

This is what all this beauty is for.

Mother Mary lowered her gaze, took a step back, and closed the door. It was a while before she could move. She felt hypnotized, and gone away to some place deep and still in her mind. When she came back to herself, she was in the kitchen in the middle of making breakfast. For the first time in years her hands were shaking uncontrollably. She cut her finger slicing the bread. She watched it bleed.

9.

THE BIG MAN HIMSELF, in his prized whip, a Bianco Icarus Metallic Lamborghini Aventador, drove Maya to Santa Monica Airport. This was the most expensive car Maya had ever been in, dwarfing the sticker price of the Maserati she stole that night in the desert. A mere five-minute drive from the Praetorian offices, they were ushered through a private gate. Malouf drove the half-million-dollar car straight up to a multimillion-dollar jet on the tarmac, door to door, or rather, car door to jet door.

Outside the plane, waiting with the two pilots and the one air attendant, was Randy Milman, an old friend of Malouf's and very minor real estate player who happened, strategically, to hold an elected seat on the board of education. A week or so ago, Milman had paid a visit to the Powers property out by Joshua Tree to eyeball the compound. He had gone with a local from San Bernardino social services to see how the kids were being treated, and how they were being educated.

Malouf didn't want to have a download meeting with Milman in his office, so they were getting on the jet only to talk, and to fly down to Luxivair SBD, the private facility at San Bernardino Airport where they'd pick up Janet Bergram, the social service worker, and get the skinny from her as well.

Malouf liked doing what he considered risky business off-site. In the Praetorian offices proper, he was not solely a private citizen, he was CEO, and there were rules that applied in a business office that could bite him in the ass. A mile high—different story. He also knew what a strong persuader a private jet was to a regular Joe, a big shiny thumb on the scale, and he was a firm believer in his own person-to-person charm. Most people would not want the ride to end, and they might say and do things to keep the ride going. This is what Malouf explained to Maya on the way to the hangar as the reason for this flight to San Bernardino and nowhere. "People are simpler than you think, they're like birds," he said.

"They like being up in the air?"

"No, Killer," he replied, "they like shiny things." He also knew that accepting a ride on a private jet could lead to a compromising position for most anyone, and the logbook for the Praetorian plane would record these four passengers to be recalled, or buried, perhaps when needed.

"Look at Clinton and the Dersh on the Epstein logbook," Malouf said. "No bueno."

If Malouf was slightly peeved that Milman had brought his seven-year-old son along for the ride, he didn't show it. Maya was aware of this type of behavior, where rich but not super-rich folk like Milman envied the big-boy toys of men with whom they sometimes fraternized. The Milmans would think the Maloufs didn't deserve such luxury; Milman's envy was in equal proportion to his hatred of Malouf, and he would act accordingly by partaking without gratitude. It was as if Milman knew, though he didn't know exactly what the service he was providing was going to net Malouf, that it was most likely more than Milman would ever see in a lifetime, that he was being bought cheaply. So Milman was going to be sure to take as much free stuff as he could to even the scales a little.

It reminded Maya of an old game show she saw stoned on TV Land one lonely night called *The Diamond Head*, where a contestant gets put in a glass booth, a modified wind tunnel called the Money Volcano or Cash-n-ator, that blows bills of all denominations (with one unicorn $10,000 bill) on jet engine gusts of air for a few seconds. The contestant has to grab, desperately and spastically, at the money as it flutters wildly about, an act way more difficult, and of course, tantalizing, than it seems—the money, the fortune in the air, floating like an apparition before your eyes. Like most American game shows, the funny at the heart of this was to reveal how people would humiliate themselves for money. In fact, Maya pondered, perhaps there is nothing more American than this, and she had googled the Cash-n-ator to find that it was actually, unsurprisingly, an arcade game, a staple of the carny, quite popular at bar mitzvahs. Your time in the Cash-n-ator was the American promise.

The captain gave the boy some cheap metal wings for his lapel. The boy snatched at them, bought and sold. Malouf patted him on the head. They all turned and walked the small plank up and into Malouf's Cash-n-ator for the short flight to San Bernardino.

"Remember Typhoon? The restaurant that used to be here at the Santa Monica Airport?" Malouf asked as they settled in.

"Yeah," Milman said. "Didn't they get busted and shut down for serving dolphin steaks or something?"

"Not dolphin, only a true reprobate would eat Flipper—it was whale meat, and yes, that's right."

"Put the chef in jail?"

"The chef has paid his debt to mammals and completed his probation and community service, and he is a good friend of mine, and he has prepared the food for our little jaunt today, so, if I may, I'd like to offer you some of my favorites off the menu of the dearly departed Typhoon—scorpion toast." Malouf made a maître d' type flourish to the flight attendant.

"Ah, thank you, Belinda," he cooed, as the attendant placed a covered dish amid the four of them and lifted the top to reveal what looked exactly like shrimp toast only with the unmistakable form of a scorpion grilled perfectly into the bread like a fossil in stone.

"Ew," the boy said.

"Don't be a pussy, Jackson, eat the scorpion," Milman said to his son as he took a bite of deep-fried arachnid.

Malouf smiled like a dark lord, much as Hades must have when he saw Persephone eat those pomegranate seeds. Malouf winked at Maya to make sure she was learning the lessons, learning the small, flashy price for which most men would sell their souls. She watched as Belinda slid more dishes on the table.

"Is that the whale meat?" asked Milman, pointing at a piece of sushi.

"Heavens, no." Malouf winked. "I'll never tell. You two have things to talk about. I will take Jackson up to the cockpit, if that's okay." Maya noted how the very rich like Malouf loved to play at being deferential, using "sir," asking permission obsequiously, seeming to assert their own power by this florid show of subservience. "This way, sir," he said, and off he went with the boy.

"So," Maya asked Milman, delicately nibbling at a scorpion of her own, "how did it go with Powers?"

"To be honest with you"—Milman's mouth was so full that it was hard to make out his words above the engines—"those kids are getting an amazing education. I'd have no qualms sending his ten-year-old to a community college tomorrow, and his seven-year-old makes Jackson look like a fucking retard. I thought about leaving Jackson there for those Mormons to educate. Not only the books, but those kids were disciplined and polite, worked hard around the house, could hunt and shoot and cook—"

Milman expelled what might've been a piece of scorpion from the back of his throat onto Maya's cheek. She didn't flinch. Rather, she nodded and smiled and wiped it away nonchalantly. But this was not good news, and Milman knew that.

"Do you mind if I?" He reached for Maya's piece of scorpion toast.

"Be my guest," she said.

He continued stuffing his face with scorpion. This guy was a real asshole. He certainly hadn't run for his position on the board of ed because of his great concern for the well-being of young minds and the $15K a year, but rather for moments precisely like this, where the uber-wealthy might need to court him when they were concerned about their uber-progeny. He continued, "Having said that, they also teach the kids a lot of crazy shit, *fakakta* Mormon shit that goes against public pedagogic policy, at least for now. Who knows what comes next if Trump gets impeached and that old prune Pence or some religious nutjob like that gets in. Separation of church and state, my ass. Depends on the fucking church. Though California is pretty independent of that shit, huh? It's like we're our own country within the borders of America. Fifth-largest economy in the world, bitches. We should secede." Maya pursed her lips and nodded, trying to make Milman feel that she was impressed by his political awareness and trite, pithy aperçus.

"I can wash my hands of it," Milman said, his conscience clear or nonexistent, "doesn't concern me what they do out there in that godforsaken shithole. If a Joshua tree falls in the desert and no one hears, did it fall? Who the fuck cares? Not the board of ed. I can't speak for social services, however. Janey or whatever her name is. She's a fucking cunt, a real do-gooder. But she's a peon. Good luck with her. I think she already hates me. Do you think this is really orca meat, Free Willy? You can tell it's mammalian, has that umami to it. Fuckin' Malouf. You like working for him?" He took a big swig from a $400 bottle of sake, like it was 7UP, swished it around his mouth to dislodge any stray bits of spiny scorpion limb from his gums, and burped. "I hear a woman trying to get a job at Praetorian is like auditioning to become a Raelette, you know, a backup singer for Ray Charles, back in the day. You know?" He wanted her to be interested in his old-man stories, his exotic chronicles of a former world. He wiggled his eyebrows up and down. Maya had the urge to punch him in the forehead to make him stop. She wondered if he might like that.

He knew she had to pay attention to him, if only for five minutes or so, and he was going to milk every one of those. He continued,

"Ray Charles was a blind Black guy—singer. Like Stevie Wonder before Stevie Wonder. The Raelettes danced and sang behind him at the piano. Like a Supreme. You with me so far?"

"I get the picture."

"So you know how you became a Raelette?"

"I suppose you had to be able to sing," she offered, blinking slowly to hint at her growing impatience.

"Sure, that helps. But to really become a Raelette, you had to let Ray." She forced a smile and nodded as he laughed at his own joke.

"The good old days, huh?" she said.

"Exactly." He downed a big piece of sushi in one bite and chased it with more sake. "This shit is like butter, meat butter, wonder which whale it is, so good. I'm salivating like a Saint Bernard. We are all going to hell, might as well enjoy it."

Maya smiled to herself because Malouf was subtly acclimatizing Milman, through a series of micro transgressions, to being a partner in crime. He'd gotten this milquetoast douche to break the dietary law on the way to baby-stepping him to more serious offenses with the unspoken promise that if he just continued to play small ball, this jet-setting, whale-eating lifestyle might be more available to him and his offspring.

"Janet, not Janey. Janet Bergram." Maya stared at the whale sashimi as Milman dipped it in the low-sodium soy sauce. "Here's a hot tip—people like it when you get their names right."

Milman, realizing his five minutes were up, smirked. "Whatever."

"And don't fucking say 'cunt' in front of me, asshole," Maya scolded.

That stopped him cold, open-mouthed and mid-chew. Maya could see the whale meat in his gullet. He swallowed and said, "My bad. Don't get your knickers in a twist, snowflake. Don't diss the messenger. Just saying she was a real Debbie downer."

Maya felt her ears pop with the change of altitude. In no time at all, they were descending into Luxivair at San Bernardino Airport, touching down for Janet Bergram, a short, stout, middle-aged African

American woman in sensible shoes, and climbing back up into the sky. Malouf took one look at Janet Bergram and knew that she was immune to his light show, his Cash-n-ator, and his T-shirt cannons. "I trust the car service was okay?" Malouf smiled, putting a hand on her back, a hand that Janet turned her neck to actually look at as if a city pigeon had suddenly perched on her shoulder.

"I took a cab," she replied. Uh-oh, a cab? Who the fuck takes a cab? She really didn't speak the language. She would not be impressed by scorpions or whales on her tray table. Malouf looked momentarily at sea. Maya hoped that he wouldn't pull his "I'm a minority, too, I'm an Arab" shtick that she'd seen him do in such situations. She looked at him as if to say "I got this."

Even though he had to bend his neck in the low cabin ceiling of the jet, Malouf still loomed over Janet, getting close to her and using his height to force her to look straight up at him. "Make sure to give Maya a receipt for the cab and we will reimburse you."

"That's not necessary."

Malouf looked around for an exit like an actor who had forgotten how to get offstage, and then excused himself, disappearing back into the cockpit with Milman and Jackson.

Maya felt the importance of letting Janet know she was not like Malouf. "Those shoes are so smart," she said. "I wear these heels like an idiot all day." The other woman nodded. She clearly had no interest in shoes, sensible or otherwise. Pushing aside the exotic, possibly illegal food, Maya dove right in.

"What did you think of the Powers situation?"

"Where are we going?" Janet asked.

"I don't think we're going anywhere. Where do you want to go?"

Janet looked queasily out the window. "I don't really like flying, upsets my stomach. What is that?" She pointed at Milman's remains of scorpion and whale.

"Scorpion toast," Maya said, as if the outlandishly exotic can become the mundane in the course of a twenty-minute flight. Janet burped and repressed the urge to vomit. Maya jumped up and removed the leftovers.

"I get it. Let's be quick?" Maya sat back down and leaned in. "First of all, I want to let you know that Robert Malouf and Praetorian Capital is donating one hundred thousand dollars to the San Bernardino school system."

Janet nodded. The sum was not insignificant; it would make a small difference. If the rest of the day amounted to nothing, she could live with that. She thanked Maya, then said, "But I'm not going to be bought for a hundred thousand."

"I wasn't suggesting . . ."

"My sole job is to assess the welfare of the kids, right. The Powerses are a fascinating case. I don't know anything, I don't care anything about real estate, so please keep that damn fool, Milman, away from me."

"Exactly. I know. Done. He's gonna get tossed from the plane when we're over water."

Janet Bergram did not smile. "The kids are clean and well fed," she said, "they seem to have plenty of attention. You're not looking at a Turpin-type case. They are very different from their peers because they don't share the same culture or cultural references, they don't have phones or computers, though I don't think that is necessarily a hardship."

"Nor do I," Maya said, paying lip service to hating phones, as all adults do, right before buying the next model.

"Here's the law." Janet dug in. "The state of California is not a fan of homeschooling. The state's education code does not even explicitly mention homeschooling. There are relevant statutes, however. One—they'd need to establish a private school in their home. They have not done that. Two—they'd have to employ a private tutor or hold California teaching credentials themselves. Though they all seem capable of getting credentialed, they have not. Three—they would have to enroll their kids in a public school that offers independent study. Obviously, that hasn't happened either. They're supposed to keep a portfolio of the kids' work. I asked for that. They didn't have a portfolio per se, but they showed me some beautiful work. I was very impressed by their levels across the board. Those kids are being educated rigorously, if somewhat idio-syncratically. Again, you mentioned the Turpin family and the Angulos . . . this is nothing like that. The kids are outside all the time, very healthy. I saw no evidence of what I would deem child abuse, though you have this polygamous situation with the multiple wives, which is certainly . . . unorthodox."

"And illegal," Maya added. But she had anticipated this soft left-of-center censure. She knew that the Powers kids were being edu-cated well. She knew that the mission statement for San Bernardino Child and Family Services was "to protect endangered children, preserve and strengthen families, and develop alternative family settings." With that absence of imminent danger in mind, Maya knew Janet Bergram most likely wouldn't suggest removing them from their home, and that if the Powerses decided to call Praeto-rian's bluff, they might very well walk away with the whole pot. But this was the most direct, prosaic approach, and Maya figured it wouldn't be that easy. So she tacked back.

"Do you know the Mormon bible actually teaches the inferior-ity of dark-skinned races?" Maya asked, knitting her sugar-threaded brow in disapproval.

"Yes, I do," Janet said. "But beyond their amazement at seeing another human being for the first time in years, the looks I got from those kids were not the kinds of looks I get from a lot of white kids in the San Bernardino school system."

"What do you mean? They looked at me like I was from Mars."

"They looked at me like I was from another planet, too. Healthy curiosity. But none of those Mormon kids looked at me like I was a nigger." The word landed like a slap. Maya wasn't sure what to say.

"I'm sorry, I don't know what that looks like," Maya said. An awkward silence followed that Janet was content to extend. Maya added, "They shot an arrow at me."

"What?"

Maya showed Janet the scar on her upper arm. Janet pursed her lips. "Well, I guess you win, but unless you wanna file charges and try to get a felony case going, I don't see how that justifies taking the kids away from their parents. And I can't say, won't say for certain, that those kids would be better off, by any quantifiable metric, removed from their present caregivers. I think it's a waste of time. For me. I have cases in San Bernardino that are much, much worse and more pressing. Do you have any idea how many cases I am working at the moment?"

"Well, I do know that the standard recommended caseload for your position is, what, thirty to forty-five?"

"Yes, exactly. I have sixty-seven. The Powerses would be ten more."

"Right, ten kids."

"I'd like to close the Powers case because of the sixty-seven other families. More than a hundred and fifty children whose lives and futures depend on me doing my job every day and not flying around in a private jet. I have one young boy of six whose job it was to feed his dad's prize-fighting pit bull. The dog lost some weight 'cause the kid would forget to feed him sometimes. The dog lost a fight and had to be put down. The father decided to teach the kid a lesson by having him trade places with the dog. The kid was forced to sleep outside in a small shed with a collar on and eat dog food for a month." Maya shook her head, dumfounded by the cruel stupidity.

"Now multiply that by a hundred and fifty," Janet added.

Maya was on her heels. "I appreciate your concern for your community. And I share it."

"You do? Have you ever set foot in San Bernardino? I mean, I know you've flown over it . . ." Janet smirked.

"Yes, I have." Maya did her best to ignore the sarcasm. "And be assured that we would love to help, that our use of the land nearby will create thousands of temporary jobs and hundreds of permanent ones, and bring billions into the community."

"Like Walmart. Yeah, I heard the pitch."

"Yes, like Walmart, but even better. But we have to get there first, move into the neighborhood, which brings us back to the Powers kids—are they being prepared to be adults, to enter into the world and the workplace? I mean, aside from being taught those fucked-up anti-science and racist beliefs, which might be seen as abusive."

"Yes, in the age of Trump, unfortunately, neither those anti-scientific idiocies or the pseudo-scientific racial ideas are so far out of the mainstream that we don't see public schools pressured in certain parts of the country to, say, teach creationism along with evolution, and certainly some private schools, walking, or rather tiptoeing or dog whistling, up to that same line. Children being used as pawns and test cases in adult culture wars."

"That's a shame," Maya said, and she meant it. Janet was nodding skeptically, alert to the cant of this line of anti-racist argument parroted back to her from this young white woman.

"Would they be better off in a public school in San Bernardino? Maybe. Maybe not," Janet wondered. "I'm inclined to look the other way and let the situation remain as is."

Maya asked, "And who decides, ultimately, you or the law?"

Janet fixed Maya in her glare. "Let me tell you something, ma'am . . ."

"Maya, please. Maya Abbadessa. Italian father, Mexican mother." Oh yeah, she was able to work the Mexican mom thing seamlessly into this conversation with an African American woman. Beneath the stark difference in wardrobe, this was a minority-to-minority deal here. That was the angle. "But call me Maya."

Janet stared at the white woman across from her. "Maya. Nobody gives a shit about these kids in the desert. You don't give a shit either. Not even my heart bleeds for them—they're sitting on a land inheritance. They'll be fine. I care about the disadvantaged children of regular, hardworking San Bernardines. The kids of color whose parents aren't sitting on a gold mine, who work two jobs, or work for an unlivable wage. The kids at the border."

Suddenly, Maya got sleepy, as she often did when a lecture began. She caught Belinda's eye and mouthed, "Espresso, please, double."

"Kids at the border. I hear you," Maya said, and smiled her "sad, empathetic" smile. Janet all but rolled her eyes in response. But this outrage with "the system" was exactly what Maya was hoping for, and she could use her judo—this was the opening, small but visible, for the gambit with which she had teased Malouf—this good woman's Achilles, where her anger and integrity met. Janet Bergram might not be personally for sale, but she could still be manipulated by her own self-righteousness and ambition for the kids if she could be led to seeing herself as a possible savior.

"You're right, Janet, and maybe I don't care as much as you do about the kids. That's fair, that's your job. But I have a job too, and my job is to make money, and when I make money, other people make money. It trickles down."

"Doesn't trickle like it used to. If it ever did."

"I see you're between a rock and a hard place. I mean, I'm just spitballing here," she lied, her plan well incubated and ready to hatch, "but what if you do turn away from these kids and give me a little time and let me set up a kind of metric that would enable you to quantify, in a scientific way, whether those Powers kids are being damaged or not."

"I don't think that's possible."

"No, it's not possible, but it may be feasible."

"What do you mean?"

"I mean . . . what do you say you don't report these kids, give no recommendation yay or nay, or you simply close the case, officially anyway, and while your back is turned, and your attention is where it should be—on the kids of San Bernardino, like the pit bull kid,

who really need it—we do a test, we take three of the kids—he's
got ten . . . we take three of the kids and we put them in public
school in San Bernardino for a year, and at the end of the year,
we compare their growth, the growth in their levels of academic
achievement and their emotional well-being, with the kids that
stayed at home, and if the kids at home did better or comparably, I
lose—the Powerses keep it all, but you win, 'cause then you get to
pressure the embarrassed school system to be better. Armed with
the results, you shame those whose lack of attention and funding
have hamstrung the local schools, and we demand more money
for the kids of San Bernardino that you care so much about."

"That's crazy," Janet said.

"Is it?"

Maya let Janet take a few moments to imagine that playing
out, as complicated and unlikely as it might seem, before laying
out her true vision. "If the kids do better in San Bernardino, which
is the way more likely scenario," Maya continued, "Praetorian
wins and establishes a presence there, and we funnel millions into
the neighborhood, all boats rising on a rising tide, children in those
boats. Either way, you bring eyes to a broken system, and money
follows eyes."

Janet couldn't hide her curiosity in this strange wager, at least at
the possibility of its economic boon. She momentarily lost her habitual bored and borderline contemptuous look, her pride and
her self-righteousness joining hands. If the kids did better in San
Bernardino, Janet could see herself as a hero to her community
who would bring in millions of dollars of business, some of that
inevitably showered on public works and public education, the kids.

But could she do it all under the radar? She knew she could
close her slim file on the Powerses and they would drift down and
disappear into the overloaded system. Through the haze of bullshit,
she started to view the Cash-n-ator as a possible source of good.

For her part, Maya had entered the part of the soul seduction where she would wait to let Janet fill the silent spaces and betray her own growing interest to herself; to let the woman now rev herself up. Janet started speaking louder, a dead giveaway. "The local schools need so much, so much. And the criteria by which you judge the growth over the year will be by necessity somewhat subjective, no?"

"Yes," Maya agreed, "but we would do what we could to make it as objective as possible. Maybe have them all take a standardized test before and after the year?"

"Sure. That's a start."

Maya had the hook in, she needed to jerk the line now and sink it into the soft flesh of Janet's mouth. But Maya paused again. She wanted Janet's to be the next voice. She wanted Janet to continue moving this idea forward, to run with it, she needed complicity, agency. They stared at each other for about thirty seconds.

Janet caved again, and asked out loud, "So the three kids—they continue on in the San Bernardino school system and then onto college hopefully, but what happens to the kids that stayed home?"

"When we win, they gotta move off too, the whole family, and back to civilization. For the good of the kids and to abide by the law of the land. 'Cause that's what our little social experiment has taught us. Your gut and the law are satisfied either way. That's the moral of the story."

Janet Bergram, a civil servant with a master's degree in social work as well as a J.D., who would be paying off her student debt until she died on the $68K a year she made before taxes, looked out the window of a private plane, the world at her feet. She stared past the clouds and allowed herself to dream of doing so much good for the kids of her hometown, and for the kids of this strange Mormon enclave that she didn't know existed until a couple weeks ago. She didn't like this "Maya," the somewhat Mexican across from her, but she didn't dislike her; sure, she was ambitious and greedy, but she was also imaginative.

Janet was pretty sure she was smarter than Maya, she could take her. Only a fool would pay as much as she did for her shoes. She knew what Manolo Blahniks were from *Sex and the City*. Janet had served her community for a long time, and had longed to do something big for them all, to enable them to make a leap. These were just three kids that didn't even have a record or social security number. She knew very well they could be hidden easily in a school for a year and no one would have to know—not the local government, not her boss, not the board of ed. The end could easily justify the means.

"You know, Janet—may I be frank?" Maya was smiling at her, almost goading her, letting the fish run with the line; she knew that some bureaucrats, in their heart of hearts, imagined a rebel hero when they looked in the mirror. "You talk about how you have no power, you talk about the inaction of government, you talk about the lack of imagination and the sluggish bureaucracy, what you would do if you had the power—and here you are being offered an end run around the bureaucracy, here you are being offered a chance to be a maverick, an innovator, a visionary advocate for the tens of thousands of kids in your district. I can't believe you will hide behind some of those same bureaucratic barriers and pass up this chance of a lifetime."

"These three kids don't have social security numbers. They barely exist." Janet was speaking almost to herself, convincing herself of what Maya had convinced her. All that remained was to pull the fish up into the boat. But Maya was so good at this sport that she wanted to see this fish jump onto the boat of her own free will, walk over to the grill, and squirt lemon on herself.

"That's right," Maya said. "Our test will be over in about nine months and no one will have noticed. Three kids no one ever heard of came into town and spent a year at a local public school and then moved to another town and another school. Happens all the time."

Janet sighed. It did happen all the time.

"If I drop the case, or close it, and walk away in any official capacity . . . You'd have to get the parents' permission, of course, to enter into this agreement—an agreement the legality of which, or any binding nature, is going to be highly debatable. They would have to willingly enter into it, willingly let three kids move to San Bernardino and go to school there. And I don't see that happening."

"Leave that to me."

"If you threaten or coerce them in any way using my name or the authority of my agency or the government of California . . ."

"As I said, leave that to me. I won't mention your name. All I need is for you to officially close the case and walk away at this point. See to the other kids. They need you. That was your instinct. I'm not asking for your help or involvement; I'm just asking that you don't get in our way or call attention to the family or us. It fits into your mission."

"How so?" Janet asked.

Maya spoke from memory: "The mission of Child and Family Services is accomplished in 'collaboration with the family, a wide variety of public and private agencies and members of the community.' That's what Praetorian is—a private agency; that's what I am—a member of the community. This is our collaboration."

Janet nodded. Yes, she could get in trouble, but wasn't the upside worth it? The agency was woefully understaffed; in fact, 22 percent of the positions in her line of work were unfilled. The system wasn't working. Maybe the system needed a jolt. She had no idea how Maya would get the Powerses to agree to it, but maybe that didn't concern her anymore. She could just close the case for a year, turn her valuable but overtaxed attention to the more needy. Nobody knew or cared about a few Mormons in the desert.

"Where are we going again?" Janet asked wearily.

"Nowhere. Joyride. That's San Bernardino down there," Maya said.

Janet looked down, and yes, she could make out some familiar landmarks, and that was San Bernardino Airport almost directly below them. Her city, full of so many sad stories, looked small and simple and untroubled down there; she could see the whole thing in its geometric simplicity. Her stomach felt sour. Janet had a moment of panic where she imagined that these folks wouldn't return her to terra firma until she gave them what they wanted. Held hostage on a private plane.

"You mean we're just flying in circles? Jesus Christ."

Maya smiled and nodded. She was twenty-seven years old and doing big business on a private jet. Millions, maybe billions, of dollars were fluttering around the Cash-n-ator fuselage because of her. And kids might even benefit. She felt high on herself.

Janet Bergram, who made $33 an hour, shook her head in disbelief at the waste—of time, of oil, of food, of energy, and the sheer gall of wasted movement, and underneath that, the potential power for good. She felt like she might throw up.

She repeated to herself, "Flying in circles."

10.

IT WAS THE SECOND TIME that Maya would visit the Powers family at their desert compound, but as far as she could tell, it was the first. She remembered nothing substantial of that peyote night a couple months ago. The roads were not familiar, and then there were no roads, and they had to switch to ATV trails, and then there were no trails even. She was beginning to think she had hallucinated the entire thing. Though the terrain had a sameness to it, it also shone with a hard beauty, and the park ranger, whom she had contacted to drive her through and past Joshua Tree, pointed out what he thought might be of interest, as if she had hired him as a guide. "Seven hundred fifty species of vascular plants found here."

She'd google *vascular* later, but "plants" was enough, she got what she needed to get. He didn't seem to see she was not that interested. "Half of those are annual plants that bloom in the spring. So it's like a different planet, depending on when you come. Used to be a sea here but there's not a ton of water now obviously, so not a lot of energy to burn, and energy is time, so time is different here in the desert. Slow. Not man's time. Rock time, sand time, lizard time, geologic time. Look at those saguaro over there."

"Oh, is that how you pronounce it?"

"Yeah, *sawaro*. They can live two hundred years." He pointed: "Those guys over there knew Abe Lincoln. Imagine that. Look like men doing different things with their arms. Stick 'em up! Scare the shit outta me outta the corner of my eye sometimes. Cacti are to trees what man is to exoskeletal insects. They, like us, are soft on the outside, hard on the inside, have their bones, their wood, their structural integrity on the inside. Ever seen a dead cactus? You'll see the wood. You can use the wood to splint a broken limb. Natives did. The original Spanish speakers called the Joshua trees *izote de desierto*—the desert dagger. That's the nomenclature I prefer. Don't worry, there won't be a test." Maya nodded and forced a smile. He was making her drowsy. "Over yonder that way is where the Chump administration, the Bureau of Land Mismanagement, wants to let Eagle Crest Energy Company build a hydropower plant and drain local aquifers in this drought-riddled world."

"Oh, I've heard of Eagle Crest," Maya said, without judgment.

"The fuckin' devil if you ask me. I gotta watch my BP when I think about that orange ass clown." He took a few deep breaths and shook his hands free of the bad juju.

"Anyway—you'll see jackrabbits, horned lizards, kangaroo rats, tortoises, if you're lucky." Maya was gamely trying to smile his way; he was showing off, lecturing, like a proud cabbie in a favorite city. "Predators here are the coyote and Mojave rattlesnake, bobcat, golden eagle, you might wanna be careful of tarantulas, too." The guide watched her face cloud over. "Not a spider fan? What about Spider-Man?"

"I don't like snakes," she said, pulling her knees up under her chin involuntarily.

"Snakes are misunderstood," he said. "They really only mess when messed with."

"I'm working on it."

"They're not for everybody. What are you doing out here, if you don't mind my asking? Research? You from Hollywood? Netflix?"

"Something like that."

"Netflix and chill."

"That's what the kids say."

"The government?"

"I'm really not at liberty to say."

"Ah, I get it. Top secret." He nodded. "'Not at liberty to say'—that is so cool."

He smiled and checked his GPS. "I've never been to this place you wanna go. Heard tell of it but never been. Thought it was an old wives' tale. According to this gizmo, won't be but about ten more minutes now. Tough going."

After about thirty minutes, a house finally became visible like a mirage up ahead, seeming to oscillate on the flat terrain. "Thar she blows. Look at her waving at us. You know why heat makes waves like that?"

"Heat waves? No, I don't."

"Has to do with refraction," he said proudly, "when light passes between substances of different refractive indices—hot air and colder air—when it mixes, makes vibration and shakes the light, looks wavy."

"That's cool."

"No," he said, "it's cool and hot. And it's just another way the desert messes with your head. Seeing is not believing."

The sound of the ATV must've carried for miles unimpeded in the wilderness, because the whole family was waiting outside the house, looking more like palace guards than a welcoming committee.

"They expecting you?" the park ranger asked. "'Cause they don't look so friendly."

"More or less."

"Looks like less to me."

"If you wanna wait here, that's cool. I don't want them to feel ambushed anyway. I can walk the rest." They were about two hundred yards away now.

"Yeah, I think I will. Rattlers, bobcats, desert animals—I know them. Desert people? Not so much. That's an animal I can't read. They look odd to me, and honestly, I've heard tall tales that they've got the whole place booby-trapped like some horror movie. Ever see *The Hills Have Eyes*?"

"No."

"Well, the sand probably has eyes, too. You tread carefully. I'll be waiting right here. How long you gonna be?"

"Could be five minutes, could be a while."

"Well, shit. Go do your thing. You're paying for the day. I'm here if you need me. Just whistle."

"Thank you." She got out of the ATV and walked toward the house.

As she approached, the younger kids looked at her like she was an escaped zoo animal, and she searched out the one who had stuck her with an arrow. Though her memories from that night were disjointed and surreal, she retained an image of her redheaded attacker as clear as if he'd been minted on a commemorative coin. She went to him.

"Hi, my name is Maya," she said, bending down.

"I'm Hyrum. And I'm sorry I stuck ya. I thought you were a coyote."

Maya laughed. "That's harsh. Coyote ugly, huh?" she joked.

"What?" Hyrum asked. She tousled his red-blond hair, which was so dirty, thick, and matted with sand that it felt like animal fur. He looked like what she remembered of Huck Finn drawings in books from her childhood.

"Hyrum," one of the women said, stepping to them and pulling the boy away from her. She couldn't make out if she was protecting the boy from Maya or protecting Maya from the boy. The woman introduced herself without extending her hand. "I'm Yalulah. You met me the other night but you probably don't remember."

"I'm sorry, I was in no shape . . ."

"No, you weren't. Don't touch the children, please. They've had no vaccines and have no defense against bacteria and viruses you bring to them from out there."

"Oh," Maya replied, mortified. "I hadn't thought of that."

"Why would you? How's your arm?" Yalulah asked. "It shouldn't have gotten infected; that boy may not bathe, but he keeps his arrows clean."

"Good to know." Maya tried to make light. It landed soundlessly.

Bronson, who'd been hanging back under the shadow of the roof, stepped forward and said, "We figured you'd be back. Come on inside out of the heat." And then he raised his voice: "Does the ranger wanna come in, too?"

"I'm good!" came his overquick reply.

The kids were drifting toward the stranger in uniform, fascinated, like drivers who slow down at an accident scene. Bronson stopped them. "Hey, Beautiful, Deuce, Pearl—help me out here, wrangle the young ones. All of you—you got work to do. Leave the man alone. Don't touch him." Maya became aware that she was afraid, and wished the ranger and his holstered gun would come inside with them, but he was being a chump, and, to be fair, she'd only hired him for transportation, not protection.

Once inside the house, Bronson led Maya, Yalulah, and the dark-haired woman into what she figured was a huge classroom. Books everywhere, chemistry sets, paintings and instruments, none of it familiar to Maya from that night. Yalulah was intensely watchful and Maya was aware that she was clocking everywhere Maya touched and that she would scour the area clean of pathogens as soon as she left. Bronson began, "You met Yalulah, this is Mary, you can speak in front of all of us. We are one."

"Would you like some water?" Mary asked. "It's hot as the devil's cunt today."

Bronson barked a laugh and then admonished his wife, "Mary . . ."

"Thank you, and thank you for taking care of me that night," Maya said, as Yalulah left for the water. Maya continued, "And I'm sorry for the unwanted attention that my visit has brought to your family. But here we are."

"Yes, here we are. At home. My home. Where are you?" Bronson asked.

Maya noticed his forearms as he leaned forward in his chair, the strongest she'd ever seen, as sinewy as the roots of a small tree. She'd dated muscle-heads and gym rats before, but had never seen anything as naturally and functionally powerful as this man's forearms. Maya handed them each a card that identified her as a vice president of Praetorian Capital. They each looked at the card in the same contemptuous fashion, exactly as if she'd handed them a shiny, laminated turd.

As succinctly as she could, Maya laid out the scenarios that now seemed to be facing the Powers family. She said that the new awareness of this family off the grid by the government was a cat out of the bag, a Pandora's box that, try as she might, she could not close once it had opened. She apologized for that, as she knew she was the reason for this exposure. She showed them clippings of the Turpins and the Angulos. "I'm not saying you guys are at all like the Turpins, but the law can be a blunt instrument if you involve it and none of us could control where it ends."

Mary looked at the photocopy of the newspaper article. "It's 2018?" she asked, looking at Bronson, too.

"It's 2019," Maya said. "That case was last year."

"My God. Time. Wow. Oh. So you're accusing us of child abuse?" Mary asked.

"I'm not accusing anyone of anything. I'm not a cop, or a lawyer, or the state of California. In fact, I'm trying to keep the cops, lawyers, and state out of this."

"We're listening," Mary said.

Bronson looked at his wife and said, "You're listening. Not me."

Good, Maya thought, cracks already in a unified front. This

Mary could be her wedge in. She focused in on her. Now Maya floated the first scenario, where her company would buy a portion of the land, which would enable the Powerses to stay where they were while giving them the money they would need to play ball with the government—to pay their land taxes, or to relocate fully or partly or to use the money to engage in lawsuits if they saw fit. "No way," Bronson said. "This is our land in full. Or not at all."

"That's right!" Yalulah yelled from the kitchen.

She felt no warmth at all from any member of the throuple for that option. And as she was talking, she was also thinking of the logistics of this arrangement in front of her. They were not one, they were three. Who had sex with whom and how often? Did they do it all together all the time or kind of alternate? Was he more into one than the other? Maya couldn't help herself. It's silly, but it's human nature to wonder, she thought. The Mary one seemed gay to her; the way she looked at Maya was intense. Or maybe that was hatred. Hatred looks a lot like sexual attraction. Plus, there were definitely some wires crossed and soap opera shit among these three. Did Mormons go to throuples therapy? Did they have quadruples retreats?

She had to stop this line of thinking. She was joking in her head and these folks could be the Manson Family for all she knew. Anyway, she was no expert. She knew plenty of monogamous parents who fucked their kids up royally. And after her dad died, her mom was with Bill, her stepdad, forever, and still they were shitty parents despite the traditional configuration, so whatever . . . who the fuck knows . . . whatever floats your boat . . . rock on, Mormons.

"That's bullshit," Yalulah said, as she returned with a mason jar of water. "Once we sell a little, it's a slippery slope. You'll keep wanting more and more, governments will change and change laws, and we will have to sell more and more, and before you know it, my kids will be living like zombies in the suburbs."

"I can see where you might feel that," Maya said, and feeling her mouth dry, took a sip of water. "What about mineral rights?" she asked.

"I'm not selling mineral rights so you can drill and tear the ground from beneath our feet," Bronson said.

"That's another slippery slope you're trying to get us on," Yalulah added.

Maya watched Yalulah note exactly where her lips touched the rim of the glass jar, a nexus between the outside world and hers to be sanitized as soon as possible. Maya was secretly pleased that the Bronson family wasn't biting at the first option; she was made to go for broke. She started with some swift business school platitudes. "There's four types of deals in life—the i-deal, the or-deal, the no deal, and the real deal. This is not ideal. Unfortunately, you don't have the legal option for no deal, and I don't want this to be an or-deal for your family—so the deal I'm looking for is the real deal, and here's what the real deal might look like. Because I disagree with Janet Bergram and the state of California, who would very possibly remove your children from here."

Thus positioning herself on their side, and betraying her promise to Janet that she would not use her name like that, Maya launched into the idea for the grand wager—they would have a secret test in good faith, comparing the learning of the kids who stayed at home versus the kids who studied away in town. If the kids did better at home, Praetorian would walk away. If the kids did better in town, then the Powerses could either make a deal and sell a good bit of land to Praetorian with a promise that the company would be as noninvasive as possible or Janet Bergram would make this family known to the authorities, and hell could very well break loose.

When she had finished, she drained the rest of her water. Yalulah took the empty jar away and disappeared into the kitchen. Nobody said a word. But Mary's aspect had changed. She was no longer looking at Maya like she wanted to strangle her. That look had changed to one resembling a person who is lost getting directions back home. Maya heard a glass shattering in the trash.

Bronson stared at his boots quizzically like he wasn't sure why they didn't just walk on their own and get him the fuck out of here. "That's the most bullshit cockamamie thing I ever heard of. That's like out of a bad movie." Still without looking up, he said, "To your deal I say no fucking way. You stand to make a lot of money out here?"

"Yes, yes I do."

"I don't trust you."

"I don't see that you have much of a choice."

"Seems like," Mary interjected, "we can trust her or the government. I'd rather trust her."

Surprised, Bronson looked up at Mary, like he was trying to see through her. Maya knew longtime couples spoke in code, and she was alert to decipher this throuple code, but unsure. Yalulah walked back into the room, drying her hands.

"We can wait them out," Yalulah said. "They'll get bored. Something else will catch their eye. I say we do nothing."

Maya tried to shoot that down, lying again about Janet's involvement precisely the way she'd promised she wouldn't. "You could try, but I wouldn't bet on it. This woman that works for the state, Janet Bergram, is a terrier—I don't see her going away and forgetting about the kids. Statute 48293, subsection C—the court may order any person convicted of subdivision A (the provision to send your kid to school or do the appropriate paperwork and proof to show they are being educated) to immediately enroll the pupil in the appropriate school." Normal folks would be intimidated by a woman naming and numbering statutes at them, but this family didn't scare easily.

"I doubt that," Yalulah said. "That lady seemed very impressed by our school, how we teach. And besides, that's just paperwork."

Mary and Bronson both looked at Yalulah to see if she wanted to keep that fight going.

Bronson eventually looked away, but Mary held her gaze on Yalulah as something deep and difficult passed between them. Mary said, "Yaya." And that's all she said. Yalulah looked down and shook her head for a good long while. Nothing had happened, but something momentous had been decided. Maya somehow felt the weight of the room shift toward where Mary was sitting.

Yalulah exhaled deeply. She looked pained. She took Bronson's hand and said, "This could be a test of our faith."

"That it surely is," Bronson said.

"The strength of our faith and what we've taught our children. What is our faith if it can't survive a challenge from the outside?" Yalulah probed.

"What are you doing, Yaya?" Bronson asked.

"It's not that simple anymore, Bro'," Mary added cryptically.

Yalulah continued, "Don't the Amish have their Rumspringa where the teenagers leave for a year or so and if they come back, they come back into the faith with renewed vigor because they've chosen this world over that one of their own free will?"

"We've given them no free will, Bro'," Mary stated.

"Not free?" Bronson was incredulous. "They are as free in their lives as natural savages."

"Not that type of freedom. In the mind. Of the will. Against temptation. Like we had before we came here," Mary said.

"And how did that work out for you?" Bronson demanded, now standing right between Mary and Yalulah, as if trying to keep them from joining. "The children are free from the thought control and groupthink and despair of that diseased world and culture out there." Maya sat back, fascinated, clever enough not to get in the way of this unit as it fought and processed; they no longer seemed like one three-headed being from Greek mythology.

"In Kirtland," Yalulah said, "where Joseph Smith himself did not want to go, they doubled the Church in one day."

"You're talking about a mission?" Bronson sought clarification. "The mission is for age nineteen."

Mary was nodding. She took Yalulah's hand and said, "It's a test of faith and a mission. Maybe it's for the older kids, so maybe it's a couple years early, they're gonna go to college soon anyway, right?"

"I don't know about that. That's a couple years away, no."

"Yes, Bro'," Yalulah agreed, calming him and pushing at once. "You say yourself, we cannot pick and choose like from a 'menu' what we believe of the faith. How can we withhold our children from a mission if a mission is part of their faith?"

Mary piled on, "Maybe this is the sign you were waiting on. The sign you kept riding into the desert to see. The sign to tell you when to send them back into the world."

Bronson watched in horror as his women seemed to be siding with this other woman, this stranger, and the dominoes underpinning his life began to fall—all the thoughts and fears that kept him up at night, that troubled his sleep, were being incarnated and voiced in front of him today. Each tumbling and toppling the next. He had to stop it. He pointed at Maya. "How do you know she's not a temptation? An obstacle to be overcome?" he demanded. Usually it was Bronson's domain to interpret omens and translate the unseen will of God in things that could be seen. Mary had usurped that place and seemed unwilling to relinquish it.

"Where the path is bad," she preached his own words back at him, "the obstacle is good."

"You think this capitalist emissary, this errand girl, is sent by our God?"

"God works in mysterious ways," Mary said. Maya thought she heard something approaching contempt in Mary's voice.

Trapped between them, Bronson stared into Yalulah's eyes and then into Mary's. He seemed defeated for a moment, like he'd heard his own words fashioned into clubs by the women he loved and then turned on him, seemed less the cowboy superman of Maya's estimation and more like a beleaguered sitcom husband, and almost mortal, even old. He shook his head and looked down at his boots again, wondering at the speed at which worlds, which for years orbit in peaceful ellipses, can suddenly collide and destroy each other. Bronson's was a full solar system, and there was much to track, too much at the moment.

Maya sensed this was her moment to strike, to play the card up her bloodied sleeve. "That night," she said, "when your son shot an arrow at me. I don't remember much of it, but it has come back to me over time in dribs and drabs. And I've remembered some of your speeches by your bonfire, something about bonobo monkeys?" Bronson squinted at her, and Maya continued, "And I also remember two graves, maybe three. Two small headstones and a larger one, or markers, for something very small, like a pet, or something." She knew those were not pet graves. She let them know it, too. This was a serious threat, plain and simple.

No one moved. No one spoke. Maya swallowed and it sounded as loud as a gunshot to her. She watched as Bronson's breathing grew faster and shallower. He jumped to his feet.

"Fuck it," he said. "Fuck it to hell."

Bronson strode quickly out of his house, his wives followed him, and Maya followed them. When they all got outside, Bronson was pacing toward the horse corral and calling the kids, all the kids. The young ones, alerted by an uneasy tone in Bronson's voice, were dropping whatever chores or work they were up to and jogging to the corral. Three beautiful horses were flicking their tails at the flies on their rumps. A pretty teenager, whom Maya assumed was the eldest daughter, straddled one. Bronson lined the children up against the wooden fence. "Which one of these kids you want me to send to a public school in San Bernardino and which ones you want me to keep?"

His voice was so full of barely controlled anger, Maya instinctively took a step backward and her back brushed a horse, so she took a step forward again. It was a huge animal.

Maya tried to remain calm. "Well, I think that's really up to you."

"I haven't said I'm gonna do it, or anything, but if I did, which kids you wanna take away from their family for their own so-called good?"

"I don't know." Maya was starting to feel anxious, her mouth getting dry. She felt close to achieving her goal, but also far away to the side from it. She felt she might be duped, or hurt. She heard the ranger start up his ATV and slowly roll closer.

"Well, I sure as shit am not gonna choose." Bronson spat. "What was that movie? *Sophie*? *Sophie* something? She had to choose. I ain't choosing. You know why?"

"No."

"'Cause I am gonna win. Doesn't matter who you choose. My kids are better off here, and after a year, they will come back here, and you will see that I am right."

"There's a good chance of that."

"Oh, is there? A good chance? Go ahead, Sophie. Make the choice."

Maya looked at the kids, and at the mothers, and at Bronson. A couple of the very young ones were crying as it dawned on the children what might be happening. Maya felt like shit, but this was business, she had to be cold-blooded, like some sort of desert lizard.

"You okay, ma'am?" the ranger called from his safe distance.

"Yes, thanks," Maya called out, and turned her attention back to the group of kids lined up as in front of a firing squad.

"Well . . ." She bought time, thinking: Janet Bergram and she had decided on a couple older kids, high schoolers, and one younger kid—middle school, perhaps—as the best test group. And Mary, the mother, had just said that the older kids were probably going to college soon, so that seemed the way to go; those kids would be leaving home soon, anyway. No big deal. Time to grow up and leave the nest. That's the way it goes. She spotted the oldest-looking boy. "Him." She pointed. "What's your name? How old are you?"

"Deuce," the young man said.

"Deuce is the smartest of us all," Bronson said. "He'll end up teaching the teachers. He's sixteen, seventeen, eighteen thereabouts, we don't really keep track of ages like that."

"Okay, Deuce." Maya was relieved. "He'll be a junior in high school, then."

She could see Deuce was not happy, or at least wanted to let his father know he was not happy, maybe didn't want to betray his dad. Maybe the kid was scared. Sure, it's scary to leave home for the first time. He'll be fine. But Maya definitely thought she saw some relief in Mary's eyes; she started to think of the woman as a potential, secret ally. "So I guess you'll want to pick a younger one now, too?" Bronson sneered.

"Okay. One down, two to go," Maya said.

Mary spoke up. "Deuce has a twin—Pearl." She pointed to the pretty girl on the horse. "We don't separate the twins. And a missionary needs a companion, two by two, that's the way. Pearl will go, too."

Mary looked at Bronson when she said this, not at Maya, and not over at the girl, Pearl, seeming to dare him to contradict her. He held her eyes for a second, a look of incredulity on his face, then shock and embarrassment, before landing on the resigned but comprehending mask of a man who had betrayed and been betrayed in turn. He looked down. Then he glanced up at the sky, as if for backup. Only then did Mary train her eyes on Pearl on the horse. Something passed between them that Maya saw but did not understand, and knew that she could not ever understand perhaps until she became a parent herself. The love, protection, apology, and guidance Mary was sending the girl's way was returned in equal measure with disappointment, competition, and rage coming back at the mother from the girl. Pearl then looked over at Bronson, but Bronson would not look down from accusing the sky of some unnamed crime.

"Fuck all of you!" Pearl screamed. She kicked at the horse she was astride. The animal took off in a gallop, skidding up an angry spray of sand, jumped the fence, and soon vanished into the distance.

"Pearl!" Mary called after her.

"Leave her be," Bronson said, with a touch a venom. "She'll be back; she got nowhere to go." Then Bronson turned back to Maya.

"I think it's going well so far, don't you? One more, right? A young one, you wanted. You have two seventeen-year-olds, you want, like a ten-year-old? Ephraim? Three for the price of one. You want another girl? How about your girl, Mother Mary? Would that satisfy you? How about Beautiful? Beautiful?"

Two kids, Ephraim and Beautiful, stepped forward. Mary seemed to try to rein in any reaction, but she was wringing her hands so hard that Maya could see little specks of blood start to seep from her knuckles.

Maya looked at the kids. Her vision was blurry. She realized she was crying. She wiped at her eyes to clear them only to rub sand in from her fingertips and tear up some more. Bronson handed her a kerchief; the musk of it repulsed her. When she could see again, Maya thought she might throw up. Maybe she should have, but she hadn't anticipated a scene like this. She couldn't think. All she could see was the fucking kid with that fucking bow and arrow, the kid that had shot at her, Hyrum. It was the only name she was sure of among all the nutty Mormon and made-up hippie names. "Hyrum?" she said.

Now everything got fast. Maya heard the horse behind her make a weird high-pitched noise and rear up; she felt the air switch at her back. She watched Hyrum, impossibly fast, like watching a movie with frames missing, string an arrow on his bow and take a knee, aiming it at Maya's heart. She heard Mary yell, "Hyrum! No!" as mothers have done throughout eternity when their sons are about to do something violent and stupid. Maya couldn't turn, but heard the ranger, behind her in the distance, yell and start running toward them, pulling out his gun, bringing it up to aim at the boy, she assumed. She saw that in her mind's eye, she knew it must be happening. Maya felt herself entering a kind of special time, like a sacred time; she felt both present and absent from her body and mind, somewhere between the here and now and a premonition of things to come.

Now everything got slow. Maya saw the boy's fingers gently release, like setting free a bird, she watched the arrow fly at her, she felt she could see it from 360 degrees; even though time slowed, she had no time to move. The aim was true. She was dead. She knew she was going to die right now. That the boy had tried to kill her before, and now he was going to finish the job. She kept her eyes open and waited for the sting of the arrow through her flesh to her heart, hoped it would be quick and not too painful, hoped it wouldn't get her in the face. Did she deserve it? She was simply trying to make money, make a life. Was that a sin, the sin? Was this justice for the pain caused by splitting up this odd family? She thought briefly but completely of the things she would not do in life. Children. See Greece. See *Hamilton*. She should've had more ice cream. Her Equinox-toned ass was about to be a useless accessory on a corpse, a thing of the past, worm food. She thought of her own father, hoped to see him again, if there was an afterlife. She keyed on the sound of the shaft as it flew nearer to her, ripping the air, and then, curiously, impossibly it seemed, missed her, continued past, and made a sticking sound a few feet behind her left ear.

It was only then that she heard the rattle. She turned, and there in the dirt, in front of the spooked horse still rearing and stomping its hooves, stuck into the ground wriggling, bleeding, and dying, was a big, angry rattlesnake inches from her leg. The snake stopped writhing and died, pinned by the arrow through its open, attacking mouth, like a science-room specimen, through its small brain to the earth.

Maya turned from the snake back to look at the boy. Hyrum was still on one knee, left arm extended in a fist clutching the bow, right fingers in a cocky freeze frame, elbow high by his ear where he had released the bowstring. He had a smile on his face and a full quiver, less one, so sure of his first shot that he hadn't even re-loaded.

PART II

FAST TIMES AT RANCHO CUCAMONGA HIGH

When you're a Jet, you're a Jet all the way
From your first cigarette to your last dyin' day.

—STEPHEN SONDHEIM, *WEST SIDE STORY*

11.

THE AFTERNOON OF AUGUST 6 did not feel momentous, like it would mark the dividing line between two seasons; it seemed no different from the rest of that dry, hot summer in Rancho Cucamonga, a city of slightly more than 175,000 souls in San Bernardino County, California.

It was still near triple digits in this low desert city that had hit #42 on *Money* magazine's "Best Places to Live" list in 2006. Summer songs (the inescapable "Old Town Road") still blasted from cars on the main street (quaintly named "Mainstreet") like everyone was trying to keep it mid-July. The better the car, and there were many Porsches and Ferraris in the hands of wannabe gangsta teenagers, the louder the speakers, the bigger the bass. Up in LA, Lebron and the Anthony Davis–loaded Lakers were rounding into shape at the Staples Center and the Dodgers were looking good for another postseason run. Sunny business as usual all across Southern California. If there was a chill in the air at all, it was mental, for school was about to restart, marking the end of something for all the kids and the adults whose brains had been patterned by the programmed ebb and flow of a school calendar.

But not so for the transplanted Powers kids moving into a four-bedroom house (rented by Praetorian for $3,200 a month) on the 6000 block of Catania Place, which was a short drive, even walking distance from Rancho Cucamonga High School (one of the city's three high schools crammed within five miles of one another), where the kids had been enrolled for the coming year. Their desert brains were free of civilized tides, these sons and daughters of nature; there would be no familiar segue, this was a before and after as stark as BC and AD. The first day of school would be tomorrow for Deuce, Pearl, and Hyrum, and they really had no idea what to expect.

When they had moved into the Catania Place house in mid-August to "acclimate," like divers from the depths, it was the first time any of the kids had had their own room. This, then, the mere shutting of a door behind you in solitude, was already a revolution in consciousness for the three. So whatever "culture shock" was expected and forecast, mundane stuff like that, like never having actually been alone unless you walked yourself out into the desert alone, Mary considered a shift in perspective so fundamental that it was impossible to predict the rippling repercussions. She thought of the phrase "fish out of water" for them all. But then she didn't like that, because fish die out of water, they suffocate, don't they? What a stupid saying. They were more like half a pride of lions airlifted from the savannah and deposited without warning in the suburbs.

Maya had chosen, with an invisible assist from Janet Bergram, Rancho Cucamonga because Rancho Cucamonga High was one of the top-ranked schools in San Bernardino County. All of its public high schools had earned the "Silver" distinction in the 2015 rankings by *U.S. News & World Report*, and had been named California Gold Ribbon Schools by the California Department of Education. They had decided that the city of San Bernardino, Janet's proper bailiwick, with its Walmart jobs and warehouses, minimum-wage gigs, and families scraping by with multiple jobs, would be too much of a shock to the system for the kids to thrive in. Janet's endgame, so different from Maya's, was to wait in the weeds, and then call attention to the needs of the local kids and the underserved local public schools, and in fact, San Bernardino had filed for Chapter 9 bankruptcy as recently as 2012. But Janet also knew that the best way to "win" would be to enroll the Powers kids at a school that was already highly functioning. Janet's hope was to employ a successful superstar public school to prevail in this unorthodox test, and then call attention to the more needy, less thriving schools. Janet had secured a promise from Maya that if Praetorian won, they would pour a portion of their winnings into the neighborhoods and schools that were the most resource-starved in the county, especially in terms of jobs at a possible resort to be built.

Maya wanted the best school available. Even though the Powers kids were well ahead of even college graduates in history (up until 1968) and world literature (same)—seems they'd read five hundred books to every one of their peers—and practical engineering, there were exploitable gaps in biology, sociology, advanced mathematics—sciences in general. Those gaps were what Maya hoped to capitalize on and see great advancement in over the year.

But the biggest weakness that Maya saw she could take advantage of was the kids' inability, never having sat through a situation remotely like it, to do well on a standardized test like an ACT or an SAT. The poor scores the Powers kids posted when they sat their first standardized test in July reflected not on their intelligence or preparation, but only that they were not used to being tested like that. Maya knew this, and merely by exposing the kids over the year to these tests that essentially measured standardized learning, she would be able to see and claim huge, though mostly illusory, educational gains for the kids in town.

Mary's "adult" acclimation was confusing in a different way. If the children were dealing with the shock of the new, she was dealing with the shock of the old. After lying low indoors in the air-conditioning for a couple days, staring out the windows at the people like they were fish in an aquarium, the family had ventured out on walks around the neighborhood, a visit to the school grounds, and an adventure to a food court at the mall. Walking past the stores in the Victoria Gardens mall, Mary, Deuce, Pearl, and Hyrum looked at once entranced and overstimulated, like *Walking Dead* zombies with ADHD, two pop culture references that would be lost on the group. There was too much of everything—too much choice, too much color, too many smells, too many people, and too many sounds. Deuce said his ears hurt. The children had lived such a quiet life before, literally quiet, that their ears were no doubt physically pained by the synesthetic immersion. She could see Hyrum occasionally recoil from an invisible assault; he was troubled because he could "hear the light."

Hy's coping strategy seemed to consist of shouting "Cucamonga!" at maximum volume, as if to keep the town itself at bay, every few minutes. This was even after Deuce explained to him that *ku-kamonga* meant "sandy place" to the Tongva Indians who originally settled the area, and that it wasn't the dirty word that Hyrum hoped it was. That knowledge didn't dissuade Hyrum from using it as an all-purpose expletive.

Mary noticed Deuce becoming aware of the girls prowling around Victoria Gardens with their Dior sunglasses and fake Louis Vuittons in small, high-pitched packs of four or more. This imme-diately made him self-conscious, and she caught him a number of times checking out his own reflection in the many windows and mirrors of this mall. Comparing himself with the other boys, so many of whom had tattoos and piercings, sporting angular, dyed haircuts, Deuce felt self-conscious for the first time, as he compared his floppy long hair and his Charlie Brown shirt (picked out by Mary at Target because of Deuce's love of the Schulz comic strip) that even he could tell were not hip. An innocent, Deuce wouldn't know to call this self-consciousness, however; he was aware of the creeping compare/despair only by its telltale physical manifestations—jumpy, sour in the stomach, cold sweats. When he looked in one of the omnipresent mall mirrors, he saw reflected back a maybe decent-looking, pimply young man who dressed like a ten-year-old. He flashed a sideways peace sign at himself, mimicking a pose he had seen in other boys, and stuck out his tongue. Pearl saw him mugging and punched him in the arm. Hyrum shouted, "Cucamonga!"

The local kids at the mall were so loud, and struck such confusing, unnatural postures, constantly taking pictures, pulling faces, of themselves with their phones, flashing peace signs among a seemingly infinite array of hand gestures. Like they had all gone to the same frenetic, semaphoring gestural finishing school. Mary thought the girls dressed like hookers or mortician's assistants and the boys dressed like they'd all once been very fat, their pants falling off their asses, exposing their designer underwear, or had once been very thin, their tight, stretchy jeans seemingly Saran-wrapped to their asses. Well-meaning Janet had given the Powers kids lectures on the microsocial, tribal world of school that they had never navigated—the emos, the jocks, the nerds, the preps, etc.—a literally foreign language falling on deaf ears; she also tried to teach them about macrosocial media and phones, the culture of Netflix and chill. The kids had stared at her blankly. They had no reference points, no abstract schema by which way to contemplate even the theoretical—they'd never watched television. They'd never even seen a toaster. Agadda da Vida was fewer than one hundred miles away, but this was life on Mars.

Janet Bergram found herself drawn to check in on the family, even though she was off the case, which was "closed." And though she didn't have the time to spare, she made time. She felt a certain responsibility here, so she visited in a nonprofessional capacity, as a "friend." Mary appreciated it. Maya seemed to Mary too young to relate to in many ways, and Janet knew her shit, knew kids, and knew the area. Seeing the disengagement of the children, Janet had pulled Mary aside and said, "You've got your work cut out for you, and it may seem daunting as hell right now, but I will be available to you, and if there's one thing I know about kids, they're resilient, they're like saplings, they bend and do not break. I've seen kids raised on television and Sugar Pops make it back and lead productive lives. Your kids are not ignorant, they're innocent, inexperienced, that's a big difference, and they're smart, and they've been loved, which is the biggest game changer, love; just keep loving them, they're gonna be okay. I have a degree in child psychology, a master's in social work, and a law degree—I'm a phone call away."

Mary kept nodding dumbly for too long after Janet had stopped speaking. "But the way you're looking at me right now," Janet tried to lighten up, "I'm more worried about you than them."

"I'm no sapling." Mary sighed, then she asked, without a hint of humor, "What's Netflix?"

Even though they ambulated forward in a tight group, like a pack of prey animals making a circle of themselves for protection against predators, there was no way to mitigate the attention that Pearl received. From boys her own age, for sure, but, sickeningly for Mary, she caught an inordinate number of grown men eyeballing her seventeen-year-old daughter, some while strolling around with children of their own. Mary didn't sense that Pearl was made uncomfortable by the attention. In fact, troublingly, she seemed to respond more readily to the ogling of the older men than that of her peers. Mary felt a deep pang of remorse, but she summoned up an equal resolve to fight as best she could. She didn't know how to fight it, she just knew she would fight. For his part, Hyrum kept pulling at the neck of his Old Navy T-shirt, complaining that it was strangling him.

Mary was already worried about Hyrum. He had developed a full body rash from either the synthetic materials his body had never encountered, or the additives in the detergent they used. They had had to bring him to the doctor anyway to get inoculated for polio, measles, and rubella. The other two kids had been born in civilization, and had, by matter of course in their infancy, had their shots. But not Hyrum. As the apologetic doctor sank needle after needle into him, Mary watched the boy ball up his fist. She took his clenched hand in hers. The doctor never had a clue how close he was to getting smacked.

On the way out, Hyrum was given a red lollipop by the kind nurse, and Mary watched his pupils dilate as he tasted processed sugar for the first time in his life. After a couple of tentative licks, he held the sweet at arm's length, beholding it from every angle as if trying to determine its power. So many new things under the sun, Mary thought, I can't protect them from all of it; I can't protect them at all.

"You like that lollipop?" she'd asked him.

"Lollipop?" he repeated, smirking at the silly word. "Yeah, why is it so red?"

"Red dye number two," Mary heard herself say, surprised to recall an FDA controversy from her deep, unused memory and youth.

In fact, all week she'd been assaulted ceaselessly by memories she hadn't accessed in years. Everything out here reminded her of everything else she thought she had forgotten. She felt cured of a pleasant type of amnesia. Now her brain seemed like someone else's, full, pulsing uncomfortably past her skull. Her mind reminded her of a hummingbird, even sounded like a hummingbird. She felt overwhelmed, dizzy, and wished she could somehow stop the random associations bubbling up.

"It tastes happy," Hyrum said, biting and grinding the hard candy on his back molars, and swallowing the shards. "Cucamonga! When can I get more shots?"

They continued strolling through the food court. Chicken nuggets, burritos, sushi—all unknown foods to them. McDonald's, Taco Bell, Jamba Juice ad infinitum—they might as well have been brightly colored Buddhist temples to these kids.

"What part of the chicken is the nugget?" Deuce asked.

"The balls," Hyrum guessed.

"It's all the meat you can't eat, beaks and assholes, ground up and pressed, and deep fried," Mary answered.

"Gross," Deuce said.

"What's wrong with beaks and assholes?" Hyrum wanted to know. "And balls."

Mary got kind of excited for pizza. She gave some cash to each kid to go roam around and see what they wanted to eat. Free will. This is what they were doing. She wasn't gonna ride herd on their palates all year.

So if this was the experiment to save the family, the family was gonna have to save itself. And she was gonna get herself a couple thin-crust slices.

When they got home, they were all overstimulated and exhausted; the four of them piled onto Mary's bed and took a fitful, gaseous, three-hour nap.

Only Hyrum stirred, lunging into the bathroom to throw up three Big Macs, after which he sat in front of the living room television entranced but somehow not entertained by NBC's highly touted primetime fall lineup.

The rest of the family was awakened by a knocking on the front door. On her way to answer, Mary noticed Hyrum in front of the TV and asked, "Didn't you hear the door?"

"No. My ears aren't working right," Hyrum said.

She flicked on the lights. "Why are you sitting in the dark?"

"It's not dark, this TV light is on," he said, pointing at the television.

"What are you watching?"

"Nothing."

"Nothing? You're watching something."

"No. I'm just looking."

Mary opened the door to Maya Abbadessa laden with plastic bags full of gifts—clothes, books, a new electric guitar and an amp.

"Merry Christmas from your friends at Praetorian Capital," she said. "Oh wait, do you guys celebrate Christmas?"

"Yes, we do," said Mary, stepping aside and helping with all the shopping bags. "But not usually in August."

"There's tons more stuff in my car."

Maya returned from her third trip back to her car. "Back-to-school gifts. Praetorian wanted you to have phones, for safety—so here's one for Mary, the Dodgers case here for Deuce, and here's a Hello Kitty case for Pearl and Jungle Book for Hyrum."

They took their new phones and beheld them like they were moon rocks. These children had never even used a house phone. "They're all set up for you—we're really just thinking of your safety, you can't be in this world of today without a phone and we didn't want you to be at a disadvantage." The kids started playing with their phones, trying to figure them out.

"Call me on my telephone," Pearl said to Deuce.

"What's your number?"

Mary showed them the basics. They started yelling their numbers and calling one another.

"Mine has a camera," Hyrum said. Pearl's phone vibrated; she screamed with delight and surprise.

"Press the green part of the screen to answer." Maya instructed the kids like a priestess at a shrine with special knowledge of the god. "They all have cameras, and flashlights, and calculators for math class. There's also a bunch of clothes here for you guys. I just wanted you to feel comfortable, like you fit in, tomorrow." For his part, Hyrum was testing the weight of his phone as if to gauge what kind of a weapon or projectile it might make.

"Oh, this is a pretty dress," Pearl said, rummaging through one of the shopping bags.

"I thought so, isn't it adorable? Sexy, but classy."

"Does that cost like a thousand dollars?" Hyrum asked.

"You shouldn't have," Mary said, meaning it, though the clothes did look kind of cute and fun. Pearl left the room to try the dress on.

"I don't want to fit in," Hyrum said.

"You don't have to fit in, Hy," Mary said.

"I can't get these pants over my temple garment," Deuce grunted, struggling with the bulk of his so-called Mormon underwear.

"That brings me to another issue. And fitting in," Maya said. "There are a handful of Mormons at your schools, but they don't wear that, what did you call it, 'temple garment'? And it's such a thing, you know, I was wondering if you could leave them for at-home wear, maybe, just at first."

"No way," said Hyrum, his eyes back on the TV.

"What do you think, Mary?" Maya asked.

Mary had hated the undergarments at first, felt desexed by them, and they had never seemed practical to her, especially in the heat. She knew it was one of the more idiosyncratic aspects of the faith that non-Mormons tended to focus on and make fun of, had been aware of their existence even before she converted. It's easy and lazy, she thought, to make fun of the archaic-seeming underwear and the outlawing of coffee and alcohol. And then there was the rampant rumor that because of the active and strict prohibition on premarital intercourse, young female Mormons were experts at oral and anal sex. In this manner, went the thinking, they still remained technically virgins along scriptural lines. She even remembered the term "Mormon mouth hug" for a blow job from back in the day. The mass culture in which she came of age had been silly and obsessed by sex; and as a kind of pansexual being, she had checked out of it even before she ran away from the world with Bronson. From her walk around the mall today, the culture seemed to have not matured a day since she left it; if anything, it felt younger, further regressed.

"I also got some regular old American underwear for you guys. For you, too, Mary," Maya added. And although Mary knew that hers was an all-or-nothing soul susceptible to any slippery slope on any moral mountain, she was trying to be a flexible parent, even open, maybe even, god forbid, hip. She knew Bronson would probably be pissed, but he didn't wear his temple garment most of the time either.

"Well, you can make up your own mind while we're here, Deuce," Mary decided on the fly. "If you wanna try them on without, go ahead."

Deuce ran out with some clothes, and came back moments later. "I still don't think they fit," he said. "I mean they're tight on the thighs, but really loose at the waist."

"That's the way they fit. They're called 'skinny jeans.'"

"They don't seem so practical, like I couldn't do real work in these."

"I suppose not, it's more of a 'look,'" Maya said.

"A 'look'?"

"Yeah, it's kinda rad. I think you look great with that shirt. Charlie Brown in skinny jeans. New and improved Greg Brady."

Mary laughed, she got that one. *The Brady Bunch*, another undead memory sprung to life, like a zombie. Pearl returned from the bedroom in the light blue dress, stunning. Her radiance was so evident, there was really nothing cogent anyone could say. Except Hyrum, who looked up from the TV, and said, "Cucamonga!"

Maya amended that with "Whoa."

Deuce asked, "What 'look' is that?"

Maya laughed; Deuce was being funny. He'd been so serious and sincere up till that point. None of these kids had made a joke in front of her. She thought it was a good sign. If a teenager couldn't be ironic, school was going to be hell. High school was irony finishing school after all. Duh.

Pearl had taken her own initiative and removed the temple garment before trying on the short dress, exposing her thighs. Mary looked at this young woman, and wanted to cry, cry because of the child's burgeoning beauty and her sudden maturity; and the love Mary had for these children pierced her heart through and through harder than God ever had. That was her dirty secret. Her dark pride.

Mary knew that Pearl hated her right now, with the intensity that only a daughter can hate her mother, or stepmother, and even though Mary understood why, and felt righteous, there was no pain like that inflicted by an angry seventeen-year-old girl on the parent she felt didn't understand her. That pain, mixed with the pride, overwhelmed Mary in the moment, and she felt frozen. Mary had never been good at dealing with big feelings. As a child, she had swallowed them with food and become fat, and then she had buried them under the roar of motorcycles, narcotics, sex, and stunt work—hell, she had even swallowed her feelings with swords on the Venice Boardwalk. She realized she was no better at managing all this than before. Her chest was tight, her head swimming. Already, she missed Yalulah. She even missed Bronson. She missed the trinity at the top of their household; she felt illegitimate and ill-equipped as a single mom.

So Mary swallowed her tears now. She cast a disapproving glance at Maya, and then turned to Pearl—"Find another look," she said, sounding like the ghost of her mother. "You're not wearing that on your first day of school."

12.

MALOUF WAS EASILY DISTRACTED by the new thing, any new thing. As the summer months shimmered by in a blur of polo matches, Malibu beach parties, political fundraisers in Santa Barbara, and divorce proceedings from his third wife while reconciling fitfully with his estranged second wife, Malouf lost all feel for Maya's Powers deal, and as a consequence, Maya began to disappear from his radar.

This lack of stick-to-itiveness was instinctive for the man, but it was also a management style. Malouf was a dog lover, and something of a self-educated, self-proclaimed expert on animal behavior (hence those weighty books about evolution and octopuses and parrots on his desk), and he knew that the best way to train a canine was "irregular reinforcement." A dog will learn a trick better if you randomly reward him for doing a task, counterintuitively more effective than giving him a treat every time he does what he's told. The dog enters into a state of agitated unknowingness, not sure how to please the master, and therefore works harder to do so. "I sat on command once and got a treat, and then I sat a few times and didn't, must've been something I did wrong—I'm gonna sit extra hard and fast next time" is how Malouf imagined the doggy thought process.

He enjoyed trying to think like a dog. In fact, the only books Maya'd ever seen him really reading, and not merely displaying, were on animal training—dogs, monkeys, dolphins, whales—the higher mammals, but also smart birds such as parrots and crows. Trying to think like a human was no different to the boss. "Humans, most humans that is, apart from the winners, Wharton," he confided to Maya once, "are herd animals. They want hierarchy. When you get married, I'll teach you how to make the special sauce—'Least Reinforcing Syndrome.'" He never did tell her what it was, but that was the Praetorian world, with all Malouf's capitalist pups cycling in and out of favor, performing tricks for their capricious owner, never knowing when they were doing the right thing to please the alpha. In this way, sadomasochism could be rechristened as corporate "culture," and an inability to focus for any length of time ("curating ideas"), coupled with a latent violent disposition ("alpha"), could be rebranded as "business acumen," or even mythologized as "genius."

The troubling signs were everywhere if you knew where to look, and the trend was not her friend. In late September, she had walked to Malouf's office to share an update on the Powers kids at school: they seemed to be doing fine; he'd been on the phone, and waved her away dismissively. She stalled long enough in the doorway to hear that he was talking to his dog groomer. Shortly after that, she swung by to give him some data, and Darrin was sitting across from the boss. They didn't invite her in, but Malouf asked her, as she stood in the doorway, if she liked cars. "Sure," she said, "I love my Tesla."

"Tree hugger. Windmills give you cancer," Darrin sniffed, witlessly rotating his arms like a wind turbine.

"Have you ever driven a Lamborghini?" Malouf asked.

"Nope," she replied. Didn't seem like a big deal to her; she wasn't a car guy.

He tossed a key at her. "Take my whip for a spin."

Darrin impudently interjected, "Careful, big man. She steals Maseratis, you know."

Malouf blinked slowly a few times to signal his irritation. "Yes,

I know she's fast and furious, I heard all about that, but what has she stolen for me lately?" Maya didn't like all this "she" business.

"So take her for a spin," Malouf continued, "and then get her washed and gassed up, before two p.m.?"

Jesus. The fucker was sending her, with her Wharton MBA, to wash his fucking car. She had a good mind to steal it now. She laughed like she was in on the joke, rookie hazing hahaha, but she felt like screaming. At the car wash, she thought about buying a Cokie on him, but decided against it.

She started spending more time at the gym, trying to sweat out her anxiety and hoping that she might come up with another good idea under duress and iron. Her ass was getting to be top shelf. She entertained idle thoughts of fucking her trainer. She even tripped on mushrooms again at home alone, hoping for a second stroke of lightning, and came up with nothing but a couple scars on her face where she went too hard at some pimples in some stoned, anxious, self-critical stupor.

Walking through gentrified Santa Monica with its modest-looking multimillion-dollar homes, she knew that she had come on the scene many years too late. That gold rush was over here. She ran scenarios and numbers in her head, of betting on land that was undesirable now but might come into favor when climate change erased Malibu in fire, Santa Barbara in mudslides, or a major earthquake toppled Venice into the sea, and suddenly Culver City was beachfront. Carpinteria, anyone? But such apocalyptic thinking put her in a dark mood, and she knew Malouf preferred the short to the long game, which is why he'd gone so cold on and inattentive to the Powers deal.

One morning, her assistant told her that Malouf wanted to see her, and a sense of foreboding came over her. She walked into his office to a big smile. "There she is! My star," Malouf said. "Have a seat."

Maya sat and spoke: "I don't have any news from the desert. It's gonna be a while—"

Malouf cut her off with a raised hand. "See no evil. Hear no evil. It is I who have news." He wiggled his Muppet brows, convinced his archaic diction was irresistibly charming. "I have a deal I'd like you to get involved in, wet your beak."

"Amazing," Maya said, but she already knew she didn't like where this was going because his affect was weird, playful, sadistic.

"I don't know if you've heard, but Praetorian has purchased the rights to the Hammer film catalogue. Are you familiar with Hammer films?"

"Not really," she said, fearing all her darkest work scenarios were about to come true.

He produced a thick brochure titled "Hammer Films: A Legacy of Horror," and handed it to Maya. Apparently, Hammer Film Productions Ltd. was some dinosaur of horror schlock. Founded in 1934, and responsible for such gems as *Taste the Blood of Dracula* (1970), *Dracula A.D. 1972* (1972, duh), and the provocatively titled *The Legend of the 7 Golden Vampires* (1974). Many of them starring the redoubtable Christopher Lee, who she thought she might have heard of.

"Lots of vampire stuff," Maya said.

"I know, isn't it awesome?"

No, she wanted to say, not really very awesome at all. "Yeah," she said.

Feasting her eyes on the endless, blaring, screaming titles— *Maniac* ('63), *Paranoiac* ('63), *Fanatic* ('65)—a trilogy? Trilogic? Trilogiac? The goofy B movies spun before her eyes, as Malouf went on, "These were way before *Twilight* or *Walking Dead* or any of that shit. So we now own all these titles, and I'd like to figure out if there's any diamond in the rough in there, waiting to be remade. I mean, *Spider-Man* was a bullshit comic for kids, right? People would've laughed at *Spider-Man* as a critical darling or legit money-maker thirty years ago. *Batman*? Bullshit. Schlock. For kids. On TV with Adam West, that's where it belonged till it turned into the billion-dollar industry that ate Hollywood."

Maya nodded. Ah, so that was it. Here was some backdoor, bargain-basement starfuckery. Malouf wanted a Hollywood play, a shiny new toy, so he bought up this IP ghetto. Now he wanted to gentrify it and then cash in. The first step on the way to owning a studio and ownership of a world that had made a serf of his artistically souled father and paid him a pittance for backbreaking work, and had deformed him as a boy. His Moby Dick, his Rosebud. In the meantime, he'd be able to rub elbows with some stars by overpaying them to lend their names to imbecility.

"I mean, who was Robert Downey before *Iron Man*? A has-been, and who was Iron Man before Robert Downey? A never was. I want you to find me another *Iron Man* to reboot in there, and I'll find another Robert Downey."

"How can I help?" she joked, co-opting Malouf's signature line. Looking at the brochure, she said, "I feel good about *The Satanic Rites of Dracula*. Feels like a winner. Oscar bait. I'm thinking Meryl Streep?"

A little pushback; Malouf appreciated it.

"You laugh, but they laughed at Stan Lee, didn't they?"

"Stanley who?"

"Stan Lee—Stan Lee. Marvel Stan Lee."

"Just fucking with you, Boss. I don't know, I wasn't born, did they laugh at Stan Lee?"

"Probably. They had every right to."

"So I'm confused as to what you want me to do."

"I think you're a bit of an artist. The desert thing showed real imagination, vision, a real sense of drama and the long game. I don't know how it turns out, but I like you thinking outside the box. I don't trust any of the other Young Turks here with artistic shit. They actually like these movies."

"I'm not sure this is art."

"It's art if we say it's art. Create the standards by which you will be judged. People write PhDs on Batman now. I want you to go through the entire catalogue, see every movie, and report back to me. I want you to write synopses and flag ideas of interest."

"Excuse me for saying, sir, but wouldn't you be better off hiring someone with Hollywood experience? What about your friend Rob? He seems like a smart guy." She was referring to Rob Lowe, a pal of his. She'd seen Lowe around the office, always smiling and friendly and handsome, like a picture of Dorian Gray come to charming life. Why don't they go remake that?

"No!" he thundered. "Rob is a super-smart guy, believe you me, but experience is the fucking enemy. Haven't the last four years taught you anything? I want fresh eyes on this shit."

"But I count one hundred fifty-eight titles here," Maya complained.

"That was fast! You see that, Wharton—you are good with numbers."

13.

THERE WERE 3,436 STUDENTS enrolled in Rancho Cucamonga High School that August. Fifty-one percent of the "Cougars" were Hispanic, and 13 percent Afro-American, with a late addition of two more students in the junior class, Deuce and Pearl Powers, bringing the percentage of white kids to 14. Eleven-year-old Hyrum was enrolled in a nearby middle school, Etiwanda Intermediate, starting seventh grade. Deuce and Pearl had only one class together, AP History. The days were long, but the weeks seemed short, and the months even shorter. There was so much to do and so much that was new that before anyone could assess all that had changed and all that had not changed, it was already early December.

Janet Bergram seemed prophetic when she'd said it doesn't matter if it's Mormon love, Muslim love, Jewish love, Black, white, straight, gay, cis, or trans love—kids who have been loved are adaptable and resilient. Because that's what Deuce was going to need—resilience. Deuce wasn't a cool kid by any means, he didn't know how to act cool, but he had a natural ease and goodwill that was in serious danger of being suppressed by his new peers. He had a huge heart for his fellow man, in the abstract till now; it was as if you had distilled all the best qualities of the late-'60s campus radicals like Abbie Hoffman, Mario Savio, and Jerry Rubin, and bottled their cock-eyed optimism. He was smart, he was a socialist, but he was no humorless scold like Bernie Sanders—he was funny and

charming with adults. The kid could've been a walking advertise-
ment for homeschooling and polygamous parenting. Upon getting
a midterm update on his academic progress, Janet had texted—
"You are f—ed, glad they're well ;) Deuce for Pres lol." His teachers
loved him, though; he was obviously brilliant, and they were pushing him to take more AP classes. No fewer than three teachers in-
dependently gifted him a copy of Tara Westover's *Educated* for
Christmas. His English teacher asked him if he was interested in
writing such a memoir. Deuce answered humbly and slyly, "Not yet."

Though he was on track for a 4.5 GPA easily, and he was catching up to his peers in the sciences where he had been lacking, he
was also being bullied. Over six feet tall, weighing less than 120
pounds, Deuce presented with a very bad case of acne vulgaris
about a month into the move to Rancho Cucamonga. Whatever
the stressors were—the shock of relocation, the breakup of the
family, the first exposure to the antibiotics in the meat and the pre-
servatives in his food—Deuce's face was a sore, mottled, bumpy
mess. This, of course, had drawn the scornful attention of an anti-
academic strain of jock in his history class when he had tried to
initiate a Howard Zinn study group to counterbalance the more
traditional historical view taught by this school's textbook—
Thomas Bailey's antiquated, unwoke *American Pageant*.

Deuce began receiving notes in his locker addressed to "Scarface,"
"Pizza Face," and "Master Pimp," and fake prescriptions for Accutane,
which Deuce had to google. He had never really thought about his
skin before, never been forced to think of his face as something that
would attract or repel. One afternoon, a 250-pound offensive lineman
from the football team had walked up to him in the hallway between
classes and simply slapped him across the face so hard that Deuce almost lost consciousness. The boy's hand came away with pus and
blood on it from Deuce's zits. This led to the nickname "El Slimer."

Deuce played out his feelings on the electric guitar Maya had
given the family. Mary could hear him wailing away in his room

night after night, the volume knobs and effects pedals all new play-things to a kid who'd only ever had a nylon-string department store acoustic. He was a soulful player. One night, Mary found Deuce crying in bed, and he confided his confusion and hurt over what had happened. Mary was disgusted by and angry at these interactions, but assured him he was a very handsome young man and to mirror Christ by turning the other cheek, to put his head down, do his work, and that the year would soon be over. Hyrum argued for vengeance. He encouraged Deuce to "man up" and give the football player a "beatdown."

Deuce spent hours in his bathroom staring and squeezing at the angry pustules on his cheeks and forehead. He became quite withdrawn, and, not taxed enough by his schoolwork and uneasy about whatever money was being spent on him by Praetorian, he had taken a job at a local fast-food franchise called BurgerTown. BurgerTown was, as it sounded, a kind of homey, minor league McDonald's with about twenty-five franchises up and down the West Coast. Raised with no sense of time but the rising and setting of the sun and all the hard hours in a day of desert farm life, Deuce loved work, having a job, punching a clock, and hitting the pillow with the tired body and guiltlessness of an honest workingman.

BurgerTown became an unlikely refuge for the boy. It was at BurgerTown, among the mostly immigrant Mexican, less-than-minimum-wage employees, that Deuce began to feel at home. No one made fun of him there. With a bit of a language barrier, the other BurgerTown workers looked easily beneath the mask of carbuncles to the sweet, humble, hardworking soul beneath.

They taught him Spanish. They introduced him to soccer and made him play with them out back behind the restaurant during breaks, and even on weekends. Deuce had never played with a ball of any kind and was as uncoordinated as a puppy. The other guys affectionately nicknamed him "Dos a la izquierda," shortened to "Dos" or "Izzy" because, like a dancer who is said to have two left feet, he could control the *pelota* with neither of his. But Deuce was so eager and tried so hard, they stuck with him and eventually put him in goal, where, with his height and length, he began to shine a little. He loved laying his body all out, even on the asphalt, to try to make saves. He was really quite good, a bit of a natural, in fact, and it led to another work nickname that he secretly cherished, "Salvador," which morphed into "Sal" and "Sally."

Whatever he had learned about the "darker races" in Mormon scripture did not translate into his practical consciousness once he talked and interacted with actual folks of color, and his Mexican co-workers, whom he assumed were the "Lamanites" Bronson had taught him had come from Jerusalem around 600 BC, among the original inhabitants of the Americas. But the more Deuce learned at school, the more he began to perceive the historical limitations of Joseph Smith and the Mormon bible in an immediate and clear-eyed way. He spent many an hour googling Mormonism on his phone and on the school computer, and while its obvious intellectual shortcomings and the occasion it gave his classmates to make fun of him may have filled another soul with rage and accusations against the father who had inculcated him, he understood both sides intuitively—the disorder of this big, beautiful world he was now entering and his father's rage for order in his retreat to a rigidly circumscribed desert existence.

Made invisible by his own skin, he spent much of his free time alone in the school library, which was often quite empty. He was not only an exceptional student, he also had the wide-ranging, free-associative autodidact tendencies of Bronson. Late one night, reading on his phone under the covers so Mary wouldn't know he wasn't sleeping, he came across these words about Joseph Smith's bible by one of his favorite authors, Mark Twain, in *Roughing It*—

The book seems to be merely a prosy detail of imaginary history, with the Old Testament for a model; followed by a tedious plagiarism of the New Testament. The author labored to give his words and phrases the quaint, old-fashioned sound and structure of our King James's translation of the Scriptures; and the result is a mongrel—half modern glibness, and half ancient simplicity and gravity . . . Whenever he found his speech growing too modern—which was about every sentence or two—he ladled in a few such Scriptural phrases as "exceeding sore," "and it came to pass," etc., and made things satisfactory again. "And it came to pass" was his pet. If he had left that out, his Bible would have been only a pamphlet.

That, as they say, was that. Deuce saw no argument or remedy against Twain. A giant of American intellect had summarily vanquished a giant American con, with humor. Twain had struck through the root, with the blade of rationality, and the tree was felled at once. And it came to pass that Deuce lost his faith.

What was it like to realize that your spiritual education had been a joke? You could be bitter and strike back, claim abuse, victimhood. That would be most people. Or you could laugh along with the joke, and be thankful that your parents had cared enough about your spirit to cultivate it at all. He looked around and saw all his peers, and their untended spirit lives, the passionless lip service paid to the God of their parents. Tepid God the Friend. The American God of Prosperity from John Calvin to Oral Roberts to Paula White. Insufficient as he now felt it to be, Deuce had been handed down from Bronson a genuine spiritual religious passion for a wild and untamed, unreasonable deity, and even if the object of Bronson's fiery faith was now seen as misguided by this seventeen-year-old boy, Deuce was circumspect enough to treasure the brute fact of his enlarged spirit at home in the wild, which he now could empty and refill with a faith more appropriate and enlightened for him, whatever that might be. He'd been enlarged, that was a gift, and now emptied, another gift, and he was ready to be refilled.

Bronson had worked Deuce's heart out, expanded it under theological pressure like a muscle; now Deuce would empty it of dead and unworthy teachings and fill it with a more modern, fact-based, social gospel that he was in the process of devising. From Joseph Smith and from Bronson, Deuce had been raised without the nattering electronic distractions of today and, in that holy, human silence and peace, had received the ability to believe in latter-day miracles for himself, a forward-looking attitude, and he felt a miracle was happening with him now, as his spirit drained of content, and in this sacred pause he waited for a new god, a new purpose. He had been built by God the Father and his stepfather for obedience and service, but he would be the author of the new cause; in the ruins, salvaging what was useful, the child was giving birth to the new man. And though he would leave Bronson and Joseph Smith behind, he would always cherish as his life's motto a Smith quote his father had taught him when he was thirteen: "deep water is what I am wont to swim in, it all has become a second nature to me."*

And just like that, the angel Moroni packed his peep stones and funky underwear, and took the last flight back to a more welcoming Salt Lake City. Deuce's belief would no longer be pure like that, it couldn't be, but what this wise child knew without being able to put into words was that his ability to believe purely, his personal, radiant purity, was intact. He knew that his father had filled him with shiny lies and dodges, sure, but now that he'd emptied that place, he knew that's why his heart was so large, reverberative, and hungry.

Deuce spent one roller-coaster afternoon in the library watching *The Book of Mormon* on YouTube, and he laughed his ass off, but

---

* Joseph Smith to All the Saints, September 1, 1842, in PWJS 571.

he also cried, because he knew he was the butt of the joke, he and his belief, and he knew his belief had been pure; he believed that silly shit with all his heart. But he also came to see that he'd never really been a Mormon, that his belief system was way more idiosyncratic and anti-institutional. He came to know that he was raised in the religion of his father, Bronson Powers. So the barbs stung, but didn't go too deep. He looked forward to talking about all this with Bronson. Hey, Dad, guess what . . . you're not really a Mormon. Uh, maybe not.

And, as the final number of the hit musical pivoted harmlessly from ruthless irony to something approaching a sincere celebration of personal imagination as the Book of Mormon was replaced by the silly Book of Arnold, Deuce came back to a great appreciation for what had drawn his father to this religion in the first place. Deuce wondered if other Mormons could look beneath the easy contempt of that musical to its ultimate respect, as the fantastical-world creators of *South Park* embraced, storyteller to storyteller, a kindred writerly spirit in the world creator Joseph Smith. Yes, the actual Book of Mormon was unscientific, derivative, and obviously improvised by a charismatic leader, organizer, and mythmaker, but at its restless heart Mormonism sought relief from the crushing weight of the past, the old stories, and a willingness to embrace the new—new gods, new peoples and heroes, new stories. Brilliantly and falsely describing his new religion as a restoration of the old, Joseph Smith had escaped history through his imagination, lies, and will. Though he could follow him no longer, Deuce felt like he understood his father far better than he ever had and loved him even more.

Thus liberated spiritually, Deuce turned his attention to spiritual praxis and action, where the rubber meets the road, which took the form of a new obsessional trinity—climate change, gun control, and Donald Trump. Friendless, at night, he bonded with Mother Mary watching *All In with Chris Hayes* and then *The Rachel*

Maddow Show as they both stoked their hatred and disbelief of Trump through these snarky MSNBC proxies. Mary was proud of the adjustment Deuce was making in seeming to overcome some initial hazing. She was way more worried about Pearl and Hyrum. And Trump.

14.

THOUGH THEY SHARED A WOMB and 50 percent the same DNA, Deuce and Pearl could not have been more different souls, and that difference was drawn into stark contrast in the Hadron collider of adolescents that was Rancho Cucamonga High School. First, Pearl was homesick, at least that's what it felt like, but what she missed was the burgeoning and explosive secret sexual attachment that she had felt for Bronson in the months before she left the desert. She felt an emptiness in her gut that nothing could fill. She didn't quite know it, but she was heartbroken. She'd lost her mother and her lover.

She was easily distracted, not into any schoolwork, and to make matters worse, because she was so beautiful and the "new girl" and got lots of unrequited attention from boys, girls started to ostracize her. Alone, without any alliances, she was given a crash course in mean-girl dynamics. Having grown up only with siblings, Pearl was unfamiliar with this petty social Darwinism and shaming culture. But her strong sense of natural independence kept her head above these waters. She didn't feel an overwhelming need to join the herd, or the smaller subset herds like the jocks, the preps, the druggies, or to align by race or sexual orientation. It all seemed ridiculous to her, like so many masks, none of which fit her well. Unlike Deuce, who found the companionship he needed among his BurgerTown co-workers, she didn't care if the other girls made fun of her. She wasn't vain, but she knew she was beautiful, she had been loved and desired by a man, and that was a strong secret weapon. But that didn't mean she didn't feel lonely sometimes, or ostracized.

In the first few months of the year, unfriended by the girls because of her standoffish and mysterious sensuality, and appearing unapproachable to the boys because her heart was palpably still out there somewhere in the desert, Pearl came off as haughty, aloof, and disinterested. A "stuck-up bitch." She was friendless. And unlike the more methodical Deuce, she could not rationally jettison her faith, for that would mean jettisoning Bronson. In her secret heart, she could link up with Bronson through dwelling on doctrine; some nights she imagined them both reading the same scripture at the same time.

But cracks in her religious devotion were beginning to show. Her childish belief had been contaminated by Bronson's sexual love, and her removal from his daily attention and affirmations had, in turn, fatally weakened her faith. When Bronson took her as a lover, he had made himself all too human and compromised the purity of her relationship with God that existed through him. Ironically, by loving her, he had crossed too many lines between authority and attachment and had destroyed her as a believer. She was lost, but she didn't know that yet because she had no destination in mind. Her faith now, such as it was, had been hollowed out by her anger and confusion. She could no more lean on it for support than one could lean on the wind. She felt broken and needed a fix.

Like in many schools of its type, along with the bullying problem during school hours that could extend to 24/7 courtesy of social media, there was a thriving drug culture at Rancho Cucamonga, and Pearl aimlessly drifted into its slipstream. It was the only thing that made her feel whole again, and made this yearlong exercise in killing time bearable. She drank coffee, the Mormon gateway drug.

She bought herself a Juul to vape, and was given some free Adderall as a kind of stoner starter kit by one of the dealer kids who wanted to fuck her. That was the clincher. The Adderall made her feel like Bronson had, focused and free simultaneously. The comedown sucked, but the weed and nicotine helped with that. Even though she was often high and didn't work very hard, she was able to get B's and C's because she was a couple years ahead of her peers in most subjects.

One afternoon, in late November, Pearl was juuling in the girls' bathroom and ditching AP History. She took comfort seeing Deuce during the day, but recently the way he looked at her, like he knew she was tanking, made her feel guilty. She knew she was projecting, but that didn't make it feel any better or less real. So she was skipping the one class she shared with her brother. She had a good forty minutes more to kill in the toilet.

She daydreamed a little about Bronson, what a grown man he was compared with these little boys here, how hairy his chest was, and how one day she had just noticed that and it made her swoon, the way he smelled, his funk.

That killed about ten minutes. She thought about praying ("thank Thee, Heavenly Father for Thy hidden, forbidden, holy jewel"), but she really didn't feel like giving thanks at the moment. She thought of masturbating half-heartedly, but didn't quite feel like that either. She took another hit off the Juul and began singing "The Long and Winding Road." Like a few of her siblings, Pearl had perfect pitch, but unlike them, she sang with a depth of feeling that belied her age. She sang like she knew what she was singing about. She sang like a woman of experience.

The sound dynamic was excellent in the empty toilet, with the slightest harmonic reverb off the hard tiles and metal, so Pearl didn't notice another girl come in to pee, and she didn't stop singing when the door was opened, so she didn't know her song had traveled far enough outside to where a boy named Josue heard the beautiful sound echoing through the hallway and, like Ulysses with the Sirens, did not think of the hard rocks that would proba- bly await him if he, a fifteen-year-old sophomore, entered a girl's bathroom. He strode down the hallway in a trance, led by the sound, opened the door, and walked in like he'd been doing that his entire life.

"Oh my god," Josue asked of the stalls, "what is that?"

It took a few moments for Pearl to realize he was talking to her. "Uh, what?"

"What's that song you're singing?"

"'Long and Winding Road,'" Pearl answered matter-of-factly from behind the door.

"Did you write it?" he asked her feet, the only part of her he could see.

"No! What are you, stupid? It's the Beatles."

"Oh yeah, that's like classical music."

"You mean classic rock?"

"Who are you? You have the most amazing voice . . ."

And then the girl in another stall, who had been quietly going about her business, swung open her door and lost it on Josue.

"Are you fucking kidding me right now, kid?" she yelled at the boy. "You're totally standing in the girl's bathroom while I'm peeing!"

"Oh shit," Josue said, suddenly realizing what he'd done and where he was, and flailing, almost falling down. "I . . . I . . . I . . . just heard her singing and I . . ."

Pearl walked out of her stall, exhaling Juul smoke. She didn't know either of these idiots. The other girl was super upset. "I'm taking you to the principal," she yelled at Josue, and then turning to Pearl said, "That's safe-space invasion! This dude's like a rapist, right? You're a total witness!"

"He didn't try to rape anyone."

"I said, 'like a rapist.' *Rape* is a broad term."

"Is it?" Pearl asked.

"Are you serious right now? He's a space-rapist! Are you gonna back me or not, sister?"

Pearl shrugged. "Back you for what?"

"Oh my god, you're such a bitch," the girl whined, and shoved past Josue into the hallway, yelling for security.

Josue looked like he was about to throw up. Pearl shrugged at him, too. She had been perfecting her shrug the past few months.

"What's your name?" she asked.

"*Hosway,*" he said. "Nice to meet you."

"Sure," she said. They stared at each other. "How do you spell 'Hosway'?"

"J-O-S-U-E. Jose with a 'u' in there."

"You ever been in a girl's bathroom before, Josue?"

"Never."

"Whaddyou think?"

"Pretty nice."

The girl was screaming out in the hallway. "Help! Security! Help! Pervert!" bounced around the bathroom slightly muffled.

"You have a great voice," Josue said.

"You said that already."

Ear cocked, Josue was half listening to the growing commotion outside.

"Maybe you should run," Pearl said.

Josue considered that, then replied, "Probably too late."

Pearl nodded. "Probably right."

The door swung open again and a female teacher came barging into the bathroom with a security guard who grabbed Josue by the arm and hustled him out into the hallway.

"Dude, you're hurting my arm, I'm not trying to go anywhere," Josue complained to the guard.

"You are so fucked," the other girl threatened.

"Are you all right, dear?" the teacher asked Pearl, putting an arm around her.

"I'm fine," Pearl said, wriggling away from her grasp.

"I'm sorry, but we are gonna need a statement from you, dear."

"You need a statement from me?"

"Yes."

"High school sucks," Pearl deadpanned.

"Oh, snap." Josue laughed. "Legend."

"Nothing the fuck happened," Pearl added, displaying her quick acquisition of the rhythm of high school lingo, and started heading down the hallway the other way.

"Wait," the teacher called out. "What's your name?"

"Pearl," she answered, not slowing.

"Pearl what?"

"Pearl De Jackie-san."

"What?"

Pearl disappeared around the corner.

"That's that new Mormon chick," the other girl said.

15.

SUBTRACTING MARY, DEUCE, Pearl, and Hyrum from the hands available to work Agadda da Vida was a physical, as well as emotional, hardship. The family dynamic had shifted in ways that were unfathomable and changing daily, settling into new and strange configurations. Little Joe began to wet the bed. Palmyra wanted to learn how to speak French. Little Big Al was convinced his siblings had been taken away by "the cancer" that had killed one of his mothers, Jackie. Lovina Love had created an involved fantasy that her siblings were not coming back, that they had been abducted by aliens for horrible experimentation that seemed to always begin and end with the "butthole." Yalulah chastised Bronson when he egged Lovina on to describe the anus-centered miseries that had befallen her siblings, but Bronson would keep on giggling like a schoolboy.

In September, Bronson and Yalulah planted the alfalfa alone for the first time. Though the "farm" area was less than twenty acres, without the teenagers, it seemed endless. They needed alfalfa, a good source of protein, for their livestock and for themselves. In mid-November, Bronson planted the durum wheat. Bronson had to irrigate and mulch by himself. When he brought along the younger kids to teach them about irrigation, how the threading of small hoses punctured at certain lengths to drip (and save) water worked and had to be maintained, they were often as much a hindrance as a help. He explained to the children why the farmed areas were lower than both the house and the well, and how he had chosen the sites carefully so that water used for baths and cleaning in the house would be reused with very little energy since it flowed downhill from the house to the soil beds as "gray" water to feed the crops. Explaining his hard-won engineering victories in this desert to the kids, he felt renewed in his quixotic mission, his love-hate battle with God's elements, all over again. He hoped the kids fell in love with this life, too. He was not at all sure.

He showed them how he had repurposed old parachute material that he had squirreled away from stunt days, hanging it around a canopy made of light metal rods that kept the produce from burning up in the unrelenting desert sun, while still allowing enough light through for the plants to grow. This was one of his proudest innovations. Unfortunately, the younger kids were not suitably impressed, and were more interested to hear about the parachute material's original function, defying gravity, floating down gently from the heavens, than its present-day, more prosaic use.

He would also plant the carrots in late winter, and harvest them with the kids come early spring; so, too, with the seasonal onions planted in mid-winter and picked in early summer. He would plant the okra and the potatoes. He tended the grapes, as well as plum and peach trees. He prayed that nothing would go wrong with the well this year because he didn't know how he would handle that kind of predictable catastrophe, seemed every seven years or so there'd be a problem with the pump or a filter needed to be replaced, without the muscle of Deuce, Pearl, and Mary. He lived in near constant dread of that solar-powered pump failing. Lack of water haunted his dreams.

Some days, Bronson felt his age in his lower back and in the declining strength of his once-crushing grip. Once upon a time, on movie sets, Bronson could win a few extra hundred bucks arm wrestling men that outweighed him by 100 pounds. It sure beat scrapping for real. Occasionally doubling Stallone on the '87 ode to the "sport," *Over the Top*, Bronson had also doubled his paycheck going head to head, or rather arm to arm, against the pros.

But now he found his greatest tools, his fingers, cramping and locked from time to time. It wasn't that he couldn't work his hands the way he used to do, but more like he could see the day fast approaching when he wouldn't be able to. He'd need the next generation to work soon. He'd never really liked to hunt; it was more something he did to survive, and with Hyrum gone, there was less wild meat on the table. None of the young kids exhibited Hyrum's natural joy for the hunt, exhilaration at perfecting his aim and skill, or sheer animal satisfaction of the kill. Yet the meals were kept generally similar for the kids to what they'd always been, with the exception of the countless mourning doves, white-tailed antelope squirrels, and black-tailed jackrabbit, as well as the occasional treat of mallard, and once in a blue moon a gray fox that Hyrum would ambush, arrow, and drag in for Yalulah to gut, clean, and cook.

The home school suffered as well without the leadership and kinship of the older kids, and neither Bronson nor Yalulah were any good at the visual arts that Mary excelled in and taught with such contagious verve. Yalulah was concerned that the level of instruction had taken a hit across the board, and that at the end of the year, they would be judged wanting with respect to what the Cucamonga kids learned. "This is bullshit, Bro'," she said, "it's rigged. They took three of our teachers away, out of five, and then they want to judge us as teachers?"

"The change was bound to come, Yaya, they just forced us into it a little early, I guess."

"I don't know that I can prepare them for standardized testing. That's exactly the type of learning we shielded them from. That's rote memorization to program robots. They're making us play their game."

"I know it's frustrating, you've made a beautiful curriculum here."

"It's not a fair test."

"No, it's not. But the test doesn't matter, Yaya," Bronson would reply. "It's really about survival. That's the test. As it always is."

"Why are we doing it, then? If the test doesn't matter."

"The test is the test. This has nothing to do with us versus them, or their way versus our way, their teaching versus ours. This is about us. This is a test of us. That's the only test."

"The test is the test?"

"Of our pride, and of our sins."

"What sins?"

Bronson inhaled and looked down, stared down at something like a man peering into a well for a fallen child. But it was not a child who had fallen, he could see, as his eyes and his mind adjusted to the darkness, it was the light-bearing angel, Lucifer. He stared at the beast itself, and he blinked first. "Pride. Lust. Sloth. Jealousy. Our sins are innumerable and unnamable. We are human."

"Then surely we are forgiven? Why do we have to pass a test to earn forgiveness for being as God made us?" Bronson didn't answer. He didn't want to and he couldn't. He rubbed his forehead.

"You have a headache again? How long have you been getting headaches? Are you drinking water? We're working harder, so you have to drink more water. Let me make you a banana-yucca poultice tonight," his wife said, feeling for heat on his forehead.

"No," he said, brushing Yaya's hand aside and squeezing his head in his hands, "no headache."

Yalulah fetched him a glass of water. "I put some poppy-root juice in it."

"Thank you, Yaya," he said. "If we survive," he went on, "if we don't crack and give in, we will win better terms. And mark me, we will survive."

Yalulah took a deep breath and sighed. "I miss Mary."

"I know you do."

"And Jackie."

"Yeah."

"You miss her, too?"

"Sure, Yaya," he whispered. "I miss her every day. Banana-yucca—she thought that was gonna save her life."

"Bronson?" Yalulah paused a moment to signal that she wanted to steer the conversation into deeper waters.

"Uh-oh. Whenever you say my full name like that, I think some shit is gonna go down. You and Mary both. Lay it on me." He made the comic face of a silent movie actor who just noticed a piano about to fall on him from above.

"No, baby, it's just . . . I know that when Jackie died you had no one."

Bronson shook his head. "I had you and Mary. I had my family. I had my work. I had my God."

"No, Bro', Mary and I fell into each other then, selfishly, I think. I'm sorry."

"Don't apologize for love. God is love."

She took his hand. "We left you alone with your grief. We left you and Pearl alone with the grief."

"Stop it, Yaya."

"No. You need to hear this. We forced you away."

Bronson removed his hand from hers. "No. No, I don't. This is nothing but psychology. The things you are saying are not real to me, just words, false witness."

"They do exist. Psychology exists. Exists every bit as much as God."

"Not to me, Yaya. Not to me. I've got to work on the well. Excuse me." Bronson went back to rubbing his head and walked away.

The younger children remained persistently plagued by fears of being taken away as their siblings had been. Yalulah saw it as a psychological reaction to trauma that called for talk of feelings and increased transparency and vulnerability. Bronson saw it as a weakness of faith that called for more scriptural study. Beautiful began to focus on Revelation in the bible, and she alluded often to a creeping unease about some unnamed "apocalypse," a "rough beast" slouching, heading their way. Beautiful was convinced that the beast would take the shape of a huge fire in the form of a dragon, and fire was a real concern in the desert. There were small isolated wildfires that the family had confronted over the years, but nothing like the one Beautiful was convinced was coming now to consume them all. She adopted an obscure Joseph Smith utterance as a kind of half nursery rhyme, half mantra: "Noah came before the flood. I have come before the fire."

This precocious thirteen-year-old girl mixed the apocalyptic imagery of Revelation with a literal reading of Dante, Yeats's "The Second Coming," and Frost's "Fire and Ice" to create a horrifyingly detailed prophecy of doom. Pearl had been Beautiful's mentor, confidante, and champion, always able to talk the imaginative girl off a ledge of her own making. Without Pearl's mediating influence, Beautiful had a tendency to float off into a self-created darkness populated by her fantastical literary images. Yalulah could see the makings of a writer in the girl, and she encouraged Beautiful to keep a record of her images and stories—"She has an adult brain in a child's body," she told Bronson, "and we have to make sure that brain doesn't destroy the body before it has a chance to grow up. The dragon fire stuff? That's just puberty talkin'. Her mom is away and she's about to hit puberty—perfect storm. She's finding the wildest words to put on changes and feelings she can't describe."

"I don't know about puberty, but she freaks me out sometimes," Bronson said. "When she describes the dragon's features, I swear to God, it's like she's describing me, the way I look. I feel like she's afraid of me, pissed at me, judging me."

"For what?"

"I don't know." Bronson massaged his temples. "The other day, I woke up in the middle of the night and she was just standing in the doorway, staring at me, like in a bad horror movie. Like *The Omen*."

Yalulah laughed at that pop culture callback, so Bronson laughed too. "Oh God, *The Omen*," she said. "I haven't thought of that crap in ages. Maybe you dreamed that."

"Yeah, maybe."

"No," Yalulah said, reaching out and rubbing Bronson's head for him. "Every little girl loves her daddy."

Bronson pulled back a bit from her touch and tilted his head instinctively, defensively at that seemingly harmless cliché. "You call her a writer," he said, "but maybe she's more of a prophet. That's what scares me."

"I've had the thought," Yalulah said, "that watching Jackie suffer for so many years, maybe that was God opening the child up. Do you remember how she wouldn't leave Jackie's side and how involved she was with the rituals of the burial?"

"Yes. It was holy."

"It was heartbreaking. And God forgive me, I was jealous. Jealous of how she loved that woman, jealous of how everyone did."

Bronson looked at Yalulah, surprised at her vulnerability, and nodded. "That's not psychology. That's a sin."

"I know it is," she said.

Bronson accepted her confession. "Maybe," he said, "that's how God makes a prophet, by breaking the human early."

"Like you?"

"I'm no prophet, Yaya, I can only see a few steps ahead. Barely. And I struggle for clues. I beg for scraps. Beautiful sees all the way through and it flows out of her in great articulation. God chooses to speak to her, not to me."

"No, Bro', no—she's a writer. But she's just a baby writer. You know, like baby rattlesnakes are the most dangerous 'cause they can't control their venom? It's like that. She hasn't learned control yet, mastery. And a writer is a type of prophet anyway. Words are to the world as omens are to time."

"Like Joseph Smith."

"Yup. I hope she's a better writer than he was."

"She already is," Bronson said.

They were both able to laugh at that, but Beautiful unsettled Bronson. Her gift of vision into words must've come down from God himself through Mary's unnamed lover, for neither he nor Mary had the gift of words, and this facility remained foreign to him in the child, like a beguiling divine visitation. Her out-of-the-blue talent was evidence of God touching her, so all her words must be from God, he reasoned. Awe in front of a child in your charge was a vertiginous feeling. Although Yaya could allay his fears momentarily, he would often, more and more these days, go back to puzzling over her poetic pronouncements literally, trying to parse them for hidden prophecy and clues as one does with biblical texts. Fire began to consume him as well, though he kept its horrible fascination for him secret, hidden. Amid Beautiful's fascination with the apocalypse, Little Big Al's cancer talk, and Lovina's fixation on buttholes, dinners with the remaining Powers could ping-pong into a lively, unsettling, surreal affair.

Rather than the new constellation as a traditional couple at the head of this rather untraditional household driving them closer together in deeper levels of working intimacy, Yalulah felt Bronson drifting ever further from her. Alone and lonely, Yalulah found herself driven more and more to her original ways of thinking and processing for succor. More at home with the simple psychology and the terms of therapy she had learned as a child of wealth, privilege, and private education, Yalulah reverted back to a pre-Mormon, younger version of herself, and diagnosed Bronson to herself as an obsessive-compulsive (his rage for order), addictive personality (hadn't he traded drugs for God?), depressed, even bipolar, held down and blue in a tightening spiral of self-recrimination and unresolved childhood shame, an old wound that had been reopened by their world being torn asunder. He had known how to live and feel with a tight rein over his little kingdom, and the loss of control to him must have felt like a failure of character. It wasn't. She knew it wasn't, but did he? To think of him in these terms was painful, but really comfort food for her. She liked things tidy and in boxes. Words and terms made it all seem manageable. She was a script supervisor, after all.

She wanted to release him from his self-made hell, but didn't quite know how. He had a short attention span for psychoanalysis and its cocksure, seemingly rigorous, postbiblical terminology, and she feared driving him further within himself by using that rarefied language. Nonetheless, she kept going back at him to look at his life that way. He refused to acknowledge the mid-twentieth-century psychological map of the brain or the existence of an ego, an id, or a superego. "Show me where they are and I'll believe you. Show me this ego on an X-ray like I can see my spine and I'll believe."

"It's not like that," Yalulah said, "you just have to have faith."

"Aha!" he said. "Faith. Then it's just another religion, and a false one at that. I have the true religion, and I don't need another, and neither do you. The truth is hiding right there in the word, Yaya— psycho*anal*ysis—feels like I'm getting dry-fucked in the ass by some Austrian dude." She didn't laugh. He referred to psychology as, loosely quoting Karl Kraus, "the disease for which it purports to be the cure." He would mutter things like "I'm not gonna blame my father for everything. What good does that Oedipal shit do anyone? I'm a fifty-five-year-old man whining about his mommy? Disgusting."

"I'll listen if you want to whine about your mommy," Yalulah offered.

"No, thank you."

He had never talked about his mother to her, never. Yalulah didn't even know the woman's name. That was okay. Yalulah herself had worked so hard to distance herself from her own Yankee origins, she would not judge Bronson's palimpsest of a past. But maybe Mom and Dad were holding the key? How do you tell a desert prophet you think he's having a run-of-the-mill midlife crisis?

If Bronson believed there was an ego, that would surely be a blow to it. She didn't know how to begin that conversation with him and, shorthanded as they were, there was so much new work to be done that she was asleep before her head hit the pillow shortly after sundown each day.

Bronson seemed to get worse as the months passed. He grew darker and less communicative. He continued to appear lost to her, or as a man who had lost something, some part of himself, and needed time and guidance to adjust to that loss. He was often cold and distant when he wasn't working the land or tinkering on the house. He slept alone more and more, said and laughed less, and spent more time in the desert away from her and the kids. He seemed to have regressed in a way, seemed more like the short-tempered rule breaker she'd met in Hollywood so many years ago, and less like the patient rule maker he'd become. He'd survived as a rule breaker, and he'd thrived as a rule maker, but could he survive and thrive as both at the same time? Or would those dual, warring identities paralyze him?

Yalulah was truly scared for him now, and of him; and with no Mary there to run interference or confide in, she felt a panic sewn in her heart like the crops they planted—watered daily by doubt, a whirlwind of discord to be reaped. It was not even Christmas yet. Only three months into the test with six to go. Six more months of this anxious sleepwalking? She felt like running away.

16.

LESS THAN A HUNDRED MILES from her insomniac sister-wife Yalulah, Mary, consumed with worry about Hyrum, could not sleep either. The kid had spent the first two weeks of the school year indoors like a caged animal. She tried to coax him outside, but he would say, "Outside isn't even outside. It's all inside." He missed his wild outdoors like a severed limb. Those two weeks he sat numbly and dumbly in front of the TV, at least she knew where he was.

She prodded him to try out for a sports team, maybe that would speak to the competitive thrill and independence he was missing, maybe even fold him into the camaraderie of a team, make some friends, but he'd never heard of any of these games—football, soccer, basketball—let alone knew the rules or how to play. The kids today were so specialized and so deeply coached, Mary found out, after talking to the eighth-grade basketball coach at school, that it was very hard to be a beginner, even at as young an age as Hyrum. Mary mentioned Hyrum was an excellent archer and sniper. At the word *sniper*, the coach had recoiled and looked at her strangely, and said those were no longer considered sports. The coach promised to keep an eye out for him, saying that he looked athletic and maybe wrestling or track and field in the spring would be an easier fit, find a sport where his natural athleticism could get him over the finer-motor-skills hump.

That was the first two weeks. At first all he watched was the

Discovery Channel and *Naked and Afraid*, but soon graduated to *The Walking Dead* and *Stranger Things* and *Black Mirror*. He mostly liked animated stuff—*Rick and Morty*, *Family Guy*, and *The Simpsons*. Mary couldn't believe *The Simpsons* was still on the air. It had been on when she went to the desert with Bronson, two two-term presidents ago. She never got the humor of it, even back then—thought the irony was like sugar, or a synthetic sugar substitute, went down easy, but nothing about it sustained her, and it left an inorganic aftertaste.

Watching *Family Guy* with Hyrum, she felt even worse after laughing at Peter's Boston accent and horrific, surreal shenanigans. Aside from not knowing most of the people they were making fun of on the show, she felt slimed by an overall sense of meanness and smugness, making her feel inferior about feeling superior. And as for the culture in general—so mean, and crafted for teenagers. She felt old and afraid, like she'd lost the mother tongue; she didn't even know how to defend herself in this new world. She left Hyrum alone in front of his cartoons; she figured knowing this new language was a luxury for a dinosaur like her, but for Hyrum it was a necessity. In that dark room he was getting an education, and Hyrum had never been a student of books—his faith was in action, in movement, in the animal joy of boyhood. Mary prayed that that joy was being ministered to in some way through electronic adventure.

Then came a sea change, and one Mary could barely recognize or fathom. Hyrum started wearing his pants low and baggy, and began cursing a lot—trying out the "N-word" and, more harmlessly, "D'oh," whenever he could; gone was the innocence and innovation of the expletive "Cucamonga!" Even as he spent more time in front of the TV, he stopped watching programming. He was playing a game called Fortnite, had become obsessed with it, spoke of it ceaselessly. And Mary, happy that the kid was showing a lively interest in anything, anything at all, encouraged it—well, not encouraged, but at least didn't try to curtail his time on it or make him feel shitty about it.

She knew he wasn't praying, but he'd never much been one for sitting still. She wondered about how he felt about his religion in general, until one day he came up to her and said, "Hey, Mom, what do you get when you take away an 'm' away from a Mormon?"

"I don't know, Hyrum, what?"

"A moron." He walked away and Mary knew where he stood. The kid hid nothing.

In a panic about the video-game violence, Mary called Janet Bergram and Janet told her she expected as much and not to squash the kid's interests, but to meet his enthusiasms, however strange to her, with a hands-off respect. Janet said that in the "olden days," kids used to be able to go out in the backyard to be alone, or into the "woods," but now the woods were gone, and modern parents were too afraid to let their kids out of their sight anyway, so these games were the only adventurous places a young boy could be alone. What appears to be an unhealthy act is answering a very healthy call in a pubescent boy—the male need for blood, victory, and solitude in a world without women. Janet had laughed. "Wait until women become part of the equation."

"Olden days?" Mary wondered—not olden to that boy. Just a couple months ago, Hyrum was spending days alone in the desert having real adventures and getting up to god knows what, and now he sits on his ass in a darkened room killing time and virtual people, talking with strangers, some of whom are probably predatory adults and pervs. Mary didn't like it, but she understood what Janet was getting at. The desert was full of dangers that Hyrum knew, the streets were full of dangers, namely humans, he did not. And after all, Mary reasoned, he was talking to people, imagined predators aside, the other gamers online. He was making invisible friends, but he was making friends.

For her part, Mary was spending the school hours at the gym, the local Equinox. She found it a refuge, like a church, almost womb-like. She could move anonymously from Stairmaster to stationary bike to steam room and then take a yoga or Zumba class, have a drink at the juice bar—a self-contained world—and be home by 3 p.m. She couldn't believe that her years in the desert had transformed her from a scrappy, Venice Boardwalk sword swallower into this gym rat afraid to go out into big bad suburbia. Well, she told herself, I know myself, and if I stay out of the situations, I won't get into any situations. This is a safe place. I feel good here. Her abs reappeared. She met some people, parents like her, some older, some younger, and remembered half of their names. She met a couple Mormons even. She made plans to get together for dinner and tea and talk about the kids, but she never followed through. At least it was a potential social life that passed for a social life.

She missed Yaya. Missed her body and her scent, her companionship, and felt somewhat of a relief to be in the presence of all the women in the locker room. Not that she was tempted to make a move, but she couldn't help noticing that everybody shaved their pussies. She noticed women staring at her down there like she was a wild beast or something, like a prehistoric woolly mammoth. She became self-conscious about her natural, so she trimmed.

She stayed away from the too-clear intimacy of the sauna, but after years of dry heat in the desert, the wet steam was a new and welcome feeling. She would eavesdrop in the steam room, hiding within a cloak of mist; sometimes the other ladies didn't even know she was in there, listening and learning. Much of the girl talk in this cavernous, hissing, eucalyptus-scented cocoon was the same as it ever was, boring and wonderful sisterhood. Same old concerns, different manifestations in the modern-day sweat lodge. Instead of weed being the bogeyman for children, it was Adderall. A prescription drug that the kids apparently sold and abused on a black market. She heard the term ADHD for the first time. She made a note to ask Janet Bergram about it.

One early afternoon, finding herself alone in the steam, Mary suddenly had the urge to pray. She hadn't felt like it, aside from the obligatory group prayers over meals with the kids, in months. Prayer had never come naturally to her; it always seemed too needy, like begging or showing off her piety to Bronson. But deep down, she knew prayer was really a way of speaking to yourself, of slowing down enough to make your own unspoken thoughts known to yourself. That's probably the real reason she hadn't done it in a while. She didn't want to know her hidden thoughts.

Unable to see more than three inches ahead through the thick steam, she was reminded of the anonymity of the confessional from when she was a child. "Father," she whispered, "thank Thee for this body, and this life." And then she stopped. She felt false. She was full of shit. She didn't feel grateful. This was a bad beginning. Maybe she couldn't pray, but she could speak to her God, and that was prayer, wasn't it?

"I feel discouraged," she confessed. "I am so angry and confused at Thee. I don't even know what to ask for, or who to ask forgiveness from or for." She paused. She could feel herself slowing down, centering, getting more real. She'd been terrified for months, alone, running blind. She breathed the steam deeply into her lungs and imagined it enveloping her heart in a loving white cloud. "I guess I just want to know—if I'm a . . . if I've been . . . a bad mother." Saying it out loud lifted the unspoken, ever-present weight for a moment. But almost immediately, the heaviness and confusion settled back down upon her. She groaned.

Within the steam, a woman's voice came to her from across the room. "We all think we're bad mothers. Only the bad mothers don't think that."

Mary jerked back from the shock of the sound, her naked ass slipping a bit along the slick tiled bench. "Oh! I thought I was alone. Oh God, you scared me. I can't see you. I thought I was alone."

"We are alone. Mormon, huh?"

"How'd you know?"

"The 'Thee' is a dead giveaway. Thee, thou, thine: Mormon, Mormon, and . . . Mormon."

"Of course," Mary confessed, lifting Hyrum's joke. "I feel more like a moron . . . moron . . . moron . . . these days."

"You're discouraged, you said? I seem to recall the prophet said something about never being discouraged. 'If I were sunk in the lowest pits of Nova Scotia, with the Rocky Mountains piled on me, I would hang on, exercise faith, and keep good courage, and I would come out on top.'"

"Thank you. That's helpful. My name is Mary." Mary kept peering into the steam to make out a figure, but it was way too thick.

"But you're not really a Mormon, are you?" the woman asked.

"What do you mean?"

"Not a Mormon born. What happens to a woman when her justifications outweigh her foundations?"

"What? What does that mean?" Mary thought it meant something profound, but she wasn't sure.

"Wanda Barzee."

"Nice to meet you, Wanda."

But Mary thought she knew that name, Wanda Barzee, from long ago. Another name floated to her in the mist—Brian David Mitchell. It was a big news story. A crazy Mormon polygamist who'd criticized modern chemical approaches to illness and gone off his meds. Aided by one wife, Wanda Barzee, he'd kidnapped some beautiful young girl to make her another one of his wives. She couldn't remember the young girl's name.

"Elizabeth Smart," the other woman said, as if reading Mary's mind.

"Oh yeah," Mary said. "God, what a nightmare. I hope she's okay." Mary was talking like this was a normal steam room conversation, but this woman across from her was claiming to be Wanda

Barzee, an infamous figure, one of that species of sad, co-dependent criminals, women who aid and abet men in hurting other women.

"You hope she's okay? She ain't okay," the steam woman said. "Nobody is ever 'okay' after that. Elizabeth Smart. Wanda Barzee. Brian David Mitchell. Ammon Bundy. Bronson Powers."

Even in the heavy wet, Mary could feel the hairs on the back of her neck stand up now. "What?"

So many scenarios flashed through her mind about this woman across from her. Was she sent by a local Mormon church to test her faith? Was she sent by the Praetorian people to fuck with her, to weaken her? Was she a local mother who had somehow heard about the yearlong school experiment and was appalled by it? Mary didn't want to say another word until she figured out who this adversary was and what her agenda might be. But the woman kept speaking, "Who were you before you were Mary Castiglione? Jackie Young. Pearl Young Powers. Not a one of them okay."

Mary stood up quickly and got lightheaded. She'd been in the steam too long. Her legs were weak. This was getting too weird too fast. "Who do you think you are?" she demanded.

"Elizabeth."

"Elizabeth? You're Elizabeth Smart?"

"Wanda Barzee."

"You're Wanda Barzee?"

"Pearl Powers."

"You got a hell of a fucking nerve."

"I am what I am. I'm every woman, like the song goes," the woman continued. "Chaka Khan. I'm you."

"What?"

Mary moved slowly toward the origin of the voice, her hands held straight out in front like a woman walking in dark woods, like she might strangle someone. "Who the fuck are you?" she asked. "What's your name?" Mary thought she might kick this woman's ass right here, right now in the hot white cloud.

Mary got to the other side of the steam room, but there was no one there. She felt around with her hands and even her feet, trying to make contact with anything human. Was this crazy lady crouching, hiding? But there was no one else. She was totally alone in the steam room. This woman must've slipped out. But no, Mary would've noticed the door opening, felt the rush of cold air. Mary opened the glass door and looked around to see if anyone was close and wet and sweaty, a suspect. There was no one. The locker room was virtually empty, and the few women there were in street clothes and dry. She kept the door open to let enough steam out so she could see the entire room. There was no one in there. Mary's hands were shaking again as they had when she was young.

Spooked, Mary fled to her locker and was dressing quickly when a woman she had superficially befriended in the Equinox manner a few weeks earlier, named Frankie, came hobbling by on crutches. She'd had a car accident and was recovering from a broken leg. She was just gonna do arms and abs today. Having worked as a stuntwoman, Mary was quite knowledgeable about how to recover from bangs, breaks, and bruises. Frankie was appreciative for all the professional insight. Mary warned her about the Percocet she was taking for the pain, said she should throw it away, that the body had its own healing system if you let it be, and natural painkillers called endorphins, and that she could bring her local homeopathic remedies naturally available in the desert. Frankie reluctantly, then enthusiastically, agreed, and tossed it, wiping her hands clean of the devil's Big Pharma drugs. The two women high-fived. After Frankie walked out of the locker room grimacing on her crutches with nothing to dull her pain, Mary retrieved the bottle from the trash. It was almost full. She brought the pills home.

That evening, still rattled by the steam, Mary was besieged by old thoughts and memories—she wondered how her adoptive parents, the Castigliones, were. She had dropped them a line now and then when she ran away to California, along with a couple tortured calls from pay phones, but the old working-class Catholic couple had expressed only confusion, anger, and censure at their daughter's life, her hair, her sexual choices, and soon Mary had cut them off completely, cut the whole family off. It was easier that way, all or nothing. Once her new roots were planted firmly in the desert, she had resigned herself to never seeing her parents again, or her siblings, or—and this was a new thought—her biological parents, whom she knew nothing about, and had never cared to investigate for fear of wounding or betraying the Castigliones. In her mind, Mary had arrived on this planet sui generis, self-made, a true orphan.

But this computer in her hand, this phone that was new to her, inspired all the questions; indeed, like an ancient oracle, it had all the questions and all the answers, and all the answers led to more questions. She tentatively googled "Francis and Maria Castiglione Elizabeth New Jersey" and two obits popped up. Just like that, in a blink, with a wave of a fingertip, her parents, who had been alive in her mind moments before, were dead now, long dead. There was even a picture of her father. She cried for them. Three of her eight siblings were dead. Dizzy, she had to sit down, then she had to lie down. She was overwhelming herself, the electronic revelations, the sudden reckoning of the passage of time suffocating her, but she couldn't stop—easy information at her fingertips was like a drug. She was about to try to figure out how to investigate her birth parents when she told herself to turn off the phone, and that she might soon reach out to one of her siblings, maybe one day find out who her real parents were, and if they were even alive, but not now. She jammed the phone away in her pocket.

The rest of the evening, as she made dinner for the kids, she was alternately in a sleepwalking type of trance or overcome with deep sobs, rising up from her gut. She ran to the bathroom to hide the convulsions from the children. Deuce noticed that Mary didn't eat a thing. After the dishes were done, with Pearl in bed, Deuce doing homework, and Hyrum deep in a Fortnite marathon, Mary stared at the vial of pills on the sink as she brushed her teeth. The vial of pills stared back. She swallowed one down. Almost immediately, the feeling was similar to that of meeting an old, dear friend. As the warmth settled deeper, penetrating her bones, and her head got fuzzy, she recalled vaguely that this particular old friend had broken her heart, and that he had also stolen from her, crashed her car, and owed her money, and that he should not, under any circumstances, be trusted. But by then it was too late. She was not a person who could give herself structure, and away from Bronson, she had felt the old chaos encroaching again. She couldn't stand that quotidian mess, the duration of a day stretching out ahead with nothing but worry and projection. The little pills made her feel okay in the chaos.

But what was the big problem anyway? she asked herself. She was alone with three kids and no help. She had no friends and nothing to do, and besides, this was only a temp fix—the summer would roll around soon enough, and this test would be over, and they would win and get back to their lives as they were, more or less. She just needed to survive and this would enable her to. Sure, there'd be no way to get pills once back out in the desert, but out there she wouldn't need them. Problem solved. Uncomfortable maybe, but solved. No harm, no foul. Her major concern was where to get more when Frankie's vial ran out.

One night in late October, sleeping and sleeping off a high, Mary was awakened in her bed by a dark stranger kissing her lips. For a moment, she thought she was about to be raped. She tensed to push the stranger to the floor and scream, but these kisses were so gentle, and the feel familiar, and as her eyes adjusted from sleep to darkness, she could make out Yalulah smiling above her, moaning, "Baby, baby, baby, baby . . ."

17.

AFTER MAKING LOVE with an intensity they hadn't reached in years, Mary and Yalulah held on to each other. They were both so hungry for reconnection, and the time apart had lent a newness and shine to the easy routine of longtime lovers. "I'm in love again." Yalulah sighed.

"Aw, baby . . ." Mary sighed back.

"With your mattress."

"Oh my god, right? Me too." They laughed and cuddled some more; just feeling the weight of body on body was good to the both of them. "We'll always have Rancho Cucamonga," Mary joked.

Yaya stroked Mary's hair and looked toward the windows. "I forgot how it never really gets dark out here."

"Or quiet."

"I'm sorry, baby. I just missed you so. I had to disobey the prime directive."

"I'm happy you did. I didn't know how horny I was."

Yaya laughed again. "I gotta get back soon or Bro' is gonna be suspicious."

"Bro' don't know?"

"No, baby, he's not in great shape; he's spending the night out in the desert with his peep stones looking for answers. I put the kids to bed and snuck out. Hope no one wakes up. He's getting headaches again. He's going through something deep and very, very—male."

"Shit. Sometimes I dream that he comes to kidnap us and take us back to the desert."

Yalulah nodded like that was a real possibility. Distance had given, at best, an illusion of separateness and independence. A hundred miles and three months was nothing in the face of Bronson Powers and twenty years of enmeshment.

"Tell me about Agadda da Vida," Mary said. She didn't want to say, but she missed her biological daughter above all else. Yalulah knew her woman.

"Beautiful is about to get her period, I think, and she's writing some amazing apocalyptic poetry, she writes so well."

"Apocalyptic? Jesus. But she's okay?"

"Misses you, but she's okay. Alvin thinks you're all dead like Jackie, and Joseph wets the bed three or four times a week. Lovina Love thinks you've been abducted by aliens who like to do things with your assholes. Other than that, we're aces."

Mary laughed a little and nodded. "Oh, Lovina. Did we screw up her toilet training?"

Yalulah laughed too. "You know, it's like one of those mobiles with lots of different parts, if you hit one part, all the other parts move, too. We are all still joined in the same mobile."

"Yes, we are."

"Forever." They held on to each other. They'd closed a lot of the distance by making love, but there was some stubborn terrain between them still.

"Uh, what did you do to your pussy?" Yalulah asked.

Mary shot up to sitting. "Whaddya mean 'do'? Is there something wrong with it?"

"It's . . . how can I put it . . . streamlined?"

Mary looked at her quizzically. "Huh?"

"Uh, economical . . . aerodynamic?"

"Oh, yeah." Mary laughed. "Bald. I shaved it!"

"No shit. With a razor?"

"No, with a lawn mower; yes, with a razor."

"Are you a porn star now?" Yalulah teased.

"No, it's what all the women do now. Not just the porn stars. What do you think?"

"It's . . . interesting. It's just right there—like, 'Hi, nice to meet you.' Unencumbered."

"That's not a sexy word."

"Well, I like you the way God made you."

"God made me fucked up."

"God made you perfectly . . . fucked up."

"That's the nicest thing."

"Tell me about Rancho Cucamonga," Yalulah said.

"Haven't lost any of the kids, so pat on the back for me. I mean, it's hard to say. Deuce is lonely, I think. His skin is a mess."

"Really?"

"Yeah, acne, and it's made him a little withdrawn."

"Understandable. Poor thing."

"But he's such a good guy. His heart is pure. It's like he got Jackie's heart and Pearl got her soul."

"How is Miss Pearl?"

"She hasn't really made any friends either."

"That's okay, nobody is putting down roots."

"Yeah, it's okay for Pearl. Pearl is cold-blooded, you know, she's a survivor. She scares me sometimes, she's twice as tough as I am. Which is good, 'cause . . . well, as beautiful as she is . . ." Mary trailed off.

Yalulah nodded. "I wouldn't know."

Mary kissed Yalulah's creased forehead and thought about telling her of the woman in the steam room, but the whole thing was so odd that she didn't want to share it, as if sharing it with Yaya would make it more real, and then maybe Yaya would think she was losing her shit. Maybe she was. She'd rather forget about it, if that were a possibility.

"And Hyrum? How is that little Neanderthal?"

"Honestly, Hyrum is just okay. He misses the desert and the hunting and the arrows and guns and all that."

"Who wouldn't miss being Mowgli?"

"Exactly. He's come home with a couple bruises, so he's probably scrapping with other kids a little, but he's really the only one of the three that's brought a friend home, which is good, right? He talks about joining the wrestling team. I can't get him to crack a book."

"Nothing new there."

"I guess that's okay for now, though. Don't mind him not learning anything here—good for us for the end-of-the-year test, I guess."

"Yup. No girls yet for Hy?"

"Oh God, no, I don't think he has any pubes."

"Just like you."

"Ha, yeah, I guess it's a trend."

Yalulah brushed Mary's hair from her face. "Wow," she said, "your hair is so soft."

"It's called shampoo."

"Shampoo! I remember shampoo." She inhaled the sweet chemical fragrance off Mary's scalp. "I gotta get going," Yalulah said, getting up, then pausing and adding, "Do you wanna come back with me, baby? All of you. You know, call this whole thing off? I did some research and we could get loans on the worth of the land and hire lawyers and fight this thing in perpetuity. We can be the same as we were. It'll be a hassle, but our lives will go back to the way they were."

Mary still tasted Yalulah on her lips, but her mouth was dry and she wanted a Percocet. She got out of bed and said, "We can never be the way we were." She saw Yalulah's face fall. "But it won't be long now, Yaya. We can make it."

"Five long months."

"It'll go by quick." Mary disappeared into the bathroom to drink some water from the faucet. And stealthily pop a Percocet. She called out, "Water doesn't taste like water here."

"What does it taste like?"

"Almost water."

"Aw. I miss that."

"What?"

Yalulah popped her head into the bathroom. "The sound of your piss."

Mary farted, loudly echoing in the bowl. "How 'bout that? Miss that?"

"Not as much. But kinda. I saw coffee in the fridge, you rebel," Yalulah sang.

"Guilty."

"Can I have some?"

"Be my guest."

"'A friend of the devil is a friend of mine.'"

"Uh-huh. I thought you were a Starbucks gal."

"Very funny. I mean, it's just 'cause I don't want to fall asleep on the drive back."

Mary came back in from the bathroom. "Of course. You should probably put a couple gallons in the tank so Bronson doesn't notice."

Yalulah picked her shirt up off the floor, sniffed it, and grimaced.

"Can I borrow a shirt, too? I wanna wear my baby's shirt," Yalulah said as she opened the closet door and about ten Ugg boots came tumbling out like a soft wall had crumbled, a wall of Uggs that Mary had constructed against the chaos of her mind.

"What the hell?" Yalulah said. "These are all brand new." She dug deeper in the closet. It was filled with never-worn Uggs in all the available styles and colors, boots piled upon unopened boxes. She stared in amazement at Mary.

Mary shrugged. "You don't even have to go to the store

anymore, you get on your phone and order, and pay electronically. It's like you get it for free."

"But you don't, you know."

"I know. It's somehow wonderful and diabolical at the same time. I guess I got carried away, lost track. I love me some Uggs." Truth was, she'd shop while high and then forget that she'd bought anything until a package arrived, and the surprise, though embarrassing, was also pleasant—a gift. Somebody up there likes me. Like a prayer answered within three business days.

"I guess." Something in Yalulah sensed there was more here, a thread that should be pulled, that this mountain of brushed suede might be covering something more significant, and should be analyzed psychologically. But it was late and she had to go. Instead, she just asked, "Should I worry?"

Mary pouted. "I don't know why I'm the one here for this year. You were always the way more practical one. Jackie was the hardass boss and you were always the voice of reason, and I was somewhere in the middle—nothing. You should be here, not me."

"I need to teach them English and history back home. They need to test off the charts at the end of the year. And you're not 'nothing,' my baby."

"Right. I forgot. The fucking test."

"Unfortunately, they're gonna have to do without painting and music for the year, though Solomona, you'll be happy to hear, is filling in quite nicely."

"Solomona can draw a line."

"Oh, and Little Joe tried to use his poop as paint last week, though. We didn't quite know what to say."

"Multimedia genius." They laughed. "Yeah, yeah, I get it now." Mary continued, "I keep asking myself—what would Jackie do? I've been thinking a lot about her these days. Every time I pass a hospital, I think . . . maybe, you know?"

"You can't think that."

"I can't help it, and I don't think Bronson can help it either; I don't think he's been the same since she died. Something in him broke watching her suffer for so long, something broke in him about his God, why did God make her suffer so fucking long? I just know it. He lost something when she got cancer and didn't get treatment. He lost more than a wife."

"You shouldn't think about that."

"It ripped something out of him, the fullness of his belief. And it's like he's trying to replace it, but he doesn't really know what he's trying to replace. Like he's trying to fill the Jackie-shaped hole, the God-shaped hole."

"If his faith could be broken by adversity, then it was no real faith."

That sounded so hollow to Mary, she didn't even respond. Her tongue was starting to feel thick from the drug. She didn't want to give it away. But the drug also made her less guarded, vulnerable. Mary began to cry. "How can we live with a man for so long and not know him? We failed him."

Yalulah wrapped Mary in a hug. She was the larger woman, and Mary melted and folded into her like a puzzle piece.

"That's why we have each other."

"You know I was afraid," Mary sniffed, "with me gone, that you and Bronson would fall in love again, and I'd be left out in the cold, this old spinster. I thought you came here to tell me that."

"Seriously? That is so adorable."

"Fuck you."

"And wrong. No . . . baby, baby, baby . . . ssssh." Yalulah stroked Mary's fragrant hair. "I want you, and only you."

"Yeah, yeah, Yaya."

"Yeah."

Mary reached for a tissue to blow her nose. She needed fresh air, so she went to open a window. Her legs were wobbly. It had begun to rain a bit. Big fat splashes on the hot cement street below. She shook her hands out and put on a light purple pair of slippers and began prancing around the room like a Ukrainian folk dancer, yet another skill she'd forgotten she had from a childhood suddenly reappearing out of some unconscious store of muscle memory. She was naked but for her furry slippers, singing. This had the desired effect—to break the spell with comic relief—and Yalulah laughed, disarmed.

Mary hugged her sister-wife, saw the concern in her eyes. "We are good here. That's what the kids say—You good? I'm good. All good." Mary made some faux gang hand signals while she spoke.

"What are you doing?" Yalulah seemed irritated.

"I don't know, that's what the kids do when they talk now."

"Stop it." She took Mary's hands in hers a little more aggressively than she'd intended. She so often fed on and delighted in Mary's exuberance, but right now she felt annoyed by it. Mary looked hurt, so Yaya apologized in her way.

"But I do like that—'All good,'" Yalulah repeated. "All is good. Thank Thee, Heavenly Father God, Thou hast made all and all is good. Pray with me, Mother Mary."

Mary didn't want to pray. Last time she tried to pray was in the steam room and look what happened there. But with her drug coming on and covering her in slow carelessness, she felt her will leave her. She was nothing but compliance.

The two women knelt among the Uggs and prayed. They prayed for guidance, they prayed for forgiveness, and they prayed for Bronson and their children. When they had finished, Yalulah kissed her good-bye and whispered, "Look, baby, listen to me, Bronson says he'll stop."

Mary pulled back. "Stop?" If one word could make her sober in an instant, that was it. Her carelessness fled. She shook her head as hard as a dog does to rouse itself.

"Stop."

"Just stop."

"Yeah."

"For how long?" Mary demanded.

Yalulah didn't answer, she didn't have the answer.

"I don't even know that they've consummated it," she said.

"Don't be stupid."

"I don't, and neither do you."

"Well, if they didn't, it's only a matter of time. And what about Pearl?" Mary kept on. "Is she gonna just stop, too?"

"Pearl will do what we tell her."

"Bullshit."

"We're the adults. We can handle Pearl. We are only as sick as our secrets," Yaya said, throwing one of Mary's favored NA sayings at her. "And now it's not a secret; it's in the light now. We can handle anything in the light of God."

"Is that why you came here? To tell me that?" Mary's hands were tingling. She flexed them and looked at them like they belonged to someone else.

"No, I missed you. I miss us. All of us," Yalulah pleaded.

"The age of consent in California is eighteen."

"In Canada, it's sixteen."

"Fuck Canada."

"Oh, please, Miss Manners, were you a virgin at seventeen?"

"That's not the point." Mary's voice was rising. "I lost my virginity at thirteen. I got raped at fifteen, and I fucked half of Venice and a good chunk of Los Feliz by the time I was sixteen. Shit, maybe that is the point."

"Baby, baby, shhh . . . In 1889, the age of consent was fourteen. That's all I'm saying. It's relative, and kind of arbitrary." Yalulah remained even and calm, marshaling factoids to her defense. "Man's law, not God's. Man's law guesses and changes, God's law remains, immutable and sacred."

"Jesus, Yaya, it's like you use God when you need him and psychology when you don't."

Yalulah nodded in agreement as if to say, yes, that is exactly what I am doing. "He could marry her. I know that's not the fairy tale; it's not the optimum situation, and I know most of the world would look down on that, on him and on them, on all of us, but since when have we cared about what most of the world thinks? Fuck them. And God knows, it's probably what Jackie would want."

Mary felt herself falling through the air, but soberly; she wanted to hold on to something. That something was usually Yalulah, but not Yalulah right now, anything but Yalulah right now. "You're a mother." Mary said it like a curse.

Yalulah did not blink. "Yes, I am, but I am not *her* mother, and neither are you, and he is not *her* father and I'm asking you to think about it. There's nothing 'wrong' with it. It's not real incest." That dread word had been spoken and could not be unspoken. They stared at each other silently in tacit acknowledgment that there was no going back from here—from that utterance a new world born. Mary could think of some things wrong with it.

"Listen to yourself, Yaya. You just said 'real incest.'"

"I know what I said."

"Is that how he talks about it?" Mary asked.

"He doesn't talk about it directly."

"What's he said, *indirectly*?"

"He hasn't said anything, Mary. This is my interpretation. I think he's confused, and scared, and maybe ashamed of himself, and feels like he's being punished. I think he feels it's more of a modern hangup. Probably feels this is how Bible Man did it. Probably thinks Joseph Smith would have no problem with it. He's a good man, Mary—"

"I know he's a good man," Mary cut her off. "Yaya, please . . ."

"I think he will defer to you. To your feelings. To your cultural bias."

"Fuck me, did you say 'cultural bias'?"

"Yes."

"Is that what he said?" Mary asked angrily. Yaya nodded. Mary was not at all sure she was telling the truth. She couldn't imagine Bronson saying that. He didn't talk like that.

Yalulah was hell-bent on making inroads, but didn't want to press too hard right away. She could sense Mary at her limit for this at the moment. There was time. Mary would come around. "Think about it, Mary?" she pleaded. "We'll have each other." Oh.

"Right."

"I'll visit again soon, baby."

Mary nodded. "I'll think about it," she lied; well, she would think about it, all right, but not the way Yalulah wanted her to. Yalulah kissed her again; Mary didn't like the smell of her all of a sudden, something stale and off. Mary tried to hide this sudden repulsion and attempted to relax herself by welcoming the warm feelings of the Percocet back inside.

"Are you okay? All good?" Yalulah asked, lamely trying to play along, putting a Band-Aid on a gunshot wound.

"Yup," Mary said, and she started dancing again. "We good, Yaya. We good. All good." Mary laughed, pulling away farther, Ukrainian dancing, and flashing signs she didn't know the meaning of.

18.

WHILE YALULAH AND MARY communed secretly in Rancho Cucamonga on a cool, early December night, Bronson rode out to his new sacred place in the desert, where they had relocated the three graves after Maya's intrusion, to commune with the dead, and his God. His head was throbbing, as it had been for hours. The light of day caused a searing pain behind his eyes that would have sent a man with less work and will to bed with the shades drawn. The darkness of night brought a modicum of relief.

He knelt first at the graves of his two dead children, Carthage and Nauvoo. He thanked God for the short time he had spent with them. He put his hand on Carthage's marker and did his best to recall the bodily form his "first estate" had taken. Carthage had been stillborn of Jackie, her third and last child, and her only child with Bronson. Jackie had held her dead boy in her arms for hours, talking to the perfect, little lifeless form, and having the kids come to say hello and goodbye to the baby brother they had been expecting. Only after each child had said their piece, only then had Jackie allowed Bronson to take their baby away. That was Jackie's way, to meet everything head-on, eyes open. If Delilah had been the spur to Bronson's faith, Jackie was its rock and its seal. She presented with tumors for the first time just a few months after losing Carthage.

Now Bronson moved to touch Nauvoo's grave. Nauvoo had come out of Yalulah a half-formed thing herself, riddled with multiple deformities. She never ate, never took the breast. Terrified, Yalulah put this unfortunate babe to her breast, but the tiny mouth refused to latch on and suckle; as if she knew better, that it would only prolong her agony. Yalulah could plainly see that medicine could not save this poor baby, and she was deeply ashamed that in her heart, unspoken, she prayed for the child's suffering to be brief. She had no idea how to care for such a thing. It was a horrible blessing when Nauvoo starved and succumbed after a few days. But Bronson would save her soul nonetheless. Nauvoo's soul would not be deformed. Her first estate was perfect from God. He would perform a baptism of the dead for Nauvoo and Carthage. Death was nothing to a man with his beliefs, but a moment in time, time that did not really exist. Just the pause between an inhalation and an exhalation. Yalulah had been shattered by Nauvoo's birth, her faith rocked more than she would ever let on, her anger at God commensurate to her faith, but she gave birth to Palmyra thirteen months later, and then Ephraim and Alvin and Little Joe, and they had all moved on, as they say, as best they could. God took Nauvoo away, but He gave them so much more, so much more health and fertility and abundance, as if in apology.

Bronson was secretly racked with doubt for not seeking medical attention for the births and babies, or for Jackie. He was also concerned that Maya or that Janet Bergram would find out now about the buried children and accuse him of some modern crime. But this was God's will. He had trusted in God's will, and Nauvoo, poor Nauvoo, poor, half-made-up, small-headed, innocent Nauvoo— nothing, he was sure, could have saved her. He put his hand on the marker under which the infant bones lay, caressing the stone as if it were flesh, as if it could feel, and he began to weep. "Nauvoo," he said over and over to his baby girl. "Poor Nauvoo, poor, sweet Nauvoo." He then moved on to Jackie's grave.

He met Jackie at the Los Angeles California Temple in West-wood, which he'd begun to frequent shortly after his "worthiness" interview with Elder, while he was still puzzling over how to square his newfound landowning wealth and newfound faith with the hard-partying Hollywood stuntman he'd been. Elder greased the wheels for him to worship there (as far as possible from the elder Elder in Utah, of course). Bronson dug the fact that the church was built on a huge parcel of land, a million square feet, that the silent-movie star Harold Lloyd had purchased for a movie ranch in the 1920s. The conversion of the land itself from movie ranch into a Mormon church seemed to foreshadow and mirror exactly his own path.

Jackie, thirty at the time, and still sporting the sculpted thighs of a college tennis player (third singles, first doubles at BYU), had started up a conversation with Bronson in that friendly, outgoing Mormon custom. He had seemed out of place to her, in a good way. As opposed to the soft, fish-belly white, bespectacled sixty-year-old seeming forty-year-old men that populated most of her working day at the Church, Bronson was tan and strong, vital. She thought he was beautiful and rare as a movie star. Jackie had been raised a Mormon in Salt Lake and had left for Los Angeles for a new start when her marriage ended. Just two months after giving birth to her twins, Pearl and Deuce, she had discovered her college sweetheart husband in bed with another young Mormon man. She asked no questions. Jackie closed the bedroom door and filed for divorce. She was like that, irrevocable.

As she packed her bags, she told her husband that she would take the children and he would not hear from her or them again. In shock, and maybe relieved, he had not argued. She had a law degree she'd never used and got herself a tiny apartment in Westwood and a clerk-type job for the Church itself. She was getting back on her feet when she met Bronson, but she lived with the constant fear that her ex would one day have a change of heart and try to track her down and take away her kids. Eventually, she knew, she wanted to disappear more completely to ensure that from ever happening.

They were both isolated from their former selves. Jackie knew no one in Los Angeles. No longer drinking, Bronson lost the common denominator with his running crew and hung out with his stuntman Hollywood fraternity less and less. Alone together, they folded into each other, rarely leaving each other's side. They were equals, student and teacher for each other. With her Utah pedigree in the church, she gave his faith depth and legitimacy; with his newly converted enthusiasm, he reinvigorated her sleeping love of God, and reinforced any belief that might have been weakened by her husband's betrayal. Bronson and Jackie soon went deeper into the differences between Smith's original, revolutionary vector and institutionalized, Americanized Mormonism. They pushed into the fringes of the scriptures, egging each other on in a type of Mormon folie à deux.

Bronson found himself falling for Jackie's mind, the intensity of her faith, but he was also overwhelmingly attracted to her. And she to him. And even though she was a divorcee, she would not make love to Bronson out of the seal of marriage. They made out for hours and hours, though. Like they were in high school. Bronson was giddy with the flush of true romance and the idea of a new life. When Bronson told her the story of his family and Delilah's inheritance, it was Jackie's idea to get married and have a family out in the desert. It was also her idea that Bronson should take more than one wife, that polygamy was a natural state and a restoration of the biblical way—and, quoting the prophet, "with more worthy women than men, some women would not be exalted without plural marriage." When she said slyly that she might like a few husbands as well, Bronson immediately asked her to marry him, saying, "I'd like to be first in line."

They were wed in the Los Angeles Temple, officially sealed by the Mormon Church, a celestial eternal bond. For their vows, they chose 1 Corinthians 13:1–2. Jackie chanted, "If I speak in the tongues of men and of angels, but have not love, I am a noisy gong or clanging cymbal."

Bronson continued the verse from there, "And if I have prophetic powers, and understand all mysteries and all knowledge, and if I have all faith, so as to remove mountains, but have not love, I am nothing."

After the ceremony, Jackie toasted Bronson with a glass of sparkling apple juice, using the words of the prophet Joseph Smith himself as a benediction and hope for a perfectable future: "'As man now is, God once was. As God now is, man may be.'"

She was the love of his life, and the first sister-wife, and subsequently, Bronson had brought Mary and then Yalulah to her for approval. After a decade in the desert, when Jackie died of cancer, refusing Bronson's entreaties to let him take her to a hospital, he had fallen into a deep, bottomless funk. He sleepwalked through a year, maybe more. He absented himself from the kids, from Mary and Yaya, from everything except the hard work Agadda da Vida demanded. It was during that time when Bronson was "away" that Yaya and Mary had fallen truly, deeply in love as a couple. When Bronson awoke again from his grieving slumber, he was the odd man out. He'd felt more or less alone since then. Until Pearl.

Pearl reminded him eerily of Jackie. Mother and daughter had had an inexplicable bond, inside jokes, even a little made-up language that only they understood. They were like witches in a coven of two. One night near the end, as Jackie lay in her sickbed and Bronson sat beside her, stroking her hand, she asked, "You won't forget me, will you, Bronson Powers?"

Bronson did not even need to answer, but nonetheless, he said, "Never."

She goaded him sweetly, "Man is resilient. Time passes, memory fades."

"Stop it, love," he said gently. Her hand in his looked unrecognizable, like a Halloween gag, a dinosaur claw, it was so large and red and swollen, larger now than his, even. She held his eyes, and motioned for him to lean in like she would tell him a secret.

She smiled, and when her lips parted he could smell rank death on her weak breath. "Look for me in Pearl when I'm gone. She's my secret sharer. Look for me in Pearl's eyes." It was the last thing she said to him. She closed her green eyes, slipped into sleep, and died a few days later.

Pearl had taken Jackie's dying the hardest. She had refused to go in and say goodbye to her in the final days, and did not watch as she was buried. Bronson was the only one from whom Pearl would accept even the smallest solace, and indeed, she was the only one that he would accept consolation from as well. They grew very close, and as she grew up, Bronson, as Jackie had instructed, secretly looked for Jackie in the child, and he had found her. It was unmistakable, uncanny. It seemed almost a performance of his dead love, a haunting, a channeling, a cohabitation. He was both horrified and delighted. He was mystified and terrified of Pearl. For her part, Pearl doted on him as only a young girl can dote on a father.

And still he had kept a certain distance from her. Even as she grew into a woman, he remained aloof enough. When she hit puberty, he unconsciously distanced himself further and further. He saw how hurt she was that her remaining confidant and best friend had taken himself away for no reason she could fathom, but he could do nothing about that pain, could say nothing to assuage it, as he was the cause and the cure.

He had stopped himself even as she made herself so clear to him, dared him, teased him, exercising in the loneliness and safety of their desert bubble her nascent sexual power, staring at him constantly with a mixture of possessiveness and delight. Yes, he had stopped himself. He had ignored her. She would not be ignored. She was vain and proud. He didn't blame her. He knew this was natural. She was as perfect as the God that made her. He knew he was the only thing standing between them. The pressure was enormous, the thoughts constant.

He slept sandwiched safely between Mary and Yalulah, even though they didn't seem to want him there. He felt hunted. And yet in the daylight hours, he couldn't stop himself from being near

Pearl. Patting her on the head, looking at her. When she would dismiss his company or ignore him, he sulked, moody and moony as a teenager. But he had weathered the initial storm of those years. He had guided her through with paternal love and restraint. Thoughts were just thoughts. He had done the right thing.

Fifteen and sixteen passed for Pearl, and Bronson felt they had made it past their own Scylla and Charybdis. But when she turned seventeen, Pearl seemed to get hostile and antsy all over again, and with greater intensity and ingenuity. She started flirting with Bronson overtly. It pissed him off. It pissed Mary and Yalulah off. Still, Bronson knew it was natural for her. It was her life force. It was nature and God expressing Himself through this body. And as Pearl matured, she became ever more and more like her mother, Jackie. So much so that sometimes it hurt Bronson to look at Pearl and remember his dead love.

He locked the door of his room when he left Mary and Yalulah to their own devices and he slept alone. Night after night, he could hear a tentative hand try the door handle and then walk away. He knew it wasn't Mary or Yaya. He could've locked the door forever. How hard would that have been? But he didn't. He didn't. One night, he had left his bedroom door unlocked and Pearl had slipped into his bed. And then he hadn't stopped himself. He did not send her away. He did not. He welcomed her into his bed and heart. He felt love again, a kind of love for Pearl, simple and deep, complicated by circumstance.

Mary seemed to hate him for it now, sure, probably Yaya, too, but Mary had love with Yaya and Yaya with Mary. Where was Bronson's? For without love, as his wedding vows had proclaimed, a man had nothing. The psychology of it all was messy and confusing, and he ran from it. He did not believe in psychology. They were mere animals, hairless apes, after all, without faith. Baboons. Without faith, we are all beasts engaged in endless violence and domination in different dress over the epochs. Same-o same-o. He did not believe in the march of progress. He did not believe in cultural relativism. He was no modern man. He believed in the restoration of the ancient scripture, as commanded in Acts 3:21, a "restitution of all things." Restoration and restitution was his calling. He remembered Holden Caulfield catching those kids in the rye. That was him, too. A catcher and a savior, a restorer of things and souls. He had restored the word of God in the desert. He was a king in the desert. A desert king like David.

David and Bathsheba, he thought.

And then came this rupture. His kingdom had been split apart, his faith challenged, weakened. His pride and fear had made him rise to the bait of this stupid wager. But it was only pride, wasn't it? Had the rupture happened even before that woman had stumbled upon them? Had he done what he'd accused his wives of—treating the whole belief system like a menu from which he'd choose the laws that suited his taste? That was the question. All alone in his desert, he had not kept the ordinances. He had countenanced homosexuality. He had practiced sex outside of marriage. He had been lax with the law. He had loosened his hold on the reins. He felt that God had communicated to him what He would accept. But that struck him in this moment as pride, expediency, rationalization, maybe evil. He recalled Christ from the Sermon on the Mount— "whoever relaxes one of the least of these commandments and teaches others to do the same will be called least in the kingdom of heaven." Was he himself the snake in the garden? It could not be so. It could not be. What was the cure? A return to origins. Always. That was always the cure. Start at the beginning again. Reinvigorate the word, the law. The law.

He knew he was not a murderer like King David. He hadn't abused his power like that, had he? He hadn't acted in such ways as to place himself beyond forgiveness, beyond the atoning blood of Christ. He quoted out loud from memory, "When the wife of Uriah heard that Uriah her husband was dead, she mourned for her husband. And when her mourning was over, David sent and brought her to his house, and she became his wife and bore him a son. But the thing that David had done displeased the Lord."* When her mourning was over. When the mourning was over. When was this "when"? But the thing. The thing. But the thing David had done. Displeased the Lord.

Bronson hung his head and cried.

Since he had been sealed to her in celestial marriage, Bronson knew that Jackie's first estate was in Heaven, and that she could hear him. He didn't even have to speak out loud for her to hear all this about Pearl. Jackie was in his mind. She could hear his thoughts. She knew all. That was not what he had come here for tonight. He had heard his thoughts circling and circling for months now; he was all too well acquainted with them. He had come to see if he could hear Jackie. But all was silent, and that silence felt like censure, judgment. There was no wind, no rustling, no howling or scurrying of animals. His love would not speak to him. He felt a banishment; his desert paradise seemed all the world to him now a barren thing, east of Eden.

Jackie was dead. The desert was quiet. God was AWOL. This was surely his fault. He had sinned. He could not hear his beloved, his land, or his Lord. Suddenly, without a sound or warning, with neither thunder nor lightning, it began to rain.

---

* 2 Samuel 11:26–27.

19.

HAMMER FILMS HAD EATEN her mind. There was nothing left. Just crumbs of bad horror, wooden stakes, wooden acting, and rotting celluloid. That's it, Maya thought, that's the only decent movie that could come out of this pile of dreck—*Hammer Films Have Eaten My Brain*—the story of a young professional woman with an advanced degree who catches a deadly brain virus ("More of a meme, or a deadly earworm than a virus, if you will. We've located it in the amygdala, Chief, the so-called lizard brain") from watching too many shitty B movies. When our heroine tells you the plot, like that of 1970's *The Vampire Lovers* from the so-called Karnstein Trilogy ("a peaceful hamlet in eighteenth-century Europe is home to a female vampire with lesbian tendencies who ravages the townsfolk"), you barf, shit yourself, and die, and your bodily fluids infect the next poor sucker with rotten ideas till he too explodes with infectious stupidity. She listened to the actual trailer voice over and over in condescending wonderment—"Sample, if you dare, the deadly passion of the vampire lovers—perverted creatures of the night." What heinous genius!

These creatures of the night overtook her waking and sleeping hours. The long nights especially were Hammer time—her dreams seemingly directed by that Hammer mainstay, the "uncouth, uneducated, disgusting, and vulgar" stylist, Mr. Jimmy Sangster. Perhaps Malouf would like his sexy vampires younger, as in '71's *Lust for a*

Vampire, in which a "temptress does Count Karnstein's [that kooky Karnstein again!] biting at a finishing school in nineteenth-century Styria." Biting, not bidding, get it? Well played. Styria? She had to look up Styria. It's a state in Austria that borders Slovenia. Maya wondered how the real estate was there. She thought maybe she'd move to Styria, start over.

But not before she watched *The Quatermass Xperiment* (1955)— yes, that's right, you autocorrect cowards, no *E* in *Xperiment*, only one *R* in *Quatermass,* in Hammer world—wherein an "astronaut returns to Earth after an experimental space flight, afflicted by a strange fungus that transforms him into a murderous monster. After bullets and bombs fail to stop the creature, brilliant scientist Professor Quatermass [oh, she did love that name] becomes mankind's last hope of survival." She wasted more time than any human should contemplating the present-day ramifications in the gender politics of 1971's *Dr. Jekyll and Sister Hyde*, wherein "the good doctor, experimenting with ways to prolong his life, tests the formula on himself and metamorphoses into a beautiful woman" (well, she could maybe sell Malouf on that—Rob Lowe is certainly still pretty enough to do dual duty . . . and the Oscar goes to . . .).

Jekyll's alter ego turns out to have a very narrow nasty streak, killing prostitutes who, terrified of Jack the Ripper, believe they have nothing to fear from a woman. Aha—so tricky! But why, she mused, as a woman, did Sister Hyde, like the Ripper, kill hoes? Was that a prescient indictment of how strong the urge to murder, to commit violence upon the opposite sex, is in man, that it lasts even through the transformation to woman? Or, more stickily, and oh so politically inconvenient, was it an of-its-time, benighted condemnation of the trans existence itself as a freakish perversion? Or . . . was it an unconscious attack on womanness itself—because the male Jekyll/Hyde had never murdered before he had a temporary, nighttime vagina and a gravity-defying '70s vintage push-up bra? The cleavage made me do it? Maya shook her head. Her mind was mush. She fixed herself a tequila and orange juice.

Over the months that she disappeared down the Hammer universe rabbit hole, as she waited for reports on the kids from Rancho Cucamonga, subtle, troubling changes in her consciousness manifested. She lost some drive. Something about contemplating all the time, energy, and yes, love even, that must have gone into these ridiculous movies struck her at first as absurd, even tragic. To spend one's life like that, taking seriously the Quatermasses and the zombies and the lesbo vampires? To be on one's deathbed with those images swimming up in your head as you dwelled on your "achievements." Ugh.

Malouf was sadistically attentive to her Hammer work. Was he really looking for a diamond in the rough or was he slyly roughing her up, testing her resolve, because he could? He wanted ten synopses a week. He wanted her to identify at least one remake per month. He made her go to lunches with desperate writers who would pitch her and then try to fuck her. It wasn't hard work, but it wasn't what she had spent her life training for, and it hurt her somewhere inside. She lost all energy to move for a weekend in mid-November. She'd drag herself home from Praetorian wondering, And what am I making? How am I better than Hammer? I'm worse, maybe; I'm merely pushing paper, moving numbers from one side to the other. Is my entire life an abstract endeavor to move the decimal point farther and farther to the right? And at the end of it, I won't even have the slightest comfort that my pathetic contortions blissfully occupied some bored kid or social outcast in some rainy Saturday afternoon matinee. Am I a paper clip in smart business attire? She didn't have a shrink to tell or close friends or a lover. Her associates, the Turks, would tell her she needed to get laid. Her doofus trainer did mention that he thought she'd "plateaued" and maybe she'd like to try some black-market supplements from China, rhino horn or tiger penis powder or something gross and animal unfriendly like that.

One winter day, Malouf called her into his office to give a twenty-minute presentation for a remake of *The Vampire Lovers* to him and the Young Turks. Taking their cue from the boss man, the Turks sat stone-faced and grim during her pitch, with their best schoolboy "listening" faces on, seeming to perk up only whenever the word *lesbian* made a cameo. Of course, Malouf had called the meeting for 2 p.m. so the boys were sleepy and maybe even a little tipsy from lunch. A couple of the Turks twitched and drooped. When she was finished, the boss thanked her courteously and dismissed her. She was a few yards down the hall when she heard the door shut and the room erupt in muffled laughter. She thought of quitting. If this was a test, she didn't know yet how to pass—take the lumps or fight back? WWMD? What would Malouf do?

Then the pendulum started to swing back. It came when she was contemplating the life and times of Peter Cushing, Hammer's preeminent star from the '50s through the '70s. Cushing played Baron Frankenstein six times and Dr. Van Helsing five times, along with numerous other heroes and villains. Doctors Frankenstein and Van Helsing; he'd looked at clouds from both sides. She imagined Cushing on his deathbed, surrounded by loved ones in a huge mansion in the English countryside that all that child's play had bought. And she thought—he knew. He knew the truth. Not the truth of how to make a living man out of killing corpses or the best way to dispense with a gay Styrian vampire, or even the inner life of Grand Moff Tarkin, but the truth of life itself—it didn't matter. None of this shit mattered. It was all child's play after all. And that was fucking beautiful, not tragic. And the energy expended! The energy endowed by the creator, in Mr. Cushing's case, had been used, over and over again, in his mock fight for truth or evil or whatever that week called for. Cushing didn't need an Oscar on his deathbed in Canterbury in 1994 to make it all worthwhile; he was whole, and holy.

Through Cushing contemplation, Maya's condescension flipped to wonder, and her lethargy turned around. She still didn't know what exactly the fuck she was doing with her life, but it seemed to matter less. If Praetorian was her Hammer, then so be it. Was this growing up or giving up? She didn't know. She wondered if there was a difference.

She turned her revitalized attention back to the Powers deal, and thought maybe it was a good time to visit Bronson, poke the bear. She drove to San Bernardino to see Janet Bergram. For her part, Janet seemed invested in the project almost against her own better judgment. She cared about the kids. But the news Janet relayed was not good for Maya. Deuce was doing well, but not Pearl or Hyrum. The California educational system was failing them. It looked like Powers might be winning this wager and his land, and her all-or-nothing gambit would end up a zero.

Maya couldn't stand by passively and watch her unicorn die like this. Maybe it was time for some horse-trading. Maybe a little meddling was called for. Maybe if I put a stone in Bronson's boot, he'll do something stupid, and we can turn things back the Praetorian way so that my outside-the-box production of *The Mormons Come to Town* might one day soon pay huge dividends. I will move the decimal point to the right of eight zeroes. There was still plenty of time left to improvise. Conditions were ripe to hit the desert again, without the 'shrooms.

As Maya was leaving her tiny office, Janet said, "And oh, that hundred grand your boss promised the San Bernardino school system? No sign of it."

"No?" Maya bristled. Malouf was like his buddy Trump in this regard, making a show of charitable donations without any actual follow-through. It was morally disgusting—everything to men like that was gesture and signal with no meat, like a tweet, and it reflected badly upon her as well, tainted her.

"Neither hide nor hair. Not a penny," Janet groused.

"Maybe it was anonymous." Maya looked at Janet's face to see if that was a good joke. Nope. "Here," Maya said, taking a checkbook from her bag. "Can I write you a check for ten thousand, say?"

"Well, not to me, but yes." As Maya wrote the check, she flashed on that bitchin' new silver Tesla truck she could not now afford, "But ten is not one hundred," Janet added.

Maya spent a pleasurable night at Twentynine Palms, putting in some time in the spa and a few interminable hours on her iPad with soul-destroying fare—*The Devil Rides Out* and *The Gorgon*. In the morning, she drove to a meeting point arranged with her favorite park ranger to get off-roaded out to Powers's land.

Ranger Dirk was happy to see her, and very talkative; she was a big tipper. "Back for more Hollywood research, huh?"

She laughed because this time, immersed as she was in the world of Hammer, he was closer to the mark than before. "Oh yeah," she said. "I'm making money moves."

"I grew up on Westerns. I miss a good Western," Dirk confided in her. Oh God, she didn't want to talk about movies with this guy. She didn't even like movies. Period. He droned on to his captive audience, "Costner was good for a while, but Clint Eastwood. That's my man. 'Go ahead, punk, make my day.'"

"Clint Eastwood, sure." She could tell Dirk was quoting something, but she didn't know what. All she remembered of that guy was when he talked to a chair like a loon at some political convention. She always got him mixed up with the crazy gray-haired dude from *Back to the Future*.

"They shot all those old Westerns out here," Dirk proclaimed. She was pretty sure that wasn't true, though. "When I'm driving around out this way, I'm always on the lookout for a familiar backdrop. Yup, I was born in the wrong era. A six-shooter, right? Haha, I'm a Western guy."

"You sure are, Dirk," she said, thinking, I'd like a six-shooter right now.

"You look sleepy." Dirk misinterpreted her abject boredom, then added in a semi-leer, "Rough night?"

"Yeah," she said. "Do you mind if I close my eyes and try to nap?"

"Not at all, but good luck on this terrain. I'll do my best to make it smooth, m'lady."

"Thanks, Dirk. You're my hero." She closed her eyes and faked sleep for the hour or so it took to get to the Powers property.

"Last stop, Princess. Wakey-wakey." Maya opened her eyes to see Yalulah and some of the Powers kids walking toward her, drawn to the intruders the way she imagined zombies are when they smell living flesh, but nicer, if only slightly.

"Thanks, Dirk, you're amazing, but I can take it from here."

"You want a ride back?"

"I could be a while. Why don't you head back and if I need you I'll call." She really didn't want him around to annoy Bronson or any of the kids with his friendly nonsense. Maybe Bronson could give her a ride back to Twentynine Palms.

"Sounds good to me. These folks give me the creeps." Maya got out of the vehicle and walked toward Yalulah and the kids as Dirk turned tail back to civilization.

"Hi, Fam!" Maya called out, though she knew that the hipness of the salutation would be lost on them. "How is everyone doing?"

"What's wrong?" Yalulah asked immediately. "Did something happen in Rancho Cucamonga? The kids? Mary?"

Maya realized now that her mere presence might have spooked everyone, and instantly felt stupid and callous. "Oh no, no, no . . ." She calmed Yalulah down. "I'm sorry. Everyone is fine. Everyone is doing great."

"They're all dead," a little boy of about seven said. "Everyone is dead of cancer."

Yalulah chided the child, "Cut it out, Alvin, you know they're not dead. That's not funny. You're scaring your brothers and sisters."

"You're a philistine, Little Big Al." Beautiful sighed.

"Aliens took them so they could look at their buttholes," Lovina offered.

"Wow," Maya said.

"Do you have cancer, too?" Alvin asked Maya.

"Interesting sense of humor," Maya said, patting the boy on the head, secretly thinking maybe she should have chosen this loser weirdo for the test.

"Please don't touch the children."

"Oh right, I'm sorry."

"God only knows what viruses and diseases you all are cooking up out there. What have you come for, then?" asked Yalulah, not exactly rolling out the welcome mat.

"Just to give you a general update and to go over some logistical stuff. Is Bronson around?"

"No, he most likely won't be back till sundown. Maybe later."

"Shit."

The children laughed at the curse word.

"You ride a horse?" Yalulah asked.

"Well, I've ridden a horse, I wouldn't say I'm a horse rider."

"I can put you on one of the kids' ponies and give you directions."

Maya didn't know if she was joking. "Directions?"

"I can't leave the kids, can I? He might not even be back tonight. If you wanna see Bronson, that's the only way you're gonna see him today."

"You're gonna die," that little shit, Alvin, said.

"Alvin, cut it out," Yalulah scolded him, but she looked pleased. "I'll give you a compass. It's simple, head straight east."

"Well, giddy up," Maya joked.

Maya was terrified she'd get lost. She was told the journey might take over an hour and to simply head east straight for a peak that would never be out of view. Simple enough, but she was in the Mojave, all alone, a rain-shadow desert absent of landmarks to the uninitiated, with redundant, similar-looking (to her) peaks in every distance, and eventually it would get dark. She wondered if Yalulah was trying to kill her. That thought started small and idle, but grew bigger and louder as the sun passed its zenith and started angling back toward the earth. She kept hearing Alvin say, "You're gonna die." She thought she was in a Hammer flick and lizard zombies might attack at any moment. Actually, that thought comforted her in its absurdity, and she laughed.

Reception for her phone went in and out, so she turned it off to save the battery, just in case. She erased some lingerie photos she'd taken of herself a few weeks ago ('cause her abs were getting so ripped) in case she died and all that was left of her was the phone. She erased her search history just because. About an hour and twenty in, she began to think seriously of turning back, but then she feared she'd wander dangerously astray. She tried to keep her eyes on the peak Yalulah had shown her, and due east on the compass, which she began to mistrust. She began a panic spiral—how does a compass work anyway? Magnetic something or other? What if there's a disturbance in the magnetic field? That was a thing, wasn't it? Why didn't she know how anything worked? Why didn't she learn anything useful in college? Can a compass break?

She tried to swallow the rising panic in her throat, it felt like broken glass, and she realized how hot and thirsty she was. What was she thinking? Who was she trying to impress by coming out here alone? Malouf? Bronson? Nothing good happens in the desert. You get an arrow shot at you by a child, a rattlesnake sneaks up behind you, and you die of exposure. She was obsessing on rattlers and magnets when she heard Bronson yell, "What the fuck?" Maya thought she was hallucinating, till she made out a form riding fast toward her on a horse twice the size of hers.

She hadn't realized how freaked out she was getting till she saw Bronson's face and couldn't fully stifle a heaving sob. Bronson offered her some of his water. She was shaking. "Oh Jesus, you're scared to death, poor thing. Who let you come out here alone? Yalulah?"

Maya nodded.

"Jesus H. Christ." He shook his head. "You okay?"

"Now I am."

"Sorry about that. Yaya's a hard-ass, bless her."

"She gave me a compass."

"Magnanimous."

"Well, I get it. I think I know where she's coming from."

"The devil's hindquarters, that's where she's coming from. Follow me now," Bronson said, and he led them a short way to a shady spot that was quite pleasant.

Maya started to cool down and relax. She noticed again how handsome Bronson was. She'd been pursued by handsome men before, pretty men, she'd fucked a few even, and watched the power their looks had over her fade with time and bad manners. She thought she had a healthy view of what looks meant and didn't mean to her. But gazing at Bronson, and those forearms again, she got buzzed. Jesus, what was she, she wondered, a forearm freak? Was she gonna go back home to Santa Monica, get on Pornhub, and type in "big sweaty forearms"? Probably get diverted to some "fisting" movies; best not to have that on her history. There'd already been a wonky sex scandal at Praetorian about five years ago involving an exec, now fired, and the eating of much cum.

No, it was something else, 'cause Bronson wasn't young anymore, and the sun had taken its toll on his white skin, especially around the neck. She realized it was that his beauty was "functional," that Bronson worked, that everything about this man worked, and she couldn't believe how much that functionality was starting to turn her on. Shit, she thought, this is weird, maybe I'm just scared and he's like a knight in shining armor right now 'cause

I was about to bite it in the desert and this is some silly romance novel shit I'm getting off on; or maybe he's got this off-kilter, old-timey charisma that got through my protective shields and modern-day, state-of-the-art bullshit detector—he's a fucking polygamist after all, right? He keeps multiple women happy. He's like a cult leader; he's got that cult leader vibe, too, that Manson-type sneaky power. She wanted to get to the bottom of it and get away from it at the same time. Shit, she was in the desert with Charles Bronson Manson. That's not good either. She'd come out here to play him, and now she was freaking and spinning out. She realized he'd asked a question and he was smiling.

"What?" she asked.

"I asked what you came out here for. Like a minute ago."

"Oh . . . I wanted to give you an update on the kids."

"Mary's been doing that."

"Oh, right, of course. I just wanted to check in."

"Check in? Like we're on the same side? I didn't think we were on the same side. I think we want very different things."

"We do?" she asked. He nodded. "What do you want?" she asked.

He shook his head. "I know what I want. That won't change. I don't need to talk about it. What do you want?"

That was a good question. What Maya wanted, from Praetorian, from life, might have changed in the last few months. The Cushing/Hammer effect. She wasn't sure. She decided she'd start talking and they would both find out at the same time. She trusted her gut; the play would arise. "I came here 'cause I wanted to make a fortune. I saw an opportunity. I had a vision. I'm sure you can relate to that." Bronson looked inscrutable. "Remember, at first, the offer was to buy a piece of your land, less than half, and we'd keep the government off your backs? And we'd leave you with a buffer zone so you could live the way you were living? Peaceful co-existence. I think that's the best deal. I'd like to figure out how to get back to that. Get your kids back to you right now. I make a lot of money for the boss and you get to be the way you were."

"The boss?" He laughed.

"What's so funny?"

"You don't know who the boss is." He got up and roped her little pony to his horse. "And we can never be the way we were." He said, offering her his hand, "It'll be dark soon. And cold. Let's ride back. I'll help you up."

Bronson put Maya on the back of his horse and he jumped on in front. He didn't speak for ten minutes. It was starting to cool down and the early December sun was no match for his August incarnation. Maya shivered as the sweat evaporated off her skin. What was she doing with her arms around this strong man's waist? She had to be honest with herself. But, in order to do that, she'd have to know herself. And she knew enough to know that, in this moment, she was unknown to herself. She imagined seeing the two of them, from a distance, as an objective observer, this man and woman on horseback. They could be father and daughter. Or they could be lovers. They could be in love.

Finally, Bronson spoke, or seemed to speak, because Maya didn't understand what was coming out of his mouth at first, whether they were words or not. He was pointing, too, as he spoke in tongues. "*Acmispon argophyllus. Asclepias erosa. Cucurbita denticulate. Agave utahensis. Xylorhiza tortifolia.*" She realized he was identifying all that he saw by the proper Latinate names of the flora. It felt like a Catholic mass performed in Latin. It felt holy, it made Maya feel holy.

She remembered and the words cascaded through her from the deep past, "*In nomine Patris, et Filii, et Spiritus Sancti. Amen.*" Maya hadn't been to church since she was a child, with her Catholic mom, but the ancient Latin flooded back to her, smuggled in on the backs of Bronson's words. She lifted her eyes to the sky and realized she was in church again, had been all along, and that the desert was a place of worship, mystery, and revelation for this strange and powerful man. The observer at a distance in her thought now these two on horseback could be teacher and pupil, priest and penitent. Bronson continued, *"Verbena gooddingii. Stipa speciosa. Rafinesquia neomexicana."*

The old words flooded back to her from God knows where. She said, *"Judica me, Deus, et discerne causam meam de gente non sancta: ab homine iniquo et doloso erue me."*★

"Igneous rocks/skull rocks. The desert thinks with that skull." Bronson pointed out boulders that looked eaten away by millennia of rainfall fashioning divots like eyes and smooth fronts like foreheads, like nothing else but a huge skull made by the maker, a self-portrait, the earth thinking itself at the beginning of time, dreaming itself into being. "There's *Phoradendron californicum. Yucca schidigera.* Sometimes I think," Bronson continued, "that my only job is to say the names, to speak the names, to bear simple witness. That because I saw them here and spoke their names, I existed, and because I bore witness and spoke their names, they existed. Ah, *Yucca brevifolia*—Joshua tree."

"Joshua tree," Maya repeated, like a child.

"Let me tell you what I've noticed since I got here, it's getting hotter, it seems, and dryer every year."

"They call it climate change back there. Maybe we need the Latin for that."

"You can call it whatever you want, but see that ring of Joshua trees there?"

He pointed out what indeed was a circle of the Joshuas, almost as if they had been planted in such a geometric shape. "Because of 'climate change,' you say—hotter temperatures—the Joshua trees are migrating to what they call climate refugia; the trees are finding the better, more temperate climate for themselves, which is

---

★ Judge me, O God, and plead my cause against an ungodly nation: O deliver me from the deceitful and unjust man. (Psalm 43:1)

great, smart nature, but the problem is they are leaving the Yucca moth behind. The Yucca moth hasn't been moving with the Joshuas, she's a terrible flier, she can't make the trip, if you touch one, it just falls to the ground writhing, but the Yucca moth is what pollinates the Joshua tree, on purpose she does that, never eating the pollen for herself. Why? Perfect symbiosis as God ordained—she lays her eggs in the Joshua. It's a succulent, ain't a tree, and they need each other to procreate. But the moth can't keep up with the migrating plants so they're not getting pollinated and not bearing fruit, but are asexually reproducing from their roots, creating the 'fairy rings' you see there—circles of newer plants radiating out from the empty center where the living Joshua used to be. But these asexual plants don't reliably reproduce—so they die out."

"Jesus, asexual reproduction, that's like a horror movie," Maya said, thinking inevitably about Hammer films. All I ever fucking think about is dumb movies, she thought, before wondering seriously if there was the germ of a scenario in there for Malouf, playing fast and loose with the science metaphors, climate change perverting the planet, transforming it into a ghost of itself, asexual, incestuous. Stop, she told herself. She had come to realize, since working at Praetorian, how she habitually tried to monetize information. Climate change? Fascinating subject—what will it do to real estate? Or now, what's the movie? But that training started way before Malouf, at home in America and in school, she couldn't lay it all at his Ferragamo-clad feet. But wasn't this, she could almost hear Malouf in her head—and the idea that she was internalizing his voice freaked her right the fuck out—wasn't this a prime example of making Arnold Palmers when life gives you lemons? Seeing the silver lining in the hurricane.

Sure, sure it was, but soon, Bronson seemed to tell a cautionary tale, soon there would be no water anywhere, only lemons. Then what? Bronson monetized nothing. Reaching for the cliché, she thought, he knows the price of nothing and the value of everything. She wanted to compliment Bronson, but all she said was, "There's a metaphor in there somewhere. Or a movie."

She thought she saw him smile at the mention of a movie. Maybe he missed his old life sometimes? She snapped her fingers. She had the title—*The Moth Effect*. She said, "If a moth flaps its wings in Joshua Tree, a storm ravages Europe."

The smile left Bronson. He looked away. "Lepidoptera Tegeticula" was all he said, as if in final benediction for a friend. She could feel his grief for the lowly moth. It was real. "That sucks," she heard herself say. Ugh. What an inadequate and inarticulate response to his passion. She felt like a dilettante, an interloper on a planet she should be loving and taking care of. Yeah, she drove a Tesla, eschewed plastic whenever possible, and carried a metal straw in her purse, but maybe that wasn't enough to save the world.

"Do you know why it's called a Joshua tree?" he asked, like a favorite professor again, she thought, like a real-life, present-time Indiana Jones. "Named that by the Mormons who settled this area."

"Mormons settled this area?"

"Old school." She laughed at his attempt at hip lingo. He continued, "Reminded them of when Moses raised his hands up in prayer for Joshua in battle."

"Why isn't it the Moses tree, then?"

"Good question. Pearl used to ask me that exact thing. I'd tell her the definition depends on your mood. Figure you can call that tree Joshua or Moses or Bill or Ted, but he still won't come. Can you see him—Joshua or Moses or whoever it is?" He raised his arms to the sky in prayer. "Can you see him praying?"

"Yes," she said, seeing his forearms again, and raising her hands in prayer as well. "I can see him pray."

She kept her arms aloft for a while, but they got tired. There was no Equinox machine that could prepare her for lengthy horseback prayer. Bronson pointed out some surprisingly vibrant flowers beneath their dangling feet. "There's some Bigelow's monkeyflower,

Mimulus bigelovii, ain't he cute? Ah damn, look there"—he pointed to a big, gorgeous five-petaled pale yellow flower, a color so subtle no master paint mixer could ever approach—"*Mentzelia involucrata*, the sand blazing star."

"Wow," Maya said. Again with the inadequate response to the wonders Bronson was sharing. But she knew nothing about flowers except the famous "Dutch Tulip Bubble" cautionary tale she'd studied at business school. Bronson didn't seem to notice or mind.

"There's Pearl's favorite," he said, "and her mom's—the desert five-spot." He dismounted, helped Maya down, and stooped down to a light purple bulb. He didn't pluck it. He bent it Maya's way and motioned for her to join him. He gently spread the bulb. "See inside here, *Eremalche rotundifolia*, five red spots here, like the best poker hand you ever got. Royal flush." She looked inside the bulb at the painterly beauty within, the hidden order out here in what she had thought was a chaos of random desert. A sublime hierarchy that only initiates could uncover. She was thankful for Bronson, her guide to this otherworld.

The flower seemed to overwhelm Bronson momentarily. He stroked the fragile, weightless skin of the bulb comfortingly with the tip of a finger, saying, "There, there . . ." He seemed to drift off somewhere.

But just as quickly, he was already standing up and striding away. "Goddamn cheatgrass and Sahara mustard are bad out here." He began yanking the grass out of the ground angrily. "Invasive species," he said. "I consider myself a guardian, like the angel Michael with a flaming sword. Cheatgrass shall not enter." He had a smile on his face. He knew he sounded a bit pretentious. She noticed he didn't give cheatgrass or Sahara mustard the honor of a Latin handle.

"What's cheatgrass ever done to you?"

"This desert should be barren of fuel to burn. Naturally it is. Cheatgrass doesn't belong here. It'll burn. It'll make a fire burn way farther than it should and burn what it shouldn't."

"Oh." Oh? Jesus.

She watched as he pulled up the vandal roots. She got the feeling he wanted to purify the entire desert with his bare hands. He just might succeed. "You sure we should be out here? Humans?" she asked. He stopped yanking at the grass.

"You mean, like we're cheatgrass, too?" Maya nodded. Bronson inhaled. He seemed to consider the possibility. "I suppose humans are fuel for fire, too," he said. He sat back and scanned the horizon, seeming to take in the quixotic nature of one man's quest against runaway nature. "Ever fire a gun?" he asked.

"No," she replied, though the question startled her, and scared her out here all alone.

"Come here," he motioned to her, and withdrew his gun from a side holster.

"I played paintball once," she said.

"Oh—*paintball*." He smirked. "Then you'll be fine."

"Hey, don't hate on paintball."

He pointed at a cactus maybe twenty yards away. "See that saguaro?" She nodded. "Okay, here, take this." He placed the gun in her hand, way heavier than they seemed to be in the movies. "Nothing to it. Just make believe it's an extension of your finger, the barrel, just point and shoot."

"Like a camera."

"Sure, if that helps."

"Wow, it's so heavy."

"Uh-huh. That's the weight of life and death you feel."

"Show me," she said, realizing that her tone had become flirty.

Without turning around, Bronson gestured with his head. "Okay, see that boy back there over my left shoulder? He's not praying, he's got his hands up ready to go." She looked where he pointed. There was a big cactus about thirty yards away, its two branches, she didn't know what else to call them, almost perpendicular to its trunk and directed their way as if it wanted a hug or to fight. She could easily imagine a man with a gun. "He thinks he's got the drop on me, but . . ."

In one fluid motion, Bronson snatched the weapon from Maya's hand and spun around like a gunslinger in a Western, shooting from the hip. The cactus in the distance popped wetly, three times, some of its succulent flesh sprayed out right where one might assume a head would be, dead center. Pap, pap, pap. He'd shot holes for eyes and a nose, boom, like that. He spun the gun on his index finger. "Pearl calls that 'old man strength.'"

"Oh God! Don't hurt it," Maya said, surprised at how her heart went out to the ambushed saguaro.

"Nah, it'll take more than a bullet or two to take down cactus-man. He can take whatever God and man throws at him. His skin will heal. Now you," he said, handing the gun back to her. "I'll help."

He was showing off. She liked that. He got behind her and held her arms tight, his hands around her hands. He placed her finger on the trigger and said, "Inhale, exhale, pull." She inhaled, exhaled, and pulled. The bullet disappeared with a spray into the cactus again into one of its "arms"—a hit. She yelped with genuine delight.

"Sorry! Sorry, Mr. Cactus, or Joshua or Bill, Ted, whatever your name is," she called out.

"Okay," he said, "not bad. Now you try by yourself, Killer. Hit that bad man." She liked that he called her "Killer," like Malouf on a good day. She turned back and aimed at the injured saguaro. "Steady your right hand with the left."

"I know. I've seen *Law and Order*. I'm gonna hundred-percent Hargitay this shit. Or maybe go full-on *Wonder Woman*."

"Wonder Woman had a lasso."

"You didn't see the reboot."

"The lasso of truth."

"Shut up, Mr. Powers. Inhale," she said as she inhaled, "exhale, pull." She pulled the trigger, the gun recoiled, but that was that. There was no sign that she had hit anything at all.

"What happened?" she asked.

"Paintball," he said, "whiff."

"You mean I missed the earth?"

"Apparently, and that ain't easy out here, there's a lotta earth." He laughed. "Try again. Use your sight there. Inhale, exhale, pull." She did as he said. She squinted through to find the sight and fired. The bullet plunked into the lower half of the cactus. "That'll work," he said. "Good shot. You're a natural with a mean streak— you got him right in the cojones. Hyrum calls that a 'balls'-eye.'"

The sun was going down by the time they got back on the horse. She was getting tired of balancing with her inner thighs, and wrapped her arms around Bronson's waist. The desert was a beautiful peach-pink. She thought she could see the house in the distance. They must be close to home.

"Back when I used to be in movies, they'd call this the magic hour. But it's no hour, more like twenty minutes. Ain't that the way."

"All Hollywood lies, huh?"

"All lies." He sighed. The landscape was barren and lunar and glowing. Maya swelled with feeling at the sheer unwelcoming, almost hostile beauty of it all.

Maya put her hands on Bronson's shoulders and turned him to her. She liked making the first move; it jibed with her preferred image of herself. She kissed him deeply. He returned in kind. He tasted of sand and rock and sun. The observer in her watched and thought these two beautifully backlit golden-hour riders were lovers, and then flew back into her body, making her one, whole, no longer split, in that moment, between the one who observes and the one who does. She lost all thought and self-consciousness and was filled with something wordless and electric.

Though the observer in Maya had rejoined her, what the two

on horseback didn't see as they kissed was that there was still yet another observer out there in the desert, coming from the house, riding out to meet them, hidden in the lengthening shadows of sundown. Pearl, bored, frustrated, and angry at school, had come back to see Bronson, had run away from the city, unbeknownst to Mary. No one knew. She'd gotten her Adderall/Ritalin/Xanax-dealing senior buddy to lend her his motorcycle with vague promises of future favors that could haunt her one day but so what. Bronson had taught her how to ride on his Frankenbike when she was ten. She arrived quietly at the house when Yalulah and the kids were inside having dinner and, unseen, went straight to the barn, saddling up to go meet Bronson in the special place where she knew he must be. She'd only gotten a few thousand yards from the house when she saw Bronson and that woman from LA making out on the horse. Same as she and Bronson had before.

Pearl gently turned her horse back to home, before Bronson and Maya knew she was there. She easily beat them back to the house, jumped on her motorcycle, and roared back to Rancho Cucamonga. An apparition.

20.

DEUCE CONSIDERED SCHOOL and BurgerTown equally as loci of learning, but at work, he really came into his own. The industrialized, inhuman speed coupled with the very human give-and-take of fast-food service was for him an education in the modern world and its ideal of efficiency, ease, and faux friendliness. But there was nothing "faux" about Deuce. He was sincere and well intentioned, whether playing goalkeeper with the Mexicans out back, constructing perfect burgers to company specifications like a flesh machine in his silly hat, or making Spanglish small talk with customers.

BurgerTown was fast food but with a homier, more personal vibe than McDonald's or In-N-Out, and on a much smaller scale. There were fifty BurgerTown franchises in California and the Pacific Northwest. After being trained and programmed to avoid them like a killing virus his entire short life, Deuce found that he actually liked people and liked to be helpful. He liked serving people, being of service. He didn't even mind the lame, mustard-yellow-and-baby-shit-brown uniform. He made the California state minimum wage of $11 an hour, but he didn't do it for the spending money. He gave his paycheck to Mary anyway, to put into a college fund for himself and for his siblings.

He was set on going to college now. His teachers were already pushing him Ivy way as their very own "success story," but those were long shots. Even though his daddy was worth easily a couple hundred million in real estate, the family had zero liquid money. Bronson Powers didn't have a bank account or a credit card. He hadn't paid taxes in twenty years. He had a big stash of cash hidden somewhere in the house he'd pull out like a magician to pay for seeds, gas, and parts, but that was all. Deuce figured he'd get better financial aid if he stayed in state—so he was looking at UC Berkeley, UCLA, maybe Stanford.

Of the twenty-five BurgerTown employees, only a handful were students, though fast food was the quintessential American student temp job. But in the twenty-first-century economy, in Rancho Cucamonga in the county of San Bernardino, California, the United States, fast-food work had become predominantly a full-time job for an adult citizen. Deuce was one of the few white student employees. He took two eight-hour shifts on the weekends and two four-hour shifts after school, on Wednesdays and Fridays. The manager, Frank, put Deuce out front at the main register. He said, "People like seeing a white face when they open their wallets." Deuce was self-conscious out front with his skin, but he did as he was told. Raised by a strict father, he had a natural respect for the chain of command.

Deuce's favorite at work was an old Mexican man named Jaime. Old man: he was about fifty and working full-time at BurgerTown, pulling double shifts whenever he could, bringing cold burgers and fries home at the end of the night to freeze for his kids and grand-kids; he must've worked sixty hours a week, usually showed up an hour early to do what needed to be done, always a smile on his face. Deuce just dug the guy. One day, Jaime brought a guitar into work and played "some José Feliciano shit" on the nylon strings. Deuce had never heard it; he was blown away by the speed of the old man's fingers; it sounded like three guitars playing at once. Deuce asked Jaime to teach him to play like that, and he did, for free.

One Saturday, Deuce got to work about twenty minutes early to open at 6 a.m. As usual, Jaime was even earlier; Deuce saw him high up on a ladder, silhouetted by the rising sun, beholding the foot-long magnetic letters of the restaurant sign out front about twenty-five feet high. The sign was supposed to read:

BURGERTOWN
COME ON IN
OVER 100,000 CUSTOMERS PLEASED

But it had been rearranged by some Friday-night drunken tom-foolery to render the dirty haiku:

MI UGE BONERS
COME
OVER 100,000 CUNTS R PLEASED
R T NOW

Jaime looked down from the sign and sighed. "This happens three, four times a year. Pretty boring. First time I seen 'cunt' though."

Deuce looked up and said, "'R. T. Now,' huh, that's a great name, maybe it's the signature of the guy who did it, cool villain—R. T. Now!"

"They need to buy an 'h.' They don't win the jackpot, Sally," Jaime yelled down.

"What?" Deuce yelled up.

"*Wheel of Fortune*, dude."

"What's that?"

"You don't know *Wheel of Fortune*? You lyin', Sally."

As Jaime laughed and reached to unscramble the twelve-inch letters, he leaned way out over the ladder, which he had placed in the soil flower planter beneath the sign. The feet of the ladder shifted in the soft soil with his weight, the top of the ladder pitched, and Jaime came crashing down onto cement, breaking his left leg and his pelvis, and sustaining a concussion.

Somebody called 911. Deuce didn't know to do that. But Deuce went to visit Jaime in the hospital that day, the next day, and the next after school. He'd never seen a hospital before, let alone been inside one. He'd never been to the doctor. He met Jaime's wife, Lupe, and his five kids.

One day, maybe a week after the accident, Deuce came for a hospital visit and Lupe was crying in the hallway. Deuce asked her what was wrong. Lupe's English wasn't great, and neither was Deuce's Spanish, but he could make out that Lupe sure was Catholic and she sure was thankful Jesus Christ had saved Jaime's life, but that Jaime wasn't covered by BurgerTown and didn't have any health insurance, that he may have entered the country illegally twenty years ago, that he'd been fired by BurgerTown, that the hospital bill was going to be $100,000, that they would have to leave the country for cheaper care in Mexico or be thrown in prison here for not being able to pay the bill, and they'd have to stay there because Trump wouldn't let them back in the country, but the kids would stay here and get thrown into concentration camps and she'd never see them again.

Lupe was understandably distraught with these worst-case scenarios circling around and around in her head. One hundred thousand dollars seemed like an impossible sum. Deuce'd been told that's about what he'd need to get through two years of college, and when he watched the $11 an hour add up, he saw that he'd never get close, and without a scholarship, he'd be saving his pennies from Burger-Town forever, and Lupe and Jaime would never get there alone.

These were issues that Deuce was acquainted with from his nightly dose of Hayes/Maddow with Mary, but this was his first firsthand experience of such systemic pain, the pain of a family breaking up because a government was negligent and corporations were greedy. He liked what Bernie Sanders said about universal health care. He'd seen YouTube videos of the Black President Obama speaking and promising. He liked him. He saw a lot of old men say the made-up word *Obamacare*, derisively, a lot. He liked what Elizabeth Warren said about free college for all and erasing student debt. But none of that was law, it was all talk.

He read far and wide about Noam Chomsky, Naomi Klein, and Chris Hedges, and saw them as the righteous, rightful heirs to Marx, Debs, Hofstadter, and Zinn (the brilliant worldview founders that Bronson had taught him), but they seemed so grumpy and not to like anyone and to believe we were already doomed by capitalism and its careless usury of the planet. They were in possession of the Truth, he thought, they should be happy and radiant with the social gospel the way Bronson was with his Mormon truth, like Bronson had taught him to be.

Deuce wished that he could call Reinhold Niebuhr, who brought a vital, living Christ to social justice. He was unable to reach Chris Hedges to have that discussion. He wished he could call Martin Luther King, Jr., as well. He wished he could friend Sheldon Wolin on Facebook. He had arrived in the world too late for the heroes of truth and justice his father had turned him on to, but Chomsky and Klein were alive and kicking. He got their phone numbers easily enough and called both; he wanted to ask what he could do. He wanted to ask, Where is the front? Just point me in the right direction. He reached the colleges and institutes they were affiliated with and spoke to an assistant in both cases who assured him of a return call.

Neither Klein nor Chomsky had called him back yet. But he was sure they would, and then he would start the good works. He imagined they lived together, Naomi and Noam, in a simple hut somewhere, like Thoreau, cooking vegetarian meals and being grumpy geniuses together. He was gonna call them again to ask them about Jaime. He told Lupe about Chomsky and Klein and that they would know what to do. Lupe said she didn't want lawyers and didn't have time to wait. But hold on, he thought, and he tried to tell Lupe, my family was broken up over money, too. He tried to explain the "bet" that brought him to Rancho Cucamonga, but then realized this wasn't helping.

Compared with all the big problems that he wanted to address after college when he was more expert, this one seemed pretty easy. This wasn't saving a planet, this was saving one man, one good, hardworking man. He told Lupe not to worry, because he knew the boss at BurgerTown, his manager, Frank, and that boss knew the big boss, and surely once they understood what was going on and a clear line of human communication was forged, a quick remedy would be found and everyone would live happily ever after. He believed this must be a big misunderstanding and he assured Lupe that he'd take care of it.

He left the hospital and called his manager, Frank Dellavalle. Frank was at home with his kids, but he said Deuce could come right over. Frank was broken up about Jaime, too. Frank thought the world of Deuce. Called him "Ace." Thought that was clever. Deuce didn't get it. He'd never seen a deck of cards.

"Welcome to the slums of Rancho Cucamonga," Frank said, as he opened the door of his home. It seemed okay to Deuce. Certainly not as big and shiny as some other houses he'd seen, but nothing to be ashamed of, although Frank Dellavalle seemed ashamed. Frank was a smallish guy, about forty-five, the kind of average man about whom saying he was nondescript might be too much description. "What's up, Ace? You want some water? Gatorade?"

"Gatorade? Sure. Thanks, Mr. Dellavalle." Deuce had a thing for Gatorade now. Orange and red. He thought about joining the track team 'cause Gatorade was expensive and the athletes got as much as they wanted for free at practices.

Deuce sipped his Gator and led Frank through what Lupe had told him. He didn't seem surprised by any of it. Frank kinda nodded and made sad little expressions and sounds, faces like he was trying to figure out an impossible math problem, all furrowed brow and pursed lips. He said, "Here's the problem: well, first, you know I'm not the boss, right? I mean look at this house, this isn't the boss's house."

"It's a nice house."

"Thanks, Ace, but the bosses live in a galaxy far, far away. Anyway, the thing is, the accident occurred at what time?"

"Right before we opened."

"Right, that's in the accident report, before six a.m., right. Before Jaime was on the clock."

"Jaime always gets to work a half hour early, at least, sometimes an hour—he finds things to do."

"I know. I love that guy. Wish I had twenty-five more just like him, like him and you—I'd never have to leave the house. If only he was white."

"He's not white?"

Frank laughed at him. "Where you from, Ace? No, he's not white, he's Mexican."

"He's the same basic color as me or you. I don't get it, then, why is he fired, 'cause he's Mexican?"

"I didn't say that. And I would never say it. I don't have a racist bone in my body." Deuce started to get a weird feeling. Frank continued, "He wasn't on the clock when the accident happened, that was on his own time. It doesn't qualify as an accident at work 'cause he wasn't at work yet, officially."

"That doesn't make any sense."

"If he had an accident doing work around his own house, cut off his finger slicing an avocado, is his employer supposed to pay for that, too?" Deuce started to feel Frank's tone and temperature change. Frank seemed angry now. "And who asked him to go up on a fucking ladder, excuse my French, from his own truck, a truck which is nicer than mine, by the way—to do company business?"

"Some kids changed the sign to say something funny."

"I'm aware of what assholes do to that sign. And I've asked

corporate if we could change the old removable letters 'cause it happens a few times a year. But they say it's part of the company's 'legacy,' that they've had that sign since the '70s, yadda yadda, nostalgia."

"But wait." Deuce tried to get back on track. "You're saying that 'cause Jaime hadn't officially started his workday, even though he was giving you more than you pay for, that he's fired and you won't give him any paid sick leave and you won't pay his bills."

"Sick leave is like the bogeyman to a shop like BurgerTown. I got a better chance of getting a BJ off Britney Spears than Jaime has of seeing dime one of paid sick leave."

"A what off who?"

Dellavalle took a deep breath. "I'd love to pay his bills, Ace, I would, but he should have health insurance, that's on him, and Obama, but really, it's corporate. There's levels. There's me—down here, I'm a drone, a worker bee. And there's a wall for Jaime to climb between each level. There's a wall between you and me, me and my boss, my boss and his bosses, and each of those walls is higher than the one before it. So if you get past one wall, there's always another wall."

"That's why we need a union."

"What? Union? Who said anything about a union?"

"No one."

"Good. If there was a union formed under my watch, I'd get fired, and then I'd be fucked all over again. Pardon my French."

"No, Jaime is f'ed."

"You should relax, Ace, you're gonna go to college, you're on the winning side of the walls. You think I'm the bad guy? I make seventy K a year, my dude, and I got three kids and an ex, and taxes up the wazoo, in-debt man walking."

"Seventy thousand a year?! That's so much!"

"You're funny, kid."

"Why is there no union?"

"Why is there no Santa Claus? I dunno—maybe because of the high turnover of just kids working."

"Jaime isn't a kid. It was permanent to him."

Dellavalle sported an ugly smirk now.

"Maybe it's the fact that it's unskilled, excuse my French, but you don't need to know fuck-all to work at BurgerTown. A monkey can flip a burger, no offense. Takes me a week to train someone to do Jaime's job, max, and real unions are for skilled workers. It's the system, it's rigged."

"It's the Taft-Hartley Act all over again."

"Huh?"

"It was a law passed in 1947 by a Republican Congress to weaken unions, curtail their ability to force nonunion workers to pay union dues."

Dellavalle liked Deuce, but he sure didn't like to be outclassed by him, or being made to feel stupid. "Okay, Joe College. Makes sense. More money in my pocket, right? Better for the working stiff."

"Short term. That's how they'd sell it, but unions are better for the working stiff long term."

"I'm anti big government," Dellavalle said, with the certainty that he was saying something of undeniable substance.

"What does that have to do with anything?"

"The union is just like the government. Taxes, union dues—same thing."

"They are absolutely not the same thing. Can't you see that?" Deuce raised his voice for the first time. He was flabbergasted that this man was immune to reason; having met so few men, he believed Dellavalle must be unique in this.

"I see that my bosses tell me to squash any union talk I hear." Dellavale was getting tired of being lectured by this pimply faced kid. "So let's change the subject. Maybe you should think about your skin more than you think about the Mexicans, huh? Have you heard of Accutane? My niece took it—miracle drug, cleared all that shit up. Look into it. That'll change everything. When you get laid, you'll start to see what really matters and forget this union shit. Another Gator?"

Deuce was trying to put the whole rambling, surreal scenario in perspective, but the pieces wouldn't fit. Why did Frank keep saying he was speaking French and then continue speaking only English? He wished Noam or Naomi would call him back and explain everything.

Frank put his hand on Deuce's shoulder. "Bad things happen to good people, Ace. I gotta wash my hands of this. And so do you. You, me, Jaime—we all gotta dust ourselves off, get up, and move on past it. It's the American way. No freebies."

He guided Deuce to the door. "Drop it, Ace, let it go. Jaime is a big hombre, he'll survive. You want a Gator for the road?"

"No, thanks," Deuce said, wishing he hadn't accepted the first one.

As he made his way home in a kind of confused stupor, Deuce thought of his heroes, of Marx and Klein, Zinn and Chomsky, Debs and Bronson, Lennon and McCartney, Lennon and Lenin, and realized that Jaime was a hero to him too, that hardworking man with a broken leg and pelvis he could no longer afford. A "working class hero is something to be," John Lennon sang in his head. Part of the precious post-Beatle catalogue Bronson had allowed into Agadda da Vida. Deuce felt close to the edge of something. Jaime should have the power. The people should have the power. "Power to the people, right on!" Lennon sang again. Not corporate. It's what Jesus and John Lennon wanted. It's what Joseph Smith wanted. It's why Bronson had fled the world and its corruption.

And it's why, he began to see, he had been brought back to the world. To fight. And it struck him in an instant. He would fight city hall, whatever that meant. He started to feel the emptiness fill again with something new and true, the emptiness created when Joseph Smith left. He didn't need to wait for Bronson; he didn't need to wait for Noam and Naomi to call back. He heard the words of Eugene Debs, founder of the Industrial Workers of the World, echo in Bronson's voice in his mind, for Bronson would sometimes read Debs to Deuce as he fell asleep as a child, what passed for bedtime stories in Agadda da Vida—"I have no country to fight for; my country is the earth, and I am a citizen of the world." Deuce knew what needed to be done. Praxis.

He would start a union at BurgerTown.

21.

AS DEUCE BECAME MORE INVOLVED with Jaime's recovery and local BurgerTown politics, he had less time for Mary and their nightly feast of Hayes/Maddow. Trump-hating wasn't as much fun alone, but someone had to do it. She was obsessed with the president—his circus peanut–colored hair and dead lizard eyes, his intransigent stupidity and mean-girl fifth grader's vocabulary, the sheer nightly *Groundhog Day* shock that millions had chosen this impulsive dunce to be the most powerful man in the world, and might again. He makes me want to run away to the desert, she would say.

The last president she remembered was the younger Bush guy. She saw him as an upward-failing, bumbling dummy with a quirky bit of charm in the grand tradition of Wasp establishment legacy placeholders, but she had disappeared into Agadda da Vida before the tragic fruits of his unfounded self-assurance, incuriosity, and entitlement were fully manifest. She was learning only now of Obama, and was sorry she missed him, in a way. She really liked the idea of him. The last president that she had paid any attention to was the second-term Bill Clinton hounded by the abominable, jowl-ballasted, undead Newt Gingrich and the specter of Republican impeachment.

The spiritual vertigo that Trump induced in Mary was all pervasive, and threatened to redline her growing sense of dislocation in

Rancho Cucamonga. Trump's deep, blind wound had created something less than a full human, a gargoyle who fed on chaos and hurt. The hate in him, like a dark shaman, brought out the hate in this country. Mary felt the regression, the violence, everywhere, and it freaked her out. She was not even sure that the desert was safe from this unleashed primordial, Cain-like vengeance; she sensed it spreading and borderless, like air pollution. To tamp it down, she wanted a drink or something, but not only at night, all fucking day long. She could smell it in her sleep. There was apocalypse in the air. She needed a meeting. She went to a meeting, but listening to the wild tales and sob stories made her want to use even more.

Mary, like many Americans in 2019, watched the political news as daily entertainment, like a soap opera, or rather a horror movie, and she could never watch those alone, so, having lost Deuce, she asked Pearl to join her. But Pearl, though still unexpressed in this, was in the midst of a yearlong punishment of Mary for having taken her away from Bronson, and would as soon sit next to an alligator on the couch for a few hours. So she recruited Hyrum as a replacement with the promise of more of the chocolate peanut butter cups that he'd become obsessed with these days, and he gamely tried for a couple nights; in fact, every time Trump talked, Hyrum would explode into laughter, to the point of hyperventilating, and look over at Mary dumbfounded that she wasn't equally amused.

"What are you laughing at?" Mary asked. She'd never seen Hyrum belly-laugh like this at anything. She realized the guy entertained him, maybe like an Oompa Loompa.

"Everything. This guy's hysterical. Like a cartoon. Why aren't you laughing?"

"I don't see anything funny." It got to the point where Hyrum's outbursts so discomfited Mary that she asked him if he had any homework to do.

"Sure," he said. "You want me to go do it?"

"Please."

"Okay," he said, grabbing another peanut butter cup, disappearing back into his lair, and shutting his door. From the subsequent sounds coming through the walls, by "homework," he apparently meant listening to rap music and playing Fortnite.

Feeling alone in this still new place made Mary want her little pill that much more as a reward for being on high alert all day. Good thing she'd been able to forge Frankie's signature at the pharmacy across town and keep the supply of Percocet renewed, at least till she got found out. She slyly popped a pill, and, not having the gumption to face Trump alone, switched channels to a station called MeTV, Memorable Entertainment Television, that broadcast all the old shows from the '60s and '70s. She lost herself to an illusion of a simpler time and the shameless hambone of William Shatner on the starship *Enterprise*, truly warmed to the fast sad-funny patter of Alan Alda in *M*A*S*H*, and escaped mindlessly into the sublime incompetence of Linda Carter's *Wonder Woman*.

While driving Hyrum the less than three miles to Etiwanda Intermediate School (Go Wildcats!) in the mornings, Mary, at first, would fight him for control of the car radio. A ten-minute battle royal for aural supremacy. She favored the Beatles channel on Sirius that kept them in their warm Apple bubble and no doubt was what Bronson would want, but Hyrum was stepping out into his new world a little. He wanted contemporary, and Mary figured maybe this was a good sign that he was trying to be present. She was surprised he knew all the lyrics to so many songs that were new to her, and then it was kind of exciting to hear him rap along. He was really good at it. He had the rhythm and the intonation; he called it his "flow." He rapped along with a man called A\$AP Rocky, "Praise the Lord": "I came, I saw, I came, I saw / I praise the Lord, then break the law . . ."

Hypnotic as a nursery rhyme. It was actually thrilling for Mary to see Hyrum like this. Even though Mary didn't understand half the lyrics, and doubted Hyrum did either, he seemed to really believe in what he was saying; he had conviction. It was the first time she'd seen him engaged since getting into Fortnite; something about the music and lyrics spoke to him in a way that didn't speak to her. Something in it, she projected, must remind him of how he used to feel out in the desert, wild and free, the sky open and big enough for his energy, with the need to leave his mark. Rancho Cucamonga must feel like a cage to Hyrum after having known nothing but freedom every single day of his Mowgli life. This music tapped into his sorrow, his loss, and also his confusion and anger. These songs pissed high on every tree in the neighborhood. A recently caged bird had found a kind of talking song.

"Why do you like this music?" she asked him.

"I don't know."

"C'mon, tell me, I wanna know."

"Why do you like any music? Why do you like the music you like? 'Cause you like it."

"Yeah, but why, be a little more introspective. Use your words."

"What?"

"I mean, I like the Beatles 'cause it reminds me of when I was young, and of Agadda da Vida."

"I like this music 'cause it doesn't remind me of anything."

"You like it 'cause it's not the Beatles?"

"No."

"You like it 'cause I don't like it?"

"What?"

"'Cause it's new? It feels new? No associations, no baggage?"

"It feels like it was made for me. I like it 'cause it's mine, okay? Can we stop this conversation?"

It was his. So she was thankful for that, at least. He fiddled with

his phone and said, "Here, maybe you'll like this. Sounds older."
She saw that the song was "Redbone" by someone named Childish
Gambino. The name tickled her. It was a slow funk groove, something Sly and the Family Stone might've done, or George Clinton,
or even the Stylistics.

"Oh, I like that. It's like Parliament-Funkadelic. Thanks, Hy,"
she said.

He said, "Okay, boomer. Please stop dancing."

"I'm not dancing. I'm driving. I'm grooving while driving. I'm
shaking my moneymaker."

"Whatever it is, stop it, please."

She made a sad face at him, but she didn't mean it. She kept
the beat in her shoulders. She was pleased—he was trying to reach
a life compromise by making a musical compromise. She liked
that. She tried to make out the lyrics—"But stay woke / Niggas
creepin' . . .'"

She asked Hyrum, "Is he saying, 'niggas creepin'?" Hyrum
nodded. "Oh, I don't like that word," she said.

"No, Mom, it just means other guys, just other guys are trying
to get with his girlfriend, sneaking around behind his back—he
wants to stay woke, you know, awake."

"Oh, like 'Back Stabbers,' the O'Jays' song—'they smile in your
face, all the time they wanna take your place.'" That song came out
of the deep past to her tongue.

"Sure, Mom, whatever."

He didn't care what it reminded her of; he was not curious
about her nostalgia and footnoting, nor should he be. His world
was new and had no antecedents. Nothing of note had come before, and that was as it should be, Mary thought. It was incumbent
upon her to live in his world now, the current one, become fluent
in his tongue and not weigh him down, bore him with her ghost
songs.

But as soon as she dropped Hyrum off, she switched back to the

Beatles. She blasted "Helter Skelter" on her way to Equinox, where she would work out, pop a Perc, and kill time until school got out. But she would continue to try to meet Hy and this new world halfway. She would try to stay woke. She would try not to close her eyes. She would break the law, then praise the Lord.

22.

EVEN THOUGH SHE'D ALL but forgotten about it, Pearl had eventually been called back to the Rancho Cucamonga High principal, Dr. Jenkins, to discuss the "bathroom incident." It had been some time—the wheels of school justice turn quickly, but are subject to improvisational change depending on the political and social climate, and the interplay between the whim or attentiveness of the student body versus the traditional authoritarian fiat of the administration. There was nothing specific on the books addressing a boy setting foot in the girl's bathroom, but Jenkins was aware that this was the type of transgression that could go full nuclear mushroom in today's climate. He wanted to steer a course between the crime and a punishment that created no martyrs on either side of that restroom door.

It was a few days after her aborted attempt to see Bronson, when she had seen him with another woman, and Pearl was still in a dark mood from that unhappy vision. She made it clear as quickly as she could to Dr. Jenkins that the boy, Josue, had not raped or touched or made a move to touch or talked about touching anyone or even appeared rapey or creepy at all. The principal informed her that she had a right, as a victim, to justice, and equally as important, to be heard. Pearl stated that she didn't feel like a victim, that there were no victims because no crime had been committed.

She said, "I don't know why we're still talking about it."

"Yes, I hear what you are saying," Dr. Jenkins replied in his best Fred Rogers tone, "but I am also trying to hear what you are not saying."

" . . ."

"What you're not saying."

"I'm not not saying . . . anything."

"I don't want to put words in your mouth."

"Yeah, I don't want that either."

"At any time during the event did you feel unsafe?"

"Event?"

"The thing, the incident, the cisgendered boy in the girl's bathroom."

"Unsafe?"

"Uncomfortable?"

"I feel uncomfortable right now."

"You're being funny?"

"Trying to be. Guess not."

"That could be what we call a 'coping mechanism.' Your ironic affect. Sometimes we're funny when we are covering something, like pain, or abuse. Funny is one of our reddest of flags." This guy spoke so slowly and carefully, Pearl thought, as if he thought words were spiked, or booby-trapped like land mines. At this pace, she'd be staring at his sad mug all day. She found herself mesmerized by the soft pouch of skin under his chin where his goatee ended. She wanted to flick it.

"And sometimes we are funny," she said, "'cause we are bored out of our minds."

She felt that Jenkins really wanted her to feel worse than she did. She thought it was all stupid. She did have a notion to bring up the mean-girl bullying, which had intensified after the bathroom thing, but she felt that was her business, her cross to bear. There was a group of girls, maybe about five in real life, and a larger, anonymous group on social media sites that weren't known to the school, who were attacking her as a Mormon. The easy stuff. Calling her the "Notorious MMH (Mormon Mouth Hug)" and "Pearl Necklace" and "Butt Stuff Gal"—terms she had to look up that were so juvenile they didn't even pierce very deeply. She didn't want to be part of the "in" group, she was going to be out of this place in a few months, so being ostracized by a bunch of losers didn't hurt that badly. Secretly she deemed the bullying an inverse badge of honor—if these fools hated her, she must be doing something right. She could learn the lingo easily, she could sound like one of them, dress like them, but she'd never be one of them. Never.

She had resolved to do poorly in school, tanking the wager in favor of the homeschooling, and save the family that way. Let Deuce be the Boy Wonder. She'd put on the mask of the Fuck-Up, and enjoy her year of weed, Adderall, and Juul. Easily capable of getting all A's, Pearl would let her grades steadily drop to B, to C, then D, like an expert jockey throwing a fixed race, even sprinkle in a couple F's for seasoning by the final grading period. It was a simple, perfect plan, and the only thing in her life she could control anymore. Hyrum, with his video games and rap, his low-slung jeans and underwear showing, was gonna fuck up, too, without even trying, she saw that coming a mile away. She didn't even have to enlist him. His grades were already slipping. It was in the bag. Homeschooling would win 2–1, underachieving Pearl and Hyrum over high-flying Deuce, and then they'd go back to Agadda da Vida like nothing had happened. This year would be a blip.

Pearl was royally pissed at seeing Bronson on the horse with that lady, but she'd be able to forgive him with time and God's teachings, she knew that. And she knew it was his right, as a Mormon, to take as many wives as was fit. She knew he would marry her, he had said so—well, not in so many words, but he had implied a future for them, and she would ascend to her rightful place in the family. Mary would see the light. What's the big deal?

She was a woman now; she didn't belong here with all these stupid, immature kids.

She knew better than to get into any of that with Dr. Jenkins, of course, so she kept mum about the bullying, about anything controversial. It was easy because Jenkins was so focused on this boy, Josue, and the crime he'd supposedly done. Pearl allowed Jenkins's myopia to blind him.

Mother Mary and Janet Bergram were called into the meeting at the end for a recap and to sign off on any action or nonaction that would be taken. Mary'd made a quick call and invited Janet to attend as a "friend." She could tell that Janet had much worse, legit shit to attend to today as well, her proper caseload as usual in the sixties. After a few minutes with Dr. Jenkins, Janet and Mary agreed with Pearl that there seemed to be no meat here, nothing to be done but move on. No harm, no foul. Satisfaction all around.

They all got up to shake hands. "Much ado about nothing," Pearl said. "You know, if anyone got victimized here, I think it's that Josue kid, 'cause that girl was a tower of bitch."

Mary stifled a laugh; that was Jackie in Pearl right there, balls of steel. The principal was unamused. "We appreciate your input, Pearl, though as policy we discourage the use of female-derogatory terms, even if the user of said terms is female. My door is always open to a member of the student body or his / her / hir / zir / its / their family," Dr. Jenkins droned, as if reading a cue card, a futuristic, almost lifelike, PC robot. He ushered them out into the hallway, his guiding hand hovering above their shoulders, but never making contact that could be construed as physically inappropriate or emotionally condescending. Then he pressed his palms together in front of his lips, bowed slightly in a vaguely Asian manner that he hoped wasn't racist, and receded, silently as a mist, back into his office.

"What the what was that? Zir?" Mary asked in the hallway, removing from her lapel the "she / her" pronoun sticker that Jenkins's assistant had asked her to fill in before joining the meeting. "It's ze / hir, not ze/zir." Janet Bergram explained the new gender-neutral pronouns and nomenclature. "Ahhhhhhhh, I think I get it. Hir is like a him/her combo. That's cool, but complicated. Do you get it, Pearl?" Mary asked.

"Yes, my cisgendered LGBTQ progenitor," Pearl answered. "It's not complicated. I get it/she/him/hir/they/them." Mary laughed, though she had a sudden pang of loss for the unironic girl Pearl was when she was ten. Where had that kid gone to be replaced by this flashing blade, this serpent's tooth?

Pearl had the rest of her classes left, so she said goodbye to her mom, who went back to Equinox, and Janet Bergram, who went back to San Bernardino where the kids really needed her help. Pearl meandered back to class to fake that she was struggling to learn things she already knew. She was mildly irritated that the confab with Jenkins had made her miss her "Introduction to the Psychology of Mythology" class, which was really the only hour of school in which she had any interest. She had learned nothing of theories of the human mind in the desert because Bronson was adamantly anti-psychological; he was more of a Marxist who believed in the struggle of capital and classes, not psyches.

In this class, they discussed Greek gods as if they were an early version of a map of the psyche, which fascinated her precisely because it was pre-Christian, pre-monotheism, and pre-Bronson. The one-god setup started to appear so stingy to her, and limiting, and unrelatable. And no fun. Life was messier than that. Why not have a whole cast of deities? Zeus, Hera, Eros—Id, Ego, Superego. Persephone and Hades—beauty and the death principle. She really dug it. Started to make the beginnings of applying it to her life and experiences. She liked it so much, she was finding it difficult to get a D. And she'd missed it today 'cause of that stupid meeting.

At lunch, Josue found Pearl in the cafeteria, and asked if he could sit down with her. She was alone, as usual.

She said, "It's a free country."

"Thanks for this morning," he said as he sat. "I heard you were like, my advocate. So, thanks for exercising your white privilege on my behalf."

"What?"

"I'm just being a dick. Thank you is all."

"Don't thank me. I just told the truth. You didn't do anything."

"I know, but I did walk into the girl's bathroom. That was stupid."

"Yeah, that was stupid."

"But, your pipes. Dat voice dough."

"Yeah, you said."

"I sing, too."

"Congratulations."

"I sing old stuff too. Musical theater."

"That's where you sing?"

"No, that's what I sing, the style. But I also do contemporary, like *Hamilton*, *Evan Hansen*. I played Burr in *Hamilton* last year and Evan Hansen in *Dear Evan Hansen*."

"I don't even know what that is."

"Haha."

"I'm not kidding, kid, I don't know what 'musical theater' is."

"It's a play with music, where the characters speak but also sing."

"That makes no sense. Why would people just sing instead of talk?"

"Like opera. But not boring like opera."

"Why didn't you say opera, then?"

"'Cause it's not opera. We're doing *West Side Story* this year. They wanna do one that's like updated and relevant for today with the situation at the border and all the current drama between whites and Latinos. They think it's relevant again, whatever, but the music is so awesome. Stephen Sondheim / Leonard Bernstein."

"If you say so."

"Spielberg is doing a movie of it."

"Who's Spielberg?"

"You're funny. It's based on Shakespeare, *Romeo and Juliet*, you've heard of him?"

"Yes."

"You'd kill as Maria."

"What do you mean 'as'?"

"Playing. Playing the part. You playing with me?" Josue didn't know Pearl wasn't kidding. He didn't know her full story. Didn't know she was half feral. None of the schoolkids did.

"Who's Maria?" she asked.

"The female lead—the Juliet."

Pearl nodded, and then inhabited the young Capulet from perfect memory in flawless iambic pentameter: "'What's in a name? that which we call a rose / By any other name would smell as sweet; / So Romeo would, were he not Romeo call'd, / Retain that dear perfection which he owes / Without that title. Romeo, doff thy name; / And for that name, which is no part of thee, / Take all myself.'"

If Josue had been hit by a lightning bolt to hear Pearl's singing voice emanating from the girl's bathroom, now the impossible had happened twice, he was struck again. For a few seconds, without preparation, without seeming to try or care, she had transformed herself into Juliet Capulet in the Rancho Cucamonga High School cafeteria.

"Your mouth is open, buddy boy," she said, definitely back to being Pearl.

"Are you for real?" Josue could barely manage words at this point.

"What kind of question is that?"

Josue swallowed and blinked stupidly, then got back to why he'd sat with her. "So Maria's the female lead in love with Tony. I think you're fucking with me. I think you know it."

"Who's Tony?"

"Me. The cool thing is—the way they wanna be woke is—I'd be

playing the white guy, Tony, and I'm Mexican, and if you played Maria, who's actually Puerto Rican, you'd be playing it as a . . . what are you?"

"Not Puerto Rican."

"What are you?"

"I'm half my mother and half my father. I'm me. What does it matter?"

"It matters."

"I'm Mormon. I guess, if I'm anything—a rose by any other name."

"Mormon Puerto Rican and Mexican white guy. Perfect. They call it casting against type."

"So I'm in love with you?"

"No. Your character is in love with my character, and vice versa."

"You can sing?"

"Yeah, I told you that."

"Let me hear you."

"Right here?"

"Sure."

"No way."

"No way, Josue. Why not?"

"It's totally in public."

"Dude, you ran into a girl's bathroom and you're scared to sing here in the lunchroom?"

Josue accepted the challenge and began to sing "Maria." At first, Pearl wanted him to stop 'cause it was embarrassing in front of everyone, and all the kids kind of stopped eating to see the Josue show, but then he had a good voice, a really good voice, and the music, the melody and the lyrics, were so enchanting, she'd never really heard anything like it before, and she didn't want it to stop. She let him go all the way to the end. A concert for one. She wanted to sing back to him, to join, but she didn't know the words. She wanted to.

When he finished, a few kids shouted, "Josue!" and some even clapped. Josue took a few big, self-deprecating bows to the room, and sat down again.

"That was pretty good," Pearl said.

"Thanks. Will you come to auditions after school today? Will you audition for Maria? You'll get it. I promise you. You blow everyone here away."

"Maybe," Pearl said, figuring, Why not pass the rest of my time here in Hell singing beautiful music. It wouldn't get in the way, wouldn't mess up her master plan to get back to the desert and Bronson.

23.

DEUCE DID HIS HOMEWORK. He contacted the National Labor Relations Board to see what preparatory steps were necessary to unionize BurgerTown. He needed to create an organizing committee—well, that was him. Done. He had to come up with an issues program—he liked the "Fight for $15" movement, and he wanted decent health-care coverage for those not on their parents' plan. Done. Third, the NLRB rep told him, he'd have to create buzz, an excitement for the union. Deuce was an electric kid, he was a power line, he could buzz.

He armed himself with facts and figures. He'd been pigeonholing and isolating co-workers in intense one-on-one rap sessions for weeks, listening and proselytizing, educating, always educating. He knew exactly where it was okay for him to have these discussions—in the break room, or in off-work sites. He would do things the right way. His eyes had a new light in them. Mary thought maybe he was in love, and she asked him if he had a girlfriend. He said no, he was just involved in some exciting work stuff.

"Exciting hamburger stuff?" she asked absently.

"Exactly right, exciting hamburger stuff," he replied with a smile.

After he felt he'd talked enough to the BurgerTown workers individually and had sufficient interest generally to call a meeting, he organized one behind Dellavalle's back. He knew that Dellavalle, if alerted, might fight the union drive with the time-honored yet illegal weapons of the employer—offering raises and incentives off the books, threatening to close up shop because a union would break the business financially, and threatening to fire someone. But Dellavalle was still very fond of Deuce, didn't suspect a thing, and Deuce knew how to play on his boss's vanity and turpitude.

Deuce suspected the real enemies here were the apathy of the student workers on the one hand (they were gonna quit this job in a matter of months anyway—why make waves?), and fear on the part of the adult Hispanic workers (if they got fired, they had no options). Maybe they had concerns over documentation, real or imagined. There were horror stories under Trump that cowed everybody in the margins. Fear and apathy, Deuce intuited, were powerfully resistant to logic. He wasn't going to rationalize his way to heaven, and he knew from his father, from Joseph Smith, and from Eugene Debs, that righteous passion was contagious. He knew the Greek origins of the word *enthusiasm* meant literally to have God in you. *Zeal* was just another word for God.

He needed 30 percent of the workers to pledge their unionization support in order to bring a petition to the NLRB. He worked fast because he knew if Dellavalle caught wind of it, he'd try to sabotage the drive any way he could with lies and scare tactics, to threaten that the union takes more out of a paycheck than taxes—tried and true coercion.

That's what he was up against the night he got the entire staff together in the BurgerTown parking lot. Bottom line, when it came time for a vote, there were only twenty-five employees, so all he needed were those eight yes votes. He prayed for a moment, asking God for clarity, and the tongue of Aaron, the ability to inspire and the honor to be of service to his fellow man. Then he opened his mouth and spoke extemporaneously for twenty straight minutes without pause on the inherent dignity of man, the right of a man or a woman to dignified and fairly compensated work, the unfairness of capitalism, and the mercy of Christ. He knew his shit inside and out. He was possessed by a holy spirit, the spirit of God the Father and Bronson the father, the spirit of Tom Joad. Zeal. He did not hem or haw, he did not say *uh* or *um*. He imagined his father in the audience, pumping his fist, shouting approval; and that gave him courage. After fifteen minutes with barely a breath, he looked out in that dark parking lot beneath that stupid BurgerTown sign and saw grown men and women crying, crying with him, crying tears of hope and tears of joy.

When he had finished, the entire parking lot erupted into wild applause, chanting, "Union Sí! Union Sí! Union Sí!" and "Sally! Sally! Sally!" Deuce didn't feel spent; he felt he could've gone on like that for hours. He scanned the little crowd, making eye contact with each co-worker, the recognition and respect flowing back and forth evenly, until his eyes fell upon a man he hadn't seen when he'd begun his speech. A man clapping loudest of all, with the biggest tears running down his face. His father, Bronson Powers. Deuce made to go to him, but he got a little waylaid; he shook a couple hands and received hugs, a kiss and a blessing from Jaime, who, despite being fired, was there on crutches. By the time he got to where he'd seen his dad standing, it began to dawn on Deuce that the old man had never been there at all, that he'd just wanted him there, needed his presence there in his mind. For there was no one. If the man had been there, he was gone now without a trace, vanished like a holy ghost.

24.

TWENTY SECONDS INTO Pearl's audition for the lead in Rancho Cucamonga High School's spring production of *West Side Story*, Mr. Bartholomew, the head of the theater department and director, knew he had just met the girl to play Maria. He imagined the guardian presences of Bernstein and Sondheim tap him on the shoulder, point, and sagely nod. He felt like whomever the guy was who first saw a young Meryl audition. Because it wasn't only her voice, which was Broadway ready, it was her acting, or rather inhabiting. She became a credible Maria in a moment, without preparation, as soon as she opened her mouth. She went from a sullen, bored, though beautiful seventeen-year-old girl to something as incandescent and timeless as Natalie Wood, in the time it took to count in the song.

Sure, she could use some help with details and technique, clean certain things up. She was in her salad days, green, but the immediate transformation had been seamless and complete. It was a magic trick. He felt blessed. He hadn't seen a transformation like that since childhood Communion when the priest waved his hand, and cheap red wine and an unsalted cracker transubstantiated into Christ's blood and body. Maybe, he second-guessed, he'd been waiting so long for something like this in this boring little town that he was overreacting. Well, so be it. He would overreact. He was a drama queen after all, always had been, always would be. He was going to be the man who discovered Pearl Powers. Pearl, like Janis Joplin. A ready-made star handle. She wouldn't even have to change her name.

When she'd finished, he stood and slow-clapped, shaking his head like he couldn't believe what he'd heard. "It's yours, Pearl. All yours. You can play Tony, too, if you want. Sorry, Josue. Play everybody. Pearl, baby, you're the entire Mormon Tabernacle Choir. I just died and went to heaven. It's you and Josue. My job is done. I'll just sit back, watch it happen, and take all the credit."

The next couple weeks, Pearl threw herself into rehearsal. Even though she had those walls up, that glum safety was nothing compared with the spirit that entered her while she sang and acted. She'd found the first inklings of a calling. This assuredly complicated any fallback to Agadda da Vida, would seem to preclude a return even, but she didn't allow her mind to go there. Like any seventeen-year-old kid, she lived from day to day, in the moment, and the moments on the rehearsal stage, looking into Josue/Tony's eyes, watching the Jets get up to their shenanigans with Officer Krupke, were the best she'd ever had. She began to open up to Mr. Bartholomew, and to Josue. She really enjoyed the esprit de corps of the whole acting troupe; she'd found the subset of high school, of life, where she belonged.

Though Pearl was probably about two years his elder, Josue took it upon himself to be her mentor and teach her about the world after 1969. He was proud to have this beautiful, older girl—a woman, she seemed to him, with a mysterious past—under his wing. Pearl had confided in him the borders of her education and experience, that she was a pop culture blank slate, and he had devised a crash course in music and movies for her, some of which he'd be seeing and hearing for the first time himself. She liked Spielberg and Paul Thomas Anderson. *Jaws* made her happy she'd grown up in the desert. *Bagdad Cafe* reminded her of home, and she learned to sing the beautiful, haunting Jevetta Steele theme

song, "Calling You"—"A desert road from Vegas to nowhere /
some place better than where you've been." She loved loved loved
E.T. and *13 Going On 30* and *Last Tango in Paris* (Brando was a god,
but she turned it off before the end as it made her uncomfortable
to watch with Josue). Josue played her *Encino Man* because he
thought she would relate to a character from the distant past being
dropped into the modern-day Valley. She laughed. He called her
"Encino Woman."

She secretly watched to the end of the credits in some action
films, which weren't really her thing, looking for the name Bronson
Powers among the stunt crew. She was amazed and proud to find it
a number of times, most thrillingly in that cult classic (Josue's
favorite), the prophetic "Rowdy" Roddy Piper sci-fi vehicle, *They
Live*. Bronson had had a whole other existence before her, an exciting life. She began to wonder if there would ever be a record, like a
movie credit, of her anywhere, if her name would ever be written
down for some future person to read and wonder about. Or would
she disappear unseen and unappreciated like one of her beloved
desert five-spots, which bloom and die in invisible obscurity? She
wrote her name on a slip of paper and gave it to Josue to put in his
wallet, like an autograph.

"I know your name," he said.

"I don't want you to forget it," she said.

She dug the Cure, really got into Nirvana (met, fell in love with,
and mourned Kurt Cobain all in one day) and Stone Temple Pilots
(ditto Scott Weiland, honorable mention Alice in Chains' Layne
Staley), and couldn't believe Michael Jackson was human. She spent
hours in the thrall of Lou Reed, Billie Holiday, Aimee Mann, the
Kinks, and Little Jimmy Scott. Josue played her U2's *The Joshua Tree*
(he sweetly figured she would respond to a work, like "Where the
Streets Have No Name," inspired by her home), which she thought
was great, but pretentious. She could watch or listen to a work for
only a few seconds before she knew whether it spoke to her soul,

whether it had the vitality of the real or the stench of the ersatz. Her slate was that pure. There was no high or low to her, only fuel.

Josue took Pearl to see *Joker* at the AMC Victoria Gardens 12. Her first movie in a theater. On the way, he explained the Batman mythology to her. "Sounds like something out of the Mormon bible," she said. He beamed. He said his dream was to do a Batman musical with a Hispanic lead (him) in which the Bruce Wayne figure starts wearing a mask as a professional wrestler in Mexico City, christening himself Hombre Murciélago, and after suffering a wrestling head injury, which causes him to sometimes confuse his own identity with the vigilante Lucha Libre character he created, ventures from the ring to infiltrate "like, the drug cartels and organized crime" as a mysterious dispenser of rough wrestling poetic justice, and to redistribute that dirty money to the people.

"Wow," Pearl said, "that sounds so crazy. Is that possible?" He beamed some more and veered off into a synopsis of *The Pillowman*, which he said was the best, most underrated play of all time, and he wished she could see it.

When they got inside, he demonstrated how to mix the Milk Duds into the popcorn for a "sweet-and-sour effect." Pearl couldn't believe how wide the screen was; she felt like she was looking at the night sky in the desert. This was not like watching a movie on a computer or TV; this was a five-sense hallucination.

They held hands and munched snacks happily through a half hour of previews, but when the movie began, the sound was so loud and full, Pearl felt it in her stomach. She became edgy. She loved the cello in the score and the gritty, richly saturated palette of the cinematography. She thrilled to Joaquin Phoenix's oddball physicality, his crooked half smile, and his lilting, quiet, slightly effeminate voice; the barely controlled chaos within him reminded her of Bronson, and she felt, while all the other actors were in a movie, that Phoenix might leap from the screen into her lap at any moment. Suddenly, it all got to be too much—this story of tragic, comic-book paternity and a traumatized child realizing a beloved parent is crazy and bad. And the noise, her body was drowning in it; and that cello like a knife gutting her ritualistically in melodic patterns. She ran out.

Josue found her hyperventilating by the concessions and bought her a blue slushie to calm her down.

"You didn't like it?" he asked.

"More like it didn't like me," she managed to whisper. She looked like she might barf an unholy melange of Twizzlers, popcorn, slushie, and Milk Duds. Josue told her to breathe. He settled her. It felt good to run to the rescue of his distressed damsel. But he could see he'd miscalculated. She was not like others. She was pure, and her receptors were not blunted by having grown up in a world of 24/7 sensory assault. He beheld her now, charmingly unaware that her lips and tongue were slushie blue, and thought she was not so much a person as an animal, a beautiful, innocent, wild thing, like a horse, though he'd never even touched a horse. Her tear tracks had stained her cheeks. He wiped them away and turned her to look in the mirror beyond the popcorn machine, and told her to stick out her tongue. She laughed when she saw it was as blue as a paint sample strip.

"Like Joker," she said.

"No, like Pearly Smurfette," Josue replied, reaching for a sweeter, less anarchic comparison.

"Who's that?" she asked.

"That's okay, we'll get to it," he said, pulling her into a hug. She angled her head sharply into his shoulder for comfort. He wrapped his arms as wide around her as he could, like he might take her fully inside himself, like a kangaroo, he thought, another animal he'd not met. Holding her like this, he walked her out of Victoria Gardens. They had learned a lesson. The rest of the pop culture education would take place in the safety of Josue's small room at home.

She couldn't get into Disney at all, or anything animated. She didn't get Jim Carrey, but did get Will Ferrell and Dave Chappelle the most, and George Carlin. She drew a blank on *Harry Potter* and *The Lord of the Rings*. She had little space for fantasy; she was catching up on reality as best she could. Josue's curriculum was scattershot and wide-ranging, varying from day to day with his moods and memory. He had Pearl watch *The Sopranos* from start to finish in three days; she was very sad to hear that James Gandolfini was dead. She bailed on the Sex Pistols and *Sex and the City* almost immediately. She liked Flight of the Conchords and *Breaking Bad* and Philip Seymour Hoffman. She passed on *Game of Thrones* ("If I see a dragon," she told Josue, "I'm out"). She thought *New Girl* was okay (liked Zooey Deschanel), and Marie Kondo, and was fascinated by cooking shows; YouTube's *Tiny Kitchen* made her happy as well as *Chef's Table* and *The Great British Bake Off*. She'd never seen food like that prepared, eaten, or wasted.

Josue was a happy teacher with a willing student. Every day, after school, when they weren't rehearsing, they were at Josue's house, listening to music and watching movies. Josue lived kind of far away. He wasn't supposed to be at Rancho Cucamonga High geographically, but it was way better than the school in his neighborhood, so his father had an arrangement with a guy he knew that he'd pay the guy's electric bill so that Josue could appear to live in the right district and could go to Rancho Cucamonga. Josue saw himself as a tough street kid aspiring upward but holding true to his roots (he could see himself on *American Idol* as that scrappy Mexican kid from the wrong side of the tracks who fell in love with show tunes but could still channel Control Machete, Cafe Tacvba, and Marc Anthony). With his limited knowledge of her history, he appraised Pearl as an innocent who needed to be protected in the big bad city. At only fifteen, he nominated himself as that mentor and protector. He'd been hopelessly smitten with Pearl since she came singing and slinging attitude out of that bathroom stall. He'd had a couple make-out sessions with girls in the past year, but Pearl was of a different order. It was his first time falling. He knew nothing of Bronson.

One afternoon, Pearl had decided it was a good idea for them to read through *Romeo and Juliet* together to see how it informed their characters in *West Side Story*. Mr. Bartholomew had suggested this exercise. They were lying on Josue's bed, trading lines of Shakespeare while *Nevermind* played on repeat. They'd kissed before and made out heavily, but hadn't had much of an opportunity away from school to go any further. Which was fine for Josue because he was a virgin, and slightly terrified of going all the way. One afternoon at rehearsal, Pearl had found a prop sword backstage and promptly swallowed half of it as her street performer Mother Mary had taught her. Mr. Bartholomew had pulled her aside and tried to warn her of the gestural ramifications of such an act before giving up and saying, "Whatever, Miss Pearl, if you got it, flaunt it—you do you."

But Josue had nearly fainted at that demonstration, and the rumors flew. He was sure it all "meant" something, but was not at all sure what that something was. He just knew she was coming from a place he did not know. She filled him with desire and fear. Yeah, he'd seen how to do sex on the internet, he'd seen porn on his phone, of course, and porn took away some mystery for sure, but also somehow made the whole thing even more intimidating. Those guys were really big and could really fuck forever. He was content to make out with abandon with Pearl, putting everything into a kiss; going further was a big, roiling, scary unknown. "And I swear that I don't have a gun," Cobain droned. "No, I don't have a gun . . ."

But now Pearl removed Josue's shirt and lightly scratched his chest, sending shivers down his spine, literally. Pearl felt no guilt, no shame, not yet. She thought of the id she'd learned about in her psych class. She thought of Eros. She didn't think of Bronson.

Pearl removed her own shirt and guided Josue's mouth to her nipple.

"Kiss," she told him. He kissed her nipple. "Bite," she said. He did as he was told. "Harder," she said. He didn't want to hurt her, but he bit down and she moaned loudly. Her volume made him self-conscious for a moment, and even though both Josue's parents were at work and wouldn't be home until evening, he turned up Nirvana a little louder. She bit his ear and stuck her tongue inside it. Something Bronson had taught her. The top of Josue's head felt like it blew off as the horizon of sensual possibilities expanded exponentially. He couldn't believe his ear could be the location of such wet pleasure. For a moment, he was frozen, listening to, even listening with, his body. She was inside his head.

When Pearl withdrew her tongue, she used it to speak. "Take me," she demanded. And by "take me" she meant, let me take it from here. Josue, the young protector, sworn unspoken in his soul to do whatever this girl asked of him, complied and let her lead. He didn't know how she knew what he didn't, but he knew she must. He'd heard wacky shit about Mormons and their skills, maybe this was that. She was his student of the world, he was her student in the bed. He trembled in her hands.

Afterward, sweating and still full of wonder at what they'd done together, they lay in Josue's bed napping and kissing until the sun went down outside the window. Josue had so many inchoate thoughts, so many questions, so many insecurities he wanted remedied, but he contented himself simply with smelling her; the back of her neck where her hair fell seemed to have most of the answers he was seeking. Most—

Sin sangre. Sin sangre. There's no blood, though, he thought.

25.

HYRUM'S MIDDLE SCHOOL, Etiwanda, was only a couple miles from the high school, but really a world apart. A wild, redheaded stranger, Hyrum had begun as an oddity to his classmates. He was small for his age, but preternaturally strong, and Bronson had taught him how to fight, as he taught all the children. After being bullied by a couple kids, Hyrum took matters into his own hands, kicking their asses in the playground one after another until there were no challengers left. After that playground tournament, Hyrum was accepted, even exalted, as some kind of badass. Because Hyrum never "snitched," this went on mostly beyond the purview of the teachers and the parents. Mary never knew Hyrum had been getting into scuffles until she was called in one day by the school psychiatrist, Julie Harwood, and told that Hyrum probably had ADHD and anger issues. Mary couldn't believe her luck.

Just as her scam to supply herself with Percocet through her gym friend Frankie's forged signature was beginning to raise suspicion at the pharmacy across town, came this boon out of the fucking blue.

"Oh yes," she said to the school psychiatrist, "that sounds like him to a T. What's the cure?"

"Well, there's no cure, but we have had success with Ritalin and Adderall, depends on the kid, on their chemistry."

"What's that? I've never heard of those. You see, I've been

living off the grid for the last twenty years—those sound like dangerous drugs."

"Living off the grid?" she said, smiling. "Oh no, not dangerous at all. Millions of kids take them. Well, of course, any drug is dangerous if abused."

"Of course, but if you say so, you're a doctor, if you really think it will work."

"I do. I think it's worth looking into."

"I trust you."

"Thank you," the doctor said, and thus stroked, felt warm enough to ask, "And what was it like living in another age like that for twenty years?"

Mary told her the general outline of the whole Agadda da Vida story. The doctor was riveted, enchanted by the tale of the ex–sword swallower turned Mormon sister-wife describing an Old Testament harem life out in the desert—the hard farm work and hard lessons, the revolutionary curriculum, the children traumatized by helplessly watching one mother take two years to die. But she was also concerned about Mary as a woman, this "sister-wife" thing, as Mary knew she would be, as she slanted the telling this way and that for her post-#MeToo audience. So Mary cannily fed the prevailing narrative and leaned into exaggerated descriptions of Bronson's unassailable male dominance.

When Mary had finished, Dr. Harwood studied the floor for a few moments, and then intoned gravely, "That would be considered trauma, no, that is trauma, what that man put you through, as part of a harem. You have to know now you are worth more than that."

Mary looked at her through lids lowered in shame. "I am?" she asked like a little girl.

"Oh, yes," Harwood said, and came over from behind her desk to hold Mary's hand. Mary had a good mind to stick her tongue in the doctor's mouth and freak her right out, but she didn't want to kill this golden, Adderall-laying goose.

"I do get anxious," Mary said, "without reason—palpitations, sweats, shortness of breath." She'd read about the symptoms, but, fucked-up thing was, she wasn't even lying.

"PTSD."

"PTSTD?" Mary played dumb.

Harwood laughed and shook her head. "No, PTSD. Post-traumatic stress disorder—you see it in soldiers, battered wives, former cult members, even dogs, killer whales, elephants—sentient beings whose will has been violated and erased by sustained physical or psychological violence and lack of agency. My specialty, obviously, is children, but I'd be happy—*happy* is the wrong word—justified, feel just—to give you a scrip for Xanax or Ambien or both along with a scrip for Hyrum's Adderall. I'm a child psychiatrist, but I don't do any private practice anymore. I find this more rewarding spiritually, what I can do in a public school. I'm sorry, do you have a family doctor?"

"Family doctor? None of my kids had been to a doctor before this year. We rely on God through prayer to heal us." Well, she knew that might be going a little far with the vaguely Christian Scientist stuff, but no, Julie Harwood ate all that exoticism up.

"Wow, okay. Amazing." Harwood whistled. "I say Xanax and Ambien because people have different reactions, and you can choose which works better, just let me know, okay?"

"Different strokes for different folks. Different pills for different ills."

"Precisely."

"Do you really think I need help, though?"

Mary found herself in the odd position of being fully honest and dishonest at the same time—lying for these drugs at the same time she was sincerely asking for help made her feel very fragmented and powerful at once.

She'd already gotten what she wanted, the Rx, and yet she kept gilding the lily, going for style points even as Harwood was filling out prescriptions on official stationery and signing them so sloppily that Mary would be able to forge and get infinite refills. She'd passed some bad checks on Venice Beach decades ago; she knew how to bluff this system. "I think I can make it on my own."

"We all need help. Prolonged abuse can alter brain chemistry, and that sometimes calls for a chemical answer. And I think it's best to treat the family as a system, rather than individuals." Ha, Mary thought, good luck getting Bronson in here. Harwood said, "The pills are only a beginning, though. And you don't have to take them, sometimes just knowing they're there is enough, knowing the option is there. Bottom line is—you need to talk to someone. Your kids need to talk to someone. You've all been through a war."

"Okay. Can I talk to you?" Mary felt that she was playing a character in a play, and the longer she stayed in the scene, the more naturally the lines came to her.

"For now, for today, you can talk to me, sure, but we need to find you someone else long-term, okay? To start the real work and the real healing."

"You'll be my training wheels." Mary watched a change come over the other woman's face, and was afraid momentarily that she'd gone too far with the brown-nosing. But no, Julie Harwood was simply holding back tears. "Yes. Let me write down a few suggestions for you as well. Good people, good resources in this city." She grabbed a tissue for herself and reached for the pen and stationery again.

"Thank you, Dr. Harwood."

"Call me Julie. And hey, how are your other kids doing up at the high school?"

"They seem good."

"Public school success stories, huh? We need more of those. Amazing. But we should keep an eye on the high flyers, too.

Sometimes they're the ones in the most trouble. Here." Julie handed her the prescriptions and a list of local therapists she might go to. "Meet a few different ones, don't jump at the first, find your fit. It's more like Match.com for the psyche."

"Huh?"

"Oh, of course, you wouldn't . . . I just mean, shop around."

But I've already found my fit and it's in my hand, Mary thought. She hugged and kissed the doctor, bounded like a mountain goat out of that office, threw the list of suggested shrinks into the nearest garbage can, and drove straight to a more local pharmacy. Hyrum didn't need it; he would figure out what being a boy meant eventually, what to do with that energy and testosterone, and besides, she wasn't going to start the kid on fucking drugs! Are you all fucking nuts? What kind of a monster does that? You put a sane kid in a crazy world and his crazy reaction means he's sane, not crazy! All these well-adjusted, drugged-up kids? They're the crazy ones! Who could be well adjusted to this world of America and Trump and the twenty-first century? Put the sane on drugs—they're insane!

There's nothing at all wrong with Hyrum. He's a savage boy, born as all boys are, to be wild. The world will break him soon enough; he didn't need drugs to break him, denature him first. There's no cure for nature, she thought, you just gotta survive it.

But my malaise is different. I'm old and broken, I'm lost, I'm soul sick, I need help, I need this. All of it. Just say the names—Adderall/Ritalin/ Xanax/Ambien—magic words like ancient magic spells. I'm feeling better already, but not better enough. And, by taking it all, and keeping these pernicious drugs from Hyrum, I will be a good mother and protector. It's my duty.

She checked her face in the rearview mirror. She saw she was smiling.

26.

SOMETHING WAS IN THE WAY between Josue and Pearl, something unsaid and sore, buzzing and droning like a headache. Pearl could feel it and she wanted it gone. It had been that way since they'd had sex. She'd really opened herself to him, and he'd pulled away. Classic boy move, she figured. But something else wasn't sitting right; something that needed to be said hadn't been said. They had a break from rehearsal and Bartholomew told the players to all get some dinner, they were going to do a full run-through after the meal. "You guys are stinking up the joint the past few days, especially my leads—Pearl and Josue. I don't know what's up with you guys, but don't bring it onto the stage. It looks like you don't even know each other. Leave real-world *chazerai* in the real world!" That was embarrassing.

Pearl saw Josue grab his jacket and head out with Bernardo, Chino, Baby John, Anybodys, and Action.

She put her hand on his shoulder. "Can I talk to you?" Josue looked irritated.

"Sure," he mumbled. Pearl led him to a secluded spot behind the set scaffolding where they could have a little privacy.

"What's going on?" she asked.

"Nothing. Whaddyou mean?"

"Josue, come on. There's something. You won't even look me in the eye unless we're doing the play."

"You know what it is."

"I don't."

Josue looked down, he looked up, he looked all around, could see no way out, and finally said, "There was no blood."

"What? When?"

"When we . . . when we . . . had sex, *sin sangre.*"

"What?"

"There was no blood." He pointed below her waist. "No blood."

"Oh." Pearl nodded.

"Oh? That's all you got to say? 'Oh'?" He imitated her sarcastically. It hurt her.

"I guess I busted my hymen on a horse years ago. When I was like, eleven."

"Bullshit."

"You call bullshit? You're an expert on female anatomy all of a sudden?"

He suffered a hot wave of insecurity that she was alluding to his lack of sexual experience and his performance. He raised his voice. "Bullshit. Blaming a fucking horse."

"You don't really know anything about me." She was speaking gently, but firmly, trying not to attack him even though he was being mean to her. "Where I come from. What my life was like before. I'm not like anybody here."

"I know about you. I know enough."

"I'm like an alien."

"Like from outer space? Keep it up—you're a horse-riding alien. What else?"

"Josue, I thought I wouldn't have to tell you. I thought, I don't know, I could just be two different people, but I can't, you know?"

"I don't know . . . I don't wanna know."

He was pouting, but trying to look hard at the same time. It was the face he would make after he realizes, as Tony, that he just killed a man.

"Then I guess I don't have anything to say," Pearl said, and started to walk away.

He followed. "You think you're so different and so special? So you can be some kinda slut?"

"Yes, Josue. I'm a slut, okay?"

He grabbed her elbow and whispered urgently, "It was my first time, you know."

"I know."

"What do you mean?"

"It doesn't matter. Forget about it."

"No, Pearl, I fucking love you and I wanna know what's up."

That was the first time a man had told her he loved her. Bronson had never said that. She had longed for him to say it, but he hadn't. He had shown it, she reckoned, but he'd never said it aloud. He was too uptight. Josue was braver. The "I fucking love you" out of his mouth sounded like music to her. She wanted to hear that song over and over again.

"You love me?"

"Yeah, I love you like crazy. I think about you all the time. And I wanna know everything about you. I can take it, whatever it is—just help me 'cause I'm making shit up in my head that's driving me crazy. I'm sorry I'm being jealous but these questions just go 'round and 'round my mind on their own."

"Yeah, I get it. I know what jealous feels like."

"Go on, you can tell me what it's like in outer space with all the horses and shit. I'm a man, I'll take it. I want the truth of you. I don't wanna go anywhere. I wanna stay with you. 'Womb to tomb,' you know?"

She could see he was crying—oh, she thought, he's not angry, he's sad. She pulled him into a hug and put her lips on his ear and began to speak in a whisper. "'Birth to earth.'" He smiled, relieved, ready to move on, but Pearl had something she needed to say. "No, you're not the first boy I've loved, Josue," she began; he tried to pull away into his hurt again, but she held him tight. She felt strong. "I'm gonna tell you a story," she said, and then she told him everything.

After the meal break, after all the kids had shuffled back in burping and farting, Bartholomew took the stage. "Children," he said, "I am in recovery. From many things, and many people. From life. And friendship helps, being kind to one another, loving one another, and making art together. This is just a moment in your lives, when we perform our little show next weekend, just a moment in a little high school play, but look around at all the other faces. Some of you will know success, some of you will know failure, except you, Pearl, you will never fail and you'll live forever . . ."

All the kids laughed. Bartholomew continued, "All of you will know sickness, and betrayal, and death. All of you, each and every one of you will know heartbreak and death." He looked around at the eyes looking back at him and held them. He had them. He was making himself cry. He went for the heartstrings. "But not in here! No! Not tonight! And not next weekend! ALL we will know in here is love, all we will know is trust, and all we will know is truth! Now fucking act and sing like it! Act one, scene one, *West Side Story* now! Places!"

And the kids, borne aloft on an old gentleman's sincerity and passion, nailed it beyond their years. Bartholomew worried that he might have given the pep talk too early, but such was the force apparent in the players' eyes that he knew it would carry over till at least next week, and if they were lucky, for years to come. By the time the last scene had finished, the kids looked out into the audience where Bartholomew normally sat, and it was vacant. He had left at some point, happy with what he'd seen, wanting the kids to experience having been great not for him, but for themselves, they were their own audience. They all jumped up and down and hugged one another. As Pearl was hugging Anybodys, she spotted Bronson over her shoulder standing in the front row by the lip of the stage, a huge smile on his face.

Pearl wasn't sure if she was hallucinating or not. She walked toward the apparition, like Hamlet dreading and desiring equally the ghost of Claudius.

"Dad?"

"Hi, Pearl," he spoke. He was real. Up on the stage, she towered above him. From this angle, she could see he had a small bald spot she'd never noticed before.

"How long have you been there?" she asked.

"Long enough to know how wonderful you are. I've never seen anything like it. You're an angel. Better than Natalie Wood."

And it's true, he knew what he was talking about, he'd worked with the biggest stars in Hollywood. His kid had as much charisma as any of them. He found himself overwhelmed with a combination of pride and possession. Pearl thought Bronson was looking at her in a way he had never looked at her before. It was a way she used to imagine men who were in love looked at the women they were in love with, and she had wanted him to look at her like that, but he never had; and now that he was looking at her like that, she didn't want it any longer, wanted him to stop, felt sorry for him, a grown man with a bald spot looking at a seventeen-year-old girl with that stupid, sappy, puppy-dog look on his face. He disgusted her suddenly. She wanted a way out.

"Josue!" she called out. Josue came jogging over from where he'd been chatting with Officer Krupke.

"What's up, babe?" he asked. Bronson visibly flinched at "babe."

"Josue, I want you to meet my dad."

"Bronson. You make a fine Tony," Bronson said, extending his hand up to the stage where Josue could grab it. The kid was giving him a funny look, though, an impudent look, like a smirk. Bronson had half a mind to crush his soft little hand and bring him to his knees.

"Dad, this is Josue, my boyfriend."

27.

BRONSON FELT RELIEF to be back on his motorcycle again after that. It was strange to be in a high school having those feelings of rage and jealousy over a girl, because he hadn't had those feelings since high school, it seemed. Was good to get out of there fast, even necessary. He found the block in Rancho Cucamonga where Mary and the kids were staying. He was going to say hi to Mary, Hyrum, and Deuce, maybe talk to Pearl when she got home, though he didn't know what he'd say to her. He had a feeling he should wait. Either wait or take her back with him to the desert tonight. He'd see how he felt when the time came.

He got off the bike and was walking past a little park toward Mary's address when he heard a voice that sounded familiar. Kind of singing, kind of talking, kind of chanting—rapping. But it sounded like Hyrum. He followed the voice into the park to a group of kids who were huddled around an old-fashioned "beatbox." Bronson pushed past a couple kids, and Hyrum was in the center. His son was dressed like a clown. His pants were so big at the waist that they drooped to his hamstrings, exposing his underwear, no temple garment there. He wore a red bandana on his head and on his wrists bangles of all sorts; what looked to be a heavy gold chain around his neck had to be fake, it was the thickness of his finger.

Hyrum looked up at the old stranger in their midst and broke out into a huge smile. "Yo! Pops!" he said. "My nigga! What's up?" and offered his father an elaborate handshake. Bronson said nothing in reply, offered nothing. He lashed out before he could formulate a thought. He slapped Hyrum so hard across the face that it knocked the boy down.

One of the kids said, "Oh, shit!" And Bronson turned hard on that child like he was gonna knock him down, too. The kid shut up.

"Why are you speaking like that, Hyrum?"

"I speak like I speak, bruh."

"Get up."

"Why, so you can knock me down again, old man? Finna pop a cap in yo ass, nigga."

"Shut up! Get! Up!"

"Get fucked, bruh."

In a rage, Bronson yanked his son up off the ground, throwing him over his shoulder in one athletic movement, and walked out of the park. The rest of the kids recovered their courage before they were out of earshot and started making fun of both of them, Hyrum and Bronson, calling them "pussies" and "faggots," whatever they had.

Bronson didn't put Hyrum down until Mary had opened the door and let them both in. Bronson tossed Hyrum on the floor, on his back. Hyrum was bleeding from his mouth, but he didn't care. He got up slowly, deliberately.

Standing now, facing his father, Hyrum challenged him. "We done, fool?"

"What the hell happened?" Mary asked.

"I found him acting like a clown in the park."

"You the clown, Mormon."

"You hear that?" Bronson asked Mary. "How long has he been like that? Talking like that? He's eleven!"

"Hyrum, go to your room. Let's all cool down and we can talk about it later."

"Later for all y'all," Hyrum sneered as he smacked his bloody lips together in a dismissive sound and disappeared behind his closed door.

"What the fuck is going on, Mary?"

"It's when in Rome, I guess, Bronson."

"What? It's not fucking 'when in Compton.'"

"He's just fitting in. It's not real, won't stick."

"Seems real to me. Where is Deuce in all this? Why isn't he watching after his brother?"

"Deuce is at work. At BurgerTown. And Pearl is at school, at rehearsal. She's doing—"

"I know where Pearl is!" Bronson yelled, cutting her off vehemently. "And what she's doing. Come here."

"What? Why? I'm right here."

"Come to me, I said." Unable to resist, she walked to him. "Closer. Look at me."

"I am looking at you," Mary said, glancing down.

"Let me see your eyes." She reluctantly let him see. "You're stoned," Bronson said. "You're fucking stoned. Jesus Christ, Mary."

"I can't do it alone, Bro'," she cried. "I can't, I'm sorry, I'm not tough enough anymore, I need help, and I don't have any help. You don't know what it's like out here. It's fucking everything all the time. I need Yaya, and I need you."

She started to sob. Bronson was unmoved. The volume of the music coming out of Hyrum's room, the bass shaking the thin walls, made it impossible to think, or to feel anything other than rage. He didn't want to do anything stupid and he was in no shape to see Pearl again now. He turned and left.

28.

STARTING BACK TO JOSHUA TREE on the eastbound 10 freeway at about 10 p.m. on a Wednesday, there was little to slow Bronson down and the speed felt good: 85, 90, 95, 100. He missed a well-paved road like this; he could open it up. He took his hands off the handlebars and replaced them with his feet, lying back flat like he'd done as a show-off in his younger stunt days. He was older now, and his balance was not as stable as it used to be. The bike wobbled, then straightened out. On his back, he looked straight up at the stars that flew by above him like the dots on sheets of player-piano music he remembered from the black-and-white movies he knew as a child. The world brought back memories to him. It's why he didn't like to leave home. He thought of Abbott and Costello and the Wolfman and laughed; the bike fishtailed again. He sat up and gunned it straight across three lanes toward an off ramp.

Bronson exited the highway, rode a couple blocks, and got right back on the westbound side. He was going to double back and get Pearl, take her out of the world, and bring her home to the fortress of solitude. But when the time came to exit, he found himself passing the turnoffs for Rancho Cucamonga, and speeding for Los Angeles. In an hour, he was passing all the old exits for the studios he used to work in. Western Avenue or La Brea for Paramount. Overland for Fox and Sony. All the old memories were crowding in on him—the old friends, the joys and the disappointments. His Frankenbike, built from stray pieces of Harleys, Ducatis, and BMWs, was a jury-rigged time machine, and it had transported him back twenty, thirty, even forty years.

But he didn't want to go into the past anymore, the only thing back there was hurt; lack of integrity and confusion—drinks, fights, fucks, and regret. Bronson continued to find it curious how just physically being in an old haunt brought back images and thoughts from so long ago that had lain dormant, waiting for him to disturb the ground and release them like spores kicked up from the dust. Haunts were haunted. He much preferred the clarity of a barren desert that contained no human ghosts or memory. He wanted to time-travel in the other direction, into the future, to see if he had one. About ten minutes later, he gently leaned right and nudged the bike off the highway and onto Bundy in Santa Monica. At 11:30, he rang Maya Abbadessa's doorbell.

Maya slept with a baseball bat by her bed. Some wooden club she'd found in the garage when she'd moved into this house. She had played some softball in high school and was a good hitter, knew how to use the hips to swing the hands, get some torque. The bat felt good in her hands, she could swing it from either side. Santa Monica/Brentwood was a good neighborhood, but at night, the streets were empty and quiet, and the possibility of good old Southern California senseless violence erupting, as Joan Didion had memorably catalogued the Manson end-times, was always in the back of her mind, like a dark, discordant streak at the back of the sunny Beach Boys harmonies. In another age, Nicole Brown Simpson had been slaughtered not too far from her door. After shooting a gun with Bronson in the desert, she'd thought of getting one, but she hadn't yet.

She approached the door holding the bat like a righty. "Who is it?" she demanded.

"Bronson."

She opened the door. Bronson looked like hell, like someone had let out his air pressure a little, but he managed a smile. "Surprise," he said.

Maya still had the bat shouldered and ready. "Hey."

"You gonna swing that thing, Steve Garvey?" Bronson asked.

"Who's Steve Garvey?"

"Great Dodger. Before your time, I guess. Forearms like Popeye."

"I'm a Phillies fan. Who's Popeye?"

"Great sailor. Also before your time. Forearms like Steve Garvey." He was consistently funnier and more charming than she might expect. She took a little check swing with the bat.

"Ha. Depends if I see a pitch I like, I guess." She let him in, closed the door, and locked it.

Having Bronson Powers of Joshua Tree in your little rented craftsman's bungalow in Santa Monica was like having a horse or a bear as a house pet. The man felt too big indoors, like he couldn't turn or sit properly without banging into something or busting something up. He didn't drink: the Mormon thing. He collapsed on her couch like he'd been deboned, and sighed, and talked about Pearl and how great she was in *West Side Story*, how much she reminded him of his dead wife, Jackie, with whom he was clearly still in love. She didn't know if he meant it this way, but Maya found his everlasting devotion to this Jackie attractive and moving as hell. She was buried in one of those mysterious graves Maya had seen when she was high.

He talked with obvious pride about Deuce leading a union drive at a fast-food place. He had a folded clipping from a local Rancho Cucamonga newspaper with the headline "17 Year Old Changemaker" comparing Deuce's youth activism with that of the young survivors of Parkland. "'And a child shall lead them,'" he said. "You know, I had always hoped the kids would want to come back to the desert when they grew up, but we taught them, we prepared them for the world as best we could while still holding them out of the world."

"Then I showed up tripping balls."

"We don't blame you."

"Anymore."

"Anymore."

"I guess that's the way, huh? Kids leave." She didn't know.

Bronson said, "'A man filled with the love of God is not content with blessing his family alone, but ranges through the whole world, anxious to bless the whole human race.'"

"That's nice. Who said that?"

"Joseph Smith."

"Who? Never heard of him. I'm kidding. I'm just kidding."

He got it, though, he gave her a laugh. He gets it. We can vibe, maybe. He's not a total kook, she thought, maybe more like an eccentric collector of things like cars or baseball cards, only he collects the memorabilia of a religion. She would talk to him like he was a regular guy.

"I wonder if they have their high school boyfriends or girlfriends yet."

"Who?"

"Deuce and Pearl."

His aspect changed. "Oh, no."

"Uh-oh—look at that face. You're one of those dads, huh? Get-the-shotgun type?"

"What?" Bronson seemed puzzled and annoyed.

"No, I love it." Maya backtracked a bit. "I wish I'd had a dad like that. It's sexy. I mean, like, on somebody else's dad it's sexy, not on mine, on you."

"Oh. Okay."

"I'm just trying to say, it sounds like you did a good job raising the kids."

Bronson seemed to come back to her a bit, from the uneasy place he'd just gone. "That's bad news for your company. I can quote you, right? Game over."

"I'll deny it." Maya forced a little smile. "I don't want to talk business."

Maya began to realize that what she liked about this man was how unpsychological he was, if that was a word. It was like he'd been born in a time before therapy, before Freud, before Christ even. She had subtly, she thought, brought up her own fatherless childhood for him to ask about, but he had declined as if that impulse never occurred to him. But it wasn't that he was selfish, it was more that those types of details were insignificant in some larger truth to which he held the keys. He was like a Greek hero to her, like Odysseus, a man of action and integrity. His certainty was intoxicating, it informed his every movement—the way he stood tall, the way he walked, the way he touched things. She didn't even have to agree with him to feel a bit drunk on it.

Bronson got up and started looking around. He kept thinking about an old *SNL* skit with Phil—who was it—Kevin Nealon? No, Bill, Phil . . . it was Phil Hartman who played a Neanderthal in hilariously bad prosthetic makeup, who is discovered frozen in ice, subsequently thawed and reanimated, and goes to law school and practices law in fur skins. So silly. But that's what he felt like tonight. Like he'd been thawed out after centuries. Usually scripture floated to his mind, tonight it was network television. He couldn't remember what it was called. Ice . . . Lawyer . . . Frozen-lawyer-man or something.

The little house was so spare and uncluttered. It looked like a "staging home." Maya had no books. She watched Bronson roam around, snooping. "You look like you're looking for clues," she said.

"Where are all your books?"

"On my iPad."

"I what?"

"Are you fucking with me?"

"No."

"It's a screen, like a portable electronic screen, can hold thousands of books."

"Unfrozen Caveman Lawyer!" he said, and snapped his fingers.

"Say what now?"

"Nothing. Was just trying to remember something." He tried describing the old skit to her; it was absolutely not funny in the telling, his retelling anyway. He gave up.

"Guess you had to be there," she said with a smile.

"Just means I feel out of place. Out of place and out of time."

"*Saturday Night Live* is still on, I think."

"Bullshit."

"No, I think it is."

"Why?" He asked like it was an existential question.

"I don't know, I'm just catching you up, I guess."

"Oh, like a public service?"

"Precisely. We put a man on the moon, too."

"Okay, that's enough."

"Still no woman president, though."

"Well, I'm happy to see some traditions remain."

"Okay, that's enough, you."

Maya felt like she might be taking part in the strangest rom-com in history. Then she remembered her mom's favorite movie, *Splash*, which Maya had seen a hundred times, and thought if she fell for this sneakily charming Mormon cowboy-stuntman plural-marriage guy, it still wouldn't be as weird as fucking a fish.

"It said 'Parkland' in that article about Deuce. What's Parkland?" Bronson asked.

"A mass shooting at a Florida school. High schoolers were shot and killed by another student."

"Like Columbine? Columbine was one of the reasons that made me want to raise kids away from the world."

"Happens a lot." She sighed. "We had shooter drills in my high school in Philly."

"A lot? It's happened since Columbine?"

"Over and over. Like once a year, at least. More. I think he killed about twenty."

"With one gun?"

"It wasn't, like, just a gun gun. It was a rifle, maybe many rifles, weapons of war. And there was that kid Dylann Roof who shot up a Black church."

"A religious killing?"

"Religious/racial, I guess."

"That is irredeemable. What kind of child kills like this?"

"Somebody that needs help."

"What kind of help?"

"Psychological, I guess. Therapy."

Bronson laughed scornfully. "Therapy? Talking will save his soul?"

"I don't . . . I don't know. To me, it's more a gun-control issue," she stammered.

"Gun control will save his soul? No. Only one thing will save his soul."

Sometimes the lack of psychological dimension charmed her, sometimes it scared her. He was dizzying and very masculine in his lack of doubt. You would always know where you stood with this man. You might not fully like where you stood, but you'd know where you were. You'd be sane. She felt sane. Not like she did with so many of the slick whiny snakes she'd dated. Her rom-com had gone a little sideways, but even this intellectual frisson was kind of a new feeling on a date. Oh shit, she thought, is this kind of a date? Or a very odd good-old-fashioned Mormon booty call?

"Who gives an evil child a weapon of war?" Bronson asked sadly.

"We do. It's not *West Side Story* anymore."

Bronson shook his head and started to cry, deep, soul-shaking sobs. Maya felt he might shake the house itself. A Greek hero, and

one that can cry. Jesus, that was attractive. Maya held him as he settled some, and he began to speak of Hyrum and Mary and how
fucked up things were and that he wanted to go with her to Praetorian tomorrow and figure out a compromise with her boss. Holding
him close, Maya noticed his odor filling up the living room. On the
horse, in the great wide open, she had been into his musk, but inside,
he seemed rank, unwashed, dirty, homeless. She thought about asking him to leave, but she didn't want him to. She was curious to see
beneath his armor. She offered him a shower and bed. He accepted.

While Bronson showered, Maya downed a couple shots of tequila
to calm herself. She was excited, but also anxious, for reasons she could
not entirely fathom at the moment. Well, there was a Mormon cowboy polygamist in her bathroom. When he'd come to her bed now,
Bronson would smell like Maya, he was using her soaps. That day
she'd visited at the ranch, they'd only kissed, they hadn't made love.
After that, she'd entertained idle fantasies about ditching the Praetorian Death Star and moving out to the desert to be with him, become
a homesteading sister-wife, but she knew that was nuts—a silly day-
dream to pass the time between writing up Hammer film synopses.

But could she date him? Would the introduction of his three
kids to the modern world be the beginning of his reintroduction as
well? Could he stop with the gross polygamy and be her sexy, older
cowboy boyfriend she could show off at parties to shame all these
soft West Side men? He could be like her personal Christopher Lee,
a tall, sexy, British actor who had played many a Dracula in Hammer films with a bounding physicality that made him much more
appealing and dangerous to Maya than the lugubrious, more famous Bela Lugosi. Or better yet, her very own Brad Pitt, who had
just made aging stuntmen sexy in the new Tarantino film.

And now here he was in her bed, her own wild man to play
with, naked and smelling good of Goop and Sephora. She had
made up so many preconceptions about the way a man like Bronson
would make love that she was almost shocked when he got into

bed that he didn't have, like, multiple dicks or some secret fanfic kung fu fuck style. She'd half expected him to introduce her to some new position, or have a third nipple or a hidden compartment somewhere like he was of a different ancient species.

He kissed her. It was a nice kiss. She liked the roughness of his stubble. She got turned on but there were so many reasons why she thought this was a bad idea, it was gonna be hard for her to let go completely; plus it was the first time, and first times were always a little weird. She could feel his cock grow big and hard against her thigh. She could smell her own sudden arousal up from under the sheets.

"I can't make love to you," he said.

"No?"

"No."

"Oh, not until we're married?" she teased. "What a pussy."

He smiled. "Now you're catching on." She kissed him hard. He returned it, then pulled back slightly.

"You're serious?" she asked.

"I'm serious."

"That's ridiculous."

"Ah, the absurdity of my beliefs is key. Any lazy motherfucker could believe in a reasonable God."

She widened her eyes and whistled, "Is that your pillow talk?"

He smiled. "Such as it is."

"You got mad game, my Mormon friend. Mad game. That is so fucking hot," she said, "so hot, it's unfair. You're just a tease?"

"I'm too old for you anyway."

"Bullshit. We'll see about that."

She made an exaggeratedly funny and obvious move to dive under the sheets to give him head. He gently stopped her, but he laughed again at the comedic move. He found her beautiful and funny, and the strangeness with which she expressed herself charming. It had been so long since he related like this with a woman. He found the sheer chasm between them, her vast difference to him and distance from him, psychologically, spiritually, and chronologically attractive. They were from foreign lands. They had the appeal of time travelers for each other.

"Come up here," he said, offering his chest to lay her head on. "I'm a tired old man. Let's get some sleep."

"I've never been turned down by a Mormon before," she mused.

"How's it feel?" he asked.

"Not bad," she said, nestling into him, "not bad at all."

Coiling up in his arms, she could feel his need was not sexual. He felt sad and strong, and unreachable. Whatever his desire was, it was unreadable to her, like an animal want. She'd never experienced anything like it in a man. This was a lark, she decided, but it would never work, and it shouldn't work, not with the wager still on the table. He might as well be a fish. She would keep her eyes on the prize. But she was taken with him all the same, not just the idea of him. Why not give in to that a little? She could compartmentalize like a dude, she thought. She could enjoy a little of this exoticism and still bring the deal home.

She could tell by his breathing that he was already asleep. She twirled some of his graying chest hair around her finger. He was the first man she'd ever known who didn't feel like he was trying to prove something to her or through her.

When she woke up alone, she wasn't surprised. But then she saw his gun on the dresser and heard sounds in the house. She threw on a robe and shuffled through to the living room to see Bronson in the kitchen engaged in a staring contest with her professional-grade espresso machine.

"Morning." Maya smiled. "What are you doing?"

"Good morning, Maya. I've been trying to figure out your goddamn coffeemaker for the past hour."

"It's a Breville—espresso. I thought Mormons didn't drink coffee."

"Exactly. I was actually trying to make you one."

"Unfrozen Caveman Lawyer?" she asked.

"Ah, you listen."

"That's sweet of you to try," she said, and made herself a double shot.

"You make it look so easy," he said, sadly.

As they drove to Praetorian, Bronson was very interested in the workings of her Tesla. "What an amazing piece of technology," he said. "It's so quiet. I used to dig the sound of a big motor. Trying to save the planet. That's admirable. Even in the desert I've seen big weather changes the last ten years. Climate change, you said? Dry season drier, wet season wetter. Life out of balance." She applied some lipstick using her rearview mirror. "Oh, that's what those are for," he joked. "I never knew."

She puckered and smiled. "Do you know what you wanna say to my boss? He doesn't know the specifics of the deal and he doesn't really want to."

"Yeah," Bronson said. "Maybe talk about selling some mineral rights."

"Okay."

"Maybe I'm good with the half/half deal, the first one you floated. I reckon that's still hundreds of millions for you guys, and you leave us be, and you get the government off our backs."

"I think that's best for everyone," Maya agreed.

She was unsure at this point, with the rocket-like ascendance of Deuce, offset by the less impressive gains made by Pearl and Hyrum, who would win this strange wager by the hazy metrics agreed upon. She had always hoped it didn't have to come to that, so she was pleased and optimistic. This compromise should satisfy Malouf and Bronson, and bring tens of millions, maybe hundreds of millions to Praetorian. It was a huge play, a great deal, a unicorn, and she had engineered it and brought it home.

"I don't know about that," Bronson said. "I think what's best would've been for us to have been left the fuck alone." They drove the rest of the way in silence.

Maya walked Bronson to Malouf's office, and the boss put on his most gracious host persona. "Welcome, welcome, two of my favorites, sit, coffee?"

"No, thanks." Bronson and Maya took seats across from him.

Malouf pointed at Bronson's feet. "Love your boots, man—I can never wear them long enough to break 'em in—Ralph Lauren?"

"No."

"Maya tells me you're quite the horseman."

"Sure."

"Do you play polo?"

"Polo?"

Malouf held up a magazine with pictures from the sport for Bronson to see.

"Oh," Bronson said. "No."

"That's a shame. What would you say is the most important thing about riding a horse?"

"Don't fall off," Bronson deadpanned. Malouf and Maya chuckled.

Maya knew that Bronson had a very low threshold for this kind of bullshit and small talk. And she knew that bullshit and small talk was all Malouf wanted to lead with. It was his way of tiring out adversaries, bore the fuck out of them so they'd agree to his terms just to get away from him and his polo talk. She said, "Bronson has a deal in mind, a compromise. Win/win, I think."

Malouf acted like Maya wasn't in the room; he didn't take his eyes off Bronson. "See," Malouf continued, "I'm always talking to horse riders—jockeys, cowboys, mounted policemen even, to get an edge, as a polo player. I'm always looking to get better with the horses, that's the key, I think. What's the single most important thing between you, as a rider, and the horse? If you had to choose just one thing." Malouf was grinning like this was a fun game they were about to play. Maya noticed his gums were receding. Bronson wasn't smiling.

"Trust," Bronson said finally.

"Ah, trust, that's interesting, thought you might say that. I respectfully disagree, brother. You know what I think is the most important aspect of the horse-person relationship?" Bronson didn't answer; he had begun focusing out the window at the ocean beyond. "Fear," Malouf asserted. "The horse has to know who's boss. Our dominance comes from their fear, then the trust comes, when the horse knows who the boss is." He winked at Maya. Malouf noticed Bronson looking out his window at the Pacific. "You a sailor, too?" he asked.

"No." Bronson stood up, walked to the window, and stared out, his head tilted to one side like a man watching a ship disappear into the horizon. "Excuse me," he said, "I have to use the head. I'll be right back."

When Bronson walked out of the office, Maya knew he wasn't coming back, and she'd most likely never see him again. Malouf took some phone calls, winking at Maya when an especially powerful figure called in, like she was part of the club, in on the big joke. "The Mnooch! How can I help?" he said at one point, mouthing silently to Maya, "Secretary Mnuchin . . ." while wiggling his eyebrows gleefully. "Loved you on Hannity last night, and love those 'oppo zones.' You're a mad genius. You behind that Milken pardon? Ha—I knew it, you wily cunt! Let's get the band back together again. You are lighting the path up ahead, my friend. Oh, I know it's all you, I know the Kush is worthless, a fuckin' puppy. And your hair is on point! How's the lovely Louise?" Maya smiled tightly back and tried to look impressed.

After they had waited fifteen minutes for Bronson to return from the bathroom, Malouf hung up the phone and pointed at his door for Maya to leave too. "Go," he said. "And please, Wharton, don't ever bring a bum into my office again. I'm gonna have to get it cleaned. Smells like Aqua Velva and piss in here."

"Yessir." She stood up quickly and walked out.

29.

"THE PARKING LOT is considered on the grounds of the Burger-Town business, you can't play soccer here, and you sure as hell can't advocate for unions here!" Frank Dellavalle called out as he strode toward Deuce an hour before opening time on a Friday in spring. Deuce had managed to assemble each and every member of the twenty-five BurgerTown employees to vote on the union before official work hours. They all showed, Jaime on crutches, even the sleepy part-time student workers who were now caught up in Deuce's time-capsule, '60s fervor and religious zeal for the people. Everybody wanted to be part of the "movement" and say they "were there when."

Deuce had become a minor local celebrity. He'd had newspaper articles written about him in the *Inland Valley Daily Bulletin*; one from the *San Bernardino Sun* even got picked up in the *Los Angeles Times*, and he had appeared on Southern California TV news (KTLA) three times. In this cowardly brave new world of social media, however, there was no such thing as purely local anymore. Deuce had a budding national profile, small, yes, but some people around the country, and even the world, were aware of the "young socialist firebrand," the "Baby Bernie," the "Cucamonga Crusader." He was no Emma González or Greta Thunberg, but he was definitely a kind of minor thing. His cause, local unionization, wasn't as sexy or global as gun control or climate change, but he had a niche. #Deuceforjustice had even trended on twitter briefly a few weeks back. Absolutely none of that mattered at all to Deuce. "Mr. Dellavalle," Deuce called back warmly, "we're about to hold the vote. I'm glad you could make it."

So Dellavalle knew this was an uphill battle, but he stood to get fired if the union passed. He was the overseer who had lost control of the plantation, and even if the bosses of bosses didn't give two cents about this one location, they cared about the contagion spreading to other franchises eventually infecting their bottom line. The precedent. The drawing of a line. McDonald's, Burger King, et al. had been fighting the unionization of their workers for decades. Dellavalle would have to go down swinging. He'd been doing work behind the scenes. He'd paid off some Mexican workers, bought their no votes with promises of raises and favors, illegally, of course. Adding them to his own no vote, he could only get to ten against. He needed to scare the shit out of them now, turn a few more.

"This is the communal parking lot for five businesses, Mr. Dellavalle, I checked. It's not considered on BurgerTown business grounds. We can have union talks here." Dellavalle walked up to Deuce, got in his face. He wished he was taller and could physically intimidate him; the kid was gangly, but he was six-two easy.

"You realize you're gonna get me fired, right?" he stage whispered. "I got three kids. They're gonna go hungry."

He took out his phone and showed pictures of his family to the crowd. "My parents were immigrants from Italy and they worked hard and I worked hard to earn what I have. That's the American Dream and you guys can get that, too! If you work hard. The union is against hard work. It's communism! It's socialism! It's Bernie Sanders and it's anti-American and now you're taking food out of my kids' mouths!"

Someone shouted from the crowd, "You're white, man, shut the fuck up, you'll get another job." The crowd agreed angrily.

Deuce held up his hand. "This isn't about Black, white, or brown, this is about the people, all of us, the ninety-nine percent versus the one percent. No color." He turned back to Dellavalle and told him, "You're one of us, Mr. Dellavalle. The union will address any recriminative action your bosses take against you, you'll be protected."

"Oh, so the union's gonna make everyone's problems go away? That's horseshit, and you know it!"

"No, it's not a panacea. But it's a part of the solution."

Dellavalle didn't know what a "panacea" was, so he forged on. "You're not even gonna be around much longer, and all these folks are gonna get fired as soon as the spotlight goes away. They'll shut us down rather than keep a union."

"That would be illegal."

"They own the law! They write the law, and if they don't like a law, they'll just write a new one!" Dellavalle raised his voice, addressing the entire crowd now, as well as Deuce. He spoke in terms that convinced Deuce the corporate headquarters had coached him.

"So what are you, the white savior? That's so racist. All these poor Mexicans need some privileged white kid to come in and 'educate' them? Lift them up 'cause they're too stupid to lift themselves up? Why are you listening to this rich white kid? He doesn't care about you!" Deuce looked out at the crowd and considered Dellavalle's point; and he considered it bullshit. Power to the people did not denote color.

Dellavalle paused like he was trying to remember a script; his eyes looked heavenward into his struggling short-term memory. "You're gonna have to pay union dues, more taxes. ICE is gonna become aware of us, of you. Maybe you guys have the right documents, but do all the people you live with? Huh? Your cousins? Their cousins? You people have big families! You know who the fucking president is?"

Deuce could see the legit fear this struck in some of his people, but he wouldn't stop Dellavalle—this was the give-and-take of democracy. He would silence no one. The people had a right to hear all arguments, no matter how mendacious or demagogic. Righteousness did not have to raise its voice or use muscle to prevail.

Jaime wouldn't hold his tongue, though. Smiling, more Zen than Zinn, partly crippled Jaime, with more than $100K in medical bills sitting by his bedside back home, addressed Dellavalle with a resigned lilt: "You are such a dick, *esse*. Fuck Trump and fuck you."

The crowd erupted in a release of laughter. "You need to vote!" Jaime said. "*Vamanos!*" The crowd took up the chant, "*Va-ma-nos! Sal-va-dor! Va-ma-nos!*"

Deuce knew the time was at hand. He rose to his full height and filled his lungs with the clean morning air. "All those in favor of union," he shouted, "raise hands and say 'aye'!"

"Aye!" came back the resounding reply, all hands raised but one, Dellavalle's. Frank looked to the nine he had bribed, and they looked back at him like they'd never seen his face before. Every single one of them was caught up in a moment. "I count twenty-four ayes," Deuce said, and his voice had a new power behind it; he seemed to grow taller every second; he wasn't leading the crowd so much as being carried high on their shoulders by collective force. "All against," Deuce was thundering now, "raise your hand and say 'nay'!"

Even Dellavalle had to mentally stop his arm from shooting up in assent moments earlier, such was the proselytizing power of this young kid. "Nay," he said quietly.

Deuce rang out the tally: "Twenty-four in favor, one against." He paused dramatically. "The union passes!"

All his buddies started chanting, "*Salvador! Salvador! Salvador!*" Somebody grabbed Deuce's ankles and drew him forward into the crowd. He felt himself falling; he impulsively tried to catch himself,

guard his head, but he didn't hit the ground. He found himself cradled, looking straight up into the cloudy morning sky. He felt lifted,
free of gravity, free. He didn't know what it was called, but he was
crowd-surfing. Being passed from hand to hand and anointed. Like
a socialist rock star. This was just the beginning.

30.

AT THE VERY MOMENT Deuce was crowd-surfing, Pearl was rising before her alarm with a feeling that was new to her. She was nervous, and she liked it. She felt alive. The first of three performances of *West Side Story* would be tonight. She made herself some eggs, at least that's what they called them here; but compared with the eggs they had back in Agadda da Vida, these tasted like yellowish Styrofoam, but that was an okay trade-off for now. She went in to say goodbye to Mary, but she was still asleep. She'd been sleeping later lately. "Mom," she said, "wake up, you gotta get Hyrum to school." Mary didn't budge. Pearl shook her gently. Still nothing. "Mom?" Pearl grabbed both Mary's shoulders and shook; Mary inhaled violently like she'd come up for air from deep water.

"Shit, Pearl, you scared me."

"You gotta get up. I gotta get to school early to help out with costumes, and you gotta get Hyrum to school, okay?"

"Oh yeah," Mary said, coming to. "Costumes for what?"

"The show tonight."

"Oh yeah, is that tonight? Of course, that's tonight. Tonight, tonight, there'll be a show tonight . . ." she sang off-key.

"Please stop," Pearl said, going back out the door.

"You nervous?" Mary asked her daughter.

"Yeah," Pearl said with a touch of insecurity.

"Good," Mary said, "that means you're gonna be great." Pearl smiled and left. Mary kept singing sleepily after her, "Tonight tonight, my daughter sings tonight and all the da da dee will shine so bright . . ."

The school day passed fitfully for Pearl. She'd see Josue in the hallway in between classes and they'd kinda check in and give each other the thumbs-up. She daydreamed through her subjects, even her beloved psychology, going over lines in her head, closing her eyes and imagining the blocking of each scene, each song, until memory merged with instinct, and by the end of the day, she was already Maria.

She saw Deuce in her AP History class; he was getting an A+, of course, and she was getting a C−. Today, he looked a little strange to her, flushed, almost high. She was slightly concerned. She sat next to him, something she never did.

"Hey, brother."

"Hey, sister."

"You okay? You look funny." She felt his forehead.

"I'm fine, thanks."

"You still growing or something?"

"Nah, I think I'm done."

"Are you shaving, dude? Growin' a 'stache?"

"With this skin? Nah, not too often. Should I? You look different, too."

"Yeah? You gonna come to the show tonight?"

"Of course, man! I mean, I got these Kanye tickets at Staples Center in LA for tonight, but Kanye Schmanye."

"You're so full of shit. That's the first time in your life you ever said the word *Kanye*. Me, too, come to think of it."

"Or *Schmanye*."

"Right."

"Break a leg, sister."

"Thanks, bruh." They smiled at each other, reveling in the

companionship and easy closeness that only twins can know. "Miss you, bro. We gotta talk more."

Deuce nodded. "You think Dad's gonna come?" he asked.

She hadn't thought of that. And for a moment, she was back in the desert, she was wholly Pearl once more. She'd have to find Maria again. "I don't know," she finally said. "Deuce, there's something I gotta tell you."

"Ahem." The history teacher interrupted them from the head of the classroom. "Am I gonna have to separate you two?"

"Later?" Deuce whispered to his sister.

"Later," Pearl replied.

After school, the Sharks and the Jets met up backstage, ordered pizza, and hung out till curtain. Bartholomew hung back; he could see them gelling, motivating on their own. He was proud of them, and of himself, but he kept an eye out for fissures in the flow; he would be there if needed. He knew he was no genius, he wasn't blind; he knew he was more Guffman than Fosse, but for tonight, he would be in the sweet spot for one time in his life where the great ones lived. And as good as Pearl had been in rehearsal thus far, he felt like her talent was still untapped, and that he could push her even more.

He glanced at her now, and the look of certainty he'd seen earlier was gone. She was pacing suddenly, appearing nervous for the first time since her audition. She dropped to her knees with her hands in prayer.

He walked over, tapped her on the shoulder, and said, "What are you doing?"

"Praying."

"If you rehearse enough, you don't have to pray."

"I've always prayed. Always."

He reached down his hand for her to take and lifted her up, and said, "Walk with me."

When they'd gotten to a quiet, secluded part of the backstage area, Bartholomew asked, "Why are you doing this?"

"What do you mean?"

"I mean, why do you want to act?"

"I don't know, it's fun?"

"Fun, huh? Fun will only get you so far. Are you nervous?"

"Yes."

"Why do you think that is?"

"'Cause I wanna do well?" Pearl sounded like she was guessing.

"Okay, for whom?"

"My family. Myself."

"Fine."

"Fine? Is that a bad answer?"

"It's not a bad answer, it's your answer."

"Do you have another idea?" Pearl asked.

"Well, Salinger—you know Salinger?"

"My dad used to read me *Catcher in the Rye*."

"Well, Salinger said, 'Do it for the fat lady,' and I like that."

"What fat lady?"

"What he means is—do it for someone else, not yourself." Bartholomew couldn't suppress a smile; he had Pearl right where he wanted her. "You see, Pearl, you're gifted, but you're selfish. I think you love playing Maria because you relate to her, loving the wrong boy, and all that." He arched his eyebrows and intimated he was talking about Josue, of course, but that's not who Pearl thought of when she performed her version of Juliet/Maria. "You love being up there because you think you're telling your story, and you're good at that, but the great ones, the real great ones: they do it to speak for those who can't speak—for them it's not selfish, for them it's a prayer for the powerless. Is there someone you want to reach with this performance, someone you want to speak for?"

Pearl totally got what he was saying. She realized she'd been selfish and that this kind man had just taught her how to go from being good to great. She realized acting could be more than fun; it could be her mission. "Well, my mom who died, my real mom, I think she's like Maria. My mom can't pray for herself anymore. So I will pray for her." Pearl hugged him so hard he inadvertently grunted. Fuck Guffman, he thought, I'm on fire. He walked away and left Pearl to her mystical preparation.

Pearl felt her mother close now. Closer than she'd been in years. And Pearl began to listen to her mother. Jackie was with her, in her. And Jackie began to speak to her, through her. Pearl felt like a conduit for her mother, for the powerless, the silent, and the long gone. She would not be selfish, she would be of service. This is how she would act from now on.

Hyrum didn't want to go to *West Side Story*, but Mary wasn't going to let him stay at home. "Come on," Mary said, "you gotta support your sister. That's what families do."

Hyrum looked at her like he could barely be bothered to respond. "Halt with that lame shit, Mom—I'll go if you stop saying shit like that." The show started at 7:30, and by 7:05 Mary and Hyrum had taken their seats; they were almost the first to arrive. Hyrum fidgeted in his suit and tie like it was a hair shirt.

Bartholomew walked out into the gathering crowd and introduced himself to Mary and Hyrum. Deuce had joined them. "I want you to know," he said, "I've taken the liberty of contacting Juilliard about Pearl."

"Who's Julie Yard?" Hyrum asked.

"Not who, what. Juilliard is the finest acting school in all of Oz. I sent them some tape I did of rehearsal; oh, they don't call it 'tape' anymore, do they? From my phone—bad picture, bad sound—and they fa-lipped out. Talking full scholarship. They want her yesterday. I also sent it to Yale Drama, and they even said somebody from the school might come to the show tomorrow night! I said, she's a junior, in high school, and I haven't even talked to her parents . . . so cool your jets, no pun intended."

Mary nodded at the torrent of words and foreign information coming her way; she could use a Percocet, she thought, or some Adderall, a glass of chardonnay, anything. She checked her watch: she still had time to get to the bathroom to take something before curtain. "Pearl has a lot to think about right now," Mary said, "as do I. We're not even sure where we're going to be next year."

"Oh please, don't tell me you're moving; I already have my heart set on crossing gender lines next year for Pearl to play the leads in both *Hamilton* and *Next to Normal*—*scandaloso*, I know!"

"I don't know those," Mary said.

"Haha." He laughed, as if there existed a person who hadn't heard of Lin-Manuel Miranda. "I see where Pearl gets her comic timing from." He winked. "Her deadpan and her high dudgeon. I gotta run. You just sit back and watch. And be blown away. You'll see what I mean. We have plenty of time to talk after."

He turned to go, but Mary stopped him. "Excuse me," she said, "but what is it that makes her so good? I mean, I know she has a good voice and she's pretty, but isn't that like thousands of other kids?"

Bartholomew turned his girth back to her and smiled as if he really liked that question. "It's charisma," he said. "Glamour—was originally a Celtic word to describe the magical haze around a fa-vored person. Some got it, some ain't. It's 'it.' She's got it."

"Yeah, but what's 'it'?"

"Ah, but that's the million-dollar question, isn't it? It's hot and cold. It's the numinous aura around a narcissistic personality."

"Narcissistic?"

"Yes, but in the best way, the Greek way. 'Gracious accommoda-tion, yet commanding impersonality.' Oh, you're taking this the wrong way. I guess the answer to that . . . life is unfair. Moses did ev-erything asked of him and ended up dying in the desert. David was an adulterer who liked young women and God gave him everything. David had charisma, Moses didn't. The 'gift of grace' in Greek, or

'favor freely given.' Even God is a sucker for 'it.'" He noticed the
dazed look on Mary's face and made a motion like he was smoothing
down a dress that had flown up too high, like the famous Marilyn
Monroe image. "Oh, I'm sorry, is my Camille Paglia showing?"

What Bartholomew said had so many personal tangents available to Mary that she momentarily could not think straight. Had
Pearl been speaking to this man about religion? Had she been
speaking to this man about Bronson? He was saying Pearl was chosen somehow. By God? By Bronson? Had there been a difference to
Pearl? Was he saying that Bronson gave her this gift? He was standing there now like he had nowhere in the world to go, and it was
already a few minutes before curtain. All Mary could muster was
"Yes, but what is 'it'?"

Bartholomew leaned in. Mary could smell sweet cocktails on
his breath. Like so many in the Program, she could separate out
ingredients forensically like a drug-sniffing dog—white wine and
cassis—he's a kir royale man. Sure, he must be nervous on opening
night. He stage whispered like it was a secret, "She makes gold out
of pain. Someone objectified her early and she's used to being an
object. Not pointing fingers, Mom. She loves letting us look at her.
Like all the great ones. Marilyn. Judy. Bathsheba. Something is broken in her and she lets us see. That a woman that beautiful has so
much masculine pain, it makes us all human and touch the unfairness of life together."

"Jesus," Mary nearly gasped. Bartholomew winked, and for
such a heavyset man, fairly glided away from them back toward the
stage.

"Who's that fat faggot?" Hyrum asked.

"Hyrum . . . not cool, dude. Not cool," Deuce gently but firmly
admonished his brother.

"Yeah, Hyrum," Mary agreed. "Not cool at all."

"Shit, my bad," Hyrum said. "By the way, Mom, *It* is a horror
movie about a clown."

It was 7:28 now. The curtain was about to go up and their row was filled. Mary wasn't gonna make it to the bathroom in time to take the edge off without making a spectacle. Maybe at intermission, she consoled herself. The lights went down and the overture, the high school band playing the Bernstein score live, started up its theme. Mary sat down and took a deep, calming breath.

When intermission came, it felt like an interruption. Mary didn't want the show to stop, even for a moment, and she didn't want it to ever end. Her cheeks were wet with an hour's worth of tears. That man had been right. Pearl was . . . Pearl was . . . Pearl was beyond her description. Her voice, her carriage, her poise. But more than that, Mary saw another figure onstage tonight through Pearl's Maria—Jackie. She couldn't believe it at first, thought she must be projecting, but then it became clear. Through some magical alchemy Pearl was channeling Jackie tonight—the mannerisms, the tone, the laugh—and it was perfect. Mary was stunned.

"Wow," Deuce said. "She's really good."

Even Hyrum had to agree. "Bitch can sing."

"Hyrum, please stop talking like that!"

"Bitch got pipes?" he offered as an alternative and a joke. Deuce laughed.

Mary smiled. "No, no, you're right," she agreed. "He's right: when you're right, you're right—bitch can sing."

Even as proud as she was, Mary still needed her bump. Any extreme jangled her—too low, and she needed to medicate, too high, and she needed to medicate—she felt safe only in the middle. Trouble is, in Rancho Cucamonga, she needed help up into the middle; this was the first time in a while she'd needed help coming down into the middle. "I gotta pee, boys," she said. "I'll be back in a minute."

On her way to the bathroom, Mary got stopped by Janet Bergram. "Oh my god!" Janet said. "Your daughter is incandescent." Mary was surprised to see her here, but Janet seemed more comfortable now associating with the Powerses in public, like a friend of the family. She felt a certain stake in their success, and pride. With her deep connections throughout the school system but relative anonymity in Rancho Cucamonga, she had her ways of keeping tabs on the children sub rosa. Whatever was going to happen with the land was beside the point for her; whatever the conflicting motivations behind the wager, they had clearly made a good move just for these kids.

She was proud. "Thank you."

"But what I really wanna talk about is Deuce."

"Okay. But, I have to pee, like forty minutes ago."

"Me, too. I'll come with."

Fuck. "Okay," Mary said.

Janet continued on the walk, "What Deuce did today was amazing." She crowed.

"What did Deuce do today?"

"You're kidding, right? He didn't tell you?"

"No."

"No? That makes him even more awesome."

"We really haven't been alone today."

"He got the union vote. They passed it. Your seventeen-year-old son unionized a fast-food franchise."

"Wow."

"Wow is right. And though it's a testament to the passion and education you and your husband and wife, sorry, gave him meeting the opportunities we've given him, that's not how we are going to spin it. We are going to claim it as a success story for Rancho Cucamonga High School, and we are going to attract attention, positive attention, that is then going to trickle down to all the public schools in the area. If you agree that that's okay."

"Sure, doesn't really matter who gets credit. Bronson couldn't give a fuck. I'm just happy for Deuce, and the union folks too, of course."

"I'm so stoked!" Janet said as they entered the bathroom and went to separate stalls. "Doesn't matter, really, who wins the bet anymore, this is win-win all around. I never trusted those folks from Santa Monica, Praetorian, and now we don't even need them. I mean, if they wanna claim some credit too, and start spending money in the area, that's cool, but I'm kind of of a mind of . . . let's move away from them."

She raised her voice over the sound of serial flushing. "How are you doing?" Janet asked, right as Mary was able to put the Adderall into her mouth.

She dry-swallowed. "Fine, I'm okay. I mean, it's a big adjustment obviously, every day brings a new challenge."

"Have you thought about what you want to do next year? It's coming up fast. Where you want to live? Oh, dammit, and I forgot to tell you, duh, why I stopped you—Harvard, Yale, and Princeton all got in touch with the admissions office here and literally begged to have Deuce apply. Berkeley, too, if he wants to stay on this coast. Some of them don't split twins, so Pearl could go too, if you wanted to go that route."

Mary flushed. "It's all so much," she said. "So much to handle."

They met up again at the line of mirrors. Janet could see Mary'd been crying, and she knew why, and smiled. "Nothing like knowing your babies are okay, is there? How's Hyrum? Sorry I've been so busy with my caseload." They heard the announcement to please get back to their seats.

"Hyrum is fine," Mary answered. "Doing some stupid 'boy' stuff to fit in, but he'll come around."

By the time the curtain went down on a shattered Maria, the crowd rose as one in a spontaneous standing ovation. The production was uneven at best; Bernardo had chosen to speak with a Castilian lisp and Baby John seemed the oldest person onstage and sported a five o'clock shadow by the second act, but Pearl had elevated the entire evening to a level these suburban high school parents had never beheld.

Mary wished Yalulah and Bro' had been there to witness. And Jackie. But especially Bro'. The kids were who they were because of him, his vision, and his rebellion, but it had taken his letting go for them to be fully themselves. It was his presence that they needed back then to steady them, and to goad them on, as much as they needed his absence now to free them. But still, she wanted him to feel this fierce pride. All Mary could think of was to get to that young girl right now, hug her, kiss her, and hold her tight.

"Deuce, will you keep an eye on Hyrum? I'm gonna go tell Pearl she was great."

"Sure, tell her 'not too bad' from me," Deuce said, smiling with genuine fraternal pride.

Backstage, Mary found Pearl embracing a few other players, and then lingering extra long and kissing one on the mouth. She'd never met this boy who played Tony. She'd heard his name—"we're rehearsing at Josue's house, Tony's house," etc.—but that was it, and Pearl had never brought it up in any other context.

"Mom!" Pearl came running over when she saw her. "I want you to meet my boyfriend. Josue, this is Mary, my mom, we call her Mother Mary."

"Like the Beatles song?" Josue asked.

"You're learning," Pearl said, with a sweet smile.

Josue extended his hand. Mary shook it, and then pulled him in and kissed his cheek. Pearl put her arm around him and looked at her mom. Pearl was apologizing—for everything, her rebellion, the vaping, the drugs, the attitude, and even though she had no need to, apologizing to Mary for Bronson. Now her arm was around her young man, dark peach fuzz on his upper lip, but she kept her eyes on Mary.

"It's so nice to meet you, Josue," Mary managed to get out before giving in to a huge sob.

"Oh God, Mom," Pearl said, hugging her. She whispered in her ear, "I love you, Mommy, and I'm sorry." Mary had been longing to hear those words for months. The simple words had a physically percussive effect on her, forcing everything out of her heart and filling it back up.

Mary sobbed in her daughter's ear, "You don't have to go back, baby."

Now Pearl was crying, too. "You don't have to go back either, Mom."

"Oh, Jeez," Josue said, looking away from the crying women.

From across the room, Bartholomew saw the tears and heard the sobs, and shouted over joyfully, "I hate to say I told you so but I told you so! Didn't I? I told you so!"

Out in the auditorium, well-wishers also besieged Deuce. Folks congratulating him about his sister or folks who'd heard about the union vote or had read about him and wanted to pat him on the back, touch him like a religious icon in the making. Even the offensive offensive lineman who had given him his nasty nickname came up asking forgiveness and slapped him again, on the back this time.

Hyrum was bored and easily slipped away unnoticed and out into the parking lot.

31.

AS SOON AS HE COULD, Hyrum ripped off his tie, removed his jacket, and unbuttoned his shirt. He could breathe again. Just having the top of a button-down shirt buttoned felt like a strangling turtleneck to him. In a stream of people, he headed toward where he thought Mary had parked. But this wasn't his school, and he kind of got turned around. Couldn't see their car anywhere. Figured he'd orient himself and walk home. He headed for a dark back corner of the lot that looked familiar to him.

In the thirty minutes since the play ended, the parking lot had pretty much emptied, but still no sign of Mary, Deuce, or Pearl. A group of about five or six kids spotted Hyrum walking the edge of the lot, lit up by the lamps; they came ambling over, menacing. Hyrum didn't know them. They looked like high schoolers.

"That him?" one of the unfamiliar boys asked. "That the Mormon faggot?"

In response, Hyrum made an exaggerated show of how boring this line of inquiry was for him. "Nigga, please," he whispered, and kept walking.

"Who you callin' nigga, nigga?" The boy stepped up.

"Sorry. Ain't no thing but a chicken wing," Hyrum said, hoping they'd just go away. He wasn't scared, but he wasn't about to fight six bigger guys.

One of the boys pulled out his phone and started filming. "You right you 'sorry,' sorry bitch-ass nigga. Mitt Romney, Opie-lookin' motherfucker." All the other kids hooted and laughed derisively.

Hyrum nodded, and said, "Good one, Lollipop."

But the leader, who Hyrum could see up close was probably Mexican, had a little starter mustache, and was easily fifteen or sixteen and a lot bigger than him, maybe 200 pounds, wouldn't stop. "And your sister, she be blowin' the football team, cuz. That's Mormon shit right there, they can't fuck, but they can suck."

Hyrum bristled at the mention of Pearl. "'Play it cool, boy, real cool.'" Hyrum quoted the play, trying to be funny and defuse. It had the opposite effect.

The big kid didn't feel he was being taken seriously enough; he kept at it. "She suck good, too. That's why she sing so good, all that dick relax her throat. She suck my dick, but my dick too big, she choke on that motherfuckin' brown mamba."

Hyrum turned to walk away, but the kid moved around to get in his face again. "What, faggot? Where you goin'? You got dick to suck like your sister, *pendejo*? You got a date, faggot? Mormon, ass-fucking, inbred fuck. You wanna suck my dick, too?"

"That's an intriguing offer, but no thank you," Hyrum said. Hyrum's cool infuriated the other kid. He turned to walk away again. The other kid ran around to get in his face again.

"Turn your back on me again," he threatened, "I'll fuck that ass if that's what you want, little faggot." The kid started pantomiming fellatio and making elaborate choking sounds in Hyrum's face.

Hyrum was breathing hard now—the stuff about Pearl really angered him—and he muttered, "Shut the fuck up, clown."

The kid punched him in the nose. The kid was strong. He bitch-slapped Hyrum across the face. Hyrum tasted his own blood. Hyrum was dizzy, but he lunged at the other boy, tying him up; and Hyrum could fight, he could wrassle and he could throw a good punch with either hand. Bronson had taught him well in the many self-defense disciplines that a stuntman must pick up over the years. Even though he was outweighed by almost 100 pounds, Hyrum held his own. The other kids gleefully circled the two combatants.

Hyrum and the boy fell hard to the ground a couple times but came back up swinging, both bloodied, neither willing to give in. The bigger boy tried to use his weight to pin Hyrum down and do some ground-and-pound, but Hyrum was as lithe and slippery as an eel, and managed to wriggle free to square up time and again. His father had taught him that if he got into a fight, to tell the other guy he was gonna kill him. Of course, he wasn't going to kill him, but his dad said that this would scare the shit out of the other guy, weaken him, make him quit. Make him think twice about fighting a killer, a guy who would stop at nothing to survive. Remembering all that, Hyrum looked over at the other boy as they both tried to catch their breath, and cursed him, "Die, Lamanite."

The big kid looked quizzically at Hyrum. He was tiring, getting frustrated, Hyrum knew he could outlast him, the older boy was a little heavy and soft, he now knew from grappling with him. The bigger boy hadn't expected a long fight like this from an eleven-year-old. He wanted this over. He wanted to quit, but he'd never live that down. Hyrum saw that fatigue segue to desperation as the kid put his head down from five yards away and charged for a final takedown. This was what Bronson had told him would happen. At some point, Bronson would say, when a man fatigues he will become foolish and desperate and charge you head down, blind like a bull, and that's when you wait, you wait and hit him coming in with an uppercut or a hook, use his momentum against him, makes your punch like the punch of two men.

Hyrum saw the dark hair, the lowered head charging at him, and he bent his knees and coiled, turning his whole body to the left. Then he uncoiled, unleashing a low left hook flush to the temple that dropped the onrushing bigger boy. On the way down, with his own momentum still plunging forward, the kid smacked his head on the edge of a raised cement wheel stop with a sickening crack.

And he didn't get up. Facedown, kissing concrete, lights out. Fight over. His body stretched out in a kind of rictus, eyes closed and neck arched over the wheel stop like he was sleeping on a pillow. KO'd.

All the boys were hooting and hollering, a couple laughing to see their buddy starched like that by a little kid, trying to film his fluttering eyes and rigid spasms. It had been a good fight. Another boy got in Hyrum's face. Hyrum assumed his fighting stance again. This kid smiled and raised his hands in mock surrender. "Walk away now, little man, you won," he said. "You slept him. We good. Tough-ass little man."

There was still no sign of his family, but Hyrum had to get out of there, so he started the walk home. He wished he'd made that decision earlier. He hadn't wanted a fight, but the fight had found him. It wasn't that far a walk, maybe ten minutes once he knew where he was, but Hyrum was already too far away to hear by the time one of the boys back in the parking lot yelled, "Oh shit! He ain't breathing! Why ain't he breathing?! He ain't breathing! Help!" The boy kept yelling, "He ain't breathing!"

PART III

BLOOD ATONEMENT

Man may commit certain grievous sins—
according to his light and knowledge—that
will place him beyond the reach of the
atoning blood of Christ.

—JOSEPH FIELDING SMITH, 1954

32.

JOHN LENNON WAS ALIVE in Mary's dreams last night. She'd gone to bed happier than she'd been in months, and could recall nothing from her sleep but that familiar, beloved, martyred, nasal tenor. She opened her eyes and still he was singing right there in her furnished bedroom in Rancho Cucamonga—"Imagine there's no heaven, it's easy if you try / No hell below us, above us only sky." This was no dream. It was her phone; a snippet of "Imagine" was her ringtone. Somebody had been calling her nonstop for hours. Her first conscious thought was "Bronson is dead." The next time it rang, she answered.

It was Janet Bergram. Hyrum, she said, had been in a fight. The kid Hyrum attacked was hurt pretty badly and still unconscious at a local hospital. Mary felt groggy, her body dumping the adrenaline from last night, and now filling up with dread. Janet said that it might be classified a "hate crime." Mary didn't know what a hate crime was. The boy Hyrum hurt was Mexican and that made a difference, made it worse.

Mary threw on some Uggs and a robe and opened Hyrum's door. He must have walked home from *West Side Story* last night. He wasn't at the car when she finally made it out after the play. When she'd gotten home, she went into his room to apologize for taking so long, and in the dark, he'd said that that was okay and he was very tired and needed to sleep.

He was still asleep, curled up in the fetal position like a little child. Some early morning light showed dried blood on his swollen bottom lip and scrapes on his elbows and knuckles. Mary couldn't breathe. She couldn't think. She needed coffee. She was going to have some coffee, goddammit. It was 5:45 a.m.

She checked on Deuce. He was also asleep. She checked on Pearl. Pearl was out, and by the looks of the bed, hadn't been home. Probably stayed at her boyfriend's house. Everything was spiraling out of her control. Yes, she remembered Pearl asking—"Can I go out for like a cast party and then a few of us are going to Josue's house for an after-party party? Don't worry, I won't drink. I love you . . ." Pearl saying "I love you" was new. It was like oxygen to Mary. She must have just stayed there. It got too late and she stayed there. Like a slumber party. Or she stayed there alone with him. That was okay, wasn't it? She was seventeen years old, a woman, almost a woman.

She didn't know how to do this. What was she gonna tell Bronson? Yalulah? The crime? Hate crime? A boy was in the hospital. What had Hyrum done?

She called Janet Bergram back. Told her Hyrum was still sleeping, but that he did show signs of having been in a fight. Janet said she'd be right over. She wanted to be the first to talk to him, before he went to school, or before the cops got involved, even before Mary talked to him, if possible. She said normally, some Mexican families might be hesitant to involve authorities, but because these folks knew Janet's reputation, they trusted her, they'd talked to her. But now, because the kid remained in the hospital, it was only a matter of time before word of the fight got out, and things could spin out wildly with news reports, school, cops, etc. It could get messy, and she wanted the freshest, most unspun facts from Hyrum to get out in front of all the noise that might come. She wanted to talk to Hyrum before they lost the "narrative."

Mary grabbed some of Hyrum's Adderall, washed it down with a cup of black coffee. That gave her some rented confidence. Janet showed up, and if she was worried about her job and the exposure this violence might bring to the gamble she had taken, she didn't show it. She seemed concerned only for the kids involved. Good woman. Mary walked Janet back into Hyrum's room and they woke him up.

"Hy, honey," Mary whispered. "We need to talk to you. Janet needs to talk to you."

Hyrum sat up in bed. "Yeah," he said, rubbing his eyes. He had the sour morning breath of a man now, Mary noted, his sweet in-nocent boy scent wrecked by the opening onslaught of hormones.

Janet sat on the bed. "You got into a fight last night?"

"Yeah."

"Tell me about it. I'm going to take some notes, okay?" Hyrum shrugged. Janet pulled a pencil and a small pad from her bag, flipping it open like an old-fashioned detective on a TV show, Mary thought.

"Some kids jumped me in the parking lot after the show," Hyrum said, his breathing calm and deep.

"Who started it?"

"I dunno their names."

"Did you start it?"

"No. There was like five of them, why would I start that?"

"I'm just asking about how it happened. Tell me."

"Some kids stepped up, were like, 'yo,' and I was like, 'yo.' And they wanted to go, called me names. Called Pearl names."

"What names did they call you and Pearl?"

Hyrum closed his eyes to remember. "'Faggot,' uh 'Mormon,' shit like that, 'Mitt Romney,' I think, which I get a lot. 'Opie.'" Janet licked the tip of the pencil and jotted down the names on her little notepad.

"'Opie'?" Mary asked. "Like . . . Ron Howard?" Janet nodded.

"Who's Ron Howard?" Hyrum asked.

"Did you know the boy?" Mary asked Hyrum.

"Never seen him before."

"His name is Hermano," Janet said.

"Okay."

"Did you call the other boy names first?"

"No. I was just walking."

"You didn't call him the 'N' word or 'Spic'?"

"Oh yeah, actually, I did." Hyrum yawned, still half asleep. "But I was like, what's up, uh . . . 'N' word, like 'yo,' you know, not like, you know, calling him an 'N' word. Excuse me," he said to Janet, "I know that's wrong for a Nephite to say."

"Jesus, Hyrum, that's ugly," Mary said.

"Everyone talks like that," Hyrum said.

"That's no excuse! You're not everyone," Mary scolded him. Janet looked at Mary to stop interrupting or leading Hyrum; she wanted as unvarnished a recollection of last night as possible.

"Thank you for the apology," Janet said evenly, "but I need you to tell me exactly the words you used last night."

"I guess, uh, the 'N' word and 'Spic,' maybe."

"But you didn't target him because he was Hispanic?" Hyrum looked blankly at Janet. "Because he was Latino?" Janet elaborated.

"Target? Kid was way bigger than me, older. I was defending myself is all. Words don't matter."

"Words matter," Janet said firmly. "It matters about your intent; words can tell us what's in your heart. And it matters because of certain things you may have been taught at home, in your bible—"

"What?" Mary interjected.

"Mary, please." Janet looked at Mary, and then turned back to Hyrum. "Ways of looking at people who are different from you, Hyrum, a different color skin, as being inferior. Do you understand that?"

"Like did I want to fight him 'cause he was Mexican?"

"Yes."

"That's stupid. I wanted to fight him 'cause he was in my face and calling Pearl names and he punched me."

"He threw the first punch?"

"First two."

"You didn't strike back after the first punch?"

"Nope."

"Second one?"

"Yeah."

"Okay, good. It's important that you be clear and honest with me, Hyrum, because you're your only witness against five other boys. One against five. And their story is very different from yours, I have to tell you, so it's important that you tell the truth now, 'cause you're gonna have to tell your story a lot to the school, maybe to the police, over and over, and it can't change, or you'll look like a liar, and if you tell the truth, the truth won't change, the truth can't change, all you'll have to do is remember, and I'll be able to say that you've been saying the same things all along. That make sense?"

"Sure."

"Anything you want to change? While you still can? Anything you want to tell me?" Hyrum shook his head. "Hyrum," Janet continued, "the other boys that were there say you hit this boy from behind. Ambushed him and hit his head on the ground. Kicked his head while he was down, and said, 'Die, Spic.' That's their story."

"Hyrum!" Mary cried.

"Please, Mary, please let Hyrum speak."

"That's bullshit. Fake news," he said. Hyrum remembered saying something like that, but it was something his dad had taught him, something between them. He wasn't ashamed, but he didn't want to share the secrets that kept them close. At the mention of "fake news," Mary saw Janet's ears prick up, and she could guess why. She instantly regretted ever making Hyrum watch Maddow with her.

"You didn't sneak up on him?" Janet asked.

"Not like that."

"What do you mean 'like that'?"

"That doesn't sound like Hyrum," Mary added. Janet shot Mary yet another look.

"You didn't kick his head when he was down, Hyrum?" Janet asked.

"No. It happened like I told you."

"Anything else you want to say?"

"Nope."

"You don't want to say you're sorry?" Mary was almost crying.

"He started it," Hyrum protested.

"But the boy is hurt. He's in the hospital!" Mary pleaded with him.

"He shouldn't have started it."

"Say you're sorry."

"No."

Mary grabbed the boy's shoulders and shook him. "Say you're sorry!" Hyrum said nothing. Just stared straight ahead.

"Mary!" Janet raised her voice, pulling her off her son. "Okay. Okay. That's enough. Thank you, Hyrum." She pulled out her phone. "Let me take pictures of your injuries before you clean up."

"I'm not injured."

"Let me take some pictures of your face and hands, and then you can clean up, okay? I need to have a record, you understand that?" Mary was still shaking, trembling, biting her lip.

"Okay. Can I brush my teeth first?"

"No!" Mary barked at him. "Which part of 'before you get cleaned up' don't you understand?"

After Janet had documented Hyrum's physical state, and the boy was showering, Mary walked Janet to the door. "You have to calm down, Mary."

"Calm down?"

"Yes, I understand how you feel, but—"

"Do you have kids?"

"No, but all the kids I work with—"

"Then excuse me," Mary cut her off, "because you don't know what the fuck you're talking about."

"I understand why you feel that way, but that's not the

argument to have right now. You need to get ahold of yourself and get him to a doctor to make sure he's okay, and have a doctor document his injuries, too."

Mary tried to take a few deep breaths, but it was like the breath would only go so far down, her chest was so tight. "Do you believe him? He wouldn't even say he's sorry. He's Bronson's fucking son from head to toe. No apologies. I try to soften him, but it's like he came to me complete, completely himself from day one." Mary was rambling now, adding, "He's such an angry kid. I don't know why he's so angry."

The sins of the father, Janet thought. Anger handed down from man to man since time began. She didn't say that. "The fact that Hyrum doesn't apologize—that may upset you, but I don't see it as a bad thing—he's unconcerned with appearing to be contrite, and that speaks more to his sense of being wronged than some coached effort at apology or faked contrition that we pull out of him or coach him to, understand?"

"No."

"He's not playing the game. From what I can tell, he doesn't play games. Feels no pressure to say the right thing, is not even that interested in what the right thing would sound like."

"That sounds psychotic. You're making him sound horrible."

"No, I'm making him sound strong and truthful, which I pray can only help him in the long run. If it's worth anything, I sensed he felt bad even though he wouldn't say it. I've dealt with psychotics. I don't think he's a psychotic." Janet was not entirely sure of that, but she needed to settle Mary down.

"That's cold comfort," Mary complained.

"But it's comfort, okay?"

"Okay."

"This is just a schoolyard fight. Happens all the time. There were no guns, no knives, no weapons involved. It's actually very innocent. The only complication is race."

"The Mexican thing?"

"Don't call it that. But, yes," Janet corrected her. "I'm in the middle. I'm an advocate for these people, you understand, and they need me, they need an advocate."

"So does Hyrum."

"Hyrum has you."

"Then he's fucked 'cause I don't know how any of this shit works." Janet could see Mary in a panic, and she got it. She imagined pulling herself out of the world for decades and trying to recreate a past from two thousand years ago and then being yanked all of a sudden back into present time. It was whiplashing, mindboggling. But no matter, Mary really had to get her shit together.

"Mary, tell me, because it will help me help you here, was your son taught to regard people of color as inferior? Did your husband ever preach that?" Mary looked like she didn't understand the question, which Janet interpreted as a positive sign.

"Not once," Mary said confidently, "not one time can I recall Bronson saying anything like that. In fact, the Mormon bible sees the Native Americans, Israelites—we would call them Lamanites—as the true inhabitants here, not the whites. Smith says something like, God denieth none that come unto him—none, okay—Black and white, bond and free, male and female . . . all are alike unto God. Smith was fucking inclusive before anyone. The kids knew this. Are you looking for a way to blame this all on Bronson?"

"No, I'm looking into corners is all. And damn, Pearl was so good in *West Side Story* last night, but maybe not the best time for a white girl in your family to be taking a role from a Latina. Shit."

"What?"

"Appearances."

"Appearances aren't the truth."

"No? No . . ."

Janet was somewhere between finding the truth, protecting the kids who needed protection, and covering her ass. Blaming Bronson could be a happy solution. Ugly, incomplete, but happy. She didn't respond directly. She was gathering mitigating circumstances for another time perhaps, partial explanations for inexplicable events.

"Can you think of any signs of, I don't know . . . indoctrination before this?"

"Indoctrination into what?" Mary had no idea.

"Internet stuff. Hate groups. Chat rooms. We need to look at his phone. Do you have it?"

Mary went to retrieve the phone from Hyrum's bedroom. She could hear him in the shower, rapping. She tapped in Hyrum's password, *Jsmith*, the same one for all their phones, and handed Janet the device. Janet scrolled through the history.

"I don't see any major red flags," she said. "There's some porn here, though."

"Jesus." Mary sighed. She looked at some of the searches the young boy had entered—vague, innocent stabs in the grown-man dark like *big boobies, naked sex people,* and *penis in vagina a lot.* The proximity of that childlike curiosity to the infinite polymorphous maw of internet perversion brought tears of mourning for innocence to Mary's eyes.

"It's not unusual," Janet said.

"At his age?"

"Not at all. I'd be more surprised if I didn't find any."

"I hate these fucking phones."

"You can't blame the phone."

"I think I can." It felt good to blame the phone, and suddenly the small, beautifully made object seemed insidious and devilish to her, like a grenade, or a Trojan horse.

"Anything else like this?" Janet asked. "We don't want to be surprised by some smoking gun here, anything that can feed an ethnic intimidation narrative, any kind of preoccupation or premeditation."

Mary thought a moment, and then went back to Hyrum's room again. She retrieved a notebook this time, thick with Hyrum's scrawls and drawings in pen and pencil.

"These doodles." Mary handed Janet the notebook. "Do they mean anything?"

Janet flipped through the pages and sucked air through her teeth. "This you should throw away immediately," she said.

"Why?"

"Probably nothing, but those are Nordic runes—it's the kind of imagery that neo-Nazis use, white supremacists."

"Nazis? Holy shit. Holy shit, I can't . . ."

"It's probably nothing, like I said, but you should get rid of it and anything else like it. It's not a good look. He's been taking his Adderall?"

"Huh?"

"I know Hyrum was prescribed Adderall. You've been making sure it's been taken?" Mary nodded, lying; well, the Adderall was being taken, and that much wasn't a lie.

"Are you going to lose your job?" Mary pivoted the attention away from drugs and onto Janet.

"That's the furthest thing from my mind right now," Janet claimed. It wasn't, but she felt justified batting away the question's implication.

"This isn't your fault," Mary said, and hugged her. That disarmed Janet. And made her uncomfortable. She liked children a lot more than adults. She let Mary hold on without reciprocating and then gently reclaimed her distance.

"I know that. Thank you, Mary. But I am complicit. I am a part of this."

The two women stood at the front door. Mary opened it for Janet, and then stopped her again. "What can we do now? I'm way better with instructions, please. What can I do? What should I do?"

"Does his father know? Yalulah?"

"No, I just found out. They're not easy to reach. I will as soon as I can. Should I get a lawyer?"

"Hold off on that for a moment. Let me see where it's at later today. I'd like this to stay quiet and not involve lawyers if possible. There may be a quiet resolution."

"Just a schoolyard fight, right? What's the big deal?" Mary tried smiling. She felt like her face might crack, like glass.

"Exactly. If we need a lawyer, I know good, honest ones. I basically took Hyrum's eyewitness testimony. I have a law degree. That's a good thing to have for now. Let's try to deal with this in-house."

Janet turned to go. Mary stopped her again. Janet could tell she didn't want to be alone. She was used to being one of three parents, not one of one. She hoped Yalulah would get here soon, even Bronson. With no children of her own, Janet marveled anew at her job of being an expert for them, from what she learned first from books and statistics, and was confronted with the fact that no one knows how to do it right, parenting, the raising of children into happy men and women who wouldn't rape and kill each other. A silly rhyme formed in her head—"One parent, two parents, three parents, none, no one knows how the fuck it gets done." She decided against sharing the rhyme with Mary.

Mary was still spiraling. She could juggle chain saws, but not all this shit spinning in her head right now. "But there's got to be something for me to do. I can't sit on my ass waiting for an ax to fall."

Out the door now, Janet turned to face her yet again. She had to get out of here. She had to get out there to gauge how fast the story was growing, what shape it was taking. She had to get on top of the narrative, shape it if she could; each minute mattered. She pointed back into the house.

"Just keep loving that kid in there. Keep your family together. Pray. That's what you can do. That's your job. Those are your instructions." All her learning, all the books, all the years, and that was the sum of her expert advice: love and prayer. The blind leading the blind. Jesus Christ, forgive me, she thought.

"Okay."

"And pray for that child in the hospital."

During the rest of that long, jumpy day, Mary got the word to Bronson via the park rangers in Joshua Tree, but someone had to stay with the kids, so Yalulah came to Rancho Cucamonga. Hyrum was taken to the hospital to get checked out. He was perfectly fine aside from a couple facial abrasions, a black eye, and some scrapes on his knuckles and knees. Then he was taken down to the police station, where he was interviewed and gave a statement that was identical to the one he gave Janet Bergram. It was chilling to Mary; that little boy had ice in his veins. It was a clear case of self-defense. Hyrum told the cops that he swung at the other boy, a sixteen-year-old named Hermano Ruiz, but that he seemed to hit his head hard on the concrete. The cops had been to the scene and they saw the bloody wheel stop, and had a pretty good idea of how the fight must have gone down. The stories of the other kids, Hermano's posse, were all over the map—five different kids and they saw five different fights every time they were asked to recount it.

Only Hyrum's account was unchanging. So the cops thought he was either a mad genius psychotic child or telling the truth. Trouble was, this wasn't just a black eye and a bloody lip; Hermano was in bad shape. Word was that doctors were saying that he might never walk again, might not talk again, a lot of rumors, but he might never be the same. With all that pain and heartache, a pound of flesh would be taken from someone, and no one was 100 percent innocent.

Pearl and Deuce came home to be with their brother. Yalulah sat with Hyrum, and Hyrum told her the same story, no detail ever changed. Yalulah sat with Mary that night, after the kids had gone to bed, and tried to figure out what the hell happened and how they were gonna get back to square one. Mary didn't tell Yalulah that she didn't want to go back to Agadda da Vida anymore.

She did tell her that Deuce had interest from Harvard, and Pearl had interest from Juilliard. They weren't going to go back, and Mary told Yalulah she supported that. Yalulah approved as well.

"How did he fall through the cracks?" Yalulah wondered, stepping up to but not over the line of blaming Mary for what had happened with Hyrum.

"He didn't fall through the cracks. He's always been wild. He got into a fight, and an accident happened—let's try not to overreact here. It's no one's fault. An accident." If she kept talking like that, eventually, she hoped, she'd believe it. Fake it till you make it, she remembered from AA.

"Just a schoolyard fight?" Yalulah repeated.

"Yup. Boys will be boys."

Mary asked Yalulah how Bronson had taken the news, and she said he had laughed when he heard scrawny little Hyrum had kicked some big kid's ass. Mary tried to warn her that the world had changed a lot in this area in the past twenty years and that people now felt entitled to answers for why bad things happened; they wanted someone to blame. That the family had to be careful of how they talked about what had happened. The way they talked about what happened, Mary said, was almost more important than what had happened.

"They want someone to blame for the world being a fucked-up place?" Yalulah asked.

"I think they do," replied Mary.

"Jesus, we left this fucked-up place years ago. We know! We are on their side."

"Yeah, I know, but we look like the enemy." Mary was doing her best to impart what Janet had told her.

"But an eleven-year-old?" Yalulah asked.

"Probably not," Mary said. "Hyrum did tell me he forgot to tell Janet Bergram that he thinks someone was filming the whole thing on his phone and if we can find that it'll show he's telling the truth."

"Well, you should tell her that. That sounds promising."

"I'm afraid to see it. Hopefully, it won't come to that."

"Maybe we should go see the kid's mom tomorrow, though. Apologize. When she sees we are sincere, that will change things." Mary smiled; that was a good idea, an old-fashioned, human idea, but she didn't have the heart to face it herself. She didn't trust herself with the intensity of a confrontation no matter how well intentioned. Yalulah was better in a crisis, less emotional. She should go.

"I can't. Can you? You're his mother, too."

"Yeah, that's what I'll do. I'll go," Yalulah said. "I'll go with Hyrum. That little shit is gonna tell that poor kid and his mom he's sorry and he's gonna promise to do everything he can to make it right."

On her way to gather Hyrum, there was a knock at the door. Yalulah opened it to three police officers who said they had to bring Hyrum in for questioning again and he'd be released to his parents in a few hours if he wasn't a flight risk.

"Why again?" she asked.

"Not sure, ma'am," the lead cop said.

"They have new information?"

"I don't know, ma'am."

"Flight risk?" Mary laughed at the cops. "He can't even drive a car. He's gonna ride his fucking bike to South America?"

Yalulah couldn't believe it either, asking, "Where the hell is an eleven-year-old gonna go?"

"Good, then." The cop ignored her attitude. "This should be over in a few hours. Unless the judge finds he should be remanded to juvenile hall, which is unlikely."

"Then what?"

"There should be an adjudication hearing within thirty days."

"Adjudication?"

"Yes, like a trial, but for children. Decided not by a jury, but a judge. You should get a lawyer, ma'am."

Mary stepped up to the cop at the door, getting in his face, and said, "We don't need a lawyer. He's innocent."

"Even the innocent need a lawyer, ma'am. You'll want to get out of my face now."

"And if he's found guilty?" Yalulah asked politely, gently pulling Mary away from the cop.

"That's a ways off, ma'am. One step at a time, maybe?"

"But if he's found guilty?" Yalulah repeated.

The cop shrugged. "I honestly don't know, ma'am. I've never taken a child this young in before."

"How guilty can an eleven-year-old boy be?" Mary asked, thinking of that stupid porn on Hyrum's phone, and the notebook drawings, hoping to God she'd found all that rune shit and thrown it away.

"Who's the mother here?" the cop asked, displaying some exasperation at the 'round and 'round.

"Both of us," Yalulah answered. The cop raised his eyebrows and turned and smirked over his shoulder at the other two cops.

"We're dykes," Mary said contemptuously. "Mormon edition. Big fat Mormon dykes . . . that turn you on, you gross motherfucker?" Mary was not good with cops; she'd been hassled and harassed frequently by them as a young homeless person on Venice Beach, and she'd never lost that flinch at blue, that reactive distrust.

"Right," the officer said, getting the picture. Mary could see some sweat beading on his upper lip, and that gave her confidence. "I see. Well, those are questions for another man, ma'am, a lawyer, like I said, a priest maybe."

"A priest?" Mary nearly spat. "Like a fucking Catholic priest? Fuckin' cop." Yalulah had to restrain her again. The cop's hand went to a canister of mace on his belt, and he left it there as a warning. The two men behind him bristled.

"Yeah, a priest," he said, "and yeah, all the priests I've ever met were Catholic."

"Oh, a cop and a comic," Mary sniped.

"Shut the fuck up, Mary," Yalulah pleaded.

"No, just a cop. But I'm also a son, and I also have a son. Look, lady, I'm just a cop, I'm not here to judge. That'll come later. Now we will need to take the boy. Is he home?"

Without waiting for an answer, the cops pushed past both women into the room. "We'd like to take a look around, if you don't mind."

33.

"IT'S A DEFINITE BLUMHOUSE TAKE, that's the template—take a hoary horror concept from the past, tweak it politically to the left of the original IP, shoot it for a price, five to ten mil, make all the villains old, white, privileged males and all the heroes women of color, or just women anyway. My heroine, Dr. Hyde, think Viola Davis or Gal Gadot or Phoebe Waller-Bridge—have you seen *Fleabag*? So dope. So Jekyll is a brilliant scientist. She already had to fight her way through a scientific establishment that's predominantly and prejudicially male. 'Women don't have those types of brains,' some old white guy with an English accent says. Plus she's a lesbian, or bi, or maybe even trans, or on the way to trans—I haven't figured that out because trans-formation is the woke allegorical theme of the movie that will make robo-critics tell you it's okay to enjoy the cheap scares and blood and guts."

Maya was sitting in the Ivy by the Shore restaurant, picking at a salad that was twice the size of her head, and listening to a twenty-two-year-old named Sammy Greenbaum pitch a reboot of the Hammer film she had targeted as promising, *Dr. Jekyll and Sister Hyde*. Malouf, sole owner of the Hammer library, had made her take the lunch meeting. Sammy had directed a short film about the relationship between a homeless man and his dog called *Friend's Best Man*, his USC senior project, that got into Sundance last year and "made a splash," and more important, he was the son of one of

Malouf's billionaire polo-playing buddies who was on the Praetorian board.

Sammy was thirsty, on his fourth Diet Coke of the lunch; he was vaping and spitballing hard. "So in the original, Dr. Jekyll is a man of course, of course we change that—that's toxic patriarchal shit—and so our Dr. Ms. Jekyll, she takes the potion, which could be hormones, would be hormones in this day and age, for the trans thing, you know, getting ready to transish, he/she kills prostitutes, which doesn't make any sense, except that she's thinking the police will think it's Jack the Ripper, aha—but I don't even set our movie in London or the past, I set it in present-day San Francisco, the main suspect will be named Jack Ripperwell, you like that? But we shoot in Vancouver for the exchange rate, west coast for west coast not a problem, anyway—in our movie—she needs to kill men, not women. That's a no-brainer. And, here's the genius part—she targets sexual assaulters. She's a doctor, twist, she's a research scientist who also has a thriving private practice made mostly of gay men—maybe even set it at the height of the AIDS crisis in the late '80s, maybe she stumbles on her potion trying to cure AIDS—shit, that's good! Twist. But the killer isn't gay, not *Silence of the Lambs* gay—can you imagine trying to make that movie now, NFW. Do you mind if I voice memo?"

"Not at all."

Sammy spoke into his phone: "San Fran '88, period? AIDS, GMHC, patient zero, cure?"

Maya's own phone started vibrating; she hoped to God it was some kind of emergency that would save her from the rest of the wild pitch, but out of courtesy, she let it ring.

"So," Sammy continued, "the good doctor, she's got friends in high places, politics and shit, she's well connected, they get her a list of sex criminal names in her area, real dark Masonic Temple–type stuff—4chan, 8chan, Charlie Chan—Q Anon to the max—the Wieners, Weinsteins, and Epsteins, but they can't all be Steins, can't all be Jews, okay, that would be fucked up, was that Keith Raniere a Jew? Raniere a Jewish name? The Nxivm dude? Anyway, he's Canadian I think, isn't he? Which is even better, Vancouver is where that went down? I gotta check. Twist. A Canadian villain offends no one. Justin Trudeau gonna mean-tweet me? That's so fuckin' woke I love it. Anyway, one can be a Catholic priest, perfect, one's like an R. Kelly, cover all the bad-guy bases—and she creates a list of these predatory men and goes to fucking town, maybe castrates them before she kills them and feeds them their own genitals, goes medieval poetic justice on their asses, right? And her signature is to leave behind this blue smoke from like a smoke bomb, like her Bat Signal—blue for boy? But blue is the new pink. Get that? She's appropriating a traditionally male color like a boss. There's a new sheriff in town, a new pope. Yeah, it's visual as fuck. That's how I write—with images. My palette is lit as fuck. They don't call it moving words, they call it moving pictures. Poetic justice! So she's like Dexter in a way, too. Maybe even finds some DNA link between a genetic mutation in these rapers and her AIDS cure, so killing them ends up saving others—no, that's not quite right, but maybe something in there, in the ballpark of there."

Sammy kind of amused Maya, in the way she could be partially entertained by those videos of animals doing human things, like a squirrel on a skateboard or a pigeon in a little suit. He no doubt misread her slight smile.

"Who's Dexter?" she asked.

"Showtime show from when I was a kid—a serial killer who killed serial killers."

"Ah. Clever. Wait, did you say she feeds them their own genitals?"

"I did, indeed."

"Rad. Raw or cooked?"

"Oh. I don't know. I'm gonna say probably raw 'cause I don't want to imply that a woman cooks, you know? That's fucked up."

"Do they know they're eating their genitals when they eat

them?" Maya became aware that a table near them had begun to listen to their conversation.

"That's a good question. I don't know yet. You ask really good questions."

"Probably depends if, you know, she serves it in a stew or just, like, puts the cock out there like a sausage." Sammy was momentarily stunned by the word *cock*, charmed and disarmed.

"Uh, I'm thinking stew. Just riffing, but, yeah, stew. But like tartar, raw, like I said."

"Fair enough. Totally. Cool. Well, that sounds like quite the ride. Excuse me one second."

She pulled her phone out of her purse and saw that it was Janet Bergram trying to reach her and that she had three voice mails from her already. The urgency was unsettling, as she hadn't heard from Janet in over a month.

"Sammy," she said, "I just need to make a quick call and make sure this isn't an emergency. You're great. The pitch is great. So many levels. Best one I've heard so far."

"No problem, and call me Sam," Sammy said, and snapped his fingers at the waiter like an entitled young white man for his fifth Diet Coke. Maya got up, dialed Janet, and walked to the bar for some privacy.

"Hi, Janet, Maya Abbadessa."

"There you are. Did I catch you at a bad time?"

"Yes, the worst, and thank you." She laughed.

"I've been trying you for a couple hours."

"I see that, what's up?"

"There was an incident."

Janet gave her the rundown on the Hyrum situation. Maya silently, hand over mic, ordered herself a tequila shot from the bartender. This was horrible news. The whole Praetorian/Powers test was fucked now, obviously, but beyond that, this was a very sad tragedy—a kid was badly hurt, she heard "decerebrate posturing"

and "anoxic brain injury"" and "intracranial pressure," and that
doctors were concerned about "brain herniation" and "unrespon-
sive wakefulness syndrome." She got dizzy, and almost upchucked
thirty-five dollars' worth of lobster Cobb. Hyrum's future was in
serious jeopardy. She downed the tequila; she wanted another, but
thought better of it. She felt like shit. She knew from watching a
million Hammer films that the explorers were not supposed to get
involved with the natives, that the scientist shouldn't play God, that
she shouldn't have fucked with Bronson and fucked up this fucked-
up family. She'd have to get right to the office to tell Malouf, and
probably get fired.

"Thank you, Janet, for telling me. And I'm sorry."

"Don't apologize to me. Oh, and the last thing, the reason I
called."

"Yes?"

"Hyrum told me he thinks one of the other kids was filming
the whole thing on a phone and that that would show that he's telling the truth about the incident. That it was self-defense, not a hate
crime, et cetera. Now, I've got my ways of trying to locate the
phone, but I'm Black, and there's limits to how much these Mexican families trust me."

"Well, I'm white, my Spanish sucks, and they don't know me
from Adam, so I don't see how I'd do any better . . ."

"No, they don't know you, but you have resources I don't,
someone from your business could flash serious money around; I
bet you could buy that phone, find the video, for ten grand, less,
they're just kids, poor kids, poor families, remember, you could get
all the phones in the neighborhood for a hundred K—might be
worth it?"

So Janet Bergram was a player, too. Even the righteous ones
had to figure the evil angles and do the dark math. Everybody had
dirty, bloody, callused hands. Maya didn't know if this revelation
made her profoundly sad or profoundly justified. She dug at a shred

of lobster lodged above her incisor. The bartender, who looked like a fifteen-year-old with huge biceps, shook his head disapprovingly at her and whispered, "No cell phones at the bar."

"Fuck you, you infant," Maya replied, then smiling, added, "You wanna be in a horror movie?"

The jacked child bartender said, "Fuck yeah, totes magotes."

"Then talk to that kid there when I leave. He's the next J. J. Abrams." She pointed at Sammy Greenbaum.

"Another tequila, sweetness?" the bartender asked. "On the casa. And use your phone all you want."

Maya downed the shot, then went to apologize to Sammy that she had to bail right now, 'cause of work shit—Trump tariffs and a volatile market roiling real estate, bullshit, bullshit—but could he, she asked semi-flirtatiously, maybe meet her for a drink at Shutters on the Beach to finish the pitch maybe tonight maybe tomorrow if he's free, and tell her more about his movie vision. She had to be nice to this kid; his dad was on the Praetorian board.

"Ah." He smiled, pleased that this attractive, powerful gatekeeper wanted to see him when the sun went down. "You wanna get in on the ground floor of the Sammy Greenbaum business, huh?"

"You know it," Maya said, kissed him on the lips, kind of, and dipped back to Praetorian.

Maya actually ran into Malouf and Darrin in the Praetorian elevator. They were getting back from lunch, too. Darrin was limping. He was sporting a brand-new pair of the cowboy boots Malouf had envied on Bronson. Malouf was making Darrin break them in for him. "How'd it go with Sammy?" Malouf asked. "Smart kid. Do you think he's handsome? You like short guys? Spinners?" Jesus, not now, she thought.

"Hammer time," Darrin blurted, trying to belittle Maya's work assignment while he attempted the famous shuffle, but he came up lame and grimacing on his sore feet.

"Yeah, Sammy's cute. Sir, I need to talk to you about the Powers deal."

Malouf nodded, deadening his eyes. The doors opened, he stayed her shoulder with his hand and guided her out of the elevator, dismissing Darrin with a curt nod as the doors closed. Malouf put his finger to his lips. "I don't like to talk about that deal in the office. Let's keep it belowground." An empty elevator car opened. Malouf ushered Maya in and pressed the button for the lowest floor, P4.

When they got to a spot deep in the bowels of the garage, Maya told him all she knew, and then asked if he thought he'd be able to find this phone that might have the fight recorded. He nodded a long time, processing, and finally said, "It's my duty to find the phone, Maya. We've created a tough situation for a kid here, it's partly our responsibility, for two kids really, and we need to make it right. And see justice done, wherever that leads. We might have to take some lumps, so be it."

Maya couldn't believe it. She waited for a moment to see if he'd break out into a maniacal laugh and say "Just fuckin' with you," but he held her gaze sincerely. His deep brown eyes even seemed moist with a species of feeling akin to guilt or empathy. She'd underestimated him all along, she thought. Maybe that's why he's where he is—he's great in a crisis. "I've got people who will get that phone, believe you me. Easy," he said. "You don't need to know. You shouldn't know. I'll need the boys' names and where they live. I'll have that phone by tomorrow night and then we'll see what's on it and where we're at. I can see you're upset, but this is how the sausage gets made. It's ugly, but it ends up tasting so good."

"Thank you," Maya said. "I'll hit Janet and get you that info ASAP."

Malouf reached his arms out. "May I?" he asked. Maya nodded and took a step toward him; she let him hug her right there on the line where P4 Yellow turned into P4 Green. She sighed with something like relief. "There, there, Wharton," Malouf said. "It's okay. This is where you learn."

She was crying now. He hugged her harder. Every time she exhaled, he seemed to squeeze her a little more. She dimly remembered a factoid from her research on her nemeses, snakes, that boa constrictors never put pressure on their prey, they do not actively strangle, they simply take up the slack of each exhale until there is no room for the lungs to expand and inhale through the lethal embrace. She felt a little dizzy and realized she was having trouble breathing now enveloped in her boss's muscular consolation. She pulled back slightly in panic. Moving his hands to her shoulders, Malouf extended his arms out of the hug, gently lifting her chin with his thumb and the remaining knuckle of his missing finger so he could stare into her wet eyes and offer his hard-earned words of wisdom. "She who can sustain the most pain wins," he whispered.

She sniffled and managed to joke, "I bet that's what you say to all the ladies."

Malouf smiled at that, nodded, and said, "Yeah, right before I ask them to turn over." Maya didn't even have time to react before he added, "Now buck the fuck up."

34.

HYRUM FINISHED WITH his second trip to the police station, and in a few hours was remanded to his mothers and ordered not to leave the city of Rancho Cucamonga. Hyrum's one suit was bloody and ripped from the fight, so Yalulah found the nicest polo shirt he had and pants that didn't droop to his hamstrings to go visit the boy he beat up at the hospital. When they got there, they were told Hermano was in the ICU and only family could visit. But this hospital seemed almost empty, no security anywhere, really, so Yalulah and Hyrum drifted off and followed the signs to Intensive Care and looked into rooms until Hyrum said, "Here."

Yalulah saw a dark-haired teenager on the hospital bed. He looked like a monster. His head was half shaved and swollen out to one side like a misshapen melon, and his eyes were puffy and shut. There was some kind of tube running liquid into or out of his head, which Yalulah soon figured was to remove the fluid from the swelling brain. Yalulah felt a sob rise up within her, as a mother, and then a wail. She grunted and swallowed it back. She composed herself.

"Is that him?" she asked Hyrum.

Hyrum nodded. "I think so." He looked scared, like it had all just now become real for him, the damage he'd caused. "I'm sorry," he said.

Yalulah could feel her legs want to give out, and she dropped to her knees, keening, "Hyrum, Hyrum, what have you done?"

Hyrum stood there impassively. He knelt down to Yalulah. "It's okay, Mom, here, get up." He put his hands beneath her shoulders and gently pulled her. "Get up."

As Hyrum was helping Yalulah regain her footing, another woman walked into the room behind them, a middle-aged Mexican lady, maybe Hermano's mother, or even grandmother. She began speaking to them in Spanish. Yalulah didn't speak the language, but Hyrum had had a year of it, this year at Etiwanda, actually. Hyrum exchanged a few words with the lady.

"What? What are you saying?" Yalulah asked, offering her hand to the woman, saying, "Hi, I'm the mother, Yalulah."

"Hold on, Mom. Her name is Esmeralda. She's his grandmother." They kept talking in simple, halting words. Hyrum pointed to his heart, and said, *"Yo lo siento."* Over and over again.

It slowly dawned on the woman that she was talking to the boy's attacker. She crossed herself and pointed at Hyrum, saying, "You? You? You?" and then she flew at him, slapping and punching wildly but ineffectively. Hyrum did not fight back; he simply covered up, waiting for the old woman to exhaust herself on him. Yalulah interceded and tried to pull the woman off, but she was screaming now and in a blind rage, and she turned her attack to Yalulah. Now Hyrum had to pull the woman off his mother. He tried to pin the older woman's arms back.

"Get your hands off her!" a man in a suit yelled, and came charging into the room, pushing Hyrum away from Esmeralda and taking the woman in his arms, where she collapsed, spent. "What are you doing attacking an old woman? How did you get in here?"

"We just asked for him and walked in," Yalulah said.

"Jesus Christ, this fucking hospital. Get out!"

"We wanted to apologize," Yalulah said. "Hyrum wanted to apologize."

"Apologize? Apologize to whom?"

"Him," Hyrum said, pointing to the unconscious boy on the bed.

"'Him'? 'Him' has a name; he's a person, goddammit. It's Hermano!"

The man seemed to realize again that he was holding this sobbing woman in his arms. "Get out, okay?" he said, in a somewhat calmer tone. "I'll be out in a minute, ma'am, okay? Please leave the room, wait for me in the hallway. I'll be out."

"Yes," Yalulah said. "And we're sorry. We are so very, very sorry."

Yalulah paced and tried to compose herself in the hallway.

"You okay, Mom?" Hyrum asked.

"Yes, dear," she said, "I'm okay."

"Is he gonna be okay?"

"Hermano?"

"Yes, Hermano."

"I don't know. Yes, I hope so. God willing. I hope so."

After about ten minutes, the man exited Hermano's hospital room, closing the door softly behind him, and walked down to Yalulah and Hyrum and out of earshot. "You shouldn't have done that," he said.

"I know. I'm sorry, we felt so bad and didn't know what to do. I didn't know how bad it was," Yalulah said.

"Yes, it's very bad. I'm sorry for yelling back there," the man said.

"It's okay." Yalulah patted him. "I understand."

The man pulled away from Yalulah's touch. "My name is Benny Ruiz. I'm one of Hermano's uncles. I'm also a lawyer."

"Oh. I'm Yalulah Powers. And this is Hyrum. Shake his hand, Hyrum."

"I know who this is," Benny said, not shaking Hyrum's extended hand.

Yalulah winced at that. "Hyrum wanted to apologize for his part in this."

"His part?"

"Yes, his part." Yalulah would not be bullied.

"Why did you really come here?"

"What? I told you. To apologize," Hyrum said.

"You think that's enough?" Benny Ruiz's breath seemed to get short and shallow again.

"I don't know." Hyrum shrugged.

"No, of course not," Yalulah added, "but it's a start."

"I shouldn't even talk to you people, you're all holier than thou, you Mormons. How old are you?"

"Eleven," Hyrum said.

Yalulah said, "Say 'sir.'"

"Eleven, sir."

Benny Ruiz smirked. "Don't 'sir' me now, kid. It's way too late for 'sir.'"

"You're an asshole," Hyrum said, waving the man off.

"Hyrum!" Yalulah grabbed the boy's shoulder.

"Ha! There's the white privilege coming out, just under the surface always. Too bad you're not older. You're gonna get away with this 'cause you're so young and so pale. No jail for the pale, but that's where I'd love to see you."

"I understand your anger, but—"

Benny Ruiz cut Yalulah off. "You don't understand shit."

"But an eleven-year-old in jail?" Yalulah asked incredulously.

"Hell yes, for this little red-haired animal. But whatever, that's the criminal justice system in America for you, slanted for the white man or, in this case, the white boy."

"You've got us all wrong." Yalulah shook her head. She couldn't believe what this man was saying. He was lumping her family in with everything she had come to hate about America, everything that she, Bronson, Jackie, and Mary had rejected and fled. Everything she said was taken the wrong way. Every time she apologized only inflamed this man more. His eyes were burning with a hurt both ancient and new, and she saw he was not looking at her as a person now, but as a thing. She was a symbol to him, of an unfair system,

and she began to fear that little Hyrum would be a symbol to everyone as well, a scapegoat in a new order. Mr. Ruiz would not let her
speak anymore. He held up his hand. He knew what he knew; he
felt what he felt.

"You've got it all wrong," he said. "Your playtime is over. You
are dinosaurs. Dead Mormons walking. Now get the fuck out. Your
apology is not accepted." He leaned in so close to Yalulah that she
could feel his breath. Beneath the coffee, she could smell that he'd
been crying, that particular deep, sour odor of sudden loss and
mourning. She stifled an urge to hold him.

"And before you go." He lowered his voice to an angry, intimate
whisper. "Listen carefully to me—there will be no trial for this
white boy, but there will be an adjudication and then a civil suit.
That beautiful brown boy in there—his life is ruined; he will never
recover fully, and we are going to put a price tag on that, a big, big
number, and we are going to multiply that number by a factor of
'hate crime,' which is going to add many zeroes to the end of it,
and consequently, every penny you have, every penny you or your
inbred, white-bread generations to come will ever have, is going to
go to that poor boy in there and his family. The record in such a suit
so far is four million in California, but this is a new day, and I think
you can multiply that by twenty. It'll take some time, a few years,
but it will happen."

"We don't have any money," Yalaluh said.

"Bullshit. I did my research, Yalulah Ballou, you and your New
England family, or your Powers husband, have a fortune in land. Or
you did. That's Hermano's land now. You just met your new land-
lord and his name is Hermano Jesus Ruiz. See you at the deposi-
tion. Now kindly get the fuck out of here."

35.

RANCHO CUCAMONGA HIGH SHUT DOWN indefinitely after the brawl. The last two performances of the musical were canceled, so the reps from Yale would not get to see Pearl. Classes were also canceled, but the doors of the school and the classrooms remained open with grief counselors waiting to "process" the "events" into a "teaching moment" if the kids wanted to come in and talk about "trauma" and "process together." Same at Etiwanda Intermediate, which Hyrum attended. The schools were in a holding pattern, the children confused and angry, rumors and conspiracy theories mixing and multiplying. Local newspaper reports called the incident a "real life *West Side Story,*" playing up the race angle and comparing it with the beating of a white man by Mexican men in the parking lot of Dodger Stadium a few years ago that left the victim permanently altered.

Then Hermano died.

As this news spread, Mary, Yalulah, Hyrum, Deuce, and Pearl holed up in the house in a type of siege. Mary sneaked away to take a pill or some Adderall whenever she felt the walls closing in. A cop was posted at their door with the dual purpose of protecting them and making sure they didn't run away. Every time one of them left, a reporter, or any blogger, vlogger, wannabe newsmaker, or self-styled vigilante with a cell phone would follow them and ask them questions, trying to badger a word out or provoke a newsworthy moment. The news had leaked that they were "Mormon Survivalists"; the spin was that they were possibly white supremacists. Janet put a lawyer in touch with them. The lawyer told them to speak to no one.

Hyrum retreated back into Fortnite and barely left his room. Pearl spent most of her time talking on the phone and texting with Josue. It was bleak and claustrophobic in the house, but they were all safe in there, for now. Mary, who was becoming more and more useless and disoriented in Rancho Cucamonga, was sent back to Agadda da Vida so she could take care of the kids in the desert, freeing Bronson to come talk to his son, and see his other children. They weren't about to expose the younger ones to this evil circus.

Bronson arrived three days after the incident. Deuce ran to him and held him tight. He was his father and teacher and he hadn't touched him in months. Deuce inhaled deeply; the man felt like food to him, sustenance.

Bronson said, "I've been reading about you, son. So proud." Deuce smiled wide. Pearl came forward, too, and hugged Bronson, as if she were a child again. "My Pearl, I've been hearing about you, too. Proud of you, too." He released Pearl, and said, "Hello, Yalulah, good to see you, where's Hyrum?"

She pointed to his bedroom. "In there, playing Fortnite."

"What's Fortnite?"

"Oh, you'll see." Bronson went to Hyrum's door and put his hand on the knob.

Yalulah stopped him. "Bronson," she said, "Hyrum doesn't know yet, but we just heard, the boy died."

Bronson ceased all motion for an instant; he hung his head and began to quietly cry. Yalulah walked toward him, but he put his hand out to keep her away. Bronson dropped to his knees for some time, his tears striking the plush carpet.

"My boy is a murderer," he whispered.

Yalulah spoke softly to him. "It was the blow on the ground that killed him, when he hit his head on the sidewalk. It was a freak thing. Hyrum didn't kill him."

Bronson looked up and shook his head sadly. "Yaya, O Yaya . . ." he moaned, and then he put out his hands to his wife and children to join him on the ground in prayer for the murdered boy. They held hands and prayed with heavy hearts and aching souls. When they had finished, Bronson said, "Give me the dead boy's name and I will make sure he is baptized and eternal life is his."

Yalulah nodded. "Hermano Jesus Ruiz."

"Jesus," he repeated softly. He stood up, walked into Hyrum's room, and shut the door.

About an hour later, Bronson emerged. He seemed less than he had been when he arrived. There had been no raised voices from behind the closed door, just a steady stream of back-and-forth—a deep voice murmuring, asking, consoling, and a young high voice answering, explaining, apologizing, and finally both high and low voices merging into groans and tears, followed by silence.

"How is he?" Yalulah asked.

"He'll be fine," Bronson said. "It'll take a little while, but he's gonna be fine. I'll make sure of that. God has a plan for this boy and his atonement, and I intend to see it through." Off the word *atonement*, Deuce looked at Pearl strangely. Bronson caught it. "Something you want to say, son?"

"No, Father," Deuce said. The budding working-class hero could still be easily cowed by his cowboy father.

"Okay, then," Bronson said.

Yalulah stood. "Oh," she said. "Maya Abbadessa from Praetorian something or other called while you were in with Hyrum."

Bronson shook his head. "Was wondering when the wolves would howl."

"They want you to come up to Santa Monica to see them. They say they have something important to discuss that they can't over the phone."

Bronson nodded and walked out of the house.

36.

THE FRANKENBIKE RIDE on the 10 west to Santa Monica and a meeting with Praetorian at something called the Hotel Casa del Mar was mild relief. The freeway wasn't the free ride that it was late at night, but any movement felt good to Bronson. When he slowed or stopped, his chest tightened and his temples throbbed with the great weight of what had happened, the killing gravity of it. At 80 m.p.h., the wind howling in his ears, he was still thinking, but it wasn't as precise or repetitive. When he got off the 10, though, the thoughts rushed back in all their dark glory and the streets of Santa Monica looked like Hell paved over. When he arrived at the Casa del Mar, the valet guy didn't know how to ride a motorcycle, which was just as well, 'cause Bronson didn't have any cash on him. He left his bike at the corner and walked into the hotel.

Malouf was easy to spot at the bar. He was alone, no Maya. Bronson wondered if that was her call or Malouf's. Malouf stood when he saw Bronson. "Sorry it's just the beast and not the beauty, too. I hope this place is okay. Of course, I prefer Shutters, but I know too many people there, or I should say too many people there know me."

"This is fine," Bronson said.

"Can I get you a drink—oh, but you don't drink, how about an Arnold Palmer—oh, but that's caffeine—you're a tough date, my Mormon friend. I know Mitt, you know. Good man. Bit of a stiff,

but a good man. Could've beaten Barack Hussein Obama—
should've. And then we wouldn't have had the recession. Guess
none of that mattered to you out in the middle of nowhere."

"I'll just have water. Do you mind getting to it, I've forgotten
your name . . ."

"Bob Malouf. Bob. Like De Niro."

"Okay."

"Maya tells me you worked with Bobby De Niro. *Midnight
Run*?" Bronson nodded. "That must've been exciting."

"Sure," Bronson said.

"'Tell me what happened in Chicago, Jack,' right? Classic. Tell
me what happened in Rancho Cucamonga, Bronson—doesn't have
the same ring, though." Bronson sipped his water. He used to know
guys like this, rich guys who were essentially geeky fans who wanted
to rub elbows with beautiful actresses and movie stars and punish
all the pretty women who didn't fuck them when they had no
money. "Did Maya tell you I bought the whole Hammer library?"

"No."

"Oh, I thought you guys talked a lot, pillow talk, thought you
guys were . . . friends. Yeah, I wanna get more into the business of
show."

"Why not," Bronson said absently.

"I'm not an artist, but I appreciate artists. My dad was an artist,
a true artist, sculptor—worked with stone and wood, but when he
moved here from Palestine, he could only find gainful employ as a
carpenter on movie sets. That's how I lost this finger." He held up
the four-fingered left hand and put it on Bronson's shoulder, squeezing and checking the strength of his trapezoids. He was one of
those guys who'd read that if you compliment people, they will
trust you, Bronson thought—I'd like to take him over to Shutters
and kick his ass in front of all his friends. "I hear you were a stuntman. Tough guy, huh?" Bronson stared straight ahead, like a still,
stalking animal attuned only to the movement of the prey that

concerned him, not the idle breeze in the trees. "Ever meet Bruce Lee?" Malouf asked.

"No."

"Think you could take him?"

"No."

Malouf pulled his hand away and continued, "Artists are shitty with money, so when they run out of it, if I like them, sometimes I buy their estates, with their debt, and then they get to live and spend again on an allowance I give them. They're like children, and I end up with their art, their output. It's a win-win. I did it with Michael Jackson, the King of Pop. King of debt, too, I might add—freed him from his financial shackles so he could sing again and delight us all. May he rest in peace. Come to think of it, Neverland reminds me of your hideaway, you know—a place where you can let your hair down and just be yourself, indulge your indulgences away from prying eyes. What did you call your place again?"

"Agadda da Vida."

"Sounds like 'Garden of Eden.' Good for you. Every great man should have his own garden of earthly delights. The original Eden was in Iraq, you know, few hundred miles from where my dad was born. Where's your dad from?" Bronson shook his head. He would not talk about his father with this man.

"Anyways," Malouf shambled on, "did the thing I did with Michael with Annie Leibovitz, too, and that's working out. You know who that is?"

"No."

"Photographer. Celebrity photographer. Does all the *Vanity Fair* covers. She did a beautiful portrait of me on my horse." Malouf was trying to make him beg. Bronson wasn't going to beg. He finished his water; the bartender filled it up again. "I know I'm talking a lot about myself right now, but I want you to relax with me. I want you to know who you're dealing with, that's why I'm gabbing like a bitch."

"I know who I'm dealing with."

"Good. 'Cause you look bewildered, my friend, and I befriend the bewildered; it's what I do," Malouf said. "Oh, speaking of photography . . ."

Malouf reached into his pocket and pulled out a banged-up cell phone. Bronson knew it was a cell phone. Malouf put it up on the bar between them with a flourish. "That's it," he said.

"It's what?"

"Look at the video."

"I don't know how."

"That is fucking adorable." Malouf took the phone and swiped at it like a magician casting a spell. "You're adorable, you know that?" He handed the phone to Bronson. "Press the play arrow. You know what that is, don't you?"

Bronson pressed and watched. It was footage of the fight between Hyrum and the other boys. It clearly showed that Hyrum had tried to avoid the fight with Hermano, that the kid had started the name-calling, actually hit Hyrum twice before Hyrum struck back. But beyond that, it showed (the audio was clear as well) that Hermano was committing the so-called hate crime, and Hyrum had acted mainly in self-defense. His son was innocent. This was great news.

But then, at one point toward the end, right before the killing fall, as the two bloodied boys caught their breath, Bronson clearly heard Hyrum say, "Die, Lamanite." Die, Lamanite. Bronson felt dizzy. He pressed the square stop shape on the phone.

"Wait," he said.

"What is it?" Malouf asked as Bronson tapped at the rewind. "Oh, look at you with the rewind. You learn fast. You see where Utah is moving fast to decriminalize polygamy? It's gonna happen. Yeah, amazing—Salt Lake City, here we come."

Bronson didn't even hear. He watched again as his son said, "Die, Lamanite." There was no mistaking it. As if he'd meant it. As if he'd meant to kill a holy man. As if he considered himself a usurping Nephite justified in killing a Lamanite. Murdering an Israelite! How had his boy come to identify with the murderous oppressors? Did his son somehow see himself in a religious war committing a ritual murder of one of God's chosen people? Was this a hate crime after all, one hidden from any but eyes that could see into the deep past? Bronson reeled. This was completely unexpected, exactly the worst thing that had come to pass. He rewound a third time and watched the video from beginning to end, the image frozen on the boy facedown on the asphalt, dying. The phone felt like a gun in his palm.

"That," Malouf said, taking back the phone, "is what our president likes to call 'complete and total exoneration.'" Bronson didn't get the reference, but that didn't matter. None of that shit mattered. "I see your face. Don't worry about the part where he says 'Die, you lame something or other.'"

Bronson was not surprised Malouf focused on that moment; as much as he'd like to think he was a jackass, the guy wasn't a dummy. Even though he'd gotten the deep matter wrong of course, Bronson wasn't about to correct him. He let Malouf continue, "We are gonna lift that 'die' part out, put a car horn over it, you'll never know it was there. That's the magic of sound editing, you know that as a stuntman. I'll have pros do it, untraceable. Hollywood."

"What are you going to do with that?"

"Nothing. Right now. It goes right back into my pocket, and before you get any ideas about trying to jump me and take it, please know that I've got people who can have it erased remotely as soon as I say so. You take that phone and I will destroy the only evidence that favors your son. Plus the 'die' part will still be in there. That's troubling." Yes, it was deeply troubling to Bronson, but not for the reasons Malouf assumed.

"Why do you have it if you're not going to use it?" Bronson asked.

"Ah." Malouf smiled. "Now you want me to keep talking, huh?"

"Yes."

"Say please."

He was a man who enjoyed nothing more than making another man beg. Bronson didn't care. This wasn't about him.

"Please."

"I didn't say I wasn't going to use it, I just didn't say when. You, my friend, are about to get sued for all you are worth. Since you have no liquid assets, your land will be used as collateral and auctioned off at a fraction of its cost. You'll end up with nothing and nowhere to live. Your little desert life, as you know it, is over."

Bronson sat still; he wanted to punch this guy, but not yet, not yet.

"Or . . ." Malouf paused overlong, drawing out the word like an asshole. "I would like to suggest something else. Because I feel complicit in this tragedy, if I hadn't okay'd Maya's idea to try to get your land out from under you—you know that was her idea, don't you? All her."

Bronson didn't know that, and the test didn't matter anymore. It was all bad human animals doing bad things to other bad human animals in this godforsaken country. He wasn't interested in assigning blame; he just wanted to make it all stop spinning away from him so he could salvage what was still holy. He had tried to make a magic circle out there in the desert and keep a small safe place for God, but the devil was too strong, too tricky.

The devil ordered another drink, and said, "I want you to keep your land and your way of life. I respect it. Like I respect artists. You're a self-made man, a life artist, a man who makes his own rules and his own Garden of Eden. So I'm gonna save you—here's my suggestion. You sell me seventy-five percent of your land at a very low rate, but not the pennies on the dollar the government will give you in five years, and I let you stay on your quarter parcel with as many fucking wives as you want—congratulations on that, by the way, I've had three wives, but only one at a time, and they each cost a fuckload. How do you do it?"

"My kingdom for a phone."

"What?"

"I sell my land to you, then what?"

"Maybe you get Maya to come out there with you, jump in the pot, make more girl stew. Three wives at once? At your age? Good Lord. You must eat Viagra like Pez. Those are those little candies that come out of the neck of the thing . . ."

"I know what Pez is."

Bronson kept looking blankly at Malouf, unblinking. Malouf enjoyed what he imagined the effort was that Bronson had to make to remain so stoic. He continued, "Maya might bail from my world. I don't think she's cut out for the game, the big leagues. Too much heart, two few balls. How is she in the ol' sackaroony, by the way? Any good? I'd think affirmative. Ambitious girls can fuck. Tits real or fakeys?"

"So I sell some of my land to you, and then what?"

"Okay, you say your heart is broken and you can't go back home anymore, you say you need liquidity to defend your son in court, to hire a dream team. I have friends that you will hire at great cost to defend you, maybe even Dershowitz is avail—the Dersh is a buddy—but anyway, guys on that level, killers that love the lime-light; you're also socking away a small fortune against the wrongful-death suit that these Mexicans will bring against your son and his family, meaning you."

Malouf took a big swallow of his drink and continued, "We let the real estate deal cool down, get the whole thing out of the papers—the way news cycles go these days, I wouldn't give it more than a month, two tops. We let the civil suit drag on—all my lawyer friends get paid, they'll run stalling circles 'round these small-town Jacoby and Meyers, Cellino and Barnes ambulance chasers; we let the left-wing media run with it, jump on the bandwagon, and go all in against whitey—and then toward the end, we say—guess what, you Mexican motherfuckers, look what we found! We found the phone! Boom! Game over!"

"Why don't we do that now? Show the phone to the cops now."

"'Cause if we play the phone card now, then we can't counter-sue!!! Oh, I'm gonna love that part where you countersue, accuse those Mexicans of a hate crime."

"I don't want to sue anyone. Seems like a waste of time."

"I fucking live for a countersuit, and—this whole MeToo, PC, open season on whitey's got me pissed off. No, this is a dish best served cold. This is the way to do it. It gives me time to make the moves I want to, develop the land, see what's underneath, look un-der the hood. Don't look at me like that, I'm a treasure seeker like your hero Joseph Smith, a money-digger. Oh yeah, I did a little research—Joe Smith originally used those stupid peep stones, Urim and Thummim, to look for silver in the ground, not God. So don't you judge me. I'm getting you back to your true roots. You, my friend, are going to make me billions of dollars of treasure and bring me great emotional satisfaction. And your son is gonna be fine at the end of the day. Plus you get to go back to screwing all your wives. Do you get tired of three the way you get tired of one?"

Yes, young Joseph Smith had been a gold digger and a silver seeker, but he had turned himself around; he had become a seeker of God, a God digger. Men change. Bronson sighed. Malouf seemed pleased that he was exasperating the other man. He extended his hand. "Do we have a deal?"

"I need to think about it," Bronson replied.

"There's nothing to think about. I've done all your thinking for you. You don't have a choice. But because you're a real man and I respect that, I'll give you a few days so you can tell yourself you're running the show." Bronson put his head in his hands. "Bet you wish you could drink now, huh?" Malouf teased. "Go ahead, I won't tell."

Bronson stood up. "I gotta talk to my family. I'll get back to you in a couple days." He turned and took a few steps, and then walked back close to the seated Malouf, looming over him. As Bronson approached slowly, he saw the other man flinch imperceptibly with the primal fear of physical harm. That gave Bronson a small kick of pleasure. He exhaled dismissively through pursed lips so Malouf knew he knew he was a coward. "I need a favor now, though," Bronson said.

"How can I help?" Malouf's voice cracked ever so slightly.

"I just need some money for gas, like ten bucks to get back to Rancho Cucamonga."

"Who's your best friend, Bronson Powers?" Malouf said as he opened his wallet. "All I got is Benjamins."

He peeled one crisp hundred-dollar bill out of a thick sheath and handed it over. "You can owe me," Malouf said.

37.

AT FIRST, not even the highway speed could clear Bronson's mind. But about twenty miles from Rancho Cucamonga, a radiant insight came upon him, a clarity he usually got only in solitude, in the desert, with his peep stones. But tonight on his bike, one all-consuming thought started to outshine all the others, and a great calmness descended upon him as it was once described when the Holy Spirit calmed the waters in the beginning of time. "Yes," he said aloud to himself, and the modern world and all its relativities and compromises disappeared so he felt like he was traveling a road in ancient Galilee or Palestine. He intuited a latter-day miracle beginning to happen, taking shape; he saw its epic outlines. He was not happy, but he was righteous. He felt absolute. "Yes," he said aloud to himself as witness, "it shall come to pass."

Bronson waited until after midnight to get Hyrum. He introduced himself as the boy's father to the cop stationed by the door and let himself into the Rancho Cucamonga house quietly so as to wake no one. He visited each bedroom separately, like a ghost. First, Deuce, then Pearl, then Yaya; he tenderly kissed his sleeping children and his sleeping wife. Then he bent over Hyrum's bed and lifted the boy in his arms. The boy's lightness surprised him. This fifty-pound thing had vanquished a thing three times its size. Even in this time of mourning, he couldn't help but be impressed by the kid's fight, his warrior spirit. Bronson grabbed Hyrum's knapsack as well and left the house quietly out the back way.

Hyrum woke up in Bronson's arms on the way to the parked motorcycle. "Where we goin', Dad?"

"Where there ain't no Fortnite," Bronson joked as he put Hyrum down on the ground.

"Come on, where?"

"Home."

"I am home," Hyrum said.

"No, you ain't," Bronson said, as he straddled the bike and motioned for Hyrum to get on as well.

Riding back to Agadda da Vida with a mind made up and his son's arms wrapped around his waist, Bronson felt a rightness rise up in him that he had not experienced for many moons. He turned his head so his passenger could hear him. "You're a good boy, Hyrum."

"Respect," Hyrum whisper-yelled in his ear.

"And I love you more than I can say, Pilgrim." Bronson tried to share some of his revelatory clarity, calling back the old affectionate handle he'd had for all his little boys, lifted from John Wayne in *The Man Who Shot Liberty Valance*. "And I hope to be worthy of my love for you."

"Mad love for you, too, Pops. You're my ride or die," Hyrum shouted over the wind. Bronson smiled. The ride was too short.

Hyrum was immediately stoked to be home. It was the dead of night, but he hollered and ran into his old spaces, got his old bow and arrow, and went careening out of the house again. Probably to go check in with his beloved cow, Fernanda, before wandering out into the desert to roam like a wild thing. Home free. Bronson didn't ask him where he was going. It didn't matter. The desert was empty of man, safe, and Bronson had a lot of work to do. He grabbed some books to consult. The well-worn edition of speeches and letters of Joseph Smith. Brigham Young, too. He must be sure. He must know the words backward and forward. He heard Hyrum's laughter somewhere outside, unencumbered and joyous. The sound filled him with hope and regret. The boy was safe. The boy was with his father now. The boy was home.

38.

IT WASN'T UNTIL MID-MORNING that Yalulah realized that Hyrum was gone. She was letting the overstressed kid sleep in, and didn't crack open his door till about 11 a.m. She freaked a bit when she saw the empty bed. Had no idea where he was. She ran out into the street, but there were those fucking looky-loos and the stray reporter, random nosey people yelling slogans and threats, and a cop car parked across the street, so she turned around and ran back inside. If you'd been basically out of society for twenty years, this was not the situation with which to reintroduce yourself. But she had no choice. She called Deuce and Pearl on the landline to see if they knew where he was. Pearl was at Josue's and said she hadn't seen him this morning, had assumed he was sleeping. Deuce said he'd be right home.

Deuce seemed very troubled by Hyrum's disappearance. He told Yalulah he didn't think Hyrum had run away; he feared there'd been some type of vigilante revenge, another fight maybe, or that maybe, and he hoped this wasn't the case, his father had taken him. Deuce called Pearl and asked her to come home. Yalulah didn't think Bronson had taken him. She kept trying to call Hyrum's phone, but it was off. She said she'd go crazy sitting on her thumbs, so Deuce showed her how she could sneak out the back of the house and through a neighboring yard to avoid the scrum out front. She put on a hat and glasses, determined to drive to the mall, check the places that Mary said Hyrum had taken to hanging out in—the park, the food court, the game room at the mall. "Call me if he comes home."

"You don't have a phone," Deuce called back.

"Oh yeah," she said as she disappeared into the neighbor's hedges. "Send up a flare."

While Deuce waited for Pearl to get home, he called Janet Bergram, but she didn't answer and her voice-mail box was full, so he couldn't leave a message. Pearl texted him to call Maya Abbadessa, that Bronson liked her and trusted her; he was able to leave an urgent message with her that he wanted to talk. Maya got the voice mail almost immediately, but Deuce didn't pick up when she called back, and, fearing something bad had happened, she decided to jump in the car and head to Rancho Cucamonga to see what the problem was for herself, see if she could help, just in case.

Pearl got home around the same time Maya got to their house. Yalulah was still out hunting for Hyrum. "Anything?" Deuce asked Pearl. Pearl shook her head. The two children looked at each other. Pearl motioned for Deuce to come to her.

"There's something I need to tell you." They drew close and Pearl whispered something in his ear, just as she had whispered to Josue. Maya couldn't make out what she was saying, but it looked very intimate and personal, so she turned away.

Deuce shook his head, pulled away, and said, "No." But Pearl held him, consoling him. "That bastard. That fucking bastard," he whisper-spat. Maya had never heard Deuce curse before. He wasn't good at it. Deuce sat down, his head in his hands, and kept repeating, "That bastard, that bastard."

Maya waited awhile before speaking. "What's going on?" Neither child answered the question.

"Family business," Pearl said. "Yaya's not gonna find him."

"How do you know?" Maya asked.

"'Cause Dad took him."

"Bronson?" Maya asked. Pearl nodded.

"Took him where?"

"Agadda da Vida."

"That bastard." Deuce was still muttering.

"You saw him?" Maya asked.

"No."

"Then how do you know that?"

"Because I know my father, okay? Deuce?" Pearl turned to her brother and said to him gently, "I need you."

Deuce looked up, his eyes wet and red. He cleared his throat a few times like something sour and sharp was stuck back there that he could not dislodge. "We're afraid to involve the police." Pearl continued to speak for both of them. "We don't want our father arrested for kidnapping. Can you figure out a way to get him under control without the police?"

"I don't know. What have you got against the police?"

"Nothing."

"If you guys don't tell me what the fuck is going on, I swear I'm gonna call the police right now."

Pearl stepped back to Deuce and took his hand in hers. Deuce cleared his throat again and finally spoke, though there was a quavering, covering quality to his voice now, as if he were holding down something weighty. "When we tell you what we're about to tell you—we don't think the police, or the government will . . . respect . . . our father enough."

"We love our father. Bronson gave us everything," Pearl added.

"What do you mean 'respect'? What are you talking about?" Maya asked.

"Respect his religious beliefs," Deuce explained. "Respect that his religious beliefs are more important to him than the laws of this country, and he may be doing things that are against the law, but that are for him, of greater moral necessity."

She couldn't believe this kid was seventeen. He was a very impressive human. When I was seventeen, she thought, I couldn't've strung a sentence like that together. She wasn't even sure she could talk like that now. Still, she wasn't exactly clear on what he was getting at. The kids seemed like they were hiding something. "Okay, I think I can promise that, something like that, though I don't know exactly what it is I'm promising. You need to keep talking. You're talking about kidnapping?"

"No," Pearl said.

Deuce took a deep breath. "Have you heard of 'blood atonement'?"

Maya's immediate thought was that it sounded like a movie she had somehow missed out of the Hammer catalogue—*Blood Atonement of the Valley Vampire Vixens.*

"Blood atonement? Seems like maybe," she said, "but I don't think so. No."

"Blood atonement is a later Mormon precept," Deuce elaborated. "Joseph Smith didn't write much about it, but later Church elders did. Brigham Young. It's a hard-line stance, not universally accepted—and it was jettisoned 'officially' along with polygamy in the late nineteenth century, but it is something that Dad, who's an originalist and deeply skeptical of any pragmatic modifications to religious truths under the influence of the government, believes in, and it's something he taught us."

"Okay. What does it mean?"

"It means," Deuce explained, "that under certain circumstances taking another man's life is such a serious crime that the sacrifice Jesus Christ made on the Cross, the atonement he gave to a fallen world with his death—is incomplete for the killer. The murderer's soul is beyond the forgiveness of Christ's Crucifixion, and the only way to come back to grace is to offer up his own blood as ransom, to be killed or sacrificed himself; only his own blood can atone for that bloodshed. Blood atonement."

"What kind of circumstances?" Maya asked.

"That's unclear."

"Unclear?"

"Seems to be a matter of personal, spiritual judgment."

"Whose personal judgment?"

"Church elders. Divine revelation. It's unclear. I suppose the person who is in the position of judging and has the power and will and the righteous inspiration to carry it out." Maya felt off balance, like she was learning the rules of a game she was already in the middle of playing in an unfamiliar country with unfamiliar customs. She scrabbled hard to make sense of it.

"So it's what, like an eye for an eye?"

"Something like that, yes. Ultimately, the Church gave up on it to show the federal government they would bow down to their laws, not God's laws," Pearl explained patiently.

"Okay, I get it, I get that concept, I think—capital punishment, basically—but—first, Hyrum didn't literally murder anyone, he was probably defending himself, and it was an accident; and two, he's eleven years old!"

"That won't matter to Dad. Joseph Smith believed that eight years old was the age of accountability."

"Eight years old? An eight-year-old accountable? Accountable for what? Wiping his ass?"

"I don't want to debate that," Deuce answered evenly. "I'm saying that Hyrum's age might concern the law, but not him. His only focus is the eternal state of Hyrum's soul, what we call his 'first estate'—Dad might see himself in the position of having to save Hyrum's first estate even if it means ending the body it's been incarnated into."

"That's insane," Maya said.

"Are you a Christian?"

"Sort of. Maybe. I guess. Sure."

"Is it more insane than the Virgin Birth, the Resurrection?"

"Well, no. But no one really *believes* believes that stuff. It's a story with a moral. And nobody kills over the Virgin Birth."

"Are you sure about that?" Deuce asked.

"The Crusades. The Spanish Inquisition, the Reformation . . ." Pearl added.

"Water into wine? Wine into blood? Heaven? Hell? Dozens of other irrational religious tenets millions have been killed and killed for—"

"Not children!" Maya cut Deuce off.

"Yes, children," Pearl said.

"Not your own child! It's insane."

"Not to Dad. I'm not defending him, I'm trying to explain him."

"And I don't think Mother Mary has the will to stop him right now," Pearl added.

Maya thought they both sounded absurd. "I don't believe that," she said. "I know Bronson a little. He's not unreasoning like that. He's not barbaric. He's a good man."

"This is beyond good and evil." Pearl had read some Nietzsche in her psych class.

"We don't think he's really himself right now," Deuce said.

"What do you mean? Like he's off his meds?" Maya was lost. Deuce looked to Pearl as if she was the one to explain this.

Pearl stepped forward now and said, "No, he's not off his meds 'cause he's not on meds. Look, let me explain something to you about our father, something that I've learned this year being away. He may look like a man you know, but he's not like any man you've ever met."

"I believe that," Maya concurred.

Pearl continued, "He's not a man of this century. He doesn't believe in psychology and feelings. He believes only in his bible and his Joseph Smith. And even though he may not believe in psychology, he still has one. Know what I mean?"

"No! I don't." Maya was getting frustrated. "Keep talking. Or stop talking. But keep talking."

Pearl spoke carefully. "Things have happened over the course of the year—the family splitting up, maybe losing the land, Hyrum, me—it's fucking with him. Bad." She looked away.

"Lots of things," Deuce added, making a gesture with his hand out by his side and behind like a parent does to keep a child from crossing a busy street, to hold something at bay, to hold all the things that might be troubling his father back from crossing into this conversation. "Dad blames himself for what's happened. He might blame the weakness of his own faith, and his reaction won't be to figure out why, like you might, to, you know, grow, learn, dig out why something in his past may have caused him to be a certain way; his reaction will be to contract, to go back to the bible, to Smith and Brigham Young, to go back to the letter of the law. And it's not like he's gonna debate about mercy either. He's a tough guy, but he's not a bad guy. Hey, Pearl, remember Black Bart?"

Pearl smiled and nodded sadly. Deuce softened. "Oh man, Dad was always trying to make me better—when we would play Wild West, when I was a kid, I always wanted to be the bad guy, wear the black hat. 'Black Bart,' he called me, and I'd make him be the white hat, the sheriff, and he'd catch me out and bring me to justice for cattle rustling or killing the previous sheriff, whatever. We'd have these great horse chases, epic chases, me on my little horse, Tamsin, and he'd run me into a dead end somewhere in the desert and pull out his *pistola*, he called it, smiling—don't get me wrong, I loved it—he'd put on this heavy western accent, he'd say, 'Ah, you think being the bad guy is fun, huh, Black Bart? But now it's time to pay the piper.' And then he'd quote Joseph Smith in that goofy voice as he twirled his gun: 'I am opposed to hanging, even if another man kill another, I will shoot him, or cut his head off, spill his blood on the ground and let the smoke ascend thereof up to God . . . now what you think of them apples, Pilgrim?'"

Maya gazed at this young man smiling fondly at a memory of his father and felt a certain vertigo, like she was on the precipice of some personal revelation, even as she was beginning to get a glimmer of what this man Bronson really was through these children who both loved and feared him in equal measure. Pearl was crying now. Deuce stepped closer to Maya, his voice tender. "If Dad questions Hyrum and decides that he killed that kid out of anger or retribution, and he was probably pissed off during the fight, right, self-defense doesn't matter and his age doesn't matter, murder is murder. God doesn't care about circumstances and excuses, does He? And maybe Dad doesn't either."

"Holy shit," Maya whispered. The man they were describing was a type of monster, like a Hammer villain for real, no joke. A man who had been in her bed not long ago. A man she had felt safe enough to fall asleep next to.

"Let me say it out loud so you can check me." Maya spoke slowly, listening to herself as she talked. "You're saying Bronson is unstable and kidnapped Hyrum and is going to kill him?" The twins looked at each other again.

Pearl controlled her sobbing and spoke. "We don't really know what Dad is thinking. He doesn't think like us. But it might be that."

"That's insane."

"Is it?" Deuce asked. "You keep using that word, but is it more insane than gun violence or ignoring climate change? Dying for a flag? Killing for a flag? Dad's trying to keep order in a world he sees as out of control with the tools that he has. His tools are blunt, but they've saved his life before."

"You were just calling him a bastard," Maya said.

"Yes," Deuce replied, but added nothing further.

Maya felt like she wasn't getting the whole story from these kids, but then again, she felt like the whole story might be impossible to get, ever. She would try to understand it rationally, psychologically, but she sensed there was something more ancient and animalistic at play here. Almost as if her first vision of Bronson—when she was tripping and she imagined he was an early man, like a *Homo erectus*, just out of Africa—was the truth. Somehow he'd been transplanted to the present day. Jesus, he really was an unfrozen caveman lawyer. That's how she understood what the kids were saying. And yes, it was nuts.

"Why won't you guys stop him?" she asked. Deuce and Pearl looked at each other again; they never seemed more like twins to Maya than they did in this moment.

"You don't understand—I can't go to him right now," Pearl said.

"Make me understand."

Deuce looked at Pearl and shook his head no, making that protective, covering gesture with his hand again to keep certain things from ever being spoken. "If we were to go against him," he said, "it would break his heart, and if we couldn't stop him, we would have to kill him to prevent him, and we can't do that, we can't kill our father any more than we can allow him to kill our brother."

"Holy shit." Maya was hyperventilating now. "And you don't want police?"

"No," Deuce said. "I think the presence of the cops will act as an accelerant, and force his hand too quickly. He doesn't recognize their authority, but he will recognize a threat, and many may die."

"Wow, okay, okay, sorry I keep saying wow, wow—how are you two so smart and calm? I'm freaking out."

"We are as our father made us," Pearl said. "He gave us everything of himself, and we won't abandon him now in his time of greatest need. Please, please, help us . . ."

These kids blew Maya away; she drafted off their focus, their seeming clarity and desperation, and said, "I think I can do something. Do you think he'd listen to me?"

"He might. That's why we're telling you. He likes you. I've seen how he likes you, and listens to you," Pearl said, as she looked at Maya with something akin to derision and thanks.

Maya thought about asking what she meant and how she knew that, but Deuce picked up the thread too fast: "And, be careful, because I also think," he warned, "that if he is dead set on this course, he will be hard for anyone to stop. My father is a capable man. He will be the Hand of God."

39.

MAYA REALLY WANTED to call the cops in, that was her instinct, but she'd given Deuce and Pearl her word, and they seemed to have insight on how to deal with Bronson and these arcane archaic Mormon beliefs. She checked her phone; she had to head right back to Santa Monica to meet with fucking Sammy Greenbaum again as she'd promised. She trusted those kids and the kids trusted her, and they were good kids, and she'd already done enough to upset this family. Possibly she could make up for it, atone. But screw atonement, blood atonement—what kind of crazy, primitive, eye-for-an-eye nonsense was that? And what of Bronson? He'd been in her home, in her bed, in her arms; she had stepped up to the edge where she could've fallen for him, and he was this irrational, hor-rific, ancient, biblical person? How could she not have seen that? He said he was a man from the past. He said it and she wouldn't hear it. Of course he was a religious zealot, that was his calling card basi-cally, but she had chosen to look past that, to see it as an attribute, one of many, like a hobby, and not the fundamental bedrock to his character. What was wrong with her radar?

Or maybe that's why she wanted to fall for him in the first place. Compared with all the cynical, moneygrubbing, Lambo-coveting man-children around her, Bronson had true conviction and felt like fresh air, like a real man. If she had to choose between Bronson and Malouf, she'd choose those serious cowboy-stuntman forearms every time. Forearms like those are made from hard work, not polo or the gym, and make for strong hands as well, hands that are grasping, and can hold fast and make love, also hands that can restrain and kill. Was she one step away from being one of those sad women you see on *20/20* who fall in love with killers on Death Row? She viewed with guilty fascination those women differently now. She saw it was her own ego that was blind to the impossibility of unmixing a man's character, that something like the intense certainty needed for a man to believe in blood atonement was part of the very fabric of Bronson's charisma for her; she just hadn't known what to call it till now. You could no more separate out that fanaticism than you could take meat off the menu for a lion and put him on a leash in the city.

She noticed that she had the Tesla up over 100 m.p.h. on her way back to LA. It was so easy to speed, the engine made no noise. She eased off the accelerator, snapped out of her own self-recriminations, and focused on the kids, on Hyrum. Forty-five minutes later, she pulled into the Shutters hotel roundabout with the Tesla near empty of charge. Before walking in and subjecting herself to Sammy Greenbaum part deux, she smelled the sea air and glanced out at the ocean, a few yards away. This is why people live in LA, she thought. Hypnotized, she walked toward the water. Proximity to this big blue was worth billions of dollars in the real estate game. She got it. She inhaled the salt air deeply and tried to slow down all that was racing inside her. Sammy could wait another minute.

She took off her high heels where the asphalt ended, slipped barefoot onto the sand, and felt an inkling of clarity. She would call that park ranger. She dialed up Park Ranger Dirk—he wasn't a cop, not officially anyway, but he had a uniform and a gun and, she assumed, some training with it. He had pulled it once before, and he seemed invested in her, wanted to impress her, maybe.

Dirk was off duty, but that was good, he said, 'cause he could more easily do a favor for her off the clock than he could on. She explained the situation to him, told him that a young, innocent boy's life might be at stake.

"That's an awful way to feel—that some are beyond hope and forgiveness. Would seem to belittle Christ's very mission: his sacrifice is not complete, they seem to be saying. I don't like that," Dirk said, dropping his usual know-it-all bravado and getting very quiet on the other end of the line. "I haven't told you this about myself," he continued, as she pondered that he hadn't told her much of anything at all, "but I lost a brother to murder when I was young. It's why I went into the Park Service, I wanted to protect the earth the way my brother hadn't been protected."

Well, that didn't make a whole hell of a lot of sense, but he was sharing and seemed receptive to the idea of stepping in to help. "Oh, I'm sorry," Maya said.

"I'll tell you what," he said. "I'm gonna get a couple buddies together right away, real tough hombres that like to flex their Second Amendment rights, if you know what I'm sayin'—these are the good guys—civilians who patrolled the park with me for free during the Trump shutdown in December 2018. Badass do-gooders, I call 'em. I'm gonna get my posse together pronto, and we are gonna pay a call on Mr. Mormon Cowboy, and we are gonna bring that kid back to you safe and sound by sundown today *no problemo*."

"Please don't hurt anyone."

"Ma'am, the gun is an instrument of peace; it's there so no one gets hurt. When words aren't persuasive enough, the gun is a strong persuader. That's how it works."

"Please, Dirk, I don't know. I don't want them hurt. I don't want you hurt. He has a gun, too."

"Ah, you're a sweetie, ain't you? I've never fired at a human being in my life, and I don't intend to change that today. He will be outnumbered and he will see reason. *Comprende*?"

"He may not see reason."

"Staring down a gun tends to make a man very reasonable, even the unreasonable ones. I promise you, I will not fire. No bloodshed. I got this."

"Promise me you'll check in with me every hour on the hour?"

"Yes, Mom, every hour on the hour." He was laughing.

"I'll pay you," Maya said. "What can I pay you?"

"Don't insult me, ma'am, this is a labor of love. I am a Christian man, a real Christian, not that Mormon nonsense, and this is about love and mercy, and a child."

People need their reasons, Maya thought. Love and mercy and a child were as good as any she could think of. "Okay," she said, "thank you so much."

There was a pause on the line. Then Dirk said, "Just let me take you out to dinner when this is over." Oh, Jesus. Small toll to pay; she'd cross that bridge when she came to it.

"I would love that, Dirk," she said.

40.

BRONSON LOOKED THROUGH his peep stones and tried to read the sky. The more decisive actions he took, the more he could see things clearly. There were four clouds above him today, and as he stared through the rocks at them, they changed shape into four men and then merged into one huge cloud and became smoke, the smoke of a fire, a conflagration so all-encompassing, Bronson for a moment doubted himself and wanted to pull back from his course. But that was fleeting. He was cold this early morning, a fire might be nice. He sniffed the air and thought of that old Dylan lyric he used to know, "you don't need a weatherman to tell which way the wind blows." He couldn't remember the name of the song now, but trouble was blowing in from the west. He knew where to lay the traps.

After that was done, he went to the back of the horse shed. The back stalls had functioned like a basement for him all these years, where he kept some of his old stuntman gear and various FX stuff he liked to amuse the kids with when they wanted a fireworks show. It was the only show he ever gave them. Every year on December 23, Joseph Smith's birthday. Two days after the winter solstice, the darkest day of the year. The fireworks were to signify light coming back to the world, light in the form of Joseph Smith, light in the form of Bronson Powers. He still had a ton of the stuff left, the tricks of his former trade. He grabbed what he thought he

might need and went back to the house, and waited, eyes and ears
to the west. Sound travels cleanly in the desert. He scanned, turning his head like a coyote, ears a better tool than his eyes. And he
heard them in the distance.

And here they came, right on time, as foretold to him by his
peep stones, the four clouds coming to him as one, four men on
ATVs, like the four horsemen of the suburban Apocalypse. Bronson grabbed his gear and went out to a spot he had chosen to meet
them by a distinctive cluster of Joshua trees. He had to get there
first. He jumped on his horse. The race was on. He handed Hyrum
a gun. "Grab your bow and arrow, too. Get on your horse, Hyrum,
come with me," he said. "Looks like we got company."

They saddled up in the barn, and met the men on the ATVs in
front of the house. Bronson held up his hand, exposing his classic
six-shooter, and asked them to stop. "You boys are trespassing,"
he said. Dirk smiled; that was like an opening exchange from a
Western, he thought, pleased. The other three men got out of their
ATVs and stood menacingly.

"Name's Dirk. We don't want any trouble, Bronson Powers,"
Dirk said, thinking, Damn, it's like these lines were written for
me—this is going to be easy, four against two, "but we need you to
give us the boy, Hyrum."

"My boy? You want to take my boy from me?" They were
afraid, he knew that from the way they stayed clumped together,
like prey animals. Apex predators stalk alone, like Bronson.

"Where you goin' on that horse?" Dirk asked. "Come back
here."

"You sound scared," Bronson said. "Is that gunpowder you painted
your face with?"

"What?" Dirk dabbed at his face; the excess sunscreen he always
lathered on came off whitish on his fingers. "No, dude," he said,
"it's sunscreen. You should wear it, too. You'll get the skin cancer.
Enough flirting, give us your gun." The three backup men moved

as one behind Dirk, their guns drawn as well, their faces nervously dripping the white sunscreen.

"This *pistola*?" Bronson slowly pulled his jacket aside again, resting his hand on his gun, and all four men pulled theirs with varying degrees of smoothness and facility. "Oh my goodness," Bronson said, "it looks like we're outnumbered. Hyrum . . ." Hyrum pulled an arrow from his quiver, smoothly loaded it into the groove with the speed it would take any of these men to aim their gun, and let the arrow fly. The badass do-gooders in the ATVs flinched and yelped in defense. The arrow stuck the front tire, air hissed.

"Shit, son," Dirk cursed. "Don't do that. We're on your side."

"We don't want trouble," Bronson said evenly. "We are just asking you to leave us alone. Hyrum doesn't like wasting arrows on tires, do you, Hyrum?"

"No, sir. I got nothing against tires."

"Just turn around and leave me to my land and my business."

"See, I can't do that, Bronson." Dirk knew from movies with hostage negotiations to keep saying Bronson's name, that it would make a human connection. "'Cause I know what your business is today, Bronson, and I can't let you harm Hyrum."

"What's he talking about, Dad?"

"He's talking out of his ass, son. He's about to step into a world he is ill-equipped for."

"He's meaning to hurt you, son. Your own father. Put your gun down," Dirk commanded, though his voice was not steady.

"No, thank you, sir." Bronson smiled. "Listen, what's your name again?"

"Dirk. Dirk Johnson."

"Listen, Dirk Dirk Johnson, you're a park ranger, right? I've seen you."

"That's right, Bronson."

"Right. So when you see something happening in the desert in the course of your job that's sad, but natural—you see a hawk take a cute jackrabbit, or you see a coyote male kill his pups in a drought or famine and eat them—do you step in 'cause you think you know better? Do you play God 'cause you think you know the happy ending? Or do you let the desert be the desert?"

"That's different, Bronson."

"It's no different, Dirk Dirk. I'm asking you to let the desert be." All the men were nonplussed and silent, and not a little weirded out by the man's preachy tone and imperviousness to their macho pressure.

"You're gonna wind up in prison, Bronson," Dirk said, as neutrally as he could. "How you gonna take care of your boy then?"

"I'm willing to go to prison for him," Bronson replied. "Fuck, I'm willing to go to hell for him. But I ain't willing to go to heaven without him."

Hyrum looked at his father, squinted, and cocked his head to almost 45 degrees, like an animal trying to figure out the exact location of a sound. But one of the badass do-gooders stepped forward suddenly, so Hyrum turned and raised his bow.

"What the fuck are you going on about?" the man yelled, gesturing with his weapon. "Just shut the fuck up and drop your fucking gun, you nutbag!"

"Hey, Sam, cool it, okay. Everybody, be cool. Chiggedy check yourselves." Dirk forced a smile and raised a calming hand to his men. "Bronson, unholster your gun—slowly—drop it on the sand, and back off. Same for you, son, drop that bow. This ain't *The Last of the* fucking *Mohicans*."

Bronson turned to Hyrum and sighed. "We tried, son. Let's go."

Bronson pulled back the reins and yanked his horse away from the men. Hyrum followed, as closely as a shadow. They got a decent lead because the two men in the flat-tire ATV had to load themselves and their gear into the other ATV to give chase. These were Bronson's two best horses, and he had the advantage of knowing this terrain. Every time the overloaded ATV got close, Bronson would detour into a ravine or rock bed where they couldn't directly follow, but only shadow from above or to the side. This tantalizing game went on for about thirty minutes.

The horses were lathered and thirsty by the time Bronson had led them to the sacred place where Maya had first discovered them. The place where his babies had been buried once. The terrain was thick with "No Trespassing" signs and weird, brown, worn scarecrows that looked like unholy half-human gargoyles. There was a sheer rock face behind Bronson and Hyrum that blocked their way, with the steep, rocky terrain and the cactus too thick on either side for a horse to run through. It looked to the men in the ATV as if Bronson had stupidly trapped himself and ridden right into a natural dead end.

Bronson turned his horse back to face the men; Hyrum shadowed his father's every move. Dirk looked to the other three men. They exchanged some nods, and then they came forward, en masse, like the prey animals, like the weak modern humans, they were.

"Keep your hands up! You, too, boy!" Dirk shouted, forgetting, in his excitement, Hyrum's name.

Bronson put his arms up in surrender, like a Joshua tree itself. So did Hyrum. While Dirk hung back a few steps, keeping his gun trained on Bronson from about fifteen yards away, the three other men crept forward together.

"Put your gun on the ground! Put the bow and arrow on the ground! Now!"

"How can I do that with my hands up?" Bronson said, feeling like maybe he'd remembered that gag from a movie in which he once doubled the cowboy lead.

"Yeah, punk-ass bitch," Hyrum added.

"Don't do that," Bronson reprimanded his son. "I don't like that stuff."

"Sorry, Pops."

"Don't call me a 'punk-ass bitch,' son, I'm trying to help you," Dirk complained.

"He's sorry. He's been in the city too much lately," Bronson explained.

"I'm sorry," Hyrum called out, "my bad."

"Thank you," Dirk said, feeling his the upper hand. "Looks like you rode yourself right into a 'box canyon.' Woulda thought a desert man like you would know better."

Bronson looked up the rock face behind him, and to the impossible terrain on either side, nodded, spat, and dropped his head. Dirk imagined the man was chastened, ashamed to have made such a novice move in front of his own son and to have been bested by another man with greater knowledge of the desert.

"Now drop your weapons and get off the horses, the both of you. I'm done playin' with y'all," Dirk ordered. The long chase had given him time to find his breath and nerve again. His Western cowboy accent was getting stronger, the more confident he got. Bronson and Hyrum did almost as commanded, dutifully dismounting and tossing their weapons, the guns, bow, and arrows about six feet away. "I said *drop* them, goddammit, don't throw them," Dirk complained. "For pete's sake." He motioned to his three men to retrieve the weapons. They coasted a bit off Dirk's recovered command and strode aggressively toward where Bronson and Hyrum had tossed their weapons.

The three men, side by side by side, got to within a few feet of the guns and Hyrum's bow, and one of them pulled up his foot, like he'd stepped on something, his eyes searching the sand at his feet curiously. "What the fuck is—?" he wondered, falling forward before he could finish the sentence, as the sand receded from him. He seemed mystified by the sudden subsidence, reaching back for balance to the other two men, but instead, latching on and pulling all of them forward as a group. Before he could finish his thought process, all three of them disappeared below the sand, like the earth itself had tired of them and had swallowed them up.

Before Dirk could figure out what was happening, before he

could move from curiosity to self-preservation, Bronson had pounced and retrieved both guns, and Hyrum his bow. Dirk, a firing-range hero, panicked and took a shot at Bronson, squeezing the trigger on the way up, like the overeager *Jeopardy!* fan he was. He missed badly. The sand kicked up a good five feet in front of his target. Bronson shot an ironically sympathetic look at Dirk, as if to say, "Don't worry, kiddo, try again."

Extending a calming hand toward Hyrum, Bronson said, "Hold, son." Hyrum held. Dirk aimed this time and shot again, overcorrecting, and missed by more, shattering some debris off the rock face above and behind Bronson.

"Sonuvabitch . . ." Dirk muttered, and he lowered his sight for another shot. He wouldn't miss a third time.

Bronson unhurriedly raised his gun with neither malice nor joy and shot Dirk right through his wide-brimmed park ranger hat, in the middle of his forehead. Dirk inhaled sharply and his eyebrows arched, looking not unlike a man in mid-conversation who had finally remembered the name of someone he'd been unable to recall. The big hat flew off behind him with a good piece of the top of his skull, and in the last act of his life, Dirk made a motion to retrieve it with his left hand, like that was the most pressing issue of the moment, like he'd be able to get his brains back in his head if he could just get his hat back on. Then his eyes rolled and he fell backward on his side, arm outstretched, his brain blood pumping, pooling, and clumping in the thirsty sand.

Bronson could hear the men screaming from down in the hole. He'd made that trap years ago with Deuce when he was a young boy, for coyotes and other bigger intruders, such as men. It was a Vietnamese Army punji-stick-type trap. Bronson had dug a number of them around the sacred site that the kids knew to stay away from. He had booby-trapped it long ago so that if anyone discovered his buried children, they would not make it out to tell. There'd never been anything that triggered the traps, till now.

He'd learned how to make those types of traps when researching and working on Vietnam-period films. *Rambo*, *Born on the 4th of July*, *Platoon*. He'd fallen into a few himself, for money. There was always a pad down there to break his fall. These men didn't get a pad, though; they got rusty spikes to run them through. Bronson hadn't smeared the spikes with sepsis-causing feces and urine like the Vietnamese had, but he'd thrown a couple of cold sleepy rattlers down there this morning, for good measure. It was a hellhole, for sure, and the sounds of the tortured and the damned were ascending to deaf heaven. He didn't get close or look down into the fifteen-foot-deep pit because he knew they still had their guns. They were yelling about broken arms and legs, and blood and snakes and mercy. Begging for help in one breath, and threatening retribution in the next. He heard them desperately trying to make contact on their cell phones.

Bronson dragged Dirk's lifeless body over to the edge of the hole, grabbed an arm and a leg, and, spinning circles, tossed him in like an Olympic hammer thrower. The three men down in the hole screamed and cried out when Dirk's corpse landed on them. It would be awkward for Bronson to safely get a shot at them. He could point his gun down there blindly and shoot around, but it wasn't worth wasting bullets, or exposing himself to their desperate aim. He admonished the overly curious boy. "Don't get too near that hole, son."

He decided to walk away. He shot the tires out of the ATVs and grabbed the keys. If the trapped men tried to claw out of the soft sand walls, they'd bury themselves alive. And if they didn't try to dig out, the blades, snakes, and heat would kill them soon enough. And if they managed to survive long enough to be rescued? That was fine as well, let it be; Bronson just needed them off his ass for a little while. God, or the devil, would decide the details.

Bronson and Hyrum got back on their horses and rode away from the wailing men back toward the house. More men, better men, better trained with better weapons, would be coming soon for his boy, to protect him, they thought, but they'd only damage him. They knew not what they were doing. He had to prepare. It would be 100 degrees in a couple hours, the hot wind was already shifting restlessly, picking up—the Santa Ana, a crazy-making wind—and there was still much to do.

41.

HOURS PASSED, and the time that Dirk was supposed to call and check in with Maya had come and gone long ago. But Maya was still procrastinating at the Shutters bar with a now sloppy (three whiskey sours in) Sammy Greenbaum. She was afraid to move and lose a call in the spotty coastal service, so she was trapped there at the edge of the Pacific on a certain barstool that gave her phone full bars. Apparently, Sammy Greenbaum was going to change the world with a horror movie.

"Like *Get Out* changed the world," he said, savoring his third maraschino cherry.

"Did it?" she asked. "Change the world?"

"Fuck, yes. For like a whole year. More even. More than fucking *Ghandi*."

"The person or the movie?"

"Both. Either. Why you keep checking your phone? You got a boyfriend or something?"

"None of your business."

"Oh, girlfriend . . . twist?" he asked hopefully, raising his eyebrows.

"No," Maya said, "no boyfriend or girlfriend."

"Well, I was kinda hoping you did," Sammy slurred, ordering that fourth whiskey sour. "I'm in the mood for an ill-advised affair with a mature woman." Fuck Praetorian, fuck Hammer, and fuck the world, this mature woman was about to deck the little prick when her phone finally, mercifully for Sammy, buzzed. But it wasn't Dirk calling, it was Janet Bergram. Sammy snooped the caller ID. "Oooooh," he cooed, "Janet . . . who Janet be?"

"The ball and chain," Maya said, winking at Sammy and excusing herself. She didn't want a sloppy Sammy to overhear anything.

She walked back outside the hotel, keeping an eye on her reception, which was holding at one and two bars, but there were people milling about everywhere, waiting for the valet, so she told Janet to hold on a moment, took off her heels again, and made a right onto the sand, which was now cold on her toes. A clear, windless night had fallen, and the beach was mostly empty, but the full moonlight was so bright, she cast a shadow.

"What the hell is going on?" Janet asked. "I called Deuce and he said to call you."

Maya walked for privacy down toward the shoreline. Though she had to raise her voice a bit to be heard above the surf, she relayed to Janet her discussion with the kids about this crazy "blood atonement" stuff and the decision to send the rangers in, not the cops. "Are you fucking crazy?" Janet wasn't on speakerphone, but it sounded like it. "Those rangers aren't cops—they're not trained like that. They're like mall security. You gotta call the cops and walk away, Maya. This is serious shit. Way too serious for me. If you don't call the cops, I will. Right now."

"Pearl and Deuce didn't want me to."

"They're kids, be the adult, use your fucking head, Maya. You wanna be an accomplice? It's time to step back. Hyrum was not to leave Rancho Cucamonga. Bronson kidnapped his kid. He broke the law. Period. I'm calling the cops right now."

"Don't."

The cops would mean the end to the deal no doubt, the end to her big score. Maya was still holding out hope for a quiet resolution followed by a land grab that would make them all rich. She also didn't like being told what to do by a holier-than-thou civil servant.

Janet didn't see it that way. "Look, Maya, you got what you wanted. Call in the cops, Bronson gets arrested and loses his kids. Why are you having an attack of conscience all of a sudden?"

Janet's righteousness and certainty were wearing thin for Maya. "Who do you care about, Janet?"

"What now?"

"You heard me."

"I don't think I did."

"You don't care about Bronson."

"Perhaps you care too much about Bronson."

Maya ignored that jibe and plowed on. "I don't know if you care about Pearl and Deuce aside from how you can use them, how it reflects on you. I'm pretty sure you don't care about Hyrum. You care about your schools and the money coming into your community." Maya waited for Janet to defend herself. Nothing. Maya thought maybe the call had been dropped. "Hello? Hello? Janet? Fuck."

"I'm here. And I'm not going to have this discussion right now with you, Maya. I'm calling the cops. But to answer your question, yeah, I care about those kids, but I care about all the kids, and I try to calculate the greatest good for the greatest number. That's what I believe in. Math. These are just three kids, three kids compared to thousands who never get a shot and more born every year. I care about the thousands more than I care about the three. You wanna call me names because of that? I can live with that. I'm calling the cops."

Janet hung up on her. A big wave curled and crashed on the sand like the roar of some infinite slouching animal, startling Maya. The frothy white water rushed up at her suddenly, hitting her at knee height with such force she almost lost her balance. She hadn't realized during the heated conversation that she had nearly walked out into the ocean. Her short black dress was soaked with cold spray as the receding wave pulled at the back of her legs, like an insistent, unreasonable being, urging her to let go of the sand, to go deeper, to sweep her out to sea. Maya looked up as a three-foot set came surging in, and beyond that, to the moonlight sparkling off the water like flashing knives.

42.

MARY WOKE GRADUALLY to strange sounds. Her sleeping ear had acclimated to the constant ambient noise of Rancho Cucamonga, so at first she had slept through the sounds of engines and men arguing. She threw on some clothes and stumbled out into the kitchen, half awake. "What's going on, Bro'? Did I hear some yelling and some ATVs?" Bronson was staring out the kitchen window, a preacher's look upon his sweaty face, agitated, faraway, mad with the prospect of salvation. She had taken the last of her Percocet stash last night and was still a bit groggy. She was gonna have to go cold turkey now, not a pleasant thought to start the day. She wanted a coffee.

Bronson chanted, "'And the Lord said unto Joshua—Stretch out the spear that is in thy hand toward Ai; for I will give it into thine hand. And Joshua stretched out the spear that he had in his hand toward the city.'"

"And a good morning to you, too, Bro'."

Bronson didn't smile. She knew what he was referring to, an alternative legend to the naming of the Joshua tree, so called not for the prayerful stance of Moses in Exodus, but rather the outstretched arm of Joshua himself holding a spear in preparation for violent battle in Joshua 8. "Today, my hands are raised not in prayer. My hands are raised holding a spear. Get the kids up and together, and Mary, get your gun." He walked out behind the house. Mary followed.

"What? What's happening?"

"They're coming for us, Mary. But I'm not gonna let any of the kids get hurt. Understand?"

"Yes, but what do I need my gun for?"

Bronson stopped; he took her in his arms. "In 1844, Joseph Smith declared martial law in Nauvoo. I am declaring the same in Agadda da Vida, Joshua Tree, today. There will not be another Hawn's Mill."

"What? Baby, you can't declare martial law."

"'One law for the lion and ox is oppression.' They're coming for us like they came for Joseph and Hyrum in Carthage in 1844. The mob painted their faces black with gunpowder and they came to kill."

Mary knew the Mormon stories, bouncing between the ancient biblical texts and Joseph Smith's nineteenth-century additions, its constellation of allusions, myths, and histories. She had learned well from Jackie and Bronson. She knew Bronson was calling out to the murderers of the prophet Joseph Smith and his brother Hyrum, and as she looked at her man, she didn't know if he, too, was back in 1844 in his mind, if he had so thoroughly identified with the founder of a family and of a religion, Joseph Smith, or was he a confused, conflicted man in 2020. Is that why he'd come to the desert in the first place? To enter into mythological time, geologic time? For what was 176 years to the dusty earth but the blink of an eye? To the boulders and sand beneath what used to be an ocean, was not 1844 barely a millisecond before 2020? And was not Bronson Powers himself mythological, a human extension of the desert? A Joshua tree come magically to life as a man with supplicant arms?

Bronson must have seen Mary processing hard, because he took her hands in his gently. "Do you think I've lost my mind?"

He asked with such a direct innocence and vulnerability that she wanted to hold him and pat his head. After Jackie had died, she had tried to take her place as his rock, though no one could replace Jackie, and Mary was no rock by nature. But she had been the first non-Mormon to tell him his vision of a life out in the desert wasn't a ridiculous scam. That was a lot. She had always tried to be, even before she fully believed herself, the solid ground beneath his feet. She could no sooner pull that ground out from under him now than jump up and pull the burning sun from the sky.

"Oh, Bro'." She sighed. "No. I think maybe you've just lost your way." She saw a veil drop from his eyes as he took this in.

"Lost my way?" he repeated, though it sounded more like an affirmation than a question. He was back, a rational twenty-first-century man who saw religion as a guideline for a loving Christian morality, not a set of intransigent, bloody rules, not the prophet on the run in 1844.

"Yes, baby," Mary gently said. Bronson looked like he might weep, like he might collapse into her waiting arms, but then cocked his head like he heard something, like he was tuned to a frequency only he could hear suddenly getting sharper; for Mary heard nothing. And just as quickly the veil, invisible but every bit as blinding as his peep stones, dropped down again over his eyes, and he hardened. He was swaying now, almost davening. Sensing that his vulnerability was quickly fading, Mary now usurped the role of preacher and reached for scripture, Malachi 4:6, hoping to call her man back to reason with the foundational words she heard in her mind. "And he shall turn the heart of the fathers to the children, and the heart of the children to their fathers, lest I come and smite the earth with a curse."

"They're coming now," he said.

Mary knew she had to say it out loud and right now. "He's just our boy, Bronson. Just a little boy."

Bronson nodded, but he was gone, gone to a past that was the eternal present in mythic time, lost to a vision of himself as an actor and stuntman, a celluloid hero in an ancient story. He was no longer acting as if, as they used to say in NA; he wasn't acting at all, he *was*; and he was certain. His original faith was not founded on brotherly love and good works, Hallmark Jesus loving his enemies and turning his cheek, but on the bloody mystery at the heart of it all, a very mortal man on a cross suffering under the passive gaze of a Father who refused to lift a hand to save His boy. Bronson felt that holy filicide in his bones, like marrow, because without it, the religion he had accepted was just a bunch of dos and don'ts and lullabies. It wasn't that he was a natural-born killer himself, no, he was a gentle man, but he needed to feel that annihilating darkness, because without darkness, no contrast or vision, no truth, no resonance. This is where it begins and ends—Christ, the perfect imperfect son, suffering all the pains a human body can offer, slowly bleeding and suffocating to death as his inscrutable, unknowable Father looks down from Heaven. This was the Father to love and to do battle with. Bronson thought of his own father and then of his own son. He felt a jolt like lightning course through him, a fortification of his soul, pushing him onward; he was filled anew with rage and love.

As he was reaffirming the origins of his faith, Bronson could see that Mary thought he was lost, and that pierced him with some sadness, made him feel alone in this, but that was only because, he told himself, he had run so far out ahead of her, yes, of all of them, that they'd lost sight of him. She would follow; she would catch up, his footsteps, solitary and visible in the sand, would show her, show all of them, the way.

"Do you trust me, Mother Mary?"

"With what?" She did trust him, absolutely, but that did not mean she felt safe with him.

"Everything. I wouldn't do anything to damage the boy. I need your faith right now."

Mary looked again at Bronson davening, revving himself up; saw that old need in his eyes. This was the man she'd thrown in with; yes, he was flawed, flawed in the way so many men were, but she'd been away from him for almost a year and had seen nothing out there that convinced her that there was a better life to be had elsewhere in civilization. This was her life, with him, with this family, for better or for worse. Pearl and Deuce were safe and free; they had futures away from here. Bless them. She'd done her job. She would stay and make sure the rest of the kids made it through and out, too. She would stay in Agadda da Vida and be a roadblock when necessary, a loving roadblock. She smelled something strange, though, and it stole her immediate attention, an odd but familiar smell from her past like rotten eggs that she couldn't pin down through her Percocet haze; and there was a clear, slightly gooey substance on Bronson's hands, almost like snot, some on hers now. "What's that smell?"

Bronson let go of her hands, wiping his palms on his pants, and headed toward the house, calling back to her, "Get your gun, Mother Mary, and take the rest of the kids to the barn. Hyrum and I will stay in the house. Just stay in the barn. Everything will be all right."

She tried to stop him one last time, putting all the love and worry and history she had into one word. "Bronson!"

The tenor of the word stopped him cold. He thought of how Mary always called him "Bro'" unless she was pissed; when she called him "Bronson," he knew he was in for it. He recalled, briefly, a cascade of earlier times of domestic bliss and squabbles, a pleasant, nostalgic pang. He turned back to face her slowly and smiled deeply, thankfully, for all of it; whatever he was up to, he was utterly in control. He winked and said, "I gotta get down with the 'boon." And then he turned his back and walked away.

43.

THE THREE COP CARS from San Bernardino were responding to a domestic disturbance/possible kidnapping at an address they'd never been to, had never heard of, and that didn't exist. They had to be helped by GPS into the middle of the desert, over terrain that damaged their vehicles. It took a few wandering, frustrating hours until they finally saw a house rise up miraculously before them, like a mirage. It wasn't a mirage. They crawled toward it cautiously, punching the siren to announce themselves, and speaking over the megaphone, "San Bernardino County Sheriff's Department." They got no response.

They got out of the vehicles, and called out again, "San Bernardino County Sheriff's Department." A bullet shattered a headlight. They ducked for cover behind the cars.

The men chattered nervously—"Jesus, guess he's not in the mood to talk."

"Some kind of crazy-ass Mormon."

"Gotta be to live out here like this."

"Mormon? Thought they were the good guys."

"We're the good guys," the sergeant, Paul Dark, said. Dark had thirty years on the job, and his sonorous, unhurried voice drawling commands through a thick gray mustache inspired confidence in his men and many a comparison to the actor Sam Elliott. He was known affectionately as "Sergeant Coors."

"How many you see?"

"I see one man by a front window left side, Sarge."

"I see a boy, window right side."

"A man and a boy? That it? There's supposed to be more kids."

"Let's call him, talk to him."

Sergeant Dark said, "He doesn't have a phone."

"No phone? Now I'm scared—that is some crazy shit."

"No, he's some kinda hoarder survivalist, off the grid."

"White supremacist?"

"No intel on that. I have no background other than Mormon and mad about his kid," Dark said.

"Man, I don't like not knowing shit," one of the uniforms said. "They sent us in to fuck with a half hard-on."

"Maybe we should wait for more intel."

"Oh, you wanna wait till the movie comes out, see what you should do?"

Dark stopped the debate: "Ladies, stop bitching."

"He's a different type of cat, huh?"

The sergeant smiled with something like respect. "Yes, a different type of cat. And our dicks are always hard. Hard but fair, right, boys?"

"Right," the boys answered.

"Okay, Adams," the sergeant continued, "get back in the car and drive it to the side of the house, on the right there, view of the back right, too. Jacko, you get up to the left side, get yourself some view of the back, too, okay? Let's pin him down and wait for more backup. He'll see the numbers and he'll quit. He's a father that loves his son. He's just confused right now. I'll get him talking, man to man, father to father, Christian to Christian."

"What if I get a shot at the white supremacist asshole?" Adams asked.

"No one said he's a white supremacist."

"Sarge, if it waddles like a duck and quacks like a duck . . ."

"Adams, hush now," Sergeant Dark said. "I haven't heard him quack at all."

"That bullet fuckin' quacked."

"If I get a shot at him, I take it?" Jacko asked. "If he's looking for suicide by cop and threatening that boy, do I give it to him?"

"Boys, boys, boys." Dark extended his arms. "Chill. This isn't that movie. No crossfire, now, okay? Nobody takes a shot. Do not give him a shot. We are gonna tire him out. No one-on-one ball. Team play. Copy?"

"Copy."

"Copy."

"Jacko? Let me hear you."

"Copy, Sarge. No one-on-one."

The men nodded solemnly at one another. They all had some training for something like this, but they were cops, not one of them had ever been in an actual deadly hostage situation. A couple hours ago, they were eating lunch in San Bernardino and bullshitting about women and sports, thinking about working out more and eating less. Now this. Life and death. They were each terrified in their own way of this sudden crucible, harboring dreams of heroism, ashamed of the growing fear in their bellies, the nightmare of potential cowardice.

"I been married three times. And I got six kids," Dark said. "I know how to deal with hostage takers." The men laughed out some relief at the cool of their beloved Sergeant Coors. "Let's keep talking to him on the bullhorn. If he comes out with the boy, shooting, do not shoot the boy, do not shoot at him when he's near the boy. If you see any children, do not shoot. Even if he is shooting—duck and cover. And stay with me on the walkie! Clear?"

"Clear, Sarge."

"There may be other children in the house that you cannot see. Is that clear?"

"Clear, Sarge."

"Nobody gets hurt today. That's the movie we're making. This ain't Waco. Let's keep him pinned down and get him talking, sit on him, tire him out. Get SWAT out here. Go!"

Two uniformed men dove at the one car, and two at the other, the sergeant and another man remaining behind the third car. The two cars drove off to separate sides of the house. A couple bullets dinged them as they skidded into position. Sergeant Dark radioed in that the situation was escalating quickly, and he requested SWAT and maybe helicopters. His radio was shit out here though. The desert scrambled everything. He felt like his request had been heard, hoped, but he wasn't 100 percent sure. The boys didn't need to know that.

From her position in the barn, Mary could see the cop cars come into view, and the guns trained on the house, on Bronson and Hyrum. Her fog was lifting now. She stayed very still, trying to ensure that the cops wouldn't be drawn to any movement, and that the kids were well hidden and silent at the back of the barn, safe from any bullet angles. The cops had taken their positions, shielded from Bronson by their cars, but Mary had a clear, and for her, easy shot at each of the four cops. She was an excellent marksman. She stayed low but lifted her gun slowly, balancing it on an empty window frame, and waited for the shot she wasn't at all sure, even given the chance, she could take.

From inside the home, Bronson saw the two cop cars pull up to the sides of the house. He knew they wanted simultaneous views of the front and back, and that's what he wanted for them, too. He wanted them to see inside, to see what he was doing, to try to get a step ahead of him. They were only about thirty yards apart; the cops could see Hyrum and him talking, but couldn't make out the words.

"Bronson Powers!" came the voice over the bullhorn. "My name is Sergeant Paul Dark. I'm with the San Bernardino County Sheriff's Department. I'd like to talk."

Bronson's response was to take a few shots at one of the cop cars, and watch the men dive down and then come back up. Bronson reloaded. Hyrum aimed his gun out of the other side of the house at the other car.

"Don't hit anyone, son," Bronson yelled across the room.

"I know," Hyrum replied. "If I wanted to hit one, one would get hit." Bronson marveled at the cold-bloodedness of the young boy. How he used to get such a kick out of what a little warrior he was, and how that same nature troubled him today—that maybe something darker was there. He smelled the scent of the spent bullets in the air, sulfurous, like the devil.

"Come back to me now," Bronson called to Hyrum. The boy did as he was told and jogged to his father's side.

Sergeant Dark's voice floated in on the bullhorn—"Bronson. Stop shooting. We don't want anyone to get hurt today. I'm here to listen. Let's find a solution."

Bronson yelled out to the cop cars, "Hey! Hey!" till he made eye contact with them. Then he quickly grabbed Hyrum by the throat and held the gun to his head. "I'm gonna kill him now if you make another move! He's mine to do with what I want!"

"Help!" Hyrum yelled. "He's gonna kill me! He's fuckin' crazy! Please help me now!" Bronson was taken aback that the kid was such a good actor. He seemed like he really meant it.

He whispered, "Good," in Hyrum's ear. "But don't say 'fuck.'"

From her vantage point, Mary could see the cops react, reposition slightly, and point their weapons. She couldn't see Bronson and Hyrum inside, but she knew enough about a gun to know that the cops were aiming at a hard target now, not just covering a general direction. She aimed, too. She had a clear shot at the side of the head of both cops. Resting the gun on the window ledge took the shake out of her hands. She felt the trigger metal fold neatly into the crease of her finger. She used to like to shoot. She knew she couldn't kill a cop; she also knew she might if they started shooting at her man and her boy.

One cop spoke into his shoulder radio: "Sarge, he's got his gun on the kid, he's threatening the kid. The kid is crying out for help."

"Clear shot on the dad?" Dark asked.

"Negative."

"I got an angle, but it's not great. He's . . . the kid."

"What? Do . . . sh . . ." The walkie was cutting in and out. "What? What do I . . . ?"

"Get ready to . . . nothing."

"Ready to what, Sarge?"

"Ready."

"I got a cl . . . got a . . . no . . . shot." The walkie was garbled and inconsistent.

"What?"

"Missed."

"What? Fuckin' walkie! Fuckin' desert is fuckin' with us."

"Missed."

"Jesus Fuck, I told you not to shoot, Jacko," Dark yelled.

"Radio problems," Jacko said. Now there was nothing but static.

The sergeant threw down his walkie. It seemed to him that the desert was siding with Bronson. "We're a hundred fuckin' yards away and the fuckin' radios don't work. Someone get me a couple plastic cups and some string."

"Sir?"

The bullet shattered the window by Bronson, glass cutting his cheek. Mary drew a bead on the cop closest to her. She could see he was very young, in his mid-twenties maybe. She was about to pull her trigger when Bronson, still holding Hyrum by the neck in a half nelson, fired a few shots at the cop cars and then sprinted to another room off the living room, out of sight of the cops. The uniforms had ducked back down behind the squad cars. Mary took her finger off her trigger. Sergeant Dark couldn't tell if anybody'd been hurt.

"Talk to me! Anybody hit?"

"Shit! He ran," one of the cops said, hunkered down behind the car.

"Ran where?"

"Lost eyes ah . . . ! He dis . . . into . . . house. He's. . . . ing . . . gun . . . boy! Orders?"

"Fuck me! Ran where? I'm blind here. What about the boy?" Dark grabbed the walkie. "Wait! Do not . . . !"

"Don't what, Sarge?"

"Don't . . ."

"Sarge?" The cop waited. "Orders? Sarge? Can't hear you. We're going in, Sarge! He's gonna kill the boy! We're going in!!" The radio started crackling again.

Sergeant Dark threw the walkie down, stood up, waving his arms, and screamed to his men near the house—"No! Don't go in! I think he wants you to go in!"

He had just gotten the attention of the men when a shot dinged his shoulder. He went down. "Fuck!" he said, gritting his teeth. "The man's got good aim. Thought I was outta range. That was a rifle. This guy's good. Give me the bullhorn."

The cops nearer to the house hadn't heard their sergeant yell for them to stay out, but they saw him take a hit and go down. They tried the walkie again—nothing. "They shot Coors. Go time!" Jacko yelled.

The four cops charged out from behind the flanking vehicles toward the house. The decisive movement emboldened them, and the righteousness of their rescue mission fortified them. By the time their sergeant got on the bullhorn again to try to stop them, their adrenaline and the blood rushing to their ears made them deaf. They were almost to the house. Bronson peeked out a window and saw them making their move. He didn't shoot.

From the barn, Mary saw the cops running too, and she was about to start shooting when it came to her, that rotten egg smell—it was a smell from the Hollywood sets, from her working days, her time as a stuntwoman and sword swallower. Of course she knew that smell. From stunt days of fire. It was an accelerant, carbon disulfide. What the hell was Bronson doing with accelerant on his hands?

Before she could hazard a guess, the answer came from without. The cops had charged the house, breaking down the door, four of the six storming inside. They hadn't been in the house ten seconds when the first explosion came, a good one, a real professional FX doozy. The force and heat of it drove Mary to the ground even out at the barn. She yelled at the kids to stay down, and by the time she got back up, she saw two of the cops on fire, running around, screaming inside the house. It looked like a movie, Bronson's movie, but it smelled like real life.

Now another explosion shook the wood planks, and knocked her down. "What's happening, Mom?" Beautiful wailed. "It's the fire, isn't it? The fire!"

"Alvin! Get back, Beautiful! Get down, all of you and shut up!" Mary ordered.

"It's the fire! I told you! The fire!" Beautiful shouted.

Mary turned back momentarily to look at Beautiful, who was lost in her own prophecies of doom now seemingly coming true. Mary made a move to console her, to lay calming hands on her, when a third explosion rocked her sideways, driving her head against the side of the barn and drawing blood from her brow. The children shrieked. Beautiful bolted. Mary recovered quickly and caught Beautiful up in her arms to soothe her, but the child was mesmerized by her own visions, inconsolable and desperate, looking to run like a spooked horse.

Mary heard/felt another explosion, the fourth, in the house, and now the fire caught and the wooden structure went up like kindling in a huge flame in the hot dry desert air. Mary held tight to Beautiful as she stood up again to see. Bronson and Hyrum were still in there. She heard the screams of the other cops, as smaller pops rocked the house like a cache of fireworks. All the tricks of Bronson's former trade making illusions now bearing real, deadly fruit. She saw glimpses through the windows and heard the dark-uniformed, burning men hurl themselves, writhing and lurching in agony, unable to find an exit in the heat and smoke. She held Beautiful's face against her breast, keeping the child blind, repeating mindlessly the lie, "There's no fire . . . there's nothing . . . there's no fire."

"I can smell the fire!" Beautiful screamed. "It's here! It's happening! This is the end!"

Suddenly, the back door of the house flew open and a Hollywood-worthy fireball came rolling out, hungry for more oxygen, and inside that fireball, Mary made out two burning figures running within it, like they were riding in and on an orange wave—a man and a boy. "Oh Jesus, God," she prayed to herself. "Don't make me watch my loved ones burn to death." Her mouth opened instinctively, as if she were preparing to swallow fire again, as she had on the Venice Boardwalk long ago. She closed her mouth; she could not swallow this fire.

Beautiful kept chanting, "It's here. It's happening!"

Mary was going to lose her temper. "Beautiful—that's not helping! Children, stay down! Look away!"

Mary turned again and watched in horror as the larger burning figure grabbed a fire extinguisher that she hadn't noticed was lying out back there with a couple of knapsacks, and pushed the smaller one down and doused him, rolling him over, rolling him until the flames had been smothered, and he was just smoldering and smoking. Then the smaller figure took the extinguisher and doused the still burning larger one until his fire was out, too. White foam was flying and dark black smoke rose into the air off their bodies.

And there, under the foam and ash, standing now, the larger figure grabbed the smaller one's face in his hands and ripped it off, up and over his scalp. Mary felt the bile rise in her throat, till she recognized the face was not a face, but a mask, a flame-retardant barrier, a Pyrex faceplate (she'd worn a few in her day), and under the mask was Hyrum, gulping for air. Now she recognized the flame-retardant suits from yesteryear, as the figures quickly removed their hot, charred Kevlar outer layer. The larger figure pulled his face off too—also gasping. Neither would have been able to breathe the last minute or so with their faceplates affixed over their noses and mouths. Their masks on the ground, Bronson and Hyrum stood there, hands on their knees, gasping hard for air, but alive, and seemingly unhurt. Bronson had been holding on to this rarefied special effects equipment, squirreling it away, for years. Once every five years or so, when he would make small burns to control the invasive cheatgrass around the property that gave too much cover and fuel for a possible wildfire, he would also do a burn for the kids where he put on a flame-retardant suit and set himself alight, and then come back to life.

"Gives them the right sense of respect for the old man," he'd say. "When you see a man burn and live, you tend to do what that man says—worked on Moses . . ." He'd laugh. "Plus, it's fucking fun."

She was frozen in place. Bronson and Hyrum stripped off the layer of Insulite and the rest of their flame-retardant suits, threw on the two knapsacks, and stumbled to the horses, who were spooked by the explosions and fire, stomping, crying out, and banging at their stalls. As she watched Bronson and Hyrum run, she had the thought that she'd never seen either of them so alive. They passed right by her, close enough to touch, but she didn't reach out or try to talk to them, but rather let them pass by; it was like they were on a movie screen to her. Her attention was drawn to the embers from the burning house buffeted on the wind in all four directions. These glowing handfuls of fire were beautiful, sentient-seeming, like fireflies, but bigger, like incandescent butterflies dancing and landing where they would. She, almost smiling, watched some settle on the barn as if they would pollinate with fire. She snapped out of her appreciation of this beauty when she realized the broad beams of the barn had caught too. The desiccated wood would go up like kindling in min-utes. She ran to release the other horses from their stalls.

Before getting on his horse, Hyrum made a detour to the pens that held the cow, the pigs, the chickens, and the ostriches. He pulled his gun from the knapsack and jogged up to the milk cow. He put the muzzle to the animal's head.

Bronson turned back from his horse and saw. "What are you doing, Hy?"

"Fernanda's gonna burn. They're all gonna burn. I don't want her to suffer." Bronson was moved by this act of mercy.

"Don't shoot her," he said, "just open the gate and shoo her out. She'll run to safety." He didn't know if that was true or not, but on top of everything else, he didn't want his son putting a bullet through a beloved cow's head.

"Okay," Hyrum said. He unlatched the gate. The cow didn't budge. She licked the boy's face instead. Hyrum hugged the animal around its broad neck and started to weep. "Dad? What do I do? Fernanda won't leave."

"Shoo her. Smack her ass!" Bronson jumped off his horse. They didn't have time for this shit. He ran into the pen and kicked at the old cow's rear end. She turned around at him, accusing, refusing to budge her 1,500-pound bulk, her big wet brown eyes hurt by this human betrayal.

The scene was bedlam. The sounds of distress at the fire and confusion coming from the pigs, chickens, and horses were horri-ble: pure animal fear. Made it hard for Bronson to think. "Shoo!" he yelled, and fired his gun right near the cow's head. She bolted at the noise and stumbled out of the gate, running blindly this way and that, toward the fire and away. "Come on, Hyrum!" Bronson yelled. He sprinted to release the other animals from their enclosures. Hyrum helped shoo the terrified beasts out into the open. "They're animals. They're smart. They'll find a way to safety. God will see to them. C'mon!"

Bronson could tell Hyrum didn't want to leave till he saw all the creatures free and clear, so he grabbed his arm. "Come on, son! That's all we can do." Hyrum wiped his eyes and mouth of tears and spittle with the back of his arm, and put his gun back in his knapsack. They jumped back on their horses, who were only too happy to gallop away from the nearby fire spreading and the madness of humans, and disappeared into the desert. "Don't look back, son," Bronson said, "just keep riding now."

"Come on, kids! Hold hands! Run!" Mary shouted. The barn was on fire now, beams crackling and shifting. Mary gathered the remaining children and ran them out a wide berth around the burning house toward the policemen by the cop car in position directly about fifty yards away. Even so, they could feel the heat of the flames. Beautiful stopped, frozen, staring into her burning home like she was seeing the future unfold. Mary picked the panicked child up in her arms. The girl was almost her size, but Mary had the mother strength born of unfolding catastrophe.

As she hobbled carrying Beautiful, herding the rest of the children in front of her, for the safety of the cop car, Mary noticed a large dark form loom over her shoulder, like a man, or a demon, like an avenging angel. She gasped, stumbled, and turned to look back—it was an ostrich, sprinting at 45 m.p.h., passing her easily. She felt its weight and power brush by her, followed by two more of the huge birds. She met the cartoonishly large, bulging two-inch eyes, and saw nothing but a mirror reflected back to her—the mad instinct for self-preservation. She glanced farther back and saw the crazy wave of freaked-out animals behind her veering off in all directions—the pigs, the chickens, the horses—like watching a world come apart at the seams. She pulled the children into a tighter configuration so as not to be trampled by the stampede.

Mary turned and looked ahead again. She could see the two remaining cops about twenty yards away now, one down and bleeding, the other standing in firing position, eyes wide with panic, gun trained, but wavering nervously between sights. He had his finger on the trigger, confused as to what was the greater threat, what to shoot at, the 300-pound sharp-taloned prehistoric birds bearing down on them as fast as cars, or on Mary, who still had a gun in her hand, and her children. They didn't cover this particular Jurassic scenario at the academy. Mary closed her stinging eyes. Her legs felt dead, but she kept pumping them. She heard the pop of automatic weapons, she heard the children and the animals screaming in terror, and still she kept churning her family toward the sound of the guns.

44.

THE SUNSET GLOWED UNEARTHLY today because of the still raging fires. From the amount of smoke in the distance, Bronson assumed that the blaze near the house had not been contained. What he didn't know was that because of intensely dry conditions and the new extremes of global warming (hotter air = stronger wind), and firefighters who were undermanned and overworked because so much money and manpower had been diverted to other disasters and fires in the state, what would become known as the Joshua Tree Fire of 2020 had begun, and would not be fully out for almost a month. X acres would eventually burn, X lives and X dollars lost. It would dwarf the Camp Fire of 2018.

The police helicopters that had been flying low over the endless desert searching for Bronson and Hyrum had eventually given way to the fire department choppers dumping water and red PHOS-CHEK on the hungry conflagration. And then even those choppers and small planes had disappeared, called back to defend areas that were populated as the fire searched out more nourishing fuel, finding it in the nitrogen-enriched (thank you, creeping LA smog) invasive grasses.

As he watched the distance burning toward him, Bronson thought—Beautiful was right all along. The fire this time. She was the true prophet. She was Jackie's spiritual daughter. Jackie. He could no longer feel her in his head. His headaches were gone. The fire outside had put out the fire inside. He was where he was supposed to be, in the desert fulfilling the law. He leveled his eyes to civilization in the flat distance somewhere beyond the horizon. You screwed it all up. All of you. God gave you this planet to be stewards and you tore it up and gorged on its innards, its oil and its gold, and raped it till there was nothing left but dry tinder. "Fuck mankind," he thought, a scourge upon the earth. "Burn."

But it wasn't burning at the new sacred place, the second temple, where Bronson and Hyrum made their camp, where Jackie, Carthage, and Nauvoo were now buried. Though he could not feel them, Bronson hoped their spirits were still here hovering, their baptized and saved souls. Bronson was a saver of souls. He thought briefly of the men in the traps, dead or dying out there at the other place, the ruined first temple; they would be silent soon, their short sojourn on the planet over, their longer trip just begun. He would learn their names too, and baptize them by proxy, and save them, in time.

Though the air was hard to breathe and the sky looked like medieval renderings of Hell itself, by the time father and son had built their own small campfire and finished their meal, it was getting colder. They lay back to watch the apocalyptic sky turn from red to black. Though cloudless, there would be no stars tonight in the smoke-obstructed heavens. The desert world would soon be dark as a crypt.

"They'll be coming for us," Hyrum said.

"They'll be coming for me, Hyrum, not for you," Bronson answered. "They won't come for a child. Not like that, and not too soon, they got their hands full right now fighting that fire. I'm sorry it's burning like that. I didn't want that."

"I'm scared," Hyrum said.

"Of what?" Bronson asked. "The fire? Those men?"

"No. Of you. Of the way you look right now."

"How do I look?"

"Like you're on fire, too."

"You have nothing to be afraid of, son. I have only the welfare of your eternal soul in mind." Bronson stood up. "But you do sense my concern. I'm afraid because of your murderous action. I'm afraid you are headed for spirit prison."

"Spirit prison?"

"There are some sins that put you beyond the merciful blood of Christ. Sins like murder."

"I didn't mean to kill him."

". . . But you've never been afraid to kill, have you, son?"

"I guess not."

"Neither beast nor man."

"Yeah."

"What do you make of that?"

Hyrum thought awhile, and then said, "I don't know."

"Fair enough. But you said, 'Die, Lamanite.'" Bronson let the quoted threat hang swinging in the silent night, like a noose from a scaffold, he thought. He squinted at Hyrum, who seemed surprised by the reference and perhaps taken aback for a moment, but the boy was just remembering.

"Yeah, I did," Hyrum said, guilelessly. He shook his head at the memory, trying to take it back.

"Why 'Lamanite'?"

Hyrum shook his head again, trying to recall the exact moment.

"I think I was gonna say the 'N' word."

"Nephite?"

"No, not Nephite," he said with a laugh. "The other 'N' word."

Bronson had to think for a moment. "Oh, right."

"Yeah, but then that came out."

"Hyrum, I need you to tell me the truth now."

"That is the truth, Dad. It's just what came outta my mouth. It's just a word. Why is everyone so hung up on words? I dunno why I said it." The boy was an innocent or a cold-blooded killer, a simple wild angel or Satan his dissembling dark self. There was nothing in between.

Bronson nodded and said, "I don't know, either. Something in your nature. Something you came here already carrying, premortal, maybe something you carried for me, something you need to unlearn, something to atone for."

"It's just me, I guess."

"Yes. And I'm afraid, too, afraid that when they come for me, then I can no longer care for you and make sure you will dwell with me in Heaven. I'm afraid of what I must do in the short time I have. Do you understand?"

"Not really." The boy looked up, seemingly unconcerned for the moment with his father's struggle. "Not gonna be any stars tonight," he said, and then stood up with a smile. "I got some chocolate in my knapsack, you want some?"

"It's got caffeine in it."

"Come on, Dad, live a little."

Bronson watched his boy, backlit by the fire, rummage through the knapsack. They could be any father and son camping anywhere, anytime. Bronson smiled too; sometimes the cheesy archetypes come through on their own, like a possession, and they feel good, for a moment.

"You don't have to be Supermormon all the time, you know," Hyrum needled him. He was growing up, growing a sense of humor, embracing irony, tentatively challenging his father.

Bronson smiled again, welcoming that archetype too. For one short moment, he allowed himself to revel in the bullshit tropes handed down from generation to generation. The comfort food of father-son bonding. "Ha. Okay. I'll have a small piece."

Hyrum dropped the bag, walked back to Bronson, and handed him a piece of chocolate. Bronson ate it. First piece of chocolate he'd had in decades.

"Damn, that's good."

"Father, your language," Hyrum joked again.

"Reese's Peanut Butter Cups? That's a bad motherfucker."

"Ha! So close. Mom gets the Trader Joe's ones. Says they're healthier. That's my jam."

"Like father, like son."

Already the archetypes were fading, losing depth and dimension, turning into memes, commercials. Capitalism corrupting truth. Bronson sighed. He was no longer able to enjoy, just enjoy a piece of fucking chocolate. That would not change. Hyrum grinned. He had no problem with any of that.

"It's a whole new world out there, Dad."

Bronson laughed. "Yeah. Did you like the world, Hy?"

"Parts of it."

"The chocolate parts?"

"Haha. Dad joke. There's plenty more here if you want it."

"Thank you, son. No, thanks." Bronson nodded again, slowly, sadly, then asked of the air itself, it seemed, "How can you atone to nature for your nature doing what it does?"

"I don't understand what you're asking."

"How do you atone to God for being as He made you?"

"Sounds like that's on Him, not me."

Bronson nodded. The kid had a point. "Does being able to kill for an idea make that idea true?"

"It wasn't my idea to kill. I didn't mean to," Hyrum said.

"So you say. Does dying for an idea make that idea worth dying for?"

"Is that like a real question? I don't know what you're talking about."

"Maybe I don't either." Bronson sighed.

After another while, Hyrum spoke. "But you forgive me?"

Bronson blinked, a tug on his heart. "Oh yes, my beautiful boy." And he did, he really did. But he could not speak for God the Father. He was trying to listen to what He wanted, and his God had always spoken in mysterious code and tongues. The goal was so far away, he could barely see it. It seemed he stood on an endless football field and way off in the distance, a goalpost with arms upraised, like a Joshua tree. He had to get his son from here to there. Bronson got lost in this football analogy, didn't know what play to call, couldn't take that first step, but he knew the ball, his son, was in his hands. He knew that much.

"First things first," Bronson said. "Fetch me my water, son, we need to baptize that boy you killed. Add his name to the Mountain of Names."

"Hermano."

"Yes, Hermano. Hermano Ruiz. We will make sure eternal life is his. It may not be enough, but it's the least we can do."

"How you gonna do that?" Hyrum handed his father the canister of water.

"I'm gonna baptize him through you. You will be the agency of his salvation, and maybe that will be the agent of your salvation. You will stand in for him. You will be him."

"That feels weird, Dad."

"Bow your head."

Bronson began to chant the words for the Mormon baptism of the dead. The same words he'd spoken for his tragic babies, Carthage and Nauvoo, the same words he planned to say soon for Dirk Johnson and the men he'd killed today. He had no fountain, but he felt this land here his sanctified temple. He sprinkled, then poured some water over Hyrum's scalp.

"I don't know that he would want this," Hyrum said.

"I don't care. Say his name."

"Hermano Ruiz. I don't know that his family would want this."

"I'm not concerned with his family. Say his name."

"Hermano Ruiz. Water's cold."

"Be quiet, Hyrum, you're doing a holy thing. Having been commissioned of Jesus Christ, I baptize you for and in behalf of Hermano Ruiz in the name of the Father, and of the Son, and of the Holy Ghost. Amen."

When Bronson was finished and convinced that the soul of Hermano Ruiz had been given eternal life vicariously through his wild son, he lay back on the sand. He had made the first move toward the goal, toward forgiveness and restoration. He was vigilantly listening for his God now, scanning the horizon for a new sign, to see if that was sufficient. With the shadows attenuating, and the sun angling down farther to the west by the second, the arms of the Joshua trees looked one moment like they were welcoming an embrace and the next as if they meant to push him away, like a trick photo oscillating. Back and forth like that as night finally fell on this murderous day.

They watched the stars try to grow brighter, only to fade and twinkle out in the waving smoke. They stared up at the black blank sky. "That's how fathers and sons make peace, Hyrum, through baptism for the dead. The present is the son and the past is the father, and in that moment they face each other with love. The present saves the past."

"If you say so."

"I say so."

Bronson laughed at his boy's prosaic honesty. He had always thought of him as a perfectly made but alien thing, organized differently from the other children. It's not that he's disorganized, he used to advise Mary and Yaya, it's that he's organized differently.

"That was fun today, wasn't it?" Bronson asked.

"Respect."

"Righteousness is always fun, to feel God's hand in your hand."

"True dat."

"You would've made a helluva stuntman."

"Yeah?"

"Better than me."

"Yeah? I liked being on fire. That was fire."

"Yeah, of course it was fire."

"No, Dad, fire means, like, really good, like hot, or, you know, good. Anything can be fire if it's good."

"Oh, okay. Cool. And you're a tougher man than me, at eleven, already you're more of a man than just about any man I've known. But you don't wanna be a stuntman—that's just a shadow of an actor, and an actor is just a shadow of a real person making shadows on a silver screen in the dark. A shadow of a shadow. It's a bullshit existence, but you coulda aced it."

"Thanks, Dad. Big ups."

"Big ups?"

"Means, like, thank you."

"Ah, okay. *Up* being a positive," the autodidact in him pushed forward, "used as a plural noun and *big* meaning a lot, or in this case, many. That's fire. Many thanks."

"Okay, boomer. Way to kill it, Dad. I'll never say it again."

Bronson laughed. He was happy that, as soon as he'd gotten back to the desert, Hyrum, for the most part anyway, had stopped relying on all that stupid language and macho posturing, as if he'd spoken a foreign language in a foreign land, and now he was getting back to his native tongue. He was just using it to tease the old man now. It's like the city boy had been a changeling, and now he'd been returned to himself. This boy was his.

"Close your eyes, Hyrum."

"Why?" Hyrum began to breathe heavily. It was the first time Bronson had ever seen the boy show any sign of distress. It gave him pause. Their identities strobed back and forth in the flickering firelight from lame father and son in a TV commercial to biblical father and son from the oldest stories of man.

Bronson intoned, "'The voice of thy brother's blood crieth unto me from the ground.'"

"He wasn't my brother."

"All men are your brothers." Bronson stood, his old knees crackling like the fire. "Do you trust me to deliver you from evil, to close this distance from your God? For, as the prophet said, in Alma 42, 'God ceaseth not to be God, and mercy claimeth the penitent, and mercy cometh because of the atonement; and the atonement bringeth to pass the resurrection of the dead; and the resurrection of the dead bringeth back men into the presence of God; and thus they are restored into his presence.'"

"I feel restored out here with you, Dad. We did the baptism thing. I think that's enough for today. I feel fine."

"You may feel that way, but it is not so. I shall restore you to His presence. We preach to the living and the dead. We teach revelation to the dead and we baptize the dead, Hyrum—there is no difference to your soul between the estates of life and death. It's just a body. Hyrum, your eyes, please close them."

"You get mad at me for the way I talk. Why do you talk like that?"

"Like what?"

"Like a movie. Like a book. That's not you either."

"Pray with me, Hyrum."

"I don't want to pray."

The boy was right. The words were speaking him, not the other way round. The words sounded crazy and fake, but Bronson believed them. He had to. He had to regain his faith through sacrifice and through the law. It was all he had left, his lack of certainty and his duty; the only way to regain his certainty was through duty. Bronson knew what he must do, but he couldn't meet his boy's eyes. Bronson was too weak. Burying Jackie, and then Nauvoo and Carthage, had been the hardest things he'd ever done. Till now. This felt impossible, like he was trying to breathe underwater, his instinct at war with his mind.

"Stand up, Hyrum," he ordered. Hyrum stood slowly. "Do you remember the story of Abraham and Isaac?"

"Yeah."

"How God asked Abraham to prove his devotion by sacrificing his son, a burnt offering, like what's still burning today?"

"God's kind of an asshole, huh?"

"It can seem that way, son, but it's only because we are not smart enough to understand his plans. Brigham Young said, 'There are sins that can be atoned for by an offering upon an altar, as in ancient days; and there are sins that the blood of a lamb, of a calf, of turtle doves cannot remit, but they must be atoned for by the blood of the man.'"

Hyrum scrunched up his face. "The fuck's a turtle dove? That a turtle that can fly or a dove that looks like a turtle?"

"Hyrum . . ."

"Uh-huh. Okay, I got it, focus—that's what my Cucamonga teachers say. Okay. But Abraham, he didn't do it, did he? He pussed out."

"No. God stayed his hand."

"Because God changed his mind?"

"I guess so. I guess God saw that they were willing, that their love was true, and that was enough."

Hyrum formulated his next thought slowly and carefully, as if his life depended on the wording. "If God is perfect and he changes his mind, doesn't that mean he's not perfect?" Ah, that old chestnut. Bronson had spent years struggling with that paradox himself. He was ready.

"No, because God's mind is so large it can contain a thing and its opposite and not be untrue."

". . ."

"God's mind, not my mind."

They fell silent again until Hyrum asked, "How do you know when God's had enough?"

Bronson did not have an answer to that quite so ready. "I don't know, son. We have to be willing. And give up hope. Are you willing?" Bronson walked behind his son and stood still, both of them facing the fires glowing in the distance.

"Maybe that will happen again," Hyrum said. "Maybe God has had enough. Maybe He's gonna change his stupid mind again."

"Maybe He has."

"I don't like God."

"That's okay, I don't like him much right now either, but we do have to love him, as you love yourself, for you will be a god, too."

"That doesn't make sense."

"It's the sense beyond sense. It will get clearer if you give up hope, son. Are you willing?"

"My eyes are closed, Dad. That's what you want, right? I'm tired of talking like this. It makes my head hurt."

Bronson raised his gun and held it less than an inch from the back of his son's skull.

"Yes, Hyrum, I understand. And I love you." Bronson had to choke back a sob. "Do you forgive me?"

"Forgive you for what?"

Quickly, smoothly, in one motion, Hyrum reached into his bag, pulled something out, spun around, and held it out to his father. For a moment, Bronson thought he was offering him another piece of chocolate, a piece of chocolate for his life, and the childish, pathetic hopefulness of that tore at Bronson's heart. But as he looked more closely, and the shape became clearer in the firelight, he saw that his son had pulled a gun on him. They stood there, a couple feet apart, father and son with guns trained on each other in the so-called Mexican standoff position that Bronson had enacted countless times in a previous life. A staple of Hollywood. Another archetype, another tired old story pushing through.

"Forgive you for what?" the boy asked again, his tone now assertive, aggressive.

"What I need to do," Bronson answered.

"What about for what you've done? What about that?"

"What do you mean?"

"To the family."

"You mean—my family. It's my family."

"So?"

"Do not judge me, boy."

"You're judging me."

"You've got Satan in you, Fred. You said, 'Die, Lamanite!'"

"What? Who's Fred?! What's wrong with you, Dad?"

Bronson was half hoping the boy would shoot him, keep him from doing what he had to do.

"Dad, there's something wrong with you. Maybe you need help."

"There's nothing wrong with me. Give me the gun, Hyrum."

"No. You give me yours."

"No. I won't do that. You'll have to kill me to get it."

"I will if I have to."

Bronson laughed at the balls on this kid. He was so fucking proud of him, and maybe even a little scared of him as well.

"You have to. I want you to."

"No. Please, let's stop."

"We can't stop this. Only God can stop this."

"Bullshit. Why?"

"You'll have to shoot me to stop me."

"I will."

"Go ahead, then, boy."

Bronson took a step forward.

"Stay back, Dad."

"No, I feel like walking. Shoot your fucking father."

"I don't want to shoot you."

"Shoot me, please!"

"No!"

"Then give me the fucking gun!"

"No!"

Bronson made a sudden move at the gun in Hyrum's hand. Hyrum backpedaled. Bronson backhanded him across the face and grabbed for his gun. Hyrum stepped backward into a lunge and aimed.

Hyrum squeezed the trigger, the gun recoiled in his hand, and he shot his father in the chest. He could smell the spent powder. Hyrum looked into Bronson's eyes.

"Why, Dad? Why did you make me do that?" He moaned, then retched, doubled over, and threw up again. From his knees, he looked over and waited for his father to drop back down to the dust from where he'd come.

But nothing happened. Bronson didn't even flinch. He stood straight. He was breathing easily. Hyrum could see no blood.

"I thought so. I thought you could do it," Bronson said. "I thought you could kill me." He nodded slowly, like a lawyer who had gathered all the evidence he needed. "But I can't die, son, don't you know that? Shoot me again."

Hyrum stood up, spitting vomit. Bronson walked toward him, reaching for the gun. Hyrum stepped back again, screamed, and squeezed the trigger again, almost point blank. Bronson took the hit above his heart, his left shoulder jerking back, but still he did not go down. He squared up to Hyrum, dropping both hands to his sides, and said, "I'm a monster. I am man exalted. Where man is, God once was. Where God is now, man will be. I am God." Hyrum's entire body was trembling now—this was no woman intruder or snake or bigger kid, this was his father. The gun was shaking in his hand.

Bronson was a superhero and a monster, a god of the past and a man of the future, unkillable. Hyrum, tasting real panic for the first time in his life, bit his lip and pulled the trigger over and over. Bronson kept taking the hits and jerking back only to shrug it off and continue forward, as if in a nightmare. As Bronson advanced, Hyrum retreated step by step, as if they were synchronized, partnering in a dance, and the boy fired into his father's body till the gun did nothing but click. Hyrum stared at the impotent weapon in his hand, powerless against the mythical power of the father.

"Is that all?" Bronson asked. Hyrum checked the chamber. It

was now empty. Bronson reached out slowly and put his hand on the boy's gun. Hyrum released the metal easily. He stared at the omnipotent father, looked him up and down for any sign of mortality or weakness. All he could see was a little dried blood on his cheek from where a glass shard had cut him during the standoff with the cops earlier. Hyrum's mouth dropped open. He shook his head from side to side in disbelief. His knees were still rubbery.

"But I shot you," he moaned.

"Blanks," Bronson said, holding the gun up proudly. "Like the Carthage Greys. I loaded blanks before I gave it to you this morning."

Hyrum was astonished. "But I shot you, I saw you jerk back when the bullets hit, I saw them hit."

"I'm a stuntman, son. That's how a pro sells a hit."

Hyrum fell to his knees, head bent in shame, and faced away from Bronson, weighed down and confused at the knowledge that he could kill his own father.

"I'm sorry," Hyrum whispered.

"I know, son. If only sorry was enough. I didn't want any more blood on your hands, you understand?" Bronson explained, "You've got enough to atone for as it is."

Bronson now trained his own gun on the back of Hyrum's head and willed his entire consciousness into his trigger finger, gently placing it against the frame in a safety position.

"I love you, son," he said. "You know that?"

The boy did not answer.

If only love was enough, Bronson thought, and stared unblinking at the back of his boy's head, the thick red hair, and on his neck, the treasured desert shark's-tooth necklace. Bronson's gun felt heavy in his hand, pressed down as if by an invisble hand; he curled his finger to the trigger, but the trigger itself seemed sentient and unwilling, locked, like it had a thousand pounds of force pushing back against him. But this boy, his rough stone rolling, was a stone-cold killer. Always had been. Yes, he'd shown mercy for those animals today, that was encouraging, but he'd shown no mercy to that poor Lamanite. What if it *were* a hate crime, a religious crime, the worst type of murder? What if it were that unholy? The boy would need a radical absolution. He wouldn't get that in America out there. They'd blame the murder on video games, blame it on race, his parents, his religion, exonerate him, free him of responsibility. They'd take him and put him in juvie, special schools, get him therapy, *psychoanalyze* him, put him on drugs, get him in the system, cut his balls off, and he'd live to die a natural death, unsaved, unforgiven, damned.

My boy, my beautiful violent boy—damned? That was the worst thing a father could do to a son. Worse than neglect. Worse than absence. Worse than death. And Bronson didn't have time. They would be coming soon enough for him. He wasn't going to be taken alive so they could psychoanalyze him, too. Call him a fanatic with mental health issues. Father issues. Mother issues. Fuck that. Sex issues.

Bronson extended his finger off the trigger and placed it alongside the body of the gun again. He repeated this motion back and forth a few times. He was stalling, waiting, feeling for a sign that the bloody God of Moses, Jesus, Mohammed, and Joseph Smith had had enough suffering for today, to call an end to this endless repetition of an ancient crime. His shoulder ached. He longed to put down the gun. He longed for ongoing revelation. Was he a Lamanite, and a righteous restorer of God's original intent, or one of those fools who puts on a uniform to reenact Civil War battles? He felt so weak, surely that was God staying his hand. Maybe he had done enough to pass this test of faith. He had walked, like Abraham, right up to the edge of the abyss with a willing, hurting heart. Maybe that was enough.

His jittering mind randomly flashed to his grandmother Delilah, a woman he'd never met, but who was the prime mover of why he stood where he did today. For some reason, he gave her Mary's face when he thought of her now, and that was disconcerting. He thought he heard rustling nearby, the sound of hooves or snakes, the devil. He suspected he might be hallucinating under pressure and fatigue. He turned to look in the direction of the sound but saw and heard nothing. He was alone with his son. To center himself, he whispered fragments of a Brigham Young sermon, bending his index finger one last time from the frame to the trigger. "'It is true that the blood of the Son of God was shed for sins through the fall and those committed by men, yet men can commit sins which it can never remit . . . There are sins that . . . '"* He choked. It didn't make sense. Could there really be no forgiveness? Nothing made sense. He couldn't say another word, his or anyone else's, be they man, angel, prophet, or devil. He was powerless.

But then his finger twitched, the trigger seeming to give way a little: a sign, the sign that soon it would be over. His duty would be done. He would . . . bury the boy, and then, wretched child-killer that he was, he would take his own life. Blood atonement. Let it be. He would be remembered as a polygamist and pedophile, a child murderer, rapist, incestophile, and a cop killer. A mythic pariah. An evil thing. They would get the story wrong. They would talk about him in the same breath as Bundy, Manson, Koresh, and Jones. He didn't give a fuck. He never wanted to be known. He didn't care if they got him all wrong. They'd gotten Joseph Smith all wrong, too. He whispered, "No man knows my history." He knew what he really was, and so did his God. He would be reunited with Jackie and they would make love and the offspring of their celestial lovemaking would be more souls to be incarnated into more men and women on their way to becoming more gods. But first this sin, this ancient sin, through this sin to redemption. Let it bleed. He winced and began to pull with the final, horrible effort.

He heard the fatal shot ring out and his heart broke.

---

* Brigham Young, delivered in the Bowery, Great Salt Lake City, September 21, 1856.

45.

BRONSON FELL FACE-FIRST to the dirt, moaning at Hyrum's feet, his voice muffled. "Oh, Lord, my God," he said, then rolled onto his back peacefully, like he was contemplating the stars. He smiled up at Hyrum, saying softly, "He stopped me, Pilgrim. Fire devouring fire. Fire." Bronson Powers then looked back to the sky with the expression of a man seeing a familiar face in a crowd, exhaled, and died.

Hyrum saw the blood oozing from Bronson's shirt, his chest blown wide open from a bullet, his red heart pumping out, atoning, into the brown-black desert. Hyrum opened his mouth to scream, but nothing came out. There was nothing left inside him. He looked behind his dead father in the dirt, and saw his mother, Mary, standing, swaying at the edge of the firelight a few yards away, the smoking gun in her steady right hand. She was crying. She dropped the weapon to the desert floor. Hyrum ran stumbling to his mother. He went to hold her, and to be held by her.

AN
EXALTED MAN

In-a-gadda-da-vida, honey
Don't you know that I'm lovin' you
In-a-gadda-da-vida, baby
Don't you know that I'll always be true
Oh, won't you come with me
And take my hand
Oh, won't you come with me
And walk this land
Please take my hand

—IRON BUTTERFLY, "IN-A-GADDA-DA-VIDA"

ABOUT THREE WEEKS LATER, Malouf left a message on Maya's phone—"A great man, my friend Karl Rove, once said, 'We're an empire now, and when we act, we create our own reality. And while you're studying that reality—judiciously, as you will—we'll act again, creating other new realities, which you can study too, and that's how things will sort out. We're history's actors . . . and you, all of you, will be left to just study what we do.'* You can come back to the office now. Seven p.m. tomorrow."

The next day, Maya entered the Praetorian parking structure for the first time in nearly a month. As she waited at the entrance for the gate to rise, she spotted Randy Milman, whom she hadn't seen since the Cash-n-ator joyride, exiting in a brand-new Porsche Cayenne. She'd never noticed him at the office before, or even in this building. His windows were tinted almost as dark as a movie star's, but she felt sure that she caught his eye momentarily as he slowed, and that he appeared to mouth "cunt" right at her. This did not bode well.

A little shaken, she circled down the levels and parked in the spot reserved for Abbadessa, took a few deep centering breaths, and then made the familiar walk into Malouf's office a little after 7 p.m. She'd seen no one else on her way in.

* Karl Rove as quoted in an interview with Ron Suskind.

Malouf was alone, the only one in the entire Praetorian office. "There she is. Wharton, sit down, but first . . ." He rose and walked toward her, smiling and opening his arms as if for a hug. Maya did not want to be touched by him. He saw the disgust on her face, and said, "Oh no, not a hug, not in this day and age, I'm gonna pat you down."

She held her hands away from her sides and he ran his long, bony fingers around her waist, kneading across her shoulders and down her arms. He kneeled before her and ran his hands up her thighs to her crotch, and down the jeans-clad crack of her ass to see if she was wearing a wire or recording device.

"Someone's been working out. Keto? Pilates? That's the best— strength and flexibility. Phone, please." She handed him her phone.

"I'll hold on to it till the end of the meeting, if you don't mind. Now turn around, please." She blushed with anger at the humiliation and violation. She flushed some more when she thought he might see her scarlet as weakness. "Okay, all good," he said. "My apologies, now sit, please." Maya sat down. He went behind his desk again and sat as well, knitting those nine fingers together. "Missed you at the funerals. Beautiful funerals," he said.

"I wasn't invited."

"So many funerals. I made great speeches. People are saying I should run for office."

Maya raised her eyebrows, scrunched up her mouth, and nodded sarcastically, her telltale cheeks still red and hot. She wanted to tell him that men that look and "feel" like him, like a cheesy, gross, nine-fingered Hammer villain, don't get elected, but she didn't want to be mean. And he knew that already. His painful knowledge of his own handicaps made him smart, and dangerous.

She was very careful of when to engage him; she didn't want to get trapped. Malouf's version of reality was a mendacious hall of mirrors, spun harder than a web; you would have to argue the meaning of basic words first before you could ever share common ground—"depends on the meaning of what *is* is." A soul-sucking, litigious eternity. It wasn't her natural habitat. She'd get lost in the swampy weeds where fine-print, escape-clause men like him live. So she let him ramble on, with his crocodile tears and alligator empathy.

At home in that swamp, he dove back in. "You really made a mess of things. You're lucky you work for me, because I cleaned it up. That's what I do. You ever see *Pulp Fiction*? I'm like Mr. Wolf, the Cleaner. Harvey Keitel?" Maya still didn't feel the need to respond to this bullshit yet—the outlaw macho world according to Tarantino, Coppola, Scorsese, and Mamet for these guys, always.

"First of all, you're fired." That came as a relief. She was going to quit anyway. Maya exhaled. "Don't act surprised—I told you this would happen. You're lucky there will be no charges brought against you. Janet Bergram will also lose her state job. Good riddance. She did a stupid thing. Talentless paper pushers. Those who can't do, work for the government. But—Deuce Powers is going to Harvard next year, a year early. Thumbs-up to that brainiac. By the way, the BurgerTown franchise he unionized is closing—I know, it's a shame they couldn't make enough money in that location. And ICE is looking into this Jaime Rodriguez for trying to scam worker's comp. He's a bad hombre."

"That makes no sense. That BurgerTown—they'd been in that location for forty years."

"I know—weird, right? To just lose business so suddenly— volatile market—I guess you'd need a degree and a bunch of logarithms from Wharton to figure out why. Good news is they're going to open another new nonunion BurgerTown a couple blocks away in a few months. All new staff—everyone Deuce 'helped' is now jobless. Some hero. C'est la vie. But there was a drive by the Rancho Cucamonga Historical Society to save the original sign, so that monument to American small-town values will remain! Love it."

Maya wanted to spit at Malouf, strangle him, but she knew he was like one of those sci-fi creatures in a schlock Hammer film that feeds off anger and grows stronger. So she swallowed her outrage for now. Malouf seemed almost disappointed that she didn't lunge at him from across the desk. He sighed and continued, "Pearl Powers is enrolled in Juilliard, a year early as well. Pearl and Deuce are success stories, and I guess they have you to thank for that, partially. The lawsuit against Hyrum and the Powers family by the Ruiz family will be dropped. The evidence on the phone video is too damning. I'm thinking of countersuing the schmucks who brought the case against us—seems their lawyers knew about the existence of the phone all along and tried to suppress it. Hate-crime this, assholes!" He made an absurdly lengthy, elliptical jerking-off motion with his right hand.

"Nine men are dead," she said. It sounded like the refrain to a '60s protest song when it came out of her mouth: Four dead in O-hi-o.

"I'm getting to that, sunshine."

"You're getting to it?"

"I am buying the entirety of Powers's estate for a song, a penny on the dollar. I don't know what I will do with it, but it's a billion-dollar deal. You brought me a unicorn."

Maya smirked. That had been her dream; so much for dreams. Malouf continued, "When Joshua Tree stops burning, I'll drill down into its mineral worth, and its oil, and I'll look into casino licenses—you were right, there's a lot of Indian sovereignty out there to be bartered for, also zoning for residence, commercial, at the very least entice the warehouse-hungry Walmarts and Amazons out of San Bernardino, spas, golf courses. What Michael Milken is trying to do in Reno, I'm gonna do in 'Dino—that's what we're . . . how we're gonna rebrand San Bernardino—the 'Dino. Kicky, right? You like that?"

Maya could taste the acid bile rising in the back of her throat. She consciously slowed down her breathing and tried to relax the clenching muscles of her jaw. "The Mnooch got those opportunity-zone tax breaks passed in 2017, and you brought me the opportunity. Oh man, did we get taught a lesson in 2008—we learned how to do it even better this time around. Tom Price got the ball rolling, and Zinke did some great groundwork at the Department of Interior, we just need some roads—infrastructure! And DJT, visionary that he is, supports America being returned from the government back to the people, where it belongs—he's opening up Bears Ears and Grand Staircase–Escalante over in Utah, and the trend is our friend. All this National Park land that's going to waste; it's a shame. Trump is handing it back to where our Founders wanted it, with the people, to use it. It's the only way we're gonna beat back the yellow peril. You know the Declaration of Independence originally read, 'life, liberty, and the pursuit of property,' don't you?"

"Yes."

"Of course you do, Miss Ivy League. Property and happiness were synonymous to the Founding Fathers."

"That's not what that means."

"Agree to disagree."

"No, let's just disagree."

"Yeah, agree to disagree," he said.

"I'm not agreeing to anything," she said.

She shook her head quickly from side to side, to shake herself out of that dumb back-and-forth. She had to stop herself from saying more. She wouldn't be baited by his ostentatious racism or vintage sexism; she couldn't be pulled into quibbles and semantics now, and murky side issues. That's what he wanted. He waited. She waited.

He shrugged and continued, "I've set aside a small chunk of *happiness* for the Powers kids. They earned it—you've put them through enough. I want to make sure they're comfortable. They can live there, or they can sell it back to me at fair market for a nice nest egg."

"Nine men are dead. How do we atone for that?" She immediately regretted saying "we." She felt a physical aversion to being enjoined with this man in any way, even in theoretical contrition.

"The Joshua Tree Fire started by the Bronson house arson and explosions is still raging, forty percent contained as of this morning; still threatening more populated areas of San Bernardino County; it's estimated that it will have cost untold tens of millions of dollars in damage before it's done. My thoughts, thanks, and prayers go out to the heroic first responders and those threatened in the neighboring communities. I feel for them because I own land there, too, now I do, in the 'Dino."

He smiled, pleased with himself. "I've already made sizable contributions to the PAL, who lost some men as you know, and also to the San Bernardino school system. As one of the area's largest landowners I intend to make a lot of friends, do a lot of good, help a lot of kiddos."

"And nine men are dead."

"Sammy Greenbaum got a green light from Sony Pictures to remake *Dr. Jekyll and Sister Hyde*. He's writing and directing. Sensible fifteen-mil budget. Can't lose. We're in talks with Nicole to produce / star. Sammy's making the villain Canadian. Jack Ripperwell's a Canuck! How smart is that? The reanimation of Hammer horror by Praetorian is under way!"

"And nine men are dead."

They stared at each other. "But how can I help that?" Malouf asked, feigning helplessness.

Backlit by the sun setting over the Pacific behind him in the window, he seemed like a hologram to her, a weird, inhuman color; a trick of the light lacking depth or dimension. She rubbed her eyes as he continued, "What's done is done. This was your game, and the game proved deadly. That's on you. Now, I don't have to buy your silence, I think you know. But if I hear you so much as accept a lawyer's card, believe you me, I will crush you and make the rest of your life a living, litigious hell, and you don't have the mental or financial wherewithal for that, we both know. Prison time for you would not be out of the question, but I will protect you as long as I can, as long as you play nice."

Maya sat in silence; she felt hapless, weak, without muscle. The man across from her was willing to fight her every day for the rest of her life. She could only marvel at his perverse stamina, his evergreen lust for competition and destruction.

Malouf smiled. "But why should we part like this? I prefer to part as friends. You were mistaken about yourself. You thought you were something you're not. Not so very uncommon, just a little sad. You didn't have what it takes to make it here at Praetorian, but that doesn't make you a bad person."

"You'll never hear from me again."

"Attagirl. I'm gonna cut you a check."

"I don't want your money. You still owe the San Bernardino school district a hundred grand. Why don't you write that check?"

"Meow. Don't be silly. It's not my money, it's just money; it goes from my pocket to yours and presto, it's your money. Five hundred K. It's not much, but it should give you some time to figure out what you want to do when you grow up."

"I don't want it."

"I'm going to have two hundred fifty K deposited directly into your account, think of it as severance, and a friendly reminder, in addition to the NDA you signed with your last contract, not to even gossip about me. It's our own little green new deal. You can do with it as you please. Spend it on clothes, get more tattoos, fuck more married men, cover your Wharton student loans, give it to charity like a fool if you want, it doesn't concern me."

"Is that all?"

"That's all from me. I'm sure you have a lot to say, but I don't want to hear it. I'm pretty sure I know what it is, and I don't want you to feel bad later about hurting my feelings, so let's spare us both, shall we?"

He turned in his chair, his back to her, to face the ocean. The sun was about to dip into the sea at the horizon, as if it wished to extinguish itself in water, as if it were tired of burning this day, too.

"Parasite," Maya heard herself say.

Her lips remained slightly parted, stuck in a kind of sneer, the tip of her tongue holding against the back of her top front teeth in surprise that this particular word, not one of her everyday go-to epithets at all, had flown out of her. She hadn't even formed the word in her mind before it took shape in her mouth and escaped, like a fugitive, into the room.

Malouf swiveled back to face Maya, and his eyebrows arched so hard and high that they seemed to momentarily disappear over the top of his smooth head. "Parasite? You call me a parasite?"

He rose from his chair, ceremoniously, it seemed to her, slowly inhaling to full height. "Amazing. And what have you done, big shot? What have you made in your life, Miss Wharton? Huh? You did your little homework assignments and got a free pass into the white man's capitalist slipstream—bravo. You got the random luck to be born in a country at a time in history when women, vaguely, comfortably ethnic women like you, are put on second base and told they hit a double—yay, everybody gets a trophy. You got that affirmative action. How's the view?"

"What view?"

"The view you have standing on my fucking shoulders."

She had the urge to giggle—this change had come over him so suddenly, like a switch thrown, like a practical joke. Sure, she was expecting some kind of attack, but this harangue had come scat-tershot out of left field and turned so nasty and offensive so quickly that Maya found herself checking out a bit in mild shock and idly wondering what the feminine version of *ad hominem* was—*ad femi-nam*? Her Latin had ended in seventh grade of Catholic school.

"And what did you make of your golden ticket?" he continued, his voice rising, seething sarcasm. "You made straight A's. Wow.

Congratulations. Gold star, smiley face, good girl. You know what I made? I made myself!"

He pounded his chest with both cupped palms like a silverback gorilla. Again, Maya thought she might scoff aloud at the cliché of the gesture if he weren't so serious and pissed off. He was looming over her now. "Out of nothing. Ex nihilo. I made all this!" He spread his arms wide in an embrace of the room and its fabulous furnishings, the floor-length offices of Praetorian, but he might as well have been referring to the entire world outside his window—Santa Monica, America, Earth. Robert Malouf made it all.

Maya felt nailed to her seat by this eruption, which was authentic, and scary, the self-righteousness and spittle sparking out of Malouf. "You think I'm a lowlife—a Vichy Republican, a mini-Trump con artist, a malignant narcissist, a bald, ugly, toxic old man with a tan—stop me if you've heard this one! Holy shit, you're right! Guilty! All of the above."

He laughed, as if that string of condemnations had made him lighter. "What choice did I have? What did God give me? What? I'm not white like you, not really, no. You ever been called a 'sand nigger' during a real estate negotiation? Doubt it. You think I don't know half the motherfuckers who work for me call me 'Sirhan' behind my back? Not sir—Sirhan. Get it? The guy who shot Robert Kennedy. So fucking clever. Why aren't you laughing?"

Maya shook her head slightly. She might feel sorry for him, but he was in the way, feeling sorry for himself, blocking any genuine goodwill she might have, taking up all the light and air. The only pity he could feel was self-pity, and it was bottomless. He continued eviscerating both of them, turning himself inside out in a rage.

"I ain't pretty like you, you beautiful, entitled bitch. I don't have a nice wet pussy to get me free dinners. I can't dance or sing or act or fight or hit a baseball or write books. I have no inheritance like your boy, Bronson. God gave me shit! A shit hand. And I took it and bluffed it into a royal flush. All. By. My. Fucking. Self!" He pointed at the heavens. "No money, no beauty, no talent, nothing—the Almighty gave me nothing!"

Malouf lowered his hand and his eyes, in shame it seemed, and sat back down. Maya thought he'd exhausted himself, but he hadn't. He looked up and met her eyes, and in a much lower, softer voice spoke with what could pass for religious conviction. "Except for one thing." He held up that ghost index finger. Maya imagined it extended upward. "God gave me one thing, and he gave it to me bigly." He paused for effect. "Can you see it?"

She wasn't sure what he was asking—could she see his finger? Could she see where his finger used to be, what it used to look like? He looked as proud as a little kid who'd stumped his mom with a riddle. She sure hoped he wasn't talking about his dick. "It's hard to see," he said, still waiting for a guess from her. Maya tried to arrange her face into an expression that conveyed total lack of interest, but she was curious; she had no clue what he was about to say and he knew it.

"Emptiness," he finally said, touching gingerly at the air before him like a blind man walking in an unfamiliar world, like it was a tangible thing, the dark presence of an endless absence. "Yes. Need. I want. And my want is infinite. I want everything."

He stood up again, reenergized, patting his polo-toned belly. "I want what He has. I want what you have. I want what they have. I want. I want. I want! It's my one gift. I'm a genius of want. That's what God gave me—a fucking hole the size of the world."

He pointed to where his heart must be. "Parasite. Yes! Thank you! Right on! All I am is a mouth, eyes, asshole, and a cock—seeing, eating, talking, taking, buying, shitting, fucking, and making money. One of God's ugliest, simplest, most perfect creatures. A parasite farming out the grunt work of living to the host. All it does is feast. And fuck you, by the way, you took this job because you wanted to be just like me, learn from the master. You wanted to use me for your host—a parasite in training. So fuck your sudden righteousness."

"Fair enough."

"Fair enough is right. I'm the more moral one here. At least I know what I am. You were my host for a year. You thought you were sucking on my tit. Wrong! I was sucking on yours. I took your vision, your dream, your unicorn and I curled up inside it—suckling and waiting—eating away at the fairness—sucking out the humanity, fucking your empathy in the ass—forget about your kumbaya, win-win fantasies—life is zero sum, you ignorant little shit. Oh, I sucked—until nothing was left of your dream idea except the husk, the land, and now your dream is dead, but the land remains, and it's all mine, the land, and I'll suck that dry, too. And you, poor thing, pushing thirty already, huh? You're drying up, too—uh-huh, don't blink, baby cakes, you'll miss it."

He exhaled heavily and his skinny shoulders sagged. He looked spent at long last, and like he might cry. He seemed as surprised at what he'd just said as she was. He smiled, almost apologetically. "You think I'm the bad guy, the villain of your story—call me in twenty years, when you're fifty—I'll take your call, you'll want to tell me you got it all wrong—you'll want to tell me I'm the hero."

Maya smiled, too—sincerely this time. Because Malouf had finally drawn back the curtain of his friendly, even obsequious persona; he had let her into the control room behind the mask. She smiled, also, because she understood now what had drawn her into an orbit around these two powerful men, Bronson and Malouf. In very different ways, in their vehemently anti-psychological worldviews, they were both throwbacks to men of earlier times. Bronson had tried to leapfrog the human, the messy twenty-first-century human, with his primate-centric vision of a monkey-like man who needed the yoke of the Law to bend him from a beast into a king-saint. Malouf perceived man as regressed even further back in geologic time, further than even his beloved Pavlovian dogs, telescoping back a billion years to the earliest microbes that joined together for protection and efficiency in the primordial soup to form more and more complex beings. His was a brutal, predeterministic, robotic vision of man as a kind of parasite-haunted zombie (thank you, Hammer films—it was all of a piece, suddenly, all connected) doomed by the ancient, self-preserving demands of his chemicals to make preconscious choices with only the illusion of free will. Malouf Man was relegated to life as a flesh automaton by encoded mitochondrial, chromosomal desires and selfish genes to do deadly battle where only those soft machines would win who were not hamstrung by such weakening notions as empathy, integrity, neurosis, guilt, shame, penance, contrition, or spiritual love.

Both restless men found majestic power in one-dimensionality—the monolithic, animal presence of an apex predator or lowly parasite, built to do one thing, to move, to act, not to dither or prevaricate; built to win unencumbered by the second guesses of conscience and psychology. She had been blinded by their heat and simplicity, by their charm and her own projections, mistaking intensity for integrity. But now her eyes had been washed by blood, razed by fire, cleansed and cleared by death and destruction; she could see the true shape of things. She could see herself. She wasn't sure who she was, but she was beginning to see what she was not. She was guilty, yes, of many sins, but she was not what they were. Not quite. Not yet. She was released. She felt aglow, an immense gratitude suffusing her insides in a sweeping, narcotic warmth. "Thank you," she said, without a trace of irony.

Her genuine gratitude seemed to baffle and annoy Malouf more than her diffidence and anger. He frowned, giving up on her once and for all, and swung his chair to face the ocean again, his back to her. Over his shoulder, he made a dismissive gesture for Maya to leave, to get the fuck out. She watched the back of his head tilt forward to the window and imagined that the ocean, his nemesis, was cursing him now as well, taunting him with his severed finger and mortality. But still, she knew he must be grinning, sure that he was winning, winning all the battles on the way to losing the war. As she walked out, she heard him whisper to himself, to the ocean, and maybe to his version of a God, "Nine men mean nothing."

On the way home, Maya thought about what she could do. She thought about a lawyer, hell, she thought about becoming a lawyer—she was young enough, though she felt decades older than a year ago. She thought about writing, not horror films, but real films about real people doing real things, maybe documentaries; she thought about teaching. Nine men were dead, many more were still alive. She needed to make amends, atone for the damage she had caused by her hunger for money and safety, her ambition, and her innocence. The future was wide open, but its direction was clear. It pointed back to helpfulness, gratitude, responsibility. Circuitous how we come to a kind of religion after all—mysterious ways and all that, she thought. Her anger at Malouf, her confusion and sadness at the tragedy of Bronson, morphed into a type of jangly feeling of freedom. She realized Malouf had stolen her phone. More freedom.

Instead of heading back for the phone, or home, Maya steered the Tesla toward the 10 freeway and its 2,460 miles that didn't stop till Florida across the entire country, clear from the Pacific to the Atlantic. Yeah, she'd have to recharge every 300 miles or so, and that wasn't entirely free, but right now she could go anywhere, be anything; she had molted her form like the snake on her arm, was as limitless now as this great American highway. Bronson had taught her that. The art of radical reinvention. He had forsaken the world to escape himself, and his tragedy was that he found himself, in the shadows of the Joshua tree, waiting out there in the desert, too. He could no more restore the biblical past than he could escape his own past.

Bronson's vision was faulty, human, but his reach was divine. Maya had learned something from him, everything. The holy act of restoration, reclaiming lost times, and proclaiming that the present matters and miracles can still occur—she learned all that from a mass murderer. Whatever happened from here on out, whatever she did and whoever she became, she would dedicate silently to the doomed expansiveness at the heart of Bronson Powers. The West was done, burning out, over and out; Bronson had feared that, too, he just hadn't known when to let go. She would let go. There was nothing left for her in LA. She would head east.

The smoke from the Joshua Tree Fire had turned the LA sunset sky a burnt smoky peach that stung her eyes. She pointed her planet-friendly electric vehicle straight east on the 10 toward the source of the still dangerous wildfire. Mary and Yaya and the Powers kids, including Hyrum, were with Yalulah Ballou's old Yankee family in Providence, Rhode Island. The plain Jane, prodigal Wasp daughter had returned home to her *Mayflower*-pedigree folks, with an eye-talian, pill-popping, pistol-packing wife and a bunch of wild Mormon kids in tow. Okeydoke. From culture shock to culture shock. Diet Coked–up little Sammy Greenbaum should take a stab at writing that story, she mused.

The young Powers children would be given new names and raised with as much privacy as they could achieve in the state that began as a penal colony and guarantor of religious freedom, Rogue's Island. Ah, the true American story of genocide, slavery, and rape hidden beneath the beautiful, obfuscating, July Fourth words. Those kids had been through a lot and had a long hard road ahead of them, but as Janet Bergram might say—they are loved, and that's a start.

At seventeen, Deuce would soon be in Boston, the cradle of the Revolution, at Harvard. Deuce had actually called *her* last week to make sure *she* was okay. He said there's only one trinity worth addressing, one that consists of capitalism, racism, and climate change, and like the Holy Trinity, he felt that those three issues are at base one in the same, and that he hoped to find the common root and yank it from the American soil. He got to talking about universal income, "data dignity," and "unionizing the internet"; he was going to take a French-language intensive this summer so he could read Thomas Piketty and de Tocqueville in "the original." The kid's learning curve was a vertical line. She had no idea what he was lit up about, but his empathetic zeal, his humble certainty, filled her with hope nonetheless. She felt some small solace that a boy like that was coming of age in this world.

In a few months, Pearl would be in New York City at Juilliard, although Maya didn't think any school could hold on to her for very long. Pearl and the Big Apple. Maya smiled at that marriage to the only city commensurate with that young girl's talent and ambition. Both children were a testament to Bronson's original vision. He had filled them with the past to transform the present, to be themselves the latter-day saints and miracles.

For today, though, she would drive toward disaster. There were many people there that needed succor. The children of San Bernardino who were going to lose a good advocate in Janet Bergram, the Ruiz family, the families of the men Bronson had killed, the family of cops, the family of the park rangers, those hurting from the conflagration still burning. Loss, loss, everywhere loss. She must give the loss meaning. It was her only hope. She had a sudden, vivid memory of her grandmother, the worn rosary beads sliding through her arthritic fingers. "To thee do we cry, poor banished children of Eve. To thee do we send up our sighs, mourning and weeping in this valley of tears."

She would mourn, yes, and she would make atonement for her blindness, pride, and greed to the living, not to the God of Mammon, nor to a God that sent a man alone into a desert and put stones on his eyes to see. Her eyes were open and clear; she would make amends by giving away the strength of her blood, youth, intelligence, sweat, and her love, not by some useless bloodletting, symbolic or otherwise. She had seen the perfect face of God, experienced His appetite for obedience and death, and she would turn away from Him now to His banished children, to the imperfect face of man, and woman, and all living, suffering things. She would risk her soul to save it. She merged onto the freeway, put her foot down, and headed straight into the fire.

ACKNOWLEDGMENTS

THE GENESIS OF THIS story began years ago when I read Harold Bloom on the Mormon founder, Joseph Smith. I had the once-in-a-lifetime privilege of studying with Professor Bloom when I was a graduate student in English literature at Yale in the mid- to late '80s. His was a unique and comprehensive mind. He was inspiring, charming, daunting—a universe unto himself. His death, while I was at work on this book, sent me into a surprisingly more complicated mourning than I would have imagined, since I did not really know him, nor he me, had never had a personal conversation with him, and hadn't laid eyes on him in more than thirty years. And yet the man left a mark on me. Bloom is actually one of the reasons I became an actor. It was in his seminar in about 1985 or 1986 that I decided I was outclassed in this academic field and, already twenty-five years old, started casting about nervously for other things to do with my life. (Oh, it's a good story—sad, funny, and absurd—the punchline is: "A world without adjectives." I know, I know—that's not enough, but there are other names involved, big names, so I only tell it to friends. Close friends. That's a story for another time. The memoirs, perhaps. The memoirs I'll never write.)

Fast-forward. It must have been the year 2000. I hadn't been in New Haven for probably fifteen years. Living in LA, I was writing an episode of *The X-Files* to direct that would eventually be filmed as "Hollywood A.D." For the plot, or crime, or caper, or gag, or "X-File," I had conceived of a character loosely inspired by a case I'd read about—Mark Hofmann, a Mormon and forger, and eventual bomber and convicted murderer. I was taken by the fact that Hofmann, when forging extremely sensitive and valuable religious documents as Joseph Smith in Smith's hand, seemed to believe that he, in very real essence, became Joseph Smith—actually, and therefore in some deep sense, his forgeries were not forgeries, but more like channeling, or ongoing revelation, a return to authenticity. He thought and wrote like an actor who has completely lost himself in the character. He became his role. I was in the midst of the worldwide phenomenon of the show and its demands upon me and its claims upon my very identity. For millions of people all over the globe, I was not David Duchovny; I was Mulder. The X-Files were real, right? The government was hiding the truth. Mulder was real to people. More real than me. But I knew that was a lie. Wasn't it?

I was very interested to develop this line between the possession by a character, acting, and truth, and I tried to portray it through a kind of whimsical lens using the frame and characters of the show I was doing at the time. Thanks to Chris Carter for giving me the reins to hijack his great show to work out my existential problems with fame and identity for a week. I offered Oliver Stone the lead guest-starring role ('60s radical turned religious fundamentalist), and he seemed into it, but after some spirited discussions, we couldn't make the dates work. The actor and poet Paul Lieber auditioned, got the role, and did a super, wonderfully off-kilter job. I did get to have my great friend Garry Shandling play me—I mean play Mulder—in the movie being made about the forgery/murder case within the TV show that constitutes the shifting frame and questioning of narrative and actual, historical truth. In 2020, these still seem like good questions to be asking.

Anyway. In the course of researching Mark Hofmann in 2000

(I called the character in the show Micah Hoffman—so many bread-crumbs, so many fingerprints at the scene—I wanted to be known, you see, to be found out, and my Hoffman was a forger of Jesus Christ, not Joseph Smith—go big or go home, right?), I came upon Bloom's 1992 work, *The American Religion*, in which he professes something more than mere admiration for Joseph Smith. He saw genius in him. Say what? Now, I had no feelings either way or natural interest in Mormonism. I came to it merely through my voracious ambition to hang a story, to use the singular, fascinating, human tragedy of Mark Hofmann as a way to discuss/meditate upon forgery, fakery, authenticity, acting, crime, and charisma while hanging out with my buddy Garry on a Fox network TV show. Like most Americans, I simply knew the Mormon broad outlines—very straight, very white, no coffee or alcohol, no premarital intercourse, and polygamy. The "prophet" Joseph Smith on the run, murdered young. I knew Danny Ainge of the Boston Celtics and Steve Young of the San Francisco 49ers were Mormon. That was the extent of my knowledge on the subject.

But I found in Bloom's brooding upon Joseph Smith all the things that my character Bronson Powers finds when he converts by chance and necessity to Mormonism. The organization and otherness Bloom sees in Mormons, their abstract true Americanness. More than anything, it was this sense of latter-day vitality rather than end-time entropy that I found freeing and right, story-worthy. As a devout man of literature, before becoming an actor, I had felt the crushing weight of the past and its genius, what Bloom himself would call the "anxiety of influence" in his best-known work. How to escape that weight, the past? One way is to forget, or not know it, to not read, to become incurious, and to call anything but self-interest fake. I don't see that working out well today. People of good conscience look on in horror at the power of daily self-reinvention in politics and on Instagram. Is that what it is to be American? Is

Gatsby Everyman? Were we heading there all along? I see the in-toxicating freedom, but it's a freedom from, not of, truth.

How to honor and escape the genius of the past? Those are the binding questions. Those are bonds. Those are questions only a big soul like Smith or Bloom would grapple deeply with, and hope-fully, Bronson Powers's wrestling with that adversarial angel would also merit attention, shed light, and give pleasure. How to feel primary when you've come so late upon the scene? All these vec-tors were in play with Bloom and Smith, and America itself.

So I took what I needed at the time in the year 2000 to write my X-File, and I moved on. But the seeds were planted, the interest accumulating. Eventually, I came upon Richard Bushman's excel-lent 2005 biography of Joseph Smith, *Rough Stone Rolling*. Clearly, I was not done with the subject. Another story I'd been contemplat-ing as a novel or movie was about a disaffected, drug-dealing high school kid who undergoes a sexual and political awakening in the course of organizing a fast-food franchise union drive (I refer you to Magnus Isacsson's 2002 documentary, *Maxime, McDuff & McDo*). I was calling that story "Uncle Samburger," and it got stripped down, transformed, and folded, as Deuce's BurgerTown war, into the larger frame of the Powers family saga. The whole enterprise started to grow, take on a shape and life of its own. Add to this my ongoing interest in climate change and the vanishing health and beauty of natural worlds such as Joshua Tree, and the abject ob-scenity of the Trump administration—I name-check some of them in the book; their names should not be forgotten. Price, Zinke, Mnuchin, Pence—say their names, do not forget—villains all. Real villains, unlike the paper tigers they rail against, whose crimes will not be fully rendered and appraised for years. And here we are in 2021, and here is *Truly Like Lightning*.

Patience. I also want to acknowledge an earlier teacher at Princ-eton, Maria DiBattista, who, while weighing me down with the greats—Woolf, Beckett—did not impart to me the inescapable belatedness and fatalism of a Bloom. She conjured more of a sense of a reciprocal love for literature, a positive, mutually nurturing vision more than a patriarchal struggle, a gloss on the unrequited or at least dangerously lopsided love affair I saw in Bloom. I guess I'm a bit of both. They are my literary/critical parents.

Heartfelt thanks to Jonathan Galassi, who had me pitch a few ideas to him for a next book, lit up at this one, and said, "I'd like to see you do that." And then he kept at me and made me see it through before I got distracted by other work, lost energy, then hope, and abandoned it. Ideas are so fragile when they begin, their immune systems so underdeveloped, anything can kill them before they bloom. Jonathan is a wise and gentle gardener. And he knows how to prune. His editorial hand was sure and inspiring again this time around. I don't think I'd have written one novel, let alone four, had we not begun to work together.

And big ups to my agent, Andrew Blauner, who, when I told him that Jonathan liked this new (old/new) idea, said, "Let's get a contract."

I said, "No, then I'll be legally impelled to write it."

And he said, "Haha, exactly."

He knows me.

Thanks to my friend the great actor Ron Eldard, who put up with my many no doubt silly questions about Mormonism during our long-ago countless meals at A Votre Santé on San Vicente.

Thanks to Emlyn Cameron for his detailed research and wandering down roads I didn't have the patience to get lost on, and to Christian Kerr, who began casting the wide net of research for me in 2018.

Also thanks to my early readers—Monique Pendleberry, Carrie Malcolm, Matt Warshaw, Chris Carter, Amy Koppelman, Janey L. Bergam, John McNamara, and Brad Davidson.